The Wand

Book 1: Elfistra the Sorceress

Michael Ross

To Clem
With my very best wishes.
Michael Ross.

This book cover and illustrations were lovingly designed and produced by Magdalena Adić.

Michael Ross

To all the intrepid explorers of the unknown,
be you Earthan or Elvish.
Be brave and you will discover all.

All quotes at the beginning of each chapter, including the Prologue and Epilogue and the whole of the contents are Copyrighted © 2018 to Michael Ross

All rights reserved. No part of this book may be used or reproduced in any manner whatsoever including internet usage, without written permission from the Author.

ISBN: 13: 9781790203826

CONTENTS

DEDICATIONS 5
AUTHOR'S NOTE .... 6 & 486
PROLOGUE 9

CHAPTERS

1. THE SLICE 15
2. THE VEL 39
3. QUEEN HARUNTHA 57
4. ELFISTRA & MANDAZ 79
5. DING LING 95
6. GRANTHANDA 121
7. THE DELEGATION 145
8. A RUDE AWAKENING 179
9. ELVINA THE WAND 195
10. A TRICKLE OF BLOOD 209
11. UNFOUNDED ACCUSATIONS 229
12. THE WAR OF THE BLACK ARROWS ... 253
13. THE SOOTALANASH 279
14. MANDAZ AND THE CURSING SPELL 295
15. RETURN OF THE LAZANATH 313
16. HELLO CHARLIE ANDOVER 343
17. A DIFFICULT DECISION 359
18. AND THE WINNER IS? 379

PTO

19. KAL THE EMPATH 409
20. LINDAZOTH 431
21. THE DECISION 465
    EPILOGUE 479

APPENDIX

GLOSSARY .... 487 – 499
IMAGES .... 501 – 502
SELECTED PHONETIC PRONUNCIATION
FOR SELECTED NAMES AND OBJECTS 503

DEDICATIONS

I dedicate this book to my sons, Aidan, Ben and Oliver and to my Brother Kevin.

To the best, and most honest Beta readers an Author could have: Emma Healey, Jackie Mirfin and Josie Manning.

To Dr. Michael at FirstEditing.com

To my illustrator, who's like-minded creativeness is beautiful.

About the Author:

It was a clairvoyant that told Michael that he should write a book. The first, a comedy called 'Memoirs from the S.B.C', the second a true-life story called 'Just Five More Minutes', both published on Amazon.

But from when he could remember, he always had a strong interest in Sci Fi, and had a voracious appetite for Sci Fi books. He believes that there has to be life out there, 'But not as we know it Jim'.

And so, these Wand Chronicles are an amalgamation of his creative ideas, thoughts and experiences. Essentially, he is writing these books for himself, but he hopes you will enjoy them as well.

A Note from the Author:

You will notice at the start of each chapter, including the prologue and epilogue, an Elvish script.
This is no ordinary Elvish script, it could not be described as 'high' Elvish. It is in fact the Elvish dialect that is only spoken in Laniakeea.
It is called 'Solderran'.
Elvish is usually written in purple in Laniakeea, extracted from the leaves of the Melroon tree. (see page 430)
To the Laniakeeans, the color purple is associated with all things magical.
Immediately following the Elvish, is the translation into English.
These sayings are deeply rooted in every aspect of the Laniakeean way of life.
Our own word, 'affirmation', loosely comes from the Laniakeaan word, 'Palnath'an', or ꙮ

One of the most well-known sayings on Laniakeea is –
ꙮ
Which translates as –
'If you say it, you'll believe it, then you will do it'

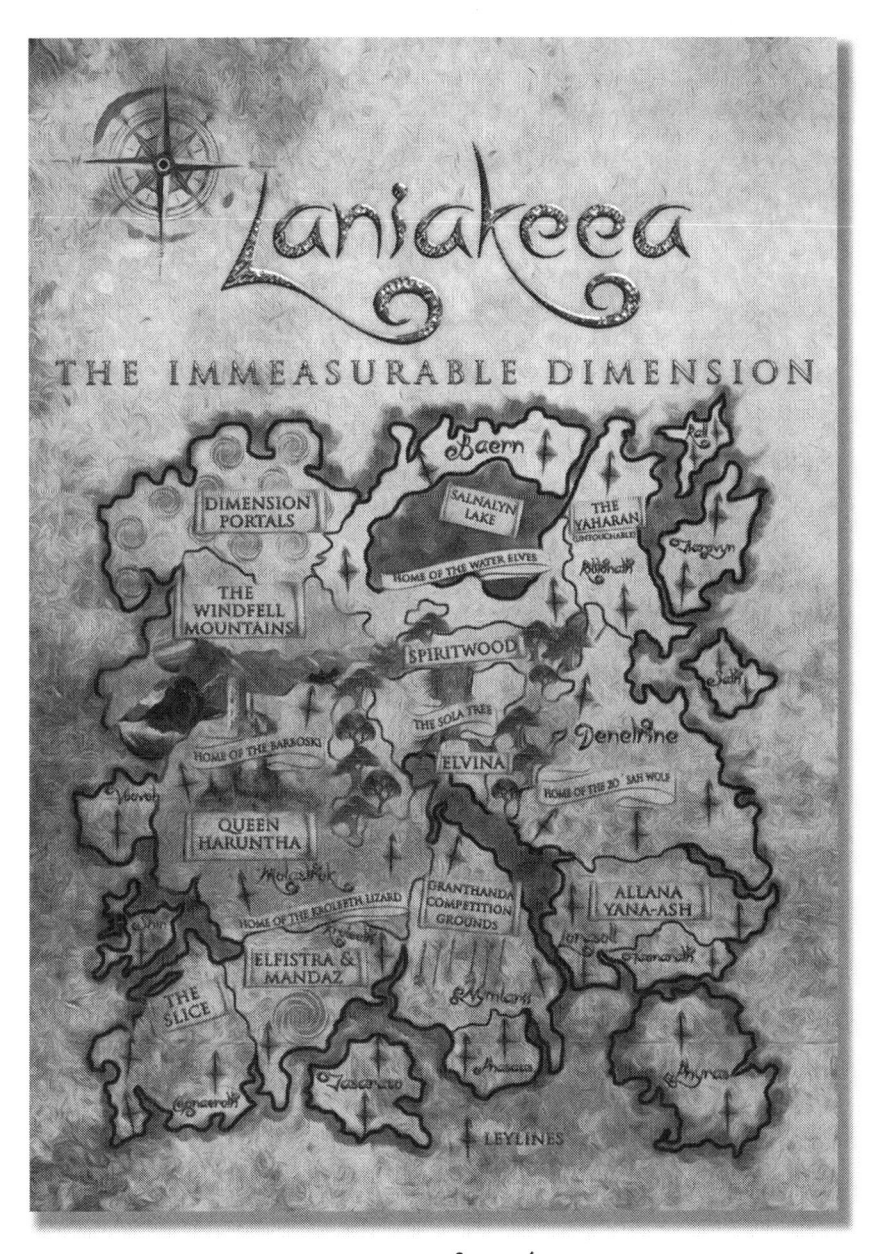

Map of Laniakeea
(The Immeasurable Dimension)

Winberry Wood
(New Mills, Derbyshire, United European Landmass)

PROLOGUE

(Challenges are there for a reason. To learn. To live. To love)

9.05pm, 30th June, 2087
Winberry Wood

General Hugo Brough, sat on Firemaker, his favorite stallion, listening intently to the beaters drumming and shouting behind him in the forest.

Dressed in brown military leathers, he was a handsome man, tanned, with a short beard and a curious scar running down his cheekbone from the side of his left eye. A retro gun, was strapped to his back, preferred by him as it was very basic and needed much-developed skill to wield effectively, giving an animal a fairer chance to escape.

At only twenty-three years of age, he was a force to be reckoned with, known to have a wise head on his shoulders. He did not suffer fools gladly and shied away from petty, small-talk-laden social gatherings.

He was hunting wild boar on the Brough family estate, which was smack bang in the middle of the United European

Landmass. He was riding with two of his army companions, Jeremy, his second in command and the other, Gavin, a close associate who had enrolled at the same time as himself. They both looked ready but nervous. However, to Hugo, the anticipation, the waiting, was just as much of a thrill as the chase.

Suddenly, below him, at breakneck speed, came a family of wild boar, grunting loudly. On cue, he dug his spurs deep into the flanks of his horse and they were off!

The now squealing wild boar were scattered in front of the posse of riders, threatening to upset them. At the front, Hugo twisted the reins of Firemaker. The spittle from the horse's mouth ran in rivers of white across its neck, which, along with the wild-eyed look in its eyes, made it look possessed.

They were now gaining on the boars.

Now the light was now fading fast, and the riders knew that time was running out. Very soon they wouldn't be able to see a thing.

Suddenly, a deafening crack was heard to their right; a flash of lightening, a glow of incandescent light, and Hugo and the other two riders were instantly thrown off their horses, high up into the woody damp air.

Hugo hit the ground face first and slid along the forest floor, through the damp detritus of soil, twigs and small stones. He eventually came to a stop and lay there, face down, winded and dazed. He slowly picked himself up and sat upright, spitting a mixture of dirt and blood from his mouth. He turned around to look for the others.

They too were coming around slowly, cursing and groaning. "What the hell was that?" Hugo groaned.

The mesmerizing bright light to his right caught his eye. The forest around him was now bathed in a white crackling fluorescent light.

He stood up, wiped the mud off his tunic, and slipped the retro gun into his right hand, looking at the white light. One by one, the two other riders joined him, mouths open. They too were hypnotically drawn to the phenomenon unfolding before them.

The pulsating light formed a column stretching up from the forest floor through the canopy above them and into the darkening sky, as far as the eye could see. It was approximately ten feet wide with constantly changing hues, pastel shades of yellow, green, blue and pink.

Hugo picked up a large stick and tentatively threw it at the column. The stick was swiftly sucked in and enveloped by the light, disappearing within a fraction of a second.

Silently inching their way towards it, they could feel a slight warmth on their faces, and a curious smell of ozone that reminded Hugo of the seaside. A constant electrical buzz emanated from it. They stopped near it, transfixed, feeling nauseous. Their hair was standing up on end!

Suddenly, a long thin slender arm, covered in red material and marked with strange patterns, shot towards them from the column, stopping just short of its shoulder. It appeared that it was struggling to penetrate the column. After two or three attempts, the arm retreated into the throbbing multicolored light. Shocked, they stumbled back and stood looking at each other in disbelief, wanting answers.

They turned their attention to the light and were trying to examine it, looking up and down, when they heard the sound of something hissing through the air. All of a sudden, an arrow shot towards them from the column, neatly embedding itself into the neck of Gavin. He collapsed to the ground, writhing in agony, holding his neck as the blood spurted out.

Hugo and Jeremy turned on their heels and sprinted as quickly as they could in the opposite direction. They had covered only three or four yards, when Jeremy was lifted slightly into the air, then nosedived into the ground and slid into a crumpled heap.

Hugo stopped mid-stride to help him up, but before he could do so, noticed helplessly as another arrow pierced the base of Jeremy's skull, the arrowhead protruding through his left eye socket.

Hugo bolted. Nothing made any sense to him. He ran with all the energy he could muster, hearing voices in his head, loud voices, strange voices!

He heard the loosing of another arrow, and in an instant knew this one was meant for him He started to dart left then right, in an effort to be out of the line of sight of the arrow. His left toe caught the root of a small tree, and as he stumbled forward, he felt the arrow nick the top of his right ear. He hit the ground at breakneck speed, head first and slid into a large rock and came to an abrupt stop.

He lay in a pool of dark stinking mud and started to pull himself up, wiping off the blood that was now pouring down the side of his face. As he looked up, he saw a tall man standing in front of him.

Hugo noticed the tops of his ears were pointed, and he was wearing strange red clothes, unlike anything he had seen before. He was holding a large bow in his left hand.

The figure was gesturing at him. Suddenly, Hugo heard a strange voice in his head, in an unusual language, but Hugo noticed that the man's lips were not moving.

He felt the breath being sucked out of his lungs. His eyes started to un-focus, as a warm tingling sensation spread quickly throughout his body, and he crumpled to the ground unconscious.

The Slice
(The portal between the Earthan dimension and the Elvish dimension of Laniakeea.)

CHAPTER 1

The Slice

(If a difficult problem comes your way, you can either ignore it, or welcome it with open arms. This is your chance to grow.)

As Hugo started to gain consciousness, he couldn't open his eyes. He could feel he was being gripped firmly underneath his arms with the sensation of the tips of his boots dragging along the ground.

He was now beginning to open his eyes, but he couldn't focus, and they were watering badly. There were those strange voices in his head again. He had the mother of all headaches, then remembered hitting his head violently when he tripped and fell, *'That must be the reason,'* he thought.

He wanted to break free, but couldn't summon an ounce of energy, so didn't put up any resistance when he was dragged to wherever it was his captors were taking him.

They stopped on what appeared to be a circle drawn in the ground. Strange letters and arrows were marked all over it. He heard the voices in his head again. This time it didn't seem like a conversation, but more like words uttered in unison and as a command. Suddenly, he felt he was being transported, at unbelievable speed, across the ground. His sight was quickly coming back, but he was traveling too fast to be able to focus on anything. Feeling nauseous, he closed his eyes and waited.

Then, after what felt like only a minute, all movement stopped suddenly and abruptly. Since he now had some feeling in his legs, he was half carried forward, stumbling, to what appeared to be a low building, with a very ornate colored curved spire on the top. The walls seemed to be moving slightly, with subtle changes in differing hues of pastel colors? Hugo, shook his head, *'I still haven't recovered'* he thought to himself. He was taken over the threshold of a circular opening that didn't seem to have a door, and into a smaller room within, and was laid down, face first, on a soft sweet-smelling fur pelt.

He lay there gathering his thoughts, remembering now the violence at that white column, the fact that his companions had been brutally killed, and with that, his anger began to rise. He reached over his shoulder to grab his retro gun, off his back, but it wasn't there. He slowly and painfully pulled himself up and into a sitting position, and began to take in his surroundings.

What was that column? No matter how he thought

about it, trying to find an explanation, nothing came anywhere nearer to making any sense of it all. It seemed to slice through the air. *'That's it!'* Hugo thought, *'I'm calling it 'The Slice'. 'At least it's got a name now.' 'It's a start I guess.' 'Not much of one I know.'* He lifted his head up and slowly looked around

What was this place? His heart was beating very fast. He couldn't make any sense out of anything he saw. For the first time in his life, he wasn't in control. In fact, it was the opposite. He was a little scared if the truth be known. He took a deep breath and started to focus on his surroundings, hoping it would reveal some sort of clue to where he was and what was happening.

The walls looked almost as if they were alive. They were gently pulsating, and there appeared to be no corners anywhere. Everything was smooth. A round window, round doorway, an oval fur pelt and an array of pastel colors that were changing color, as if to a beat.

The words, **'I'm sorry'** came into Hugo's head. He couldn't quite put his finger on the accent. It was almost like a heavy Swedish accent, but not quite. He looked around quickly, then noticed on one side, in another round doorway, what looked like a woman. A tall, slim, elegant woman. He saw the tops of her ears were also pointed and she had a form of jewelry along one edge. Her clothes were a diaphanous light green, and she had very blonde hair with some colored material wrapped intricately around some strands of hair. But it was her eyes that struck him most forcefully. Not the continuous band of what looked like make-up, reaching across from one eye socket to the other, but the actual color of her eyes. They were a striking green color, but more than that, an almost fluorescent green. An emerald green. They were mesmerizing.

He was drawn towards them. He couldn't stop looking. He just sat there and stared into this woman's eyes. Well, he assumed it was a woman. She wasn't like any woman he had ever met. Now he began to feel embarrassed, almost to the point of rudeness. Hugo thought to himself, *'This is ridiculous, pull yourself together man'*. Straight away, that foreign accent came booming into his head again, *'Please don't worry, it will take time for you to adjust.'* At the same time, Hugo noticed a slight smile spreading across her lips. It must have been the quizzical look on Hugo's face as he was trying to come to terms with her voice in his head.

"I think it will help you if I speak verbally, rather than telepathically as I was doing," said the woman.

Hugo just stared at her.

"Let me tell you who I am and where you are. My name is Allana Yana-Ash. You are in a parallel dimension to your Earthan dimension, in the Elvish kingdom of Laniakeea."

Hugo just sat there and mouthed the words 'dimension' and 'Elvish' to himself. *'Nope,'* he thought to himself, *'Nothing *makes sense at all.'* She then walked towards Hugo, almost gliding, as he would imagine a ballerina would walk. Cupped in her hands was a small clear vessel, containing a light blue liquid that seemed to be slightly effervescing. "Here," said Allana, "Slowly drink this, it will help you recover and will heal the wound on your head."

Hugo tentatively took the vessel, sniffed the liquid, as if it might be poison, but noticed it had a fresh sweet spicy smell and sipped a little of it. *'Hmmm, this tastes good,'* thought Hugo, and with that, he gulped the rest down quickly. Immediately he felt a lot better, his headache almost gone and he even felt re-energized. Hugo looked at Allana and held out the cup to her, which she reached forward to take off him. Again, the charming smile appeared across Allana's lips.

"Besides being able to send words telepathically, I understand you call it, into your head, I am also able to read your thoughts as well. But I have decided I am not going to do that in your case, even though you couldn't prevent me. I feel it is essential to build up a trust between us, and wish to be courteous, so we will communicate as you do on Earth side with your kind."

"Earth side?" said Hugo.

"Ah, that is the name we give to the dimension you come from," said Allana, "But you want answers I think? I'm sorry, but I already know many of the questions you have been thinking about since I was able to pick your thoughts up earlier on. I will do my best to explain everything for you, from the very beginning. Walk with me, and we will sit outside my dwelling."

Hugo slowly stood up. He felt much better. That blue liquid was amazing. He followed Allana through into another room with a simple fireplace, in the front of which was a very large, very thick fur pelt. Hugo imagined the animal it came from as being larger than a polar bear. Again, he noticed the walls were moving and pulsating, changing hues of pastel colors. Hugo had a strong impulse to touch them, which he did. He felt they almost felt alive! The wall was warm to the touch, and when he touched it, floods of unusual images flashed in his brain, like a slide show.

He had the feeling they were happy memories, almost as if the walls were a living photo album. Once or twice he saw Allana as a little girl, and a few holding and drawing back a bow with arrows.

Suddenly he noticed Allana looking at him again, and very quickly Hugo took his hands off the wall, embarrassed. "That is perfectly ok," she said, "The walls are built using our thought processes, and traditionally we like to keep and use the happiest of our thoughts, which is why you maybe were able to see memory reflections of myself and my family, and my relationships mixed up in there. Visitors here are always invited to 'touch the walls' or '*Paldarath*' as we call it. There will also be highlights of my life so far that I wish to remember."

By now they had arrived at the smoothed edged doorway. Allana went out first, closely followed by Hugo. As Hugo raised his head, what he saw took his breath away. Here, right in front of him and filling the entire sky, was the planet Saturn. The rings were running at an angle, from bottom left to top right. The largest moon Titan, appeared even closer.

He felt like if he reached out he could almost touch it. As they walked over what seemed to be tiny purple leaves, each footstep released a scent that Hugo found very sweet and heady. Within ten feet they came to a large log on its side. Covered in a soft dark yellow mossy carpet, it had been fashioned into a seat for three people, which meant it was able to accommodate them both very comfortably.

Slowly Allana sat down. Hugo suddenly turned to her, and with urgency asked, "Am I a prisoner?"

"No, you are not a prisoner. You are free to come and go, but you need to be accompanied."

Hugo looked up then and continued to stare in disbelief at Saturn in front of him. "That's unbelievable."

"Yes," Allana chipped in, "In our dimension, we share the same solar system as you, with the same number and sizes of planets and moons. The major difference is where each planet is, in relationship to ourselves here on Laniakeea, which is why, at certain times, Saturn comes very close. You have to understand that the laws of physics, mechanics, gravity and so on, have different rules for us in our dimension. There are one or two differences. For example, we don't have a planet Earth, and so don't have the moon that circles it. We still don't know the reason for that."

A little quieter now, Allana said, "I'm afraid I don't know your name?"

"My name is Hugo. Hugo Brough," said Hugo. And he slowly sat down, looking a little nervous and bewildered.

"Well, Hugo Brough, my queen, Queen Haruntha, has asked me to apologize to you and your people for the deaths of your soldiers. She asked me to explain that it was partly a mistake on our part, in that we thought we were under attack, which we are from time to time, from other portals, all of which are in the north-west of our dimension, beyond an area called the Windfell mountains."

"To have a portal suddenly appear down in the south-west of our dimension, in the district of Cepnaeroth, took us by complete surprise. Immediately the queen's security bowmen went to investigate, and found it difficult to access through the portal to investigate."

"When they were able to see through," continued Allana, "they mistakenly thought they were confronted by warriors, with shooting machines, I think you call them guns? As the bowmen approached the portal, they thought they were under attack from arrows. It turns out later, after an investigation, that it was simply a long piece of wood, that must have entered the portal from your side, traveled through and hit one of the bowmen, so they went on the offensive and started to let loose their arrows."

At this point Hugo suddenly remembered throwing a stick into the portal to see what would happen. Was he then indirectly the cause of the deaths of his companions? This immediately made him feel uneasy and very sad.

Hugo let out a big sigh. "Yes, none of us likes to lose friends, especially if the mistaken retaliation is sudden and a surprise, but such is life. I have to admit that I may have been indirectly responsible for their deaths." He explained to Allana about the stick incident.

"Nothing can bring them back," said Hugo, "And in the spirit of understanding and forgiveness, we would need to move on. I for one would like to explore, to understand, to learn from each other, and on that basis, try to agree on common ground, and possibly how we can help each other. For now though, I admit I am struggling to make any sense of it at all."

"And yes," continued Hugo, "I have lots of questions. How can you explain that you can use telepathy and that you can speak verbally in English, even though you do have an accent? All this is so foreign to me, and yet to you, you seem to be familiar with me as a species and on our way of life."

"I have an accent?" exclaimed Allana. For a moment there was no reaction, then she laughed out loud, "You should have heard me when I was struggling to learn and speak your language in the early days of learning, never mind having to cope with accents."

"As a culture," said Allana, "the Laniakeeans have been around for nearly three and a half million years before your ancestors, and I mean apes, were walking the Earthan dimension. Even in those early days, there was a secret portal, which has since closed, through which carefully selected Elves and Elf scientists were able, in disguise, to learn all about humans, everything: human life, politics, reproduction, intellectual capabilities, advances in medicine, science and technology, and so on. We were impressed with how you began to improve yourselves, although we have also been disappointed that greed and misuse of power seems to be inbuilt into your genes and consciousness."

"If only you could channel your collective consciousness into areas that could benefit humans in other meaningful ways," continued Allana, "how much more advanced would you be? Take your, how do you say, talk machines? that you used to hold to your ears, but are now implanted in the side of your heads. Ah yes, I remember now, phones, mobile phones. The collective technology of just that one item, means you now have all information at your fingertips, that you can communicate with anyone, pay for anything, even cure yourselves, and so on, all from a little-advanced piece of technology, the size of the nail on your little finger."

"Because our culture is so much more advanced than yours, we have been able to train ourselves to use more of our brain at any one time. At the moment, it is around ninety-five percent, and with that comes the use of what you would call magic, telepathic abilities and so on."

"You, yourselves, do use one hundred percent of your brain," continued Allana, "but never at the same time. As far as our studies tell us, you would only use up to thirty-five percent of your minds at any one time. And why do I know so much about humans from your dimension? Well, in Laniakeea, I am a scientist, with specialized skills to do with communication, and I have visited your dimension in disguise many times, and I teach some of your universal languages in our teaching facilities over here in our dimension. In fact, Earth dimension has been visited regularly from when you were cavemen."

Hugo was silent for more than a few moments, trying to take so much in. Taking in the view, accepting Allana as an alien? An Elf even. He had grown up reading such very old classics like *'Harry Potter,'* where Elves were described, but essentially were always make-believe. And now, here he was, in front of a living breathing Elf?

It felt like a dream. He thought about this. *'Yes, well,*

more dream than nightmare I suppose.' But he did know this: everything that was happening was as real as it gets. So, he took in a deep breath, and looked at Allana, who had now got up and was putting her arms around a tree.

Now he noticed the tree in detail and the other trees in front of him. He hadn't taken them in at first, because he was obsessed by the sight of Saturn. These trees were quite different to the trees on the Brough estate, particularly in Winberry Wood, that he had only been riding through only a few hours earlier.

The trunks were almost translucent, and running up inside them were gold colored streams. The branches were geometric in their design, almost like crop circles, with huge floppy leaves on the ends of the branches. The leaves were a very light purple in color and furry, and hung over in a semi-circle, almost touching the ground. Hugo had the strong impression that the trees were communicating with each other. He felt an all-encompassing feeling of intelligence, but also kindness, from something that felt like it was older than time itself.

Hugo slowly walked over to Allana. As he did so he noticed his steps were very light as if the gravitational pull was a lot less than on Earth. As he was approaching Allana, she suddenly turned to him and smiled.

"Did you hear me walking up?" he asked.

"No, I didn't," she replied, "The tree told me you were

coming."

'Maybe I was concussed after all,' Hugo thought to himself, to which Allana burst out laughing. "I'm sorry," she said, "I couldn't help hearing your last thoughts. No, you are certainly not concussed, it's simply that there is so much to take on board. Please give it time, you will get used to our ways, which at the moment are bound to seem so strange."

"Try it," she said, "Put your arms around this tree, try to relax and open your mind." Hugo stepped forward tentatively and put his arms around the trunk of the tree. *'I feel such a fool,'* he thought, and he gripped and held on as if he was going to fall backwards, his eyes wide open. The surface of the tree trunk was not at all rough, and it was warm?

"No, no Hugo Brough. Relax, let your body go limp, close your eyes, think kind thoughts, press your ear against the surface of the trunk, try to hear what the tree is saying." Hugo tried this, he relaxed and held his ear to the trunk and listened.

Immediately he jumped back! "I can hear it, I can hear it," exclaimed Hugo, "I could somehow understand everything it was saying, but not just in my head. Every single cell of my body was involved in communicating." There was a pause as Hugo had to get to grips with what he had just said. He continued enthusiastically, explaining to Allana, "The tree gave me an instant history lesson, which is as clear as if it all happened a few moments ago. A great feeling of empathy and this will sound strange, not to you I am sure, but it certainly does to me, I am sure it was telling me we share a common ancestry? Me, you and the trees."

"If I were back on Earth now, this would be the time to have a very stiff drink," said Hugo. As he turned to look at Allana, she gave him a sideways quizzical look, so he made the motion of raising an imaginary glass to his lips, but that made it even worse, and now she looked more confused than ever. "You know what? I don't think I can take any more revelations please. When will I be released to go back to my, erm, dimension?"

Allana looked at Hugo and said, "Hugo, you are free to go whenever you like, but I want to make sure you are well enough. You injured your head remember. I would like to think that you have been treated with kindness, and by giving you as much information as I can, will help the process of acclimatization. Our queen, Queen Haruntha, wants to meet you. She wants to apologize for the events that occurred and wants to set up a meeting between your Earth dimension and ours, to clear up any misunderstandings. And time is of the essence. I hope you will agree to that?"

Hugo was quiet for a moment. She was right. She had been hospitable, and he wasn't feeling quite as anxious now. That was being replaced by a thirst for knowledge and an understanding of what had happened and where he was. So,

Hugo said, "Yes, ok, I will agree to that."

Allana, immediately took him back to the sitting log. As they sat down, their forearms touched, and to both of them, it felt like a pleasant static electric shock. They both jumped a little and looked at each other, *'Wait,'* thought Hugo, *'Are her eyes...? Yes! They are changing color. Her green eyes are changing color!'* They both turned away, as if embarrassed, and then sat quietly for more than a minute, both of them gazing into the distance.

Hugo broke the silence, "Do your eyes always change color?"

"All Elves' eyes change color," Allana said, "Depending on the mood and the occasion, but particularly, the emotion the Elf is feeling at the time. We can disguise many things that give away our true feelings, but eye color and the colored aura surrounding us, those we have no control over whatsoever."

Allana smiled at this point, "However," she continued, "the only way we can try to disguise our eye color, is to turn our head away, so the other Elf can't see them, but of course it then becomes obvious we have something to hide, so generally, we are a very honest species, and however embarrassing or hurtful it is, we endeavor to keep as honest as possible. Honesty is paramount to an Elf. The only Elves that can control these effects are our queen, and Elfistra, our sorceress, although she is not strictly an Elf. This will be explained to you at some stage when the time is right. They can control them to the extent that they would be able to check that an Elf, or any being for that matter, has evil intentions."

"If you like," said Allana, "It is similar in a way to you using a truth serum or a lie detector machine Earthside. As you can imagine, this could be very helpful at certain times. You will be meeting them both shortly. In their cases, an evolutionary amendment to their DNA is in their genes. It is thought that there could be times that a disguise would benefit both of them, without giving away their true feelings."

Again, they were quiet for a few moments of reflection, then Hugo said, "It's just that I noticed your eyes were bright green, but just then they changed color to that of a pinky-red?"

Now the silence was palpable. And then quite suddenly Allana stood up and very brightly suggested they prepare to meet Queen Haruntha and Elfistra.

"Have I said something to upset you?" said Hugo, "You need to tell me? You are so different in many ways, I don't want to spoil anything by putting my foot in it."

"Putting your foot in it?" said Allana, "Put your foot in what?" Hugo grinned, "No," he said, "It is just a saying we have. It means saying something, possibly upsetting or embarrassing, that I didn't realize I had said or didn't mean to."

Allana took a deep breath, and looked at Hugo, her eyes were still that attractive pinky-red. "In my case, I have green eyes, which is not common for an Elf, who normally have blue eyes. But for all Elves, the color change to pinky red indicates feelings of friendship, or affection and also, in some cases, even strong attraction and love."

"Love in this context," said Allana, "certainly is initially always friendship love, not sexual love, which I know dominates in your Earthan dimension. The color of the eyes on their own is only half the story. We would also read the color of the aura surrounding an Elf, and in particular, the intensity of the aura and how far it emanates from the body. You can't see auras, can you?"

"No," said Hugo, "I can't. But there are those that can, although not many." Allana seemed to breathe a sigh of relief mentally. "Ah well, when you can read both, you can get a pretty good idea that someone either likes you, hates you, is indifferent towards you or finds you very attractive. We too have pheromones, and again, an honest giveaway to tell if an Elf finds you attractive or not."

"In fact, when Elves meet, it is perfectly acceptable to get very close and sniff in the air close to their face and neck, without touching of course," said Allana, "Our noses and receptors in them are highly evolved and that way we can tell so much about another Elf."

"Have you tried it on someone like me, a human?" said Hugo.

"No, I haven't," said Allana. "And probably wouldn't

until I got to know you a lot better. I believe it would make you feel uncomfortable, and probably me as well."

"Well," said Hugo, "I guess it would all depend on whether the human finds you attractive as well?" And with that, he smiled. *'Well,'* he thought to himself, *'After this last five minutes, I'm guessing she doesn't hate me.'* Hugo arrived at this conclusion with more than a hint of conceitedness.

Allana, now all official and matter of fact said, "We have now been invited to go immediately to the Elven district of Molastrok, to meet Queen Haruntha. The queen's palace is situated there."

They set off, following a path that weaved itself in-between the few trees in front of them. All the time Allana was mentioning more facts about Laniakeea, the Elvish nation, and was pointing out various peculiarities that merely needed explaining and translating, so Hugo would have a better understanding.

"How far away are we from the queen's palace?" asked Hugo, "In terms of distance that I am familiar with and that we use in our dimension?" After a few moments of deep thought Allana said, "Four thousand and thirty-seven miles, more or less."

"What?!" exclaimed Hugo, "How long is it going to take us to cover that distance? And how are we going to cover it?"

"We use ley lines," said Allana, "And over the last two

millennia have been able to harness their magical and spiritual powers. You won't know that your Earth dimension is very small compared to the size of Laniakeea. Let me illustrate it like this, if you were to squash the Earth flat, it would be a minute dot if placed on a map of Laniakeea."

Hugo was finding this size comparison hard to comprehend. "Ley lines?" he said.

"Yes, ley lines, and ours are exactly like yours, only we can harness their powers to travel great distances to every district within Laniakeea. You have them, and you even know of their powers, but only from a spiritual or magnetic non-involvement point of view."

"Your spiritual scientists already know they exist in straight lines that shoot out from all points of the compass. We travel in a little invisible force-field, that isn't physical at all, but holds you in. We then use specific incantations that would take us to a particular area within a district. It will take us just over forty-five of your Earth seconds to travel the four thousand and thirty-seven Earth miles."

Hugo shook his head in disbelief. How could this be? On Earth, energy resources, to produce electricity, fossil fuels or scientifically produced nuclear fuels from the land, had long since been depleted, and indeed for transport, slowly over the years, Earth has had to revert to using horses for transportation, the harnessing of wind for ships, and so on.

By now, Hugo and Allana were beginning to approach a clearing. There was a large laterite circle, ten feet in diameter. As they came nearer, Hugo could see a ring, fixed within the laterite, of about four inches in width. It was gold in color. Then intersecting the circle, but within its diameter, much smaller lines were crisscrossing.

They all had arrowheads that were presumably indicating a direction of travel, and along the top of the lines, what Hugo assumed were instructions, in Elvish, that the traveler would need to either think or say out loud. It was the traveler's choice to be verbal or use telepathy. Some of the lines were of a different color, and again Hugo assumed this must mean that some destinations may be off-limits to certain Elves, or that they were indicating the importance of the end conduit ley line destination, etc.

But it all looked too familiar. Where had he seen this before? Suddenly it came to him: it was when he was being dragged along by his captors, in a dazed state, only a few hours earlier.

He made a mental note to ask Allana, exactly how they worked and whether she thought it would be possible to use the Elves' knowledge and technology to incorporate ley line travel back in the Earth dimension. The logistical advantages for trade and so many applications, would be a huge help across the whole of the Earthan dimension.

As they stepped onto the ley line conduit (or circle),

Allana was explaining the rules and courtesies that had to be undertaken to gain the queen's respect. She also told Hugo to keep an open mind when meeting the Laniakeean sorceress known as the Elfistra. She would be examining and observing him very carefully. She would also be reading his mind, for which she would have full permission from the queen, so he was to try to keep his thoughts clear, clean and respectful. By her side would be her aide, a deformed being called Mandaz, whom all Laniakeeans found objectionable. He was known as a troublemaker, and Allana felt sure he would be urging Elfistra to ban Hugo and have him sent back to the Earth dimension immediately.

And so, they came to the circle. "Stand exactly here please," said Alana to Hugo, "Face the direction of the gold arrow. Whatever you do, do not move, keep as still as possible. If you were to move, the consequences could be unpleasant for you." *'Great,'* thought Hugo to himself, *'Happy days.'*

Allana said, "You will notice there is only one gold colored arrow, and it will transport us to another ley line circle, which is within twenty feet of the queen's palace. We have approximately forty ley line conduits covering every part of our dimension, and each one will contain a gold arrow which will take the traveler to the conduit close to the queen's palace.

Three of the queen's elite warriors constantly guard the ley line conduit at the queen's palace, and they have to be informed who will be traveling there beforehand. I have already instructed them of this. If they are not informed (which is usually done telepathically), they would attack first and ask questions later."

"Hmmm," said Hugo, "Gives traveling to a holiday destination a whole new and exciting slant." Allana gave Hugo a quizzical look. She wasn't too sure how to interpret that statement.

So, Hugo stepped up to his mark, Allana just behind him. He briefly turned his head to look at her, at which she almost shouted "Don't move! Please! For your own safety." She then gave the Elvish equivalent of an exasperated sigh.

Hugo couldn't hear anything, so he closed his eyes and waited. His whole body felt like it was being dragged along by a jet fighter, at Mach 6.7. Being shot forward at incredible speed, all the air, for an instant, left his lungs and immediately he began to feel dizzy and nauseous. *'How long did she say this traveling would last? Just over forty-five seconds? Oh God! I feel strange.'* He then blacked out.

The Planet Saturn
(As viewed from the Laniakeean Windfell mountains)

CHAPTER 2

The UEL

(Remember, all Elves on Laniakeea are friends, you simply haven't met them all yet.)

The time difference between the Earth and the Laniakeean dimensions are almost similar, but not quite. In other words, an hour spent on Earth would relate to two hours spent on Laniakeea. Hugo would have been on Laniakeea for almost seven elvish hours, equating to only three and a half hours on Earth.

By now, all hell was breaking loose in Winberry woods. The head of the UEL (United European Landmass) was Lord Arlo Brough, Hugo's Father. He was a surly, large brute of a man. A big red beard and very broad in the chest. He was not particularly tall, but incredibly strong, and had a large girth that meant he waddled rather than walked. His strong presence that proceeded him, commanded immediate attention everywhere he went.

His mop of red greying hair was tied into a top knot on the crown of his head. Most people who were introduced to him, immediately disliked him. He had a very offhand, patronizing and rude personality, and didn't bat an eyelid when telling someone what he thought of them. He could be nasty, and condemn a man or woman to death, in his role as a judge, without an ounce of compassion.

Even though the evidence could be overwhelming in proving the guilty person was innocent, there have been rumors that Brough would summarily issue a death sentence simply because 'I didn't like the look of that low life.'

He used brute force and political maneuvering, together with a bottomless purse, to curry favor with various others in society to help him climb up the political ladder, and this, together with his obnoxious personality, had brought him to the dizzy heights of Commander in Chief of the U.E.L.

By now, in 2087, a combination of global warming and mistreatment of other natural sources, had meant that many of the Earths other landmasses were now under water, and by far the largest of the surviving landmasses were the interconnected landmasses of England (where now there was no Scotland, Wales or Ireland, in terms of geographical and political separation) and the whole of Europe and some other eastern countries. This connection meant there was free travel to any part of the whole of 'Earth Europe', as it was now known. The days of visa's, customs, immigration, separate countries, due to separate landmasses, had long since gone.

Collectively then, we had the UEL. The governing board consisted of members from all points of the landmass compass. Corruption was rife, which suited Lord Brough down to the ground. It had got him to where he was today, and consequently, he immediately blocked any judiciary moves that attempted to change the rules, thank you very much.

Lord Brough has two sons and a daughter, Hugo, Kayon and Helena. He also has an illegitimate son called Maxx. A moment of drunken passion with a mixed-race woman who was part of the cleaning staff at Brough Manor. Some say it was violent forced rape, which in actuality, most probably was.

Consequently, Maxx was born on the 17th of December, 2063. It was difficult to refute that this boy was not Lord Brough's son, and Brough was under enormous pressure to officially name Maxx as his son, the political backlash of this, if he didn't, could mean Brough losing his seat as the head of the UEL.

That meant handing back all the privileges and favors that such a position commanded, so he relented and officially named Maxx as his son. He did not however, grant him the titles to his land, in effect 'the power behind the seat', so he was deemed a son in name only, and to be fair, he was brought up in the Brough family household just as equally as Hugo, Kayon and Helena. To all intents and purposes, Maxx was treated as a true family member by Hugo, Kayon and Helena, and being only a year younger than Hugo, who was born only two months later on the second of February, to Brough's official wife, Romilly Woodbead, meant that Hugo and Maxx grew up together, played together and fought together.

However, to Maxx, he always felt his Father was much less accepting of him than Hugo, and made this quite plain in many subtle ways. This, over time, started to gnaw away at Maxx, and as it did, he began to have an all-consuming hatred for his father. All Maxx ever wanted, was to be accepted as a full equal, not just in name, just as was Hugo, Kayon and Helena

Meanwhile, back at the manor, Lord Brough was at home, when in came running two officers from his land security force. "Sir, we have some unfortunate news about Hugo and his two riding companions."

"What?" shouted Brough, "Where is he?"

"He was Boar hunting in Winberry Wood," the first officer replied, "They were late back by almost an hour, when two of the horses returned back to the stables, on their own sir, and one of the horses was Hugo's horse, Firemaker."

"Any idea what has happened?" barked Brough.

"Well sir, I'm afraid it gets worse, Hugo's two riding companions were both killed, we have retrieved their bodies. They were killed by arrows sir, arrows unlike anything we have seen before."

"What do you mean man?" questioned Brough.

"Well sir, they are very heavy, very long and thick, bright red with strange markings all along the shaft. Our investigative team are there now sir. We have comprehensively searched the whole area, but there is no sign of Hugo. We did find a pool of blood near a large rock, together with another arrow, a few feet further on, and we have already determined that the DNA from the blood on the arrow head and the pool by the rock, is conclusively Hugo's."

"Right!" shouted Brough, "Andrew?" (one of the stable hands) "Prepare my horse, I'm going to Winberry right away."

"Sir, there is one other thing you need to know," said the lead officer.

"What now?" exclaimed Brough.

"You have to be aware that in the vicinity, there is what can only be described as a column of white light, reaching from the ground and upwards through the tree tops. We are assuming that the killing of the soldiers and the disappearance of Hugo, has to be either directly, or indirectly, linked to this column of light. One of the investigative team has tentatively suggested it could be some sort of 'doorway' to somewhere, but of course, we have no idea what or where that would be."

"We have already tried placing our hands in the column," continued the officer, "To no detrimental effect, so we are concentrating our efforts on trying to conclude that this could be some sort of portal? But until we know a little more, the advice is that we keep a safe distance."

"Right," said Brough, "And if it is a doorway, and we can pass through to wherever, I am assuming it's just as possible for something on the other side to come over to us. So, first things first, I want twenty of our best security officers with a full complement of intelliguns to meet me at the scene, as soon as possible. Got it?"

"Yes sir." With that, the security soldiers quickly saluted, turned on their heels and rushed out of the conference room. Brough headed straight towards the stables. His horse had better be prepared for him, or heads will roll, he thought to himself.

And it was, his thoroughbred Arab stallion Majesty, was almost eighteen hands, his coat as black as night, he was a magnificent horse, although he was covered in scars, reminiscent of having been whipped at some point of his life. Brough would always ride him hard, and it needed a strong horse to stand up to that.

Majesty always became a little skittish whenever he was approached by Brough. It didn't take a fool to notice that this horse, no matter how magnificent and strong he was on the outside, not counting the scars, had been well and truly broken on the inside. He was quickly mounted by Brough, and with two security guards, galloped off into the distance.

By now it was dark. It was eleven-thirty pm, but the route had already been lit by torches, and after a brief ten-minute ride, they were approaching the forest. They slowed to a canter then a fast walk. The trees were thick and many at this point. Ahead of them, like a beacon reaching out into the sky, Brough first noticed the column of white light. He slowed momentarily to look in awe at this phenomenon, then continued.

Approximately twenty feet from the light, he stopped, and as he was dismounting, the noticed the twenty strong elite soldiers had already arrived, and immediately had started to form a circle around the light where possible, using trees and rocks etc. as some form of protection, but from what?

Immediately in front of Brough, were his two commanders. To the most senior one he said, "Ah, Steven, glad you are here. I assume you have come to brief me? What do you make of all this?"

"As you can see sir, we have some of the scientists and an investigative team close to the column. They are testing everything they can think of, such as electrical fields, radiation and so on, as yet we are no clearer to understanding what has happened, but we do hope to have an answer very soon."

"Good man," shouted Brough, "But one thing does worry me, if it is a doorway, what could come through to our side? I believe we need to make this area militarily very safe. I want a twenty-four-hour watch kept on that column. The men need to be under no illusion. They need to assume that something beyond their wildest nightmares could come through that column, and if it does, we need to be ready for it."

"Off course sir," said Steven, "And we have already prepared a tent for your comfort only fifty meters to the West. I can assure you sir, the moment we hear or know anything, I will personally inform you. I also wanted to assure you that finding Hugo is of course an equal priority sir. And finally, we have now all synchronized our HC's (head comms) so we will also be in direct communication with you at all times."

"Ok, Steven," said Brough, and with that he waddled off to find his tent. As he wound his way between the trees, Brough placed his right index finger on the small indentation behind his right ear. Here was the HC, a very small round flat piece of technology. These are implanted into all babies without exception, they are free, and the drawback for this 'free' gift is that the authorities will always have a record of who you are, where you are, and to a certain extent what you are doing.

For those who have them, this latest technological marvel, can act as a phone, you can access all your bank accounts, a huge information store access on every imaginable subject or object, it can also diagnose you if you are unwell, and recommend where you go or what to take to feel better. There is also a wireless sub-neural link from the right eye's optical nerve to the HC, so images are automatically uploaded to the central information bureau (CIB).

Violent crime has fallen drastically in the last thirty years because of the HC's. You can't hide them, they can't be removed, and the latest special feature, using advanced technological extrapolation statistics, means the HC, is also able to predict a crime that someone may commit in the future. So far it is ninety-three percent accurate, but that figure is creeping higher all the time. Once it reaches one hundred percent, it is hoped that all crime will be virtually non-existent! Just imagine, someone being apprehended moments before committing a crime.

The only problem is that will only work most effectively on planned or pre-meditated crimes. Stealing a newspaper when walking past a news stand of course couldn't be prevented, but at the moment, the most violent of crimes, all involve some form of planning, particularly pre-meditated murder, which is why the success rate is excellent.

Just as Brough was entering his tent, Maxx came galloping up, quickly dismounted and shouted out "Father." Brough, turned his head to look at him, and said "Oh, it's you," and continued to walk into the tent.

Maxx came running in after him. Maxx was handsome, with that attractive light honey color that only mixed-race people can have. Not particularly well built, but extremely fit and well-toned. His jet-black afro hair had been shaped into a modern style, making him look more like a model than a soldier. Something that Brough hated. His fearless attitude and looks, always meant a string of women would follow him for his attentions.

He was gay, and this was something else that Brough despised about him even more. He had trouble coming to terms with the fact that not only was he his son, but gay as well? Nope, if Brough could bury him in the ground tomorrow, and get away with it, he would do so.

Lord Brough was the very epitome of all that can be wrong with a man. His was rude, lacked compassion, his hygiene was very poor and he had an overall unkempt appearance. He would even trample on and use his own family to better himself, if he thought that was the way forward. He was never open to ideas, good or bad. He made his own and expected everyone to obey him to the letter, and woe be tide you if you didn't.

And of course, Brough's attitude to gay men and women was unbelievably crass and insulting. Even in a large public gathering, he would point out someone gay and taunt them until they left or tried to fight back, but this was a fight they would not win, this is when he would turn physically nasty.

As one notable politician was heard to say, "Nothing short of a public castration would cure him of his nasty selfish and homophobic ways. It needs to be done sooner rather than later, for the sake of everyone on Earth."

"Father?" Maxx shouted as he came into the large tent.

"Why are you bothering me?" said Brough, "Have you nothing better to do?"

"Well I just heard about Hugo. I'm worried. I have been briefed by Steven, and just want to know what I can do?"

"Nothing." shouted Brough, "If you were more of a man, you would have been militarily trained to a higher standard, just as Hugo, Kayon and Helena are, and be out there with the others, with an intelligun in your hand, ready to face the consequences, but no, in your namby pamby way, you are there, as always, on the outside, the armchair critic, not doing a lot at all, except maybe, choosing a lipstick color."

Maxx had heard this time and time again. Was he ever going to let up, accept? Accept his sexuality. Be a man even, accept him as a full son with the titles that should be afforded to him. Maxx's Mother died six years ago, the circumstances were very suspicious. There was a witness, but unfortunately, he came to an untimely end, but not before he managed to tell others what had happened and that he feared Brough was after wanting to silence him.

So, Maxx was convinced his Father orchestrated the

carefully planned murder. And for that, he would never forgive him. It was the beginning of payback time for Maxx. Payback time that would sort his Father out once and for all, but Maxx was clever, he kept his cards close to his chest. The time, when right, would present itself, so for now, he accepted the insults.

"We can't all be military personnel, although you know very well, I did my military training, and graduated with the second highest grades of all time. But I am not cut out to shoot and kill people. I can't see the point. In any case, this isn't about me, it's about my brother Hugo, and I only want some information about how he is and if there is anything we can do to help him."

"Just get out of my sight", shouted Brough, the veins on his forehead were pulsating badly, "Steven will call you if there are any developments." Brough was seething, Maxx always seemed so laid back, and would never rise to intimidation, no matter how much Brough piled on the pressure. It was this single way that Maxx acted that really wound Brough up to fever pitch. Everybody else would acquiesce, kowtow, and fall back under the verbal and mental bullying by Brough, but not Maxx. Brough even thought that Maxx was deliberately cultivating this attitude on purpose?

Brough thought to himself, '*Well, he will never ever get from me, that which he so desires. Over my dead body,*' He thumped his gnarled fists into the arms of his make-shift chair. Then very quietly, under his breath, he snarled, "I should have had him taken care of when I arranged to have that bitch of a Mother of his sorted out!" He had worked himself up to such a state, he spluttered and coughed, and fought to control his breathing and temper.

As Maxx left for his own tent, he couldn't help a wry grin spreading across his face, he knew exactly how to wind his Father up to boiling point. One day, one day soon, that will be to my advantage, thought Maxx. He couldn't wait.

Morning came too soon for Brough. He rolled off his mattress and heaved himself up and then stepped outside into the cold damp misty air. He yawned, shook himself off, and waddled towards the slice. "Morning Sir,' said Steven, as his master came towards him.

"Any developments Steven?"

"I'm afraid not sir, nothing at all, although one of the men volunteered to enter into the slice. We had him dressed up in full protective clothing, full video capabilities, and tethered him carefully, so we could haul him back quickly if needed."

"Go on?" urged Brough.

"Well sir, as the private stepped into the column, he shot into it completely, immediately his HC failed, so we lost communication. On our side, the tether rope was being held loosely by three of my men, it started to move through their hands at an incredible speed, to the point they had to let go, the speed of the rope was burning the palms of their hands, even though they were wearing gloves."

"As suddenly as it had started," continued Steven, "It stopped. Immediately the men picked up the rope and started hauling on the rope as quickly as possible to bring him back, which it did. However, as we were reeling him back, half a dozen arrows came through the column, and shot over our heads, not hitting anyone luckily."

"Well?" exclaimed Brough.

"Sir, the private was taken to the medical tent for a debriefing," said Steven, "He was very disorientated, and said he felt very nauseous. For the time he was in the column, he was surrounded by very bright warm light that was pulsating with colors. He said he felt he was being twisted around, upside down and so on, and suddenly he believed he came to what he assumed was the other side. In front of him were a group of what looked like tall men, with pointed ears, all wearing red clothes with a pattern on them."

"As soon as they saw him," said Steven, "They took off their backs what looked like very long bows, and were scrabbling for arrows. They almost got to the stage of setting them on the strings of their bows, when at that point we had started to haul the private back to us. This explains the arrows that came towards us from the column."

"What does all this mean?" said Brough, "It certainly makes no sense to me?"

"Neither does it to our team here either sir," said Steven, "But I assure you we are working hard on this and hope to have some sort of answer very soon."

"Ok, Steven, keep it up. I'm going back to the Manor for now." Steven saluted, and ran off back towards the slice.

Brough called for his horse, and made his way back to the manor for breakfast. He had only gone three paces when he spied something glinting on the path. He stopped, dismounted, and knelt down to pick it up.

It was Hugo's silver christening chain and cross. Brough assumed the chain had obviously broken in the melee that had ensued at the time. He mounted up and again set off, thinking how he was going to break all this to his wife, Romilly. She was a hysterical creature at the best of times.

'I will have my breakfast in peace first, because I'm hungry', he thought to himself, *'Then find Romilly and tell her what has been happening.'* He wasn't looking forward to her wailing crying hysterics when she finds out what has happened to Hugo.

'For God's sake, why couldn't it have been Maxx!' His anger was returning, because of it, he was wrenching majesty's neck uncomfortably, pulling on the reins violently, making him wince and snort so badly, he reared up, and Brough fell heavily to the ground, completely winded. For a few moments, he couldn't breathe in, and it looked like majesty was rearing up to trample him under his hooves. Indeed, Brough was already shielding his face and head with his arms, but managed

to roll to one side.

When he could, he stood up, anger running through his whole body, grabbed the reins, pulled Majesties head down, and using his crop, started whipping and flailing the crop across both sides of majesties head with such force, slivers of skin on the horse's cheeks were opening up and blood was beginning to spurt out everywhere, and indeed was splattering Brough across his face and hair.

When he had vented his anger on the poor horse, Brough had to wipe away majesties blood from his eyes, so he could see to re-mount. He dug his heels deeply and cruelly into the horse's flanks, and set off at full gallop back to the manor.

Queen Haruntha of Laniakeea
(Very magical, very wise and has the ability to reincarnate)

CHAPTER 3

Queen Haruntha

(If another Elf offers you the touch of friendship, accept it and put your quarrels behind you.)

As Hugo regained consciousness, he became aware of a worried looking Allana kneeling down on one knee, searching his face for clues as to how he was feeling. Two of the queen's bowmen were also peering down at him. He was still lying face down, but pulled himself to a sitting position, spitting out half a mouthful of the red laterite dust that he must have collected in his open mouth when his body slid to a stop on the ley line circle.

"This is starting to become a habit." exclaimed Hugo.

"What do you mean?" said Alana.

"Well," said Hugo, "in the space of twenty-four hours, I have landed face down conscious, semi-conscious or unconscious, with a mouth half-full of either blood, dirt or laterite dust."

Allana couldn't help smiling as she pulled a small glass phial out of one of her pockets, which contained a small quantity of the blue liquid that was administered to him when he was brought to Allana's dwelling earlier on in the day.

This time, Hugo knew what it was, and didn't hesitate in drinking the whole thing in an instant. "I like that," said Hugo, "That packs a punch, doesn't it? Makes me instantly feel, well, amazing." As he began to stand up, he was brushing the red dust off his clothes and turned to Allana and said, "What's in it?"

"Difficult to describe," said Allana. "There are special herbs, not from this dimension I might add, that we discovered over two millennia ago, and processed into a herbal infusion, but during the final stages of processing, a magical incantation is performed over each batch, a little bit of magic if you like. The liquid is then available to all Elves across the kingdom. Every household will have a phial of the herbal mixture, which is called Voovo. It is pretty much a cure-all for all sorts of minor ailments, and it seems to work for humans as well. I didn't know this earlier on when I offered some for you to drink when I first met you."

"Oh great," said Hugo, "A guinea pig, was I?"

"What!" Allana quickly replied, with a worried look on her face, "No, no. I would never be so disrespectful towards you, I am so sorry, I would never call you a pig. I know in Earthan ways, to call someone a pig, usually a male, a pig is an insult."

Hugo laughed. "No, you were not implying I was a pig. It's just a saying we have. I was actually saying, was I an experiment to you? That's all."

"Oh, I think I understand," said Allana. There was a quiet moment of reflection by Allana, then she said, "This, what did you call it? Guinea pig? Is it a very ugly pig?"

"No," said Hugo smiling, "It really doesn't matter." Allana was frowning and looking at Hugo. He could tell she still hadn't quite got the joke.

One of the bowmen interrupted Allana telepathically, to say the queen was ready to meet the Earthan. "We have to go to the queen now," said Allana. Hugo looked up, and there to his right was the most magnificent, well, he wanted to call it a palace or castle, because he knew he was meeting the queen, but it wasn't one, not in any way shape or form.

For a start, it was gold colored, it shimmered in the light, and again, like Allana's dwelling, the walls were smooth, and seemed to be moving with flashes of subtle pastel colors running through them. It was such an unusual shape, and very tall. Hugo couldn't help thinking that it looked like a tree, the most unusual tree shape he had ever seen, but nevertheless, a tree.

It was very wide, almost two hundred feet wide, and as

Hugo was nearing it, the 'trunk' if you like, he could see there were no corners to it, it must be round. The walls rose straight up from the ground for possibly another hundred and ninety feet, and dotted all over the wall were round windows of all sizes.

In the middle though, separated by a distance of almost forty feet, were two wide parallel lines, running from a little over ten feet from the ground to the very top. From these gaps flapped very long colorful flags. There didn't seem to be any spaces anywhere, flags completely filled these gaps in the parallel lines, but then Hugo noticed there were bowmen at strategic points in these parallel lines.

But it was the top that fascinated Hugo the most. And this is why he felt it resembled a tree most of all, a carefully constructed ball of branches, that were turning in on themselves and interlocking. None of the so-called branches were protruding, all the ends of the thinning branches were carefully tucked within the ball.

When Hugo looked more carefully, he noticed a few bowmen wearing the distinctive queen's livery of scarlet, but then more and more bowmen came into view, throughout the whole of the ball of interlocking branches.

Hugo couldn't begin to count them, there were far too many. He hazarded a guess at over a thousand? Talk about the feeling of being watched. He felt every pair of bowmen's eyes were bearing down on him. It made him feel very uneasy.

Allana smiled. Watching Hugo was like watching a child with a new toy. Wonder and amazement spread across his face.

They approached an enormous round opening, with what looked like a strong scarlet fine metal mesh stretched across it. When they came to within ten feet, Allana and the bowmen, dropped onto one knee and bowed their heads. Something was happening telepathically again, thought Hugo. He could hear interchanges of Elvish going back and forth in his head, and he was caught in the 'thought' stream.

He dropped down to his knee as well but was too fascinated with what was happening to lower his head.

Then, quite suddenly, they all rose and in a rolling motion, the scarlet mesh covering wrapped itself up and as it did so, rolled to one side. *'Who's doing that?'* thought Hugo. He couldn't see anyone, no matter how far he craned his neck either side to see. He looked at Allana, who simply said "Queen's Magic." And with that, they entered into the queen's palace.

It was cavernous. The ceiling was very tall. The Elves all seemed to wear soft-soled foot coverings, but Hugo's military boots, with their metal toecaps, clattered across the floor, and the sound loudly reverberated and echoed off the walls. It was amusing to see Allana, the two bowmen, and they were now joined by four of the queen's personal guards, suddenly all stop and silently look in awe at Hugo's boots, and the noise they were making on the floor.

Hugo noticed they had all stopped, so he did as well. He immediately realized the consternation caused by the noise his boots were making, so he set off again, very carefully, almost on tip toes, seriously trying not to make a sound. All the Elves found this very amusing and they were laughing. Not out loud, but weirdly Hugo could hear the laughter in his head! *'I will never get used to this telepathic business,'* he thought.

Through more doorways, some small, others very tall and wide, turning left, then right and on for what seemed like five minutes or so, when they eventually came to more of the queen's personal guards, who were all looking at Hugo intently. Now, these guards looked a little different. They were a good head taller than the rest, and more powerfully built.

Their tunics of green had ribbons of gold thread running through it, so they shimmered, even when standing still. Across their chest tunic was a scarlet flash of an embroidered red material. Behind them was a very large wooden door. This was the first piece of actual wood, he had come across since he arrived here. It looked ancient. It was very dark, almost ebony, and it was covered in strange marks that seemed to be carved into the wood.

'*Yes Earthan,*' a loud authoritative Elvish female voice boomed into his head, '*This is a wood that is older than your Human race. From a species that have long since departed from the dimension from whence they came. It was a gift to Laniakeea. The species were called The Gareen. Please come forth, my name is Queen Haruntha, and I greet you in peace.'* As these words were reverberating inside his head, the queen's personal guards and the bowmen, all stepped to one side and allowed access to Hugo and Allana.

They entered a long hall. Lined along the walls were moving yellow lights, which gave the whole ambiance a feeling of calmness.

There was also a heady scent in the air, reminiscent of lavender. It was pleasantly warm and comfortable, but Hugo just knew that this palace was older than time itself. At the far end was a magnificent throne.

Not a chair, but a very ornate tree trunk, that was shaped to resemble a throne. It was gold colored and was covered in what seemed like a very lush soft fabric in scarlet, with what he assumed was the queen's emblem embroidered into it, and the edges bordered with a white fur, which had flecks of black material within it.

When Allana and Hugo came to within ten feet of the queen, her two personal guards, crossed their longbows in front of them and they stopped. Immediately, Allana, fell to her left knee, held her right arm to the side, bowed her head and touched her forehead with the two fingers of her left hand.

But Hugo simply stood and stared at the queen. Hugo thought, *'I have never seen such beauty before. Her body, her eyes, her shape, the way she fashioned her hair, how she seemed to seductively drape herself across the throne, in absolute confidence, was enticing and very attractive, but also with a feeling full of authority.'*

Although the queen had long silver flowing hair that cascaded down her back, she was wearing a very ornate headdress, mainly emerald green in color. Every so often, it caught the light so that it sparkled and shone. The top of the headdress contained small interwoven pieces of what looked like slivers of bamboo and began to resemble the top of the palace described earlier. As he worked his way down, Hugo noticed that she had a similar pattern of eye-shadow in a band across her eyes, similar to Allana, which was green, but from the midpoint, in the middle, between her eyebrows, this band also came down her nose, over her lips and downwards over her chin and onto her neck.

Her ears had what looked like colorful miniature peacock feathers running along the leading outside edges, and from each lobe there hung a simple green leaf, flecked with gold on one side, which caught the light whenever she turned her head. Carrying on down, her shoulders were bare, then across the top of her chest was a band of rich green embroidered material, probably something like five inches in width, to which was attached a very fine diaphanous cream fabric, which fell to just above her knees.

What surprised Hugo was that at one point, the queen turned to communicate with one of her guards, and he could see that the material did not extend all the way around her body, that the back lower half of her body, from her waist to her ankles was at times, exposed when she moved. He couldn't help but admire what he saw.

When she wasn't moving, the leading edges of the material seemed to almost meet at the back. Her shoes were soft, like little booties, but made out of a thick fabric, again green, but the leading edges were bordered in what could be embroidered gold leaf. The toes of her shoes narrowed off and curled up and onto themselves.

Her presence was unbelievable. He just felt he wanted to please her! If she had commanded him to take all his clothes off and run around stark naked, he would have done so in a flash. Why?

While all this was running through Hugo's mind, Allana was now standing. Again, Hugo began to look perplexed as an interchange of Elvish was filtering into his head. He glanced at Allana, with a quizzical look, and then at the queen. They both were smiling and looking at Hugo

The Elvish stopped. The queen took a deep breath and said to Hugo. "I am sorry, Allana has explained that telepathy is not a skill you have come to terms with as yet, so, like Allana, I will now communicate with you verbally, and will refrain, out of courtesy, from mentally reading your thoughts.

May I say though, thank you for your previous thought compliments."

As she said this, Hugo felt himself blushing a little.

"And," continued the Queen, "There is certainly no need to run naked around my palace." By now, Hugo was coughing and spluttering and was blushing even more. The Queen and Allana said nothing. They just looked at each other and knowingly smiled.

Telepathically, the queen indicated to Allana, that she wished to have a conversation with this Earthan, introduce him to a little of the history of Laniakeea, and try to gauge what his intentions were, whether good or bad. The Queen was able to telepathically talk to an individual privately, without out anyone else receiving the thought streams. Allana bowed her head and started to walk backwards. Hugo looked little perturbed at this, wondering what was happening, craning his neck around to see where she was going. Allana simply smiled at him, turned on her heels and left silently.

Now in verbal mode, the queen was looking directly at Hugo and said, "So, you are known as Hugo Brough?"

"Yes, I am." Hugo replied. The queen started to slowly walk down the steps, or to Hugo, she looked like she was floating down, perfectly balanced, as a ballerina would walk, flanked on either side by two very tall members of her personal bodyguard. Their longbows were as tall as they were, and were hooked around their backs, and they each had a full complement of long thick red arrows, in very ornate silver-looking quivers, across a shoulder. They looked menacingly at Hugo, and their dedication to their queen was apparent.

"Hugo Brough," said the queen, "follow me." They had only walked for twenty feet, still within the great hall, when they came to a miniature ley line circle on the floor.

As soon as Hugo saw this, he rolled his eyes to the top of his head, and was about to tell the queen, that he couldn't stay upright when using them, when she said, "Yes, I know you have had problems with our ley line travel, but this is a very minor one. We are literally going to my secret garden just to the north of the palace. You won't experience the same problems that you have before. May I suggest you take your position within the circle, spread your legs to shoulder width, and relax and control your breathing. If you tense up, then the transition will not be pleasant."

Hugo took a deep breath, and stepped into the circle. The queen joined him to one side. The two guards squeezed in behind Hugo, and he was sure he could feel them breathing down his neck.

"Close your eyes and breathe normally," the queen advized. Hugo did as he was told. He spread his feet apart and relaxed as much as he could. Again there was a feeling of great speed, butterflies in his stomach, and suddenly, after what seemed only seconds they had arrived. And Hugo was still standing. He was so pleased with himself that he punched the air.

The queen's guards, in what seemed like a couple of seconds had whipped off their bows, and set an arrow on the strings and pulled them back to fire. One arrow was aimed at Hugo's head, the other at his heart. The queen gently raised her arm, to which the guards immediately released the tension on the bow strings, collected the arrows and returned them to the quivers. However, the two guards continued to narrow their eyes and look intently at him.

"You have to be careful Hugo Brough," the queen said gently, "Just as you have to get used to our ways, we have got to get used to yours. Any sudden movements my guards don't understand could be taken as an offensive gesture, and they will come to my defense and protect me."

"I'm sorry," said Hugo "It's just I can't believe I managed to travel and arrive standing up." To which the queen smiled. They then all stepped out of the circle.

As Hugo took in the scene all around him, he was in what we would call a sort of walled garden. Behind and along both sides were tall walls, with intricate carvings of stone sat on the top, depicting the heads of various flowers, and in front of him the edge of a forest. There were flowers of all sorts everywhere, on the sides and growing up the walls. It felt very peaceful and tranquil, and the scent pervading the air was invigorating and heady. From the flower heads on some flowers, there were shafts of light, in rainbow colors, spreading in arcs and connecting with other flower heads. Others were quite literally moving, vibrating.

He noticed as the queen started walking down a little mossy path, that lining it were flowers with very long soft tentacles, and as she walked down, she held her hands out from her sides, and the tentacles, very gently caressed her arms and hands.

"Follow me Hugo," the queen said. "And hold your hands and arms out as I am doing. Don't make any sudden movements. Try to keep calm, and let the tentacles of the plants caress you."

Hugo followed the queen, and tentatively repeated what she had done, but this time you could feel the tentacles were being a little more cautious, and their touch a lot lighter, less relaxed. At one-point Hugo could smell a scent. He raised his hand to his nose, the scent became all-pervading, and he figured out that the tentacles must somehow have little scent pockets on them, and were able to deposit the scent on the arms and hands of those passing by.

But Hugo also noticed he was feeling a little lightheaded, but in a very pleasant way. What else was in the scent deposits? All his troubles seemed to be melting away. The guards were also letting the tentacles wipe and wrap themselves over their arms and hands, and he noticed their permanent scowls were giving way to a more pleasant look, with even the hint of a smile.

Shortly, they came to another mossy trunk lying on its side. Again this was covered in a very thick fur pelt, in cream. The borders of the edges were embroidered with a gold material, again with what Hugo assumed must be the queen's personal emblems. The queen sat down, took a deep breath and indicated for Hugo to sit beside her. The tree trunk was fashioned into a gentle semi-circle, so although the queen and Hugo were close, they were able to almost face one another.

"Did you find that experience with the plants pleasant?" enquired the queen.

"Yes, very much so," replied Hugo.

"Good," said the queen, "Because if you had been an enemy of mine say, those tentacles would have transformed into razor like barbs that could quite easily have decapitated you." At this Hugo frowned, turned and looked over at the path where the plants were and started gently rubbing his wrists.

Hugo's reaction to this last statement of the Queen, made both the Queen and the guards smile.

"You see Hugo, we Laniakeean's actually have a similar sense of humor to you. The reason for this will all become more apparent as you are able to assimilate more and more information about us."

They looked over the respective shoulders at the forest in front of them, and the Queen simply said, "That is the home of the Barboski. You have horses in your dimension do you not? I was told by Allana that you rely on them as a mode of transport?"

"Yes," said Hugo, "They are very much a way of life for us. I couldn't think of how we could manage without them."

"Well", continued the queen, "the Barboski are a very distant relative of your horse. In fact, the Barboski is a distant cousin of what Earthans believe to be the mythical creature, the unicorn. Both possess a little magic. It will be explained at a later date what that means, but for now, it's sufficient to know that our Barboski are pure white, including their manes and tails, which are very long. Their eyes, though, are bright blue. They live in peace and harmony within this forest and are our companions in times of need."

"I have sent out a thought message to my favorite Barboski to see if he will join us. I would like you to meet him. He is called Halhaze. Now, don't be perturbed when you meet him. Of course, he can't speak to you verbally but can transfer images that act as a simple conversation telepathically into your head. They are supremely intelligent."

Hugo couldn't wait. The queen looked into Hugo's eyes and said "On behalf of myself and the Elves of Laniakeea, I apologize sincerely for the deaths of your companions. I understand at the time, there were misunderstandings, and a number of mistakes made. Probably brought about by the sudden appearance of the dimension portal. It was as unexpected to us, as it must have been to you."

Hugo let out a long sigh and said, "I believe I may have been indirectly involved in the deaths of my friends. An unnecessary mistake, I grant you, but a mistake nevertheless, for which I feel very sad. The safety of Earth and where we live is charged to me. I am a military general in my dimension, but will always seek a peaceful solution to any problem, no matter what quarter it comes from, and so I apologize to you for my actions."

"I would like to think," continued Hugo, "We could forge a working friendship, to share technologies, to the betterment of both our species, although I have to admit, from what I have experienced so far, we are the ones that are intellectually lagging far behind."

"Very well said," the queen smiled. "And that's just the plan of action we need to follow. I would like to set up a meeting between your leaders, with myself and my advisors. I will release you and will charge Allana to accompany you when you return."

"It would help," continued the queen, "for your leaders to see an Elf and communicate with her, and see that in many ways, there are similarities, but more importantly, hopefully, they will understand that ultimately we strive for peace."

"In the meantime, we will return to the palace, because

I wish you to meet our sorceress, Elfistra. Do not be shocked by her appearance. Although part Elf, she is also part of the sentient being that colonized this dimension. When she dies, she reincarnates, but keeps all the memories and thoughts she has collected since the very beginning, which is over six and a half million of your years ago. You can see then that she is a wise and valuable advisor to me. I can see you are trying to grasp this concept. I will ask Elfistra to explain in more detail in a way that will be more understandable to you."

"Please feel free to ask any question of her. She will gladly supply you with the answer. In return, you must answer any question she asks of you." Suddenly the queen broke off their conversation to look towards the forest edge, then she stood and held out her arms. She looked very excited. "Halhaze has arrived."

Hugo turned to peer at the forest edge and then noticed a magnificent white horse coming towards them. It was walking towards them, but what stunned Hugo, was that it was approximately three feet off the ground. It was gliding along, and he could tell, it was also very pleased to see the queen. As it approached, the last three or four feet, it started to settle to the ground and began walking as normal. It went straight up to the queen and nuzzled her neck. The queen wrapped her arms around Halhaze's head.

There was a moment's stillness, in which Hugo assumed they were communicating telepathically, then suddenly, the horse turned its head towards Hugo. Hugo could see the similarities now between the Barboski and the Earth's mythological unicorn. But maybe the unicorn wasn't mythological in the light of knowing what the queen had told him.

With a toss of its tail, a very vivid image suddenly formed in Hugo's head. It showed Hugo, stroking the horse's neck. The image was so real, in 3D, he felt he was touching it. The horse in the image was breathing, he could hear it. It felt so real. The queen said to Hugo, "I know you can see an image in your head. He is inviting you to stroke him. He is quite happy for you to do that. He accepts my word that you will be gentle with him."

With that, Hugo stepped forward and put his hands on Halhaze's neck. As he did so, immediately flashes of images of Hugo as a child to where he was now, all the experiences he had ever known, were running like an express train through his head. They suddenly slowed down, and he could see countless images of all he had experienced with his own horse Firemaker. How Hugo respected and treated Firemaker, all the adventures, either in war or for pleasure, and how, at the back of Hugo's mind even now, the concern Hugo had for the safety of Firemaker.

Halhaze reached forward and nuzzled Hugo's neck. He was very soft and gentle, and Hugo could easily sense the higher intellect here. Finally, another vivid image suddenly appeared in Hugo's head. This time it was more like a video, with images running quickly from one to another. It showed Hugo and Allana on Halhaze's back, all around them arrows were flying, red and yellow flames, strange looking dragon type creatures, and all the time, there were looks of desperation on Hugo's and Allana's faces as if they were trying to help and control Halhaze.

It all seemed so real, at some point Hugo put his hands up to defend himself, or ducked down to avoid something coming towards him. Were they being attacked? Or running away from something? Hugo couldn't quite make it out.

Just as suddenly, the images stopped. Halhaze lifted and tossed his head, snorted, turned and made his way back to the forest, and as he went, he slowly started to rise into the air.

The queen looked a little perturbed. "The Barboski are able to read very well what is going to come up in the future. There are times I come here to spend time with Halhaze to have a premonition as to what may be going to happen, and then prepare. We can prepare because we have the ability to choose to alter the outcome of the premonitions. Although, we still have to make the final choice."

"You must know though," said the queen, "that Halhaze thinks very highly of you. He tells me you have a good heart and your love for your own horse was quite evident to him, and important of course."

"Now it is time to return to the palace to meet Elfistra." And with that, they made their way back to the ley line circle, and again without incident for Hugo, arrived back within the palace walls.

As the queen made her way into the great hall, followed by Hugo and the guards, she suddenly turned to Hugo and said that Elfistra had already arrived, and that she would be there momentarily. "She is looking forward to meeting you Hugo Brough, but a little word of caution, she will read your mind. I cannot prevent her from doing that, and neither would I. She is responsible for the safety of this realm, and I trust her implicitly. Try to keep your thoughts honest and pure, for your own sake."

There was a noise at the end of the hall, the great doors were opening. "Ah," said the queen, "Elfistra has arrived."

Elfistra and Mandaz
(Inseparable. Magical. Intimidating)

CHAPTER 4

Elfistra and Mandaz

(The three hearts of the Zo'Sah wolf are large, strong and fearless - but also full of compassion.)

In a short space of time, Hugo had heard a lot about this Elfistra, so his curiosity was getting the better of him. He stepped forward to try to get a better view, and as he looked down the length of the great hall, he could make out a figure moving towards them, slowly, as if this Elf had all the time in the world. With it came a presence. It immediately made Hugo take a half-step back defensively. The hairs on the back of his neck stood on end, and the palms of his hands were becoming a little sweaty.

Hugo was a brave man, he had always been known to be fearless; however, something told him to be on his guard and be wary, so for once, he listened to his inner voice.

As Elfistra came nearer, the feeling of unease became

stronger until she was about ten feet away. She bowed before the queen, and into Hugo's head came blocks of Elvish. At one-point Haruntha motioned over toward Hugo. There was a slow turning of Elfistra's head in Hugo's direction, and an immutable stare, then she slowly turned back towards the queen, and again there was an exchange between the queen and Elfistra.

That was strange,' thought Hugo. All the Elvish messages that had passed through his head since he arrived here were almost monotone. He couldn't tell if it was a female or male, young or old, or even if there was any rank to the Elves that were communicating, but in this case, he was now assuming that the deep raspy tone of Elvish he was now hearing must be Elfistra's. There was a definite authoritative tone, almost to the point that absolute obedience was expected, even though he was quite sure that the conversation was only between Queen Haruntha and Elfistra.

'Well,' thought Hugo, *'Hopefully the queen has told this Elfistra not to read my mind, I'm not sure I would not like her in my head at all.'*

At this point, Elfistra's head, again turned slowly towards him. She was staring at Hugo, which bore straight into him. It made him feel uneasy, and he started shuffling his feet slightly, when suddenly, this very loud, and again, deep raspy voice, in very slow broken English came into his head 'And that human, is where you are wrong.'

But even more discomfiting than that, was the salacious smile that spread over her lips. From a very young age, he had been able to tell if someone's smile was genuine. He would look into the eyes, to see if their eyes were 'smiling' as well, and in this case Elfistra's eyes were unmoving and inscrutable. And that was the other striking revelation; her eyes were a vivid scarlet.

The queen turned to Hugo and said "I am leaving you with Elfistra, please be honest with her. She is the keeper of our dimension, and at this point, you are a visitor that has to convince her that you are no threat to Laniakeea or the lives of the Elves that live in this dimension. She will read your thoughts, but she has said she will also communicate verbally with you for ease of conversation. And with that the queen glided down past Hugo to a side door, Elfistra bowing very low as the queen went by her.

When the queen had departed, there was a few minutes silence. The queen's bowmen, of which there were two, stood to attention.

Elfistra then turned to face Hugo. Without saying a word, she was studying him intently with those piercing eyes, as if she was probing, trying to find something, anything, which could spell mistrust. All the while she was very slowly inching towards him. Hugo couldn't understand it, but the 'fight and flight' hormone adrenaline, was poised, waiting to be released into his body.

Hugo could now see her more closely. She was much darker than all the other Elves, to the point of being an ebony black. When any light shone on her, the black snake-like scales covering the whole of her body, became a silvery color, and that Hugo found disconcerting. Although the scales were slightly overlapping, in-between were little glints of red that would catch the eye whenever she moved, as if she was wearing a sequined dress.

In her ears, which were Elvish ears, there was ring jewelry, and along the leading edge a striped light and dark-blue pattern.

She had long dark hair which fell untidily down her back. In some of her hair, there were flashes of red color. From mid-way down her back, her hair had woven into it a smattering of beautiful small feathers, which then cascaded down to the top of her buttocks. She wasn't wearing any other clothing, not that she needed to, since her entire body was covered in scales.

She held in one hand, an intricately carved wooden staff, on top of which was a long curved blue blade. The staff looked older than time itself, and indeed it was. It has been passed down to each subsequent reincarnated sorceress. All along its length were carvings, inlaid with gold and other rare metals not from either the Earthan or Laniakeean dimensions. She wore nothing on her feet, which were scaled.

When she walked, there was a noise associated with the motion of her walking, a little like the noise produced by the rubbing of the palms of the hands together. The moment she stopped, all the scales which were slightly raised, all silently smoothed down and began to lie very flat.

"I am not strictly an Elf," said Elfistra, "I was brought into existence nearly seven millennia of your Earth years ago. This dimension was colonized by the seed of an intelligent sentient being called the Sola Tree that had been wandering throughout the multitude of dimensions that abound in this sector."

Hugo couldn't help himself and blurted out, "You mean there are more than two dimensions? And you mentioned 'this sector'?"

Elfistra's eyes bore into Hugo, "Oh yes, many sectors containing many more dimensions, which are uncountable by human standards. In fact, a Sola Tree also visited your dimension, when there were no humans. This was around three and a half million years ago. The first point of contact was the landmass known to you as India, which is no longer in existence due to the crass irresponsibility of human mistreatment of the dimension they live in.

"The records quite clearly show the existence of the Sola Tree, albeit a dormant version, but it disappeared before it was able to become fully formed. However, there was enough time for it to seed it with the human DNA genetic coding into the formation of the Earth dimension. This then was responsible for the fact that, however tenuous, there is an ancestral link between you humans and the Elves of Laniakeea.

Hugo was now struggling to take all this information onboard, but he was genuinely interested. Elfistra could sense this, so she continued, "But we have in our possession a wand. It is called Elvina. Other dimensions, as far as we are aware, have their own wands. But Elvina has a reputation of being one of the most powerful and magical of wands.

"The Sola Tree, in its wisdom, decided that this dimension of Laniakeea, should be the keeper of the wand called Elvina. The wand is kept in a simple box called a Spiriten, fashioned out of the dead wood of the Sola Tree, and has on its top surface a number of rare metal incantation symbols there to help protect Elvina.

"But know this, normally only chosen ones are able to touch Elvina. Myself, the Queen, and certain Elves that are called Elfanda, or 'chosen ones', of which Allana is one. Each of the Elfanda are assessed individually, as to their standing in society, their responsibility, but there is one other vital component, and that is, there has to be an ancestral connection with our queen. However, Elvina is not infallible in this sense, it has been known for others who have been able to briefly hold her, but was removed from them before any real damage could be done.

Hugo thought about all this, then said, "Well I know about wands, and they have been mentioned throughout Earth's history, but only in make-believe, in films, and folklore and so on, but as far as I am aware, there are no real functioning wands. Is it powerful?"

Elfistra gave him a sideways piercing look and snorted down her nose. "Is it powerful? Yes human, beyond whatever you could imagine. It has the power to revive a dead being, of whatever species, and bring them back to life. It could collectively destroy one or more dimensions. It could also initiate new dimensions if it were necessary to do so. It is magical, spiritual and will always work for the good of the cosmos. However, if it fell in the wrong hands, although it is a sentient being, it would work with the spiritual and heart desires of the being in whose possession it resides."

"However, if the intentions were corrupt, it could affect the workings of Elvina in the wrong way. It is told in the scriptures, although never had to be proved as yet, that any being, as long as it has a pure heart, and its intentions are for the good of any species, in other words to initiate peace and life, rather than death and destruction, then it could be held and used by them It has only been called upon to be used six times since its residence in this dimension, to protect from warring alien factions from other dimensions and to protect and bring back to life an Elf."

"Being such a powerful instrument, it is under full protection in a maze within the roots of the Sola tree, which is surrounded by the magical trees of Spiritwood."

Suddenly, an awful smell reached Hugo's nose. So nauseating was it, Hugo fought hard to control his feeling of wanting to retch. Hugo looked around, covering his nose with his sleeve, trying to find the source of the stench.

A movement caught his eye to his right, approximately twenty feet away. He blinked two or three times, trying to make sense of it all. *'What the hell is this?'* thought Hugo, *'The smell coming from it is horrendous!'*

"This, as you rudely call him human, is my aide, my confidant, Mandaz. He is here to serve with me. My advisor, as decreed by the Sola scriptures. Be very careful with your thoughts."

Although now controlling the stench, reminiscent of rotting meat and chicken carcasses, that was wafting towards him; he was able to take in the appearance of Mandaz. A deformed character, with one small beady eye and an abnormally large one, and a grossly misshapen yellow greasy-looking body, with a massive soft lump on the left shoulder, covered in a plethora of pustules, which seemed to be a constant state of eruption, so his body appeared slimy. He had legs, but they had withered away to long rod-like sticks, on the ends of which were oversized feet, again covered in carbuncles and warts.

He had to shuffle and pull himself along, and for this purpose, he had a very ornate staff, a Tazareth, with an orb on the top that emanated various colors. Every time he punched the ground in front of him to move his vile gross body along, sparks flew from the bottom of it. The properties of the staff seemed to propel him forward a foot or two quickly at a time.

Behind him, he left a green trail of slime, reminiscent, Hugo thought, of the slime trails large garden snails on Earth left behind. His hands were huge, with long yellowing broken nails on the ends of his fingers. His mouth was open at a slant, which resulted in a yellowish dribble constantly spilling out of the left-hand side of his mouth, down across his chest, and continuing uninterrupted towards the floor.

He slithered to a stop, and looked at Elfistra, who looked back. They were having a telepathic conversation, but unusually, Hugo couldn't hear anything in his head? It seemed though, as if this Mandaz was beginning to get irater, and all the time he moved his head somehow (since he didn't look like he even had a neck) to examine and peer at Hugo with those misshapen eyes. His mannerisms were getting more and more bizarre, and he started shaking and now beginning to jab the end of his staff into the ground, from the bottom of which, more and more sparks were shooting out in every direction.

'What the hell's wrong with him? thought Hugo.

"You are human," said Elfistra, "Mandaz simply doesn't trust you. He tells me the sight of you, he finds abhorrent, he doesn't like the odor you emit, and he finds your thoughts unpleasant."

Hugo then gave a wry smile. *'He doesn't like the way I look and smell?* he thought, *'Well, that's rich coming from him, whatever he or it is.'*

Elfistra was about to warn Hugo, this time a little more forcefully, about his careless thoughts, when into this scene came Allana. As she was approaching, Elfistra menacingly sidled along towards Hugo, stopped well within his comfort zone, and spoke to him telepathically, *'Human, it is becoming important for you to know, especially for your own safety, that Mandaz is a trusted aide to me. Any insults directed towards him will not be tolerated. Do you understand?'*

Allana walked in on this little telepathic conversation, a slight frown came across her forehead, and she said to them both, "Is everything ok?"

Hugo just smiled nervously and nodded his head, and he noticed that Elfistra appeared to be communicating with Allana, who kept looking occasionally towards Hugo. Finally, Allana nodded at Elfistra.

She then told Elfistra she had come to collect Hugo to take him back to Earthside. Elfistra turned to Hugo and said with a large, false smile on her lips, "Well human, I have offered lots of information to you, which I hope you will use wisely. My Queen hopes there will be the opportunity to forge a working relationship between our dimensions."

By now, Mandaz, was hopping around her like a wild banshee, thumping his staff into the ground, 'blips' and 'pops' coming in rapid succession from the massive lump on his shoulder. His demeanor even had Allana looking at him quizzically.

"Thank you," said Hugo to Elfistra. However, Hugo continued to look at Mandaz.

Hugo and Allana turned, and accompanied by two of the queen's bowmen, made their way out of the great hall.

Elfistra kept her eyes fixed on Hugo until they both had left the hall. All the while, Mandaz was incessantly hopping and jumping around her. Suddenly, in a loud, high-pitched telepathic shriek, she shouted out **'QUIET!'**

Mandaz stopped immediately. He said nothing; he was intently watching Elfistra. **'No Mandaz,'** she said to him, **'I don't like or trust him either.'**

She was quiet for a moment. Her eyes started to pulse and glow an even more striking red, and then she said, **'We need to devise a plan to somehow remove him from this dimension soon before he gets too intimate with the queen. But we can't be implicated with this in any way.'** She turned on her heels and left the chamber with Mandaz, who was looking very pleased with himself and the outcome, with his version of a slanted crooked smile spreading across his face.

Meanwhile, Allana, Hugo and the two bowmen had reached the ley line circle. Hugo confidently stepped inside the ring and took his position, with a slightly smug smile on his face. Allana for a second just stood and stared at Hugo, a little frown on her forehead.

Allana went in front of him and the bowmen behind. She half turned to Hugo and said, "Is everything alright?"

"Yep, sure," smiled Hugo. "Let's do this." Allana still couldn't quite understand Hugo's confidence. She faced the front, telepathically called out the necessary chants, and they were off in an instant. Forty-five seconds later they had arrived. But Hugo had 'landed' on his back. He couldn't speak. He was completely winded. The two bowmen went to help him up, but he shrugged them off, and instantly stood up. As he was yet again brushing himself down, he could see Allana looking at him out of the corner of her eyes, hands on hips, smiling. Hugo turned to her and barked out, "What?"

"One of the bowmen here told me you managed to stay upright on your travels to the queen's garden from the palace, and that you were very pleased with yourself. Hugo, a distance over twenty of your Earth seconds, takes different skills that have to be acquired with practice."

"The very short distance the queen took you on, is the

distance that we use for very young Elvish children to practice with. Sometimes they have mastered ley line travel before they can walk. I can see you are displaying Earthan pride here, an emotion we Elves don't possess. Best put your pride to one side and move on after you have removed some of the laterite dust from your mouth again, of course."

Allana couldn't help laughing now, as were the two bowmen, while Hugo took the cloth that Allana had held out for him to clean his mouth with.

Hugo could see they were close to the Elvish forest where the slice was. It seemed so long along ago since this had all started, but as Allana had said to him earlier on, time travels more slowly in Laniakeea than Earthside. Hugo was trying to work out a timescale, Earthwise, for how long he had been away, and he roughly calculated it as twelve hours. As they were walking towards the slice, thoughts were running through his head. How would they react to seeing him back on the other side? How would they react to Allana and the bowmen?

He was sure the security forces had set up some sort of security cordon around the slice. He knew they would be just this side of trigger happy, and wished he could somehow have got word to them that he was safe, had been treated well and were on their way back with a delegation, and so no need for angry, potentially dangerous dramatics.

Hugo took in a deep breath as they approached the slice.

"I am not sure how my people will react to you Allana or the bowmen, so please keep very close to me."

Allana said, "This 'slice' as you call it, is very similar to the multitudes of portals we have in the North of Laniakeea. Passing through them is usually very quick, and you will find it a lot easier than the ley line traveling you are still coming to terms with."

So, they grouped closely together, and stepped into the slice as one. A few moments later they had arrived. Everything seemed to happen at once. The ring of Earthan soldiers, already had their intelliguns raised to their shoulders, and no sooner had Hugo, Allana and the bowmen come to a stop in front of the Slice, than all hell broke loose.

With the very first crack of an intelligun, Allana cried out in pain and fell to her knees clutching her left shoulder. The bowman to Hugo's left was shot through the head, and was dead before he hit the ground. The second bowman was frantically trying to get his bow ready and arrow set. In almost slow-motion, Hugo stood up, arms raised, covering Allana and the bowman, and shouted at the top of his voice "Cease firing now!"

In that fraction of a second, the Earthan soldiers could see it was their general, and the authoritative urgency of his command, immediately made them lower their weapons. The soldiers just stood there cautious, bewildered and confused, looking at each other, then at the victims and Hugo in front of them and froze. Then Hugo went straight to Allana's aid. Other than that, nobody moved an inch.

DING LING
(Known as 'Dingy'. Of Chinese origin. Fearless warrior with a great sense of humor)

CHAPTER 5

Ding Ling

(Even the tallest peak in the Windfell mountains is climbable.
All you have to do is find the courage)

Steven, the security force commander, in charge of the unit of men surrounding the slice, immediately came running up to the kneeling Hugo and Allana. As he did so, he barked out orders to two of his men to take the remaining bowman into custody.

Hugo quickly said, "I want him treated kindly Steven." Steven called out the necessary orders.

He opened up a medikit, and knelt down with them. Allana had closed her eyes and was groaning. She was obviously in pain. As Steven reached for the coagulant pack in the medikit, to help stem the flow of blood, he turned to examine the wound more closely.

He noticed Hugo staring intently at Allana's wound, and

when he turned to look himself, he noticed that Allana's blood was a light blue color! He stopped himself from applying the coagulant pack, and looked at Hugo for permission to apply it. Hugo glanced at him and nodded.

There was a sharp intake of breath from Allana, and she then promptly fainted into his arms. "Right," said Hugo, "I need to take her to a medicentre now!"

Steven turned to Hugo and said, "I have already thought we would need the use of these facilities at some stage, so I took the precaution of ordering a medilance to transport anyone injured to the nearest medicentre."

Common transport was now virtually non-existent in the 2080s. There was hardly any fuel sources available, fossil fuel or otherwise, and what there were was very strictly rationed for emergencies only.

What there were available, under strict law, could only be used for essential purposes and medical emergencies were included. The last of the cars, airplanes, trains etc. stopped running nearly ten years before, but essentials, like medilances (old style ambulances) were sanctioned to continue to be used for emergencies. Hugo carried Allana the short distance to the medilance. Already two medics were waiting, and he laid her down on the gurney inside. The medilance set off at once and arrived at the medicentre six or seven minutes later.

Allana was quickly transported by the two orderlies,

quickly followed by Hugo, into the main examining room and laid gently down on her back on an examining table.

Immediately, the technological miracle, known as the DTC machine was switched on, and they all stepped back. Just because all fossil fuels etc. had run out, technology continued to advance at a fast pace, and here we have the Diagnose, Treat and Cure machine, similar in looks to the old MRI, but much less intimidating and claustrophobic. Allana was passed slowly through it from head to toe and back again, whilst at the same time her injuries were diagnosed and treated.

Hugo was a little worried. He felt he had to briefly explain to the senior medic what sort of species Allana was. The medic wasn't perturbed by this at all, explaining that the technology of the DTC could treat and cure any plant, insect or animal species that could be found on Earth. The differences in DNA, sub-structure and so on, wouldn't be an issue for the DTC, so he was confident that Allana would be diagnosed and cured. The medic said to Hugo "The machine is firstly determining the differences in the structure of her DNA, then on that basis, the diagnosis and treatment should be completed within ten minutes."

One of the technicians reading the results of the DTC urgently called the senior medic over to the results screen. They were in deep conversation, with lots of pointing at the screen and printouts. They seemed very excited, which made

Hugo stare at them both inquisitively.

"Well?" said Hugo, "What's all the fuss about?"

"We have double checked the readings," said the medic, "and we can't quite understand the fact that this being, has an almost identical DNA structure to a human being. It also has two hearts One much larger than the other, and from what we can determine, the larger heart pumps the blood around the body, in a very similar way to ours, but the smaller one pumps a richer oxygenated blood supply specifically to the brain."

"Apart from minor changes to some physical aspects like the composition of her blood, which is blue, the external genetic aspects like the fact the tops of her ears are pointed, and a completely hairless body except for the hair on her head, and the color pigment in the irises of its eyes, the similarities between ourselves and this species are remarkably similar! What I am saying is, that the results do show pretty conclusively, that there is an ancestral link between ourselves and this species. Why that should be? I have no idea at this moment in time."

"Hmm," Hugo pondered this information, "Anything else that you feel it could be important to know?"

"Oh yes," said the medic "The size of her brain is much larger than the average human, particularly her frontal lobes. Whereas we may use up to twenty-five percent of our brain at any one time, I am absolutely convinced she would be able to use up to at least ninety-five percent of her brain simultaneously. Fascinating. This may explain why they have a specific supply of richly oxygenated blue blood from the smaller heart, to keep this highly developed brain from, well, overheating is the best way of explaining it."

By now the DTC had finished its treatment, the wound on her shoulder was almost healed, the bullet had been removed and Allana was beginning to come around. Hugo started to walk towards her, but just before he did the senior medic, ushered Hugo to one side.

"One other major discrepancy," said the senior medic, "if you can call it that, because it may be the norm where she originates from, is that although she has the appearance of a woman, it would be impossible for her to conceive and produce children. Her body isn't designed to produce children."

"What do you mean?" said Hugo.

"Well, she has no reproductive organs, no fallopian tubes, no eggs, no uterus and so on, and I would say this is not as a result of a prior operation or genetic deformity. I would say none of the women of her species would be able to reproduce."

This stopped Hugo in his tracks. Allana never mentioned this. Maybe the time hadn't been right, but when it was right, he would ask her about this.

By now Hugo was by Allana's side. As she looked apprehensively around, her bright green eyes were taking in everything she could see. Then she felt Hugo by her side and turned to look at him. Her eyes started to turn pinky-red and she smiled.

"You are going to be just fine," Hugo assured her, "In fact when you are ready, you should be able to stand up. Just to let you know, the gravity here on Earth is a little more oppressing than it is on Laniakeea, although you probably will know that from the times in the past that you visited out dimension?"

Allana pulled herself up to a sitting position. "What happened?" she asked, "I just remember coming through the portal, or slice as you call it, a pain in my shoulder and I lost consciousness."

"I'm afraid one of the soldiers shot you, and very sadly, one of your bowmen was also killed. The second bowman, has been taken into custody, but with my strict instructions that he be treated kindly until I have had the chance to sort this mess out. I am so sorry Allana. I was genuinely worried for your safety."

"I can see that Hugo," said Allana. She put her hand on top of his hand and smiled at him. Their eyes met. That moment lasted a little longer than expected.

Suddenly Steven came running into the medicentre, "Sir, I have managed to re-boot your HC again. Lord Brough wants to speak with you urgently."

"Ok, thanks Steven," said Hugo. And with that he excused himself from Allana while she was still recovering, and went outside to speak with his father.

Hugo touched the HC behind his right ear, to reconnect and immediately his father's voice came booming into his ear. *"Well my boy, had yourself a bit of an adventure, haven't you? I need to see you as soon as possible for a full debriefing. I need to know what the hell this is all about."*

"Yes Father," said Hugo, "I am actually on my way to you right now, but as you are probably aware I have a guest with me called Allana Yana-Ash, who is an emissary from her queen, Queen Haruntha, and also a prisoner in custody. I will drop the guest, who I trust implicitly, with Mother, then come straight to the UEL command center." The UEL command, was approximately four miles to the east of the Brough mansion, and still on the Brough estate.

"Right, I will see you shortly." And with that, his father had signed off. As Hugo turned to walk back to the medi-centre, directly in front of him was his confidant, his trusted aide, Ding Ling (or Dingy as Hugo and friends affectionally called him). Ding Ling was of Chinese extraction. Hugo had rescued him from a tyrant of an uncle in one of the campaigns Hugo was conducting in the Eastern landmass region.

To say that Ding Ling was happy to have been rescued is an understatement. The physical scars on Ding Ling's back, not to mention the mental scarring and bullying he received all his younger life from his cruel uncle would have finished off a lesser man, but not Ding Ling. Hugo soon learned that Ding Ling was made of much sterner braver stuff than most men he knew. He had accompanied Hugo on every single one of his campaigns.

His English was passable, and although he wasn't sure himself of his age, he was certainly much older than Hugo. The family joke was that Hugo picked the first of April as his birthdate, and this year celebrated his fortieth Birthday. (Although they could have been out by ten years either side of that.)

He had two endearing qualities, one of which was his smile. When Ding Ling smiled, his whole face would crinkle up. In the last three years since he had been rescued by Hugo, he had found laughter, happiness and a belonging that he thought never even existed. At the same time he had an irrepressible sense of humor, and was always playing the 'Confucius says' card, which invariably made everyone around and in earshot chuckle, smile or laugh, even though, for the majority of the time he was being very serious, and the message he was trying to get across was always pertinent and important.

Sometimes though, Hugo did have to ask him to keep quiet for a while, in a friendly way, because he would keep repeating the sayings one after another.

But he was also incredibly brave, and nothing scared him. Even though he was very small and skinny, he was sinewy and quick. He always wore clothes that were oriental in style, blacks or grays. He wore jackets with mandarin styled collars, including thin black flat soled shoes. He was fearless.

Strangely enough, there was only one thing that he didn't like, and that was boar hunting. This is why he wasn't with Hugo in the evening Hugo came across the slice. He would always claim the squealing of the Boars and the shape of their snouts were the most frightening things that man could encounter.

And so it was, Hugo was facing Dingy for the first time since this whole escapade had happened, and what were the first things Ding Ling said to Hugo?

"Master, boar hunting *and* going into column light? Big mistake! You could be killed, Master. Two things like this never go together, spell very bad disaster! Confucius say, 'Never take sleeping pill, if already taken laxative tablet.'"

This had Hugo smirking. He rubbed the top of Ding Ling's head affectionately. "I have to report to my father as soon as possible Dingy, you are coming with me. But first I need to drop off my guest, Allana Yana-Ash, a female from the other side of the column of light, with my mother. This column of light I am calling the Slice."

As they walked away back to the medicentre, Dingy kept tugging on Hugo's sleeve and saying "She a woman, yes? Good looking? Yes or no? Do you like her Master? How much you like her Master?"

Hugo, whilst smiling, gently kept shrugging off Ding Ling's hand off his sleeve, and stared ahead, not answering him at all. Hugo smiled, because he knew Ding Ling wanted answers.

Ding Ling suddenly stopped in his tracks, as Hugo strode steadfastly on, at which point Ding Ling shouted to Hugo, "Master very quiet, means Master fancies this female person? Dingy must be right yes?"

"Just hurry up will you?" shouted Hugo.

"Ok, ok Master, just remember, virginity like bubble. One prick, all gone." Hugo was laughing as he entered the medicentre, Ding Ling close on his heels.

Allana was up and hunched over the various monitors in the medicentre with the senior medic. They were pointing at something on screen and were in deep discussion as Hugo and Ding Ling came in.

Allana and the medic both looked up. The medic approached Hugo and said, "I must say that Allana here is fascinating. Her scientific knowledge is very advanced. There is a real chance here for us to learn so much from the Laniakeeans."

"Well," acknowledged Hugo, "that is one of the topics I wish to discuss at an emergency meeting of the UEL I am attending, and I genuinely do hope we can all work together?"

Allana smiled at Hugo. Again, her eye color changed from the bright green to the pinky red. She then looked down towards Ding Ling who was transfixed by the color change of her eyes.

"Hello?" Allana said to Ding Ling. There was a silence, which dragged on to the point of bordering on embarrassing, certainly for Hugo, and all the time, Ding Ling was looking intently at Allana's eyes. Hugo turned to look at Ding Ling in a quizzical way.

"Well?" said Hugo, and at the same time, he gave Ding Ling a little dig in the ribs. That seemed to bring him out of his hypnotic stare. Ding Ling simply raised his arm and forefinger and pointed at Allana. "Eyes Master?" said Ding Ling. It was almost whispered. Everyone, including the medic and Allana, all started laughing.

Hugo quickly said to Ding Ling, in a serious authoritative tone, "You need to apologize, now."

Ding Ling immediately got his composure back, was bowing to Allana, and saying "So sorry! So sorry. Pleased meet you, but my master not told me about you? Have many questions would like to ask? Sometime, when you not busy?"

"Of course," said Allana, "I only want to help in every way I can. Maybe there is a question I can answer for you now?"

Ding Ling was still staring, but not in such an obvious way as before, and again, it seemed he was staring at her head? This time, Hugo was keeping a watchful eye out for some of Ding Ling's inappropriate social skills.

"You very pretty lady. Make-up done nicely. And very tall, but me know it's because I am very small," and with that Ding Ling's face crumpled up into a million little creases as he laughed an infectious, almost child-like laugh. When they had calmed down, Ding Ling suddenly put his forefinger in the air. "Ah, remember first question now, why eyes change color? And why ears so pointy? Oh no, two questions, it's ok?"

"Dingy," barked Hugo, "that's enough!"

"No, no Hugo," said Allana, "That's ok. They are good questions." She turned to Ding Ling and said, "It is all to do with the way our bodies are made. From the very beginning, from a seed, little messengers tell the growing body what it should look like. Where I come from, our eyes change color to tell others how we are feeling anger, love, happiness for example and my ears are pointed because that is also in the little messengers that tell the body what appearance we should have."

"But there are messengers in your body and others as well. They told Hugo and the medic to have round eyes, and you to have slightly different shaped eyes, and very nice they are too."

Hugo thought that was very well explained, but now he was inwardly chuckling, the look on Ding Ling's face was a picture. He looked like a lovesick puppy, and that creased up smile came back, even more than before.

"And the color of your skin, it's a little darker than Hugo's, isn't it?"

"Yes," said Ding Ling, "I am Chinese, different part of Earth dimension, but now, nearly all my country under water."

"Do you have any family?" asked Allana.

There was a momentary silence while Ding Ling thought about this, but then he looked straight at Hugo and said "Hugo is my family. He is now my father, my mother, my brothers and sisters. Can you not see? We look so alike? yes?" And again, Ding Ling creased up and wagged his finger at Allana. His little eyes sparkled, and the others fell under the spell of Ding Ling's infectious humor and laughed out loud.

Hugo felt the headcomm behind his right ear crackle. "Hugo, are you on your way?" crackled Lord Brough, in his usual gruff voice, "We can't wait all day. Almost all members are present, either in person or via internet connect video."

"Yes Father," said Hugo, "We are just leaving the medicentre now."

"Right," said Brough, "We will see you at twelve noon

precisely." And with that, Brough signed off. Never a pleasant goodbye, always short and curt, never knowing if the conversation had actually ended. And Hugo knew by now that pleasantries were never forthcoming from his father. He would never show any concern whatsoever for his well-being, not only for Hugo but also for his brother and sister and of course, in particular for Maxx.

They said their goodbyes to the medic team and went outside. There were already three horses waiting, one being Firemaker, Hugo's horse. This had been organized much earlier by Steven, the task force commander.

Immediately Firemaker came trotting up to Hugo and nuzzled Hugo's neck. "How are you boy? None the worse for wear I hope?" Hugo then reached up for the reins, held them on Firemaker's neck, stepped into the stirrup and hauled himself up and over onto the saddle. He turned to Allana who was looking a little nervously at the horse offered to her. Hugo could see she was looking a little apprehensive and said, "Can you ride Allana?"

"I have ridden my bonded Barboski, who is called Julow. Although it's not strictly riding as you imagine it would be. Julow would go wherever I like, using the thought images I send to him. And of course, he would leave the ground, to around in Earthan measure, thirty feet or so if needed, in emergencies or battles, he could rise much higher. So, transport is very smooth and secure."

"When we reach a certain age, a chosen few of us are sent by the queen to search for a Barboski and create a bond with it. It has to be of mutual consent. A lot of trust is involved, and the bond lasts a lifetime, although the Barboski lives for considerably longer than we do. I could be anywhere in Laniakeea, and if in need of help, I would simply think of him and he would make his way to me."

"Besides the levitation powers," continued Allana, "the Barboski have a number of powers that mean they are our allies in times of need. These range from completely confusing the minds of any attacker that enters our dimension, even to the extent of turning the attackers on themselves, although all the Barboski have to work together to produce this effect, rendering their bonded rider and themselves almost invisible. I say almost, because you can still see the Barboski and rider, only more like a colorless reflection."

"So, Hugo, I do admit it probably is a skill I have to learn to ride one of your horses without falling off."

"Well, that's not a problem," said Hugo "You can ride side-saddle with me." Hugo leant over to offer Allana a hand. Immediately Ding Ling came up and offered his clasped hands as a step up for Allana. She then gripped Hugo's outstretched hand and deftly stepped up and sat across just in front of Hugo. He brought his hands around her to grip the reins and held Allana tightly and said, "Let's make sure you don't fall."

The closeness of their bodies had an impact on both of them. They obviously both enjoyed the proximity, the touch of skin on skin. It was quite clear to see, by anyone watching, that they were enjoying each other's company. None more so than Ding Ling who, with inscrutable eyes, was staring at both of them. Ding Ling was feeling just a little envious of the attention that Hugo was offering to Allana nothing serious at all, but noted by him, nonetheless.

To Hugo, he hadn't felt this way about anyone for a long time. It was taking all his mental discipline to curb his enthusiasm, to play it cool. But it didn't fool anybody, least of all Allana.

Shortly they arrived at Brough Manor, dismounted and made their way to the Blue Wing, where Lady Romilly Brough, Lord Brough's wife, tended to busy herself with her day to day activities. On the way there, Hugo had already contacted his mother using his HC. She was so pleased to hear Hugo was fit and well, and looking forward to entertaining Hugo's guest, Allana.

As Hugo, Allana and Ding Ling entered the Blue Wing, Lady Romilly Brough was already waiting to receive them. Hugo went straight to his mother and hugged her.

"My dear, I am so pleased to see you are alive and well. As always, your father was uncommunicative as to your well-being. Just so typical." She hugged Hugo and then broke off as she saw Allana to the side of Hugo. "And this must be your guest?" said Lady Brough, she turned to face Allana directly and said, "Well my dear, how very pretty you are." At the same time, Lady Brough was giving Allana the warmest of smiles. "I understand you are called Allana?" said Lady Brough, and briefly looked at Hugo, who nodded yes. "Well, my dear, you are most welcome."

"I hope you like flowers?" continued Lady Brough, "I have a beautiful walled garden, and the honeysuckle and jasmine at this time of the year are quite exquisite." Lady Brough walked gently forward, linked her arm in Allana's and they started to walk towards the west door that led, via the summer kitchens, to the walled garden.

"Not too sure what sort of sustenance you would like? Shall we have a look?" Lady Brough turned and briefly looked over her shoulder towards Hugo, and said, "Hugo, grab a bite to eat, but be quick, your father and the UEL are expecting you, and we will have a proper catch up later." And with that, still linking arms with Allana, who was now smiling, they exited through the west door.

Hugo and Ding Ling rushed back towards the horses, grabbing some prepared sandwiches on the way and eating them. When they had reached the horses, Hugo said to Ding Ling, "Dingy, hang around here and wait for my call, then escort Allana to UEL central command, where I will be waiting to present her to my father and the other members."

"Yes Master," said Ding Ling. And as Hugo mounted

Firemaker and quickly started to gallop off at high speed, Ding Ling shouted after him loudly, "Careful master! Man, who ride like hell, bound to get there!"

Fifteen minutes hard riding later, Hugo arrived at the UEL command center. He quickly dismounted, was greeted by two of the security staff and escorted to the high-tech control center which occupied the whole of the basement floor. Hugo was ushered in. Although the large room was dark, it was lit in an eerie way by numerous projection screens of all sizes, set in a large semi-circular floor pattern.

Directly facing him, was the largest of the screens. Displayed on it were the live profiles of ten members of various states of the UEL who were unable to be present in person. Hugo was facing a horseshoe-shaped table, at which were seated ten more members of the UEL, and at the head of this table, in a raised seat was Hugo's father, Lord Brough.

Every single pair of eyes, from those on the screens and those sitting around the table were watching Hugo intently. Including those of Lord Brough who immediately said, "Right Hugo, you can start your de-briefing now. Do not leave anything out, no matter how insignificant you feel it may be. We all want to know what happened, what you discovered and most importantly, how it affects us, not only within the UEL but Earth itself. Are we in danger of being compromised? You can conclude by stating your suggestions and plans to carry this investigation forward."

And so Hugo described in detail everything that had happened, from the killing of two of his men, the discovery of the column of light, which he said he had named the 'slice', meeting Allana and Queen Haruntha, the queen's palace, the ley lines, the Barboski, Elvina the wand, the Sola Tree, Elfistra and Mandaz. How the Elves communicate, and how they had studied Earthan's, as they called us, for over three million years.

Hugo went on to suggest that there is an ancestral link between ourselves and the Laniakeeans, whose dimension was colonized by the Sola tree over six million years ago, and finally, how he came back with an emissary called Allana Yana-Ash sent by the queen, with two bowmen, one of which was killed instantly, and the other in custody, immediately on appearing out of the slice.

Almost an hour later, without interruption or questioning, Hugo had concluded his general overview of all the events as he experienced them.

Lord Brough ordered a recess at this stage for fifteen minutes, for all members to construct their questions to put to Hugo, and to then organize a plan of action to deal with it.

Hugo went outside for some fresh air and decided to take the opportunity, using his HC, to contact Ding Ling to ask him to start to prepare to bring Allana to the UEL.

The fifteen-minute recess passed too quickly for

Hugo's liking but he went back to the control center. The questions came thick and fast, and many were answered relatively simply by Hugo, but it was obvious that the main gist of the questioning centered around the wand and its powers. Could the Laniakeeans be taken to be a formidable military threat? Could there be a peaceful and constructive conclusion to working with the Laniakeeans? and so on.

Finally, Hugo told the members that Allana Yana-Ash was on her way now to address them all, and was bringing an official invitation to a peaceful meeting with the queen. This would be an opportunity to engage in official discussions, to learn each other's culture, lives and aspirations, to instigate a basis of trust, and to explore the possibility of sharing technology and medical knowledge, with a view to working together in harmony and forming a peaceful union of the two dimensions.

Hugo was thanked for his very comprehensive and candid report, and Lord Brough said to Hugo, "Fine. We will await the emissary and then we will conclude our thoughts and actions on the basis of what is presented to us. I will also choose a small group of us to travel back to meet this queen."

Hugo went outside to wait for Ding Ling and Allana, and no sooner had he walked outside than he saw they were approaching. Again Allana was transported side-saddle, with Ding Ling holding the reins. The soldiers on the two security gates all did double takes. Ding Ling's horse was quite short, and since Allana was quite tall, all anyone could see from the front, was what appeared to be this giant of a woman, riding side-saddle on her own, simply because Ding Ling was hidden from view by Allana's body. Her feet were almost touching the ground.

As Hugo was watching this, he smiled and wondered how Ding Ling was steering the horse, when he couldn't see in front of him?

They stopped literally a couple of feet in front of Hugo. All Allana had to do was to push the top half of her body up and step onto the ground, and then suddenly facing Hugo was Ding Ling, sitting in his saddle, with the most worried look on his face Hugo had ever seen.

Hugo greeted Allana and indicated that she would need to be gently security checked just inside the command center, and that he would join her shortly. As Allana was accompanied up the step by a security officer, Hugo walked up to Ding Ling and said: "What's up Dingy?"

This seemed to shake Ding Ling out of his trance-like state, and he blurted out, "Master, she talk in head, my head? Her voice, lips no move. You know me master, very brave Chinese, but this make me shake with fear! She kept saying, 'Left, right, left, right' and helping me pull on reins. Still scary master, nearly make me poop my pants master."

Hugo laughed out loud, then said, "Calm down Dingy, she was using something called 'telepathy,' where she can transfer words and sentences into other people's heads. All the Lanaikeeans can do it. Not many, I understand, use their voice anymore, although they could do if they wanted to. It is very normal for them. She can also, if she wants, read all the thoughts that you are thinking, although, certainly for me, she has said she won't read mine out of courtesy."

As soon as Hugo said this, Ding Ling went a whiter shade of pale. "Oh dear master," said Ding Ling, "If Allo? Allas? Alin? This Lady has seen my thoughts, she may want use Chinese torture tricks on me."

"What do you mean?" said Hugo

"I'm thinking my thoughts," said Ding Ling, "and they are saying, she smell like no woman I smell before, different, unusual, and I can't stop looking at pointy ears, smooth arms, no hairs at all, and… and, her tattoo's master, v-e-r-y different, maybe black magic?"

"Oh, for God's sake Dingy, just dismount and wait inside. I'm going up with Allana, that's her name by the way, and we will pick you up on the way out. All she was doing was helping you steer your horse because you couldn't see."

It was a lightbulb moment for Ding Ling, who's face suddenly lit up. He said, "Ah yes. I see now. Very clear. Ding Ling breathe sigh of relief. Phew. I feel like man who sit on tack. I get the point."

Hugo made his way up the steps into the command center, followed closely by Ding Ling who was now laughing and chuckling to himself shaking his head. As they walked inside they collected Allana. Ding Ling looked at her, started laughing and waggling his index finger at her and said: "Very clever, very clever." To which Allana just looked at Ding Ling in the most quizzical way. She hadn't a clue as to what he was going on about.

Hugo and Allana arrived at the control center, and as they were approaching, there was Maxx Brough standing at the control center door waiting for them. Hugo and Maxx hugged, slapped each other's backs and were genuinely pleased to see each other. Hugo introduced Allana to Maxx, explaining that Maxx was his brother, then all three were ushered in. After Hugo made the necessary introductions, Allana went on to explain as much as she could, that would be understandable by those present: the history of Laniakeea, the differences in culture, the major attributes that all the Elves in Laniakeea were able to use for day to day living. She even mentioned their diet, their magical abilities, and some of the more diverse plants and animals that are part of the fabric of Laniakeea.

When she had finished her presentation, it was then that she extended an invitation to the members of the UEL to visit Lanikeea, to meet Queen Haruntha and have a brief tour of the more interesting parts of their dimension.

Questions were then asked, and again there was a lot of interest to do with Elvina, the wand and what it could and couldn't do. Each of these questions was instigated by Lord Brough himself. He seemed to be very interested in knowing the precise location of the wand, how it was protected, and why only certain people could handle it.

Allana was very aware of this and tried her best to only offer a minimum amount of information regarding Elvina She was cautious only from the aspect of the security and protection of Elvina, she didn't want to say anything that could compromise its safety.

She finished off with some minor demonstrations of her telepathic abilities and mind reading for those members that wanted to experience it. This lightened the mood, and there was head nodding and smiles and generally, the members seemed to be showing a very positive response to Allana and Laniakeea.

During this last section, Lord Brough was very quiet. As if he was contemplating and planning something. More than once, he glanced over to look at Maxx. Maxx noticed this and thought to himself, *'What's he up to now? I've seen that look before. It doesn't bode well and probably involves me.'*

Then it was all over. Lord Brough came over personally to Allana to thank her. He commented that she had an accent that was somewhat similar to Swedish, to which she smiled and glanced at Hugo, and said, "You are not the first Earthan to have told me that."

Lord Brough suggested that the sooner a small delegation could go over, then the best chance there would be for a positive outcome. So, they agreed preparations would be put into motion. And then the delegation would travel across that afternoon.

"Would this be too soon?' said Brough to Allana.

"No, not at all," replied Allana, "The queen anticipated you would want to do this. She does request, however that any weapons you carry are made inoperative for the time you are visiting, and of course, our security forces will be expecting you this time, so a warm welcome will be afforded to you."

"Perfect," said Lord Brough. And without a smile or a goodbye, he turned and marched off. As he did so, he caught Maxx's eye, went over to him and gruffly whispered to him, "You are coming with me," to which Maxx looked at Hugo, rolled his eyes to the ceiling and shrugged his shoulders. He followed Lord Brough out of the control center.

Hugo sensed something was afoot with his father, but couldn't quite fathom it out. It was niggling away at him, frustrating him. If ever there was a time that he could have used Allana's thought reading abilities, it would be now.

Granthanda Competitors
(Teams comprise of three Elves, one archer and two assistants)

CHAPTER 6

Granthanda

(Become as one with your bow and your arrow, and you will become as one with your soul.)

Maxx made his way to Brough's office within the UEL building. It was situated on the second floor. Maxx knocked and walked in. It was too spacious for one man, but then this was for the head of the UEL Even the desk was enormous with all sorts of papers and paraphernalia that had been strewn across it. It was very untidy. Typical of Lord Brough.

Brough looked up briefly from reading some documents as Maxx walked in. "Sit your arse down there," said Brough, indicating a chair to the left of his desk, and then continued reading his documents. Maxx sat and twiddled his thumbs. He saw the obligatory family photographs on a side desk. Everyone was there, except of course Maxx. This made Maxx frown.

"Right," said Brough, "You are joining myself, and Hugo, together with two of the elite security guards and two members of the UEL central committee when we go over later to meet this Queen."

"You will be accompanying us for a reason. And that reason is, I want you to steal this wand, Elvina, they are all talking about. That Elf woman has practically described exactly where it is. In the right hands it could be invaluable. I want you to steal it and get it back to me over here."

In your grubby hands, thought Maxx. *What is he up too?*

"What?" said Maxx, "Steal the wand? We have a peaceful delegation, a representative of their queen, and they want to forge a trusting working friendship, and you want to steal the wand? Really? I can't believe you."

"Don't be so insolent," shouted Brough, as he struggled to control his anger. "You will do this for me, because, in return, I will do something for you. Something you desperately want and have wanted for years."

Maxx frowned. He immediately went on his guard. He was still clueless as to what Brough was intending on giving him. Maxx sat there, silently, waiting for the proposal from Brough. And then it came.

"For years you have been harping on about wanting the rights to the titles of my property and land, on an equal basis to that of Hugo, Kayon and Helena. I am prepared to grant this wish, IF, you steal the wand and bring it back and give it to me."

"Let me get this very clear," said Maxx, "You will recognize my true place in the family as an heir, and with it an equal share of the deeds and titles to all your land and property?"

"Yes," said Brough, "That's it in a nutshell."

"And if I refuse?"

"Well then, besides formally disowning you, I will issue you with a permanent transfer to the South Eastern Russian landmass. An area that is desolate, very underpopulated. The weather conditions at times can be very extreme. You will, of course, wish you had never been born."

Maxx thought about this. Did he have a choice? And if Brough were willing to grant him equal rights to his titles and lands, then at least his future would be much more secure. It still didn't feel right though, but what he was being offered, was the one thing he had always wanted.

"Ok," said Maxx, "But I am not happy doing this. The ramifications of this other dimension could be catastrophic. I don't trust you. I want to see the documents drawn up before we leave for the slice. And your guarantee that these documents will be duly signed and handed to me, on the exchange of the wand into your hands."

"Yes," said Brough. "In fact, the documents are being typed up as we speak. You will have the opportunity to read them through to guarantee that everything I am offering you is true and bona fide before we leave for the slice."

"Does Hugo know anything about this?" said Maxx

"No, of course he doesn't. Nobody does. The fewer people that know, the more chance of it being a success."

Maxx was very uneasy. He had a strong feeling that something was going to go very wrong, and he was caught up in the middle of it all.

An hour later, the delegation had collected ten feet from the slice. Hugo had already released the lone Elvish bowman, and the deceased bowman was in a coffin, ready to be transported across by two security guards. Hugo, Maxx, Ding Ling, and Lord Brough were there. Included were also UEL members Raja Ahmed from the Southern Indian region and Patrick Villiers from the higher Netherland regions.

En masse, they started to walk through, after being briefed as to what to expect by Allana. When they appeared on the Laniakeean side, facing them were a substantial contingent of Elvish bowmen. Although not necessarily in aggressive stances, they had their arrows poised and on the strings of their bows. The arrows though were pointed towards the ground, but everyone knew they would be up and ready to use in the blink of an eye.

One of the queen's personal guards was there to escort the delegation to the palace. After a short telepathic conversation that Allana had with the guard, she turned to address the group stood before her. She asked that the two UEL members and Lord Brough accompany the queen's guard to the palace for discussions.

Allana turned to Hugo, Maxx, Ding Ling, and the two Earthan soldiers and said she wanted to take them to a Gruthanda practice, involving bows and arrows, since the Laniakeean championships were due to commence in a few months' time. She felt it would be an interesting sojourn for those not meeting the queen, and to experience the spectacle of Laniakeea's national sport.

Two of the waiting bowmen collected the Elf that that had been arrested and the deceased Elf and escorted them away.

They were all briefed on how best to deal with travel via the ley line conduits. Allana suggested that they all kneel, close their eyes and breathe normally.

First off was the delegation, and with a swirling of dust and air they were gone. Then it was the turn of Allana and the rest. Hugo opted to stand, feeling he was more familiar now, and wouldn't fall this time. Allana looked at him and raised an eyebrow questioningly, but Hugo, who dismissed the look and steadfastly stood in position.

The Gruthanda competition and practice grounds were in a region called Nymlarii, which was almost directly to the east of the slice. It was a little nearer than traveling to the palace, so the traveling time was thirty-five seconds.

They arrived in a swirl of red laterite dust. Allana was

standing of course, Maxx, Ding Ling and the soldiers were still kneeling with their eyes tightly screwed up. Hugo was again lying on his right side in a fetal position, coughing and spluttering and cursing. Hugo began to stand up shaking his head. Allana just smiled.

They started to make their way down a mossy path, through a relatively thick undergrowth of scented multicolored vines. The vines also grew upwards and then met above their heads around eight feet off the ground, forming a tunnel.

The trunks of the vines were quite thick, and dotted around them were little semi-circular bowls that were clipped onto the trunks. Ding Ling and Maxx stopped at one of these and were studying it. Allana stopped, saw them, went back and said, "These are drinking vines, anyone can unclip a bowl and drink the contents. It should taste delicious, and is ideal for us in this dimension because there are times when the temperatures can be very hot. We also can suffer from dehydration. Why don't you try some? I assure you, you will not be harmed. We call it Lalan.

With that Ding Ling unclipped a bowl and looked at the yellowish pearlescent liquid inside. He screwed his face up, smelled it, then lifted it to his lips to taste. When he did, his face relaxed, and he nodded and said, "Very good taste. Taste like prunes? I wonder if it make you regular like prune too?" They all laughed at that, except Allana, who hadn't a clue what he was talking about. Hugo was trying to think how you would send an image of that to Allana. Nope, so he just smiled at her instead.

They came to a small clearing, and before Allana suggested they look up, they were already doing that. Filling the sky was the planet Venus. It felt like you could reach up and touch its surface. Just as Saturn had appeared before Hugo in Allana's garden. It looked angry, a gaseous yellow color, its surface a bubbling cauldron. But it seemed so close, they all ducked down at first.

"It's ok," said Allana, "That is Venus. In this dimension, we see the same planets as you, but some of them are considerably closer. Although you can feel some warmth, there is also a light chemical odor due to the clouds of sulphuric gas covering the surface, and you probably know that it is the hottest planet in both our systems. The physics of this dimension doesn't allow the true searing heat of Venus to penetrate our atmosphere."

They all just then stood and looked at the spectacle with open mouths. Then they continued down the green tunnel of vines for another five minutes before it then came to an end.

What lay in front was a view that was truly spectacular. Imagine a huge bowl cut into the surface of the Earth. The diameter of the bowl was approximately three-quarters of an

Earthan mile. The sides fell away smoothly (although at regular intervals there were steps cut into the sides of the bowl all the way around). It was vast. As the sides fell away, they went down then in at a shallow angle, to a depth of approximately three hundred feet and leveled out.

In effect, you had a flat circle on the bottom that was around half a mile in diameter.

If you looked to the left and right of where they came out of the vines, there were rows upon rows of bench-like structures and these continued all the way around the periphery of the edge of the circle. The whole thing, the sides and the bottom were covered in a short purple colored moss.

Hugo turned to Allana and said, "How many people could you get to fill all these seats?"

"Oh," said Allana "around one hundred and ninety-five thousand." Allana then said to everyone, "Let's sit here, and I will explain what Granthanda is, how you play it, and why it's our national sport." So, they all sat, while Allana prepared to give them an insight into the complexities of the game.

Just before Allana began, two Elves approached them with some bows and some 'Skaeloth' arrows (arrows with no arrowheads on them)

"Ah, good," exclaimed Allana, "Just so you realize the strength and skill needed to actually draw back the string, and fire the arrow a great distance, my two assistants here have brought these for you to try."

The bows themselves were approximately six feet tall, from tip to tip. This immediately ruled out Ding Ling, who felt he was way too small to be able to have any leverage on the bowstring, so he sat where he was and observed.

Hugo and Maxx though instantly stood up. Both quite confident. They had learned archery when they were growing up, and were very proficient. Maxx strode forward and took the bow out of Allana's outstretched hand.

"I was pretty good when I was younger," said Maxx, puffing out his chest. "In fact, I regularly used to beat Hugo in local competitions." You could see he was very proud of his achievements, but when he grasped the bow in his left hand, he noticed how heavy it was, and the same height as he was. The string was also, he realized, under enormous tension. He plucked it and produced a very high-pitched note.

Allana handed him a skaeloth, and he managed to fit the skaeloth nock onto the bow string. Maxx prepared himself in the left-footed stance, since he was right-handed, took a grip either side of the arrow feathers with his forefinger and middle finger, lay the middle of the skaeloth across the arrow shelf and prepared to draw the bowstring back. As he took the strain, he began to pull harder and harder, but the bowstring only moved six or seven inches. No matter how hard he tried, he just couldn't pull it back any further.

Maxx was now beginning to go red in the face. Sweat was dripping off his forehead. He was gritting his teeth, and he thought to himself, *'Why is this damn string so tight?'* So, eight inches back, eventually, was the most he could pull the bowstring, his arms were beginning to tremble.

Hugo was starting to chuckle now, he had a feeling this was not going to end at all well for Maxx.

What happened next, happened in a fraction of a second. Maxx lost his grip with his left hand on the bow's handle. The bow spun around, and as it did so, the string snapped back under tremendous force and hit him on the right-hand side of his face. The snapping sound of the bowstring hitting him on his face was so loud, it made Ding Ling and Hugo wince and simultaneously shout out "Ow!" The skaeloth, by now pointing downwards, slid slowly to rest, laying across Maxx's feet.

Maxx could hear Ding Ling and Hugo and the soldiers laughing behind him. All the while from the beginning to this point, Maxx had been facing forward, but now he slowly turned to face the others.

When they saw his face, Hugo and the others fell into further uncontrollable fits of laughter. Down the right-hand side of Maxx's face, from his hairline, down over his right eye, his cheek, the edge of his chin, was a very nasty red-looking line, where the bowstring had snapped into his face. Maxx screwed up his face, and wiped his right eye, and threw the bow to Hugo, saying, "Ok then Hugo, think you are so clever, you try it."

Allana went straight to Maxx and asked his permission to wipe a healing herbal balm on the red-looking line traveling down his face. The moment she applied it, Maxx breathed a sigh of relief.

"That's better," he said. "Thank you Allana." And with that, he went and sat down. It was Hugo's turn. He took the bow and the arrow and prepared his stance. But just as Maxx had difficulties drawing back the bowstring, so did Hugo.

Hugo did in fact manage to draw back the bow string maybe three of four inches more than Maxx, and when he released the skaeloth after lots of arm straining and grunts, it may have only traveled three feet in front of him.

Allana came to Hugo, stepped in quite close to him from behind, and began to instruct him on getting the subtler points of technique right, before loosing the skaeloth. Hugo could feel her breath on the back of his neck, the warmth of her body. Her left-hand was over his on the handle of the bow, and the fingers of her right hand on top of his. She whispered to him to relax, for him to breathe in deeply only when drawing back the bowstring.

She explained to him, that the preparation, the movement of drawing back the string, the loosing of the string, and then of finally still standing in the pose and letting the bow swing horizontal, was a very spiritual, meditative moment.

"Don't rush. Try to not to let anything interrupt your

thoughts."

"Do you understand what I mean Hugo?" said Allana. But Hugo was only thinking of her.

There were no two ways about it; he was becoming very attracted to her, in a way he had never felt for any other woman. He was very quiet, and wasn't responding to her. She lent very close to his ear and whispered, "Hugo Brough, I am sorry, I wasn't sure why you weren't answering me. So please forgive me, I just listened to your thoughts."

Hugo let out a deep sigh and rolled his eyes skywards. He turned around and stared at Allana. Her eyes were the pinkiest red he had seen them so far, and she had a slight smile on his lips. She telepathically said to him, *Hugo, I can feel that you are attracted to me, and I have to admit it is very mutual, but it cannot go anywhere. My queen has already sensed that there are mutual feelings between us and has warned me that I am strictly to break off any thoughts that might mean we might try to make something more of this. There is one very good reason, and when the time is right, I will explain.'*

Although this exchange between Hugo and Allana all happened while they were facing away from the others, no one noticed anything untoward; they couldn't hear Allana's telepathic conversation with Hugo.

The others just thought Allana was helping Hugo adjust his stance and grip except of course, for Ding Ling. He was giving Hugo his coldest inscrutable stare: he knew exactly what was happening. He knew he was going to have to give his master a talking to at some stage. The fact that his master was falling for a strange smelling alien woman, from another dimension, with pointy ears, and excessively smooth skin, was not the way forward.

As Hugo went to sit down, Maxx said to Allana, "Well why don't you give us a demonstration of your bow and arrow skills?"

"Of course," said Allana. One of her assistants was right there handing Allana a bow and skaeloth. This bow looked a little different. It looked a lot older, and had strange markings all along the wooden leading edge. At both ends, where the bow nocks were, there were orbs, of differing colors, again with markings all over them.

The same markings were to be found on the arrow she was handed; this arrow was a bright green. "This bow," she explained, "is over five million years old. It has been in my family all that time. I will now only use this bow for recreation or competition. You may think that it should be looking worse for wear, but the materials are quite magical. When not being used it is regenerating.

"The magical incantations that were issued to it, are as strong now, as they were when it was first formed. All the best bows are fashioned from the dead wood of the Sola Tree, our spiritual home."

"Not only does it now fit so well in my hand, the bow itself also recognizes my hand, and in a sense, we meld together, as one. Similarly, with the arrows or skaeloths, which you can see are also a bright green color, they too are covered in incantation symbols."

Allana now moved into a very relaxed staggered stance, her left foot forward slightly, with the bow horizontal to the ground. She then quickly and deftly attached the arrow to the bowstring. "I am going through the motion of firing the skaeloth high up into the air, and my assistants will use mild magic to keep the arrow up there, then move it across the sky, and finally, bring it down gently back to the ground.

"Please try to keep very still. The loosing of an arrow is a spiritual experience for us, as well as a physical experience, and it will seem like I have gone into a mild trance-like state."

Allana took in a deep breath, held it for a moment, then slowly as she raised her body up, she raised the bow and skaeloth simultaneously, until the arrow was pointing almost straight up. At the same time as she was lifting the bow and skaeloth, she was beginning to pull back the bowstring.

At this point, Hugo, Maxx and Ding Ling, gave each other knowing looks. And the looks said it all. This woman will not be able to pull that string back. This, they were convinced, would be Allana's downfall, her embarrassing moment.

But, as she slowly stood upright, and lifted the bow and

skaeloth, the string was in fact, being pulled all the way back. As she did so, Hugo, Maxx and Ding Ling's mouths fell open. It seemed effortless to the observers. Not a hint of arm tremble, the relaxed look on her face was of absolute calmness.

As she reached the highest point of elevation, she seemed to be as one with the bow and skaeloth, the bowstring came back to rest gently on the tip of her nose and downwards across her lips, her left arm holding the bow was stretched out, straight as a die.

She held this pose for almost fifteen-seconds, breathing so gently, you could hardly hear her. She was focused and looking up into the sky. She didn't seem to be straining one iota. There is a moment, when you breathe in, and before you exhale, a moment where time stands still. And Allana had reached that point.

Suddenly, her fingers released the bowstring, and with a crack, the skaeloth hissed and shot up into the sky like a missile. Hugo, Maxx and Ding Ling quickly got out of their seats to follow the path of the skaeloth. It just kept going higher and higher. They were now finding it hard to follow, to focus on.

At this point, Allana let the bow slowly swing so that it was horizontal to the ground. The position of her right arm and hand and the elevation of her head had not changed, but slowly she started to adjust and stand normally.

Allana, looking like she had just come out of a deep trance, explained what her assistants were now doing. They were moving in a sort of slow writhing dance, moving their arms in every direction, and looking up into the sky at the arrow that they could only just see. They appeared to be continually mumbling.

The skaeloth had now reached its highest point, and as it did so, two longitudinal flaps on each side of the skaeloth fell away and immediately from the sides two semi-circular parchment flaps came out and quickly extended and connected at the back of the skaeloth, just in front of the feathers. Now Hugo and the rest of the group could quite clearly see the arrow. It was green-colored with Elvish letters and images drawn on it.

"Can you see the arrow?" said Allana, "My assistants are using their mild magic skills to keep the skaeloth aloft." "And now," she continued, "they are working together to make the skaeloth move from side to side, not in a uniform way, but quite randomly. This will become very significant when I explain the rules to you in a moment."

After about a minute, Allana said. "And now they are bringing the skaeloth back to the surface, at first quite quickly; but don't be alarmed, they will slow it down as it reaches the ground. Just try to keep your eyes on the skaeloth."

Hugo, Maxx and Ding Ling were fixed on the skaeloth.

At first it didn't seem to be moving, but as it began to get nearer, the parchment flaps detached, and it started shooting downwards like a speeding missile, aiming straight for them.

Ding Ling, started inching his way to a little vine shelter just behind him. The skaeloth was picking up speed all the time. Both Hugo and Maxx were looking anxious. The skaeloth was probably down to about fifty feet above the ground, Hugo and Maxx instinctively lifted their arms defensively, and now were ducking down when suddenly at ten feet above their heads, the skaeloth suddenly slowed down and began to turn horizontal and floated gently into Allana's outstretched right hand.

And there, on Allana's face, was that gentle smile. "Please sit," said Allana. When they were all settled, Allana began, "We always have teams of three Elves, a male and two females. It would usually be the male that fires the skaeloths up into the sky, because they are physically stronger than we are, but the females would maneuver the arrows. In my team though, I am the one that fires the skaeloth into the air. I am particularly strong for an Elf female, and of course, technique plays a big part as well.

"There was an essential part that was missing today in my demonstration," said Allana, "And that is, attached to the bottom of the skaeloth, is a very strong abrasive string.

"This string is called Lulerar. It is coated with very fine abrasive crystals that make the Lulerar able to slice through another competitors string. Also coated on the string is a particular color of powdered dye in minute capsules, so when these are ruptured, as in the slicing and cutting of another string, it will give off a colored puff of smoke.

"The object of the game then is for a team member to fire their arrow high up into the sky. There is a qualifying height that the skaeloth has to reach. If it doesn't, that team has two more attempts, and if unsuccessful, that team has to retire."

"Once the skaeloth is high enough, the two assistants, using their magic, not only keep the skaeloth aloft, but more importantly, by moving the skaeloth back and forth across the sky, each team tries their best to cut the Lulerar string of an opposing team with their own.

"It takes enormous skill and teamwork to move, maneuver and dodge other teams' Lulerar, using defensive and offensive skills. This continues, with a teams' Lulerar being cut until there are three teams left. They are all then deemed finalists in the first part of the competition.

"In the second half of the competition takes place, where the three teams have to select a bowman or woman, who will try to pop inflated colored spheres high up in the sky. We now use conventional arrows with arrowheads on them. The first team to pop all their designated spheres first, is the overall winner.

"Initially fourteen teams will begin, the fourteen having

been decided by previous knockout trials from each district within Laniakeea. To win the national championships is the greatest honor an Elf can achieve."

"The winning teams would be treated like your famous footballers, there are also political rewards as well, and the opportunity to improve and hone their magical skills. The standard and extent of using magic is very carefully monitored on Laniakeea, and only the queen can approve and give permission. The reason for this is fairness. For the general population of Laniakeea, all are able to reach a similar standard of magical skills."

"My team were the grand champions last year, and we are hoping to duplicate our performance at this year's grand final. Every team has to wear their team colors. In our team's case, we wear emerald green, my bow will be decorated with green material strips and even the dye color on the Lulerar, in our case, will be green. That way, there will be no mistake in distinguishing one team from another, certainly by the referees."

"We have one main referee, who has permission to levitate to approximately twenty feet above the ceiling height for all competition arrows. He wears a very bright striped yellow and orange uniform, with bands of the same color material weaved into his hair and trailing behind him as as far as three feet. He holds a very short staff, which is used for many functions, such as indicating a foul, a winner, a point of order and so on."

Hugo interrupted Allana and said "A foul?"

"Yes," said Allana, "We have Elves who try to cheat, because the rewards are so great. There are many ways a team can cheat. The most common is the attempt by one team to hold an opposing team's arrow static in the sky using their magical skills. This would make it easy for their own arrow and Lulerar to sever the other team's Lulerar. We also have many minor referees, whose job it is to stay near the periphery of the…"

At this point, very suddenly and without any warning, an arrow thudded into the ground only a foot away from Hugo. For a moment they all turned, stopped and stared at the arrow and said nothing. This arrow seemed thicker and longer than any of the others.

The color markings were very unusual. All the way down the shaft were circular alternating bands of black and yellow. Hugo couldn't see the arrowhead, it was buried deep in the ground, but tied around the yellow feathers at the top, were little black and yellow banners with Elvish characters emblazoned on them.

And again, another arrow thudded into the ground only a foot from one of Allana's assistants. Allana shouted to them all to run for cover. The vine tunnel was only twenty feet away, and by now they were running hard for shelter, but a barrage of arrows was following them and raining down all around them. Hugo couldn't believe that none had hit any of them, and no sooner had he thought this, when there was a scream from one of Allana's assistants.

Her left foot was impaled to the ground. Hugo stopped immediately and ran back for her. He managed, after a little tugging to free the arrow, but the arrow, although now free from the ground, was still completely embedded in her foot, so he carried her and ran to the others who were now looking out from the sanctity of the vine tunnel and urging Hugo to run faster.

The arrows continued to rain down, some were too close for comfort, but they made it. As soon as they were inside, the arrows just stopped.

They were hunched over trying to get their breath back. Allana immediately went to the aid of her assistant. She poured some of the Voovo she carried all over it, and this gave the girl some relief from the pain, but she would still need to see someone to remove the arrow and deal with the wound.

Hugo looked closely at the arrow. It was thick and heavy, its weight wrenching the assistant's foot to one side as it lay on the ground.

"What's happening Allana?" said Hugo. Ding Ling and Maxx were nodding, they wanted answers as well.

"This is an arrow of a species of Elf called the Morg'Umist. They are well known as assassins. They have no scruples whatsoever. We don't have money, as you do in your dimension, but there are all kinds of favors that can be granted, normal or magical, to further their existence. If you have asked them to do something for you, and you don't reimburse them with what they want, they will kill you. There is no hiding from them."

"We have been battling with them for thousands of your years, trying to eradicate them from our dimension, but they are very clever and are always finding new ways to infiltrate and carry out their missions on the Elves of Laniakeea and now, it seems, our guests as well."

"We usually catch them," said Allana, "Since I am an Elfanda, one who has permission and the skills to practice more complex telepathic and magical abilities, I had already alerted the queens guards the moment the first arrow hit the ground, and they are already on the scene and have apparently apprehended two members of the Morg'Umist. There were two more, but they managed to kill themselves."

"They know," said Allana, "that when they come before Elfistra and Mandaz, they cannot hide their thoughts. And so, the being who set up the contract will be revealed. Whoever it is, will know two have been captured, so they will immediately leave wherever it is they have been hiding because all will be revealed to Elfistra, who will send out a search party to find the culprit or culprits."

"Such is the skill of Elfistra, she can recreate an image

of the perpetrator from the minds of the captured Morg'Umist, and then transfer the image to the searching queen's guards. Whoever set up this contract, will be caught, eventually. It is only a question of time."

"What will happen to your assistant now?" said Maxx

"Already I have alerted a medical team, and they are approaching the other end of the tunnel. So, we need to make our way there now. But she will be fine. And she has already indicated to me to give you her thanks, for rescuing her and carrying her to shelter."

This time Maxx offered to carry the wounded assistant, who was now a lot more relaxed and calmer after receiving the Voovo magical herbal liquid. They all made their way back through the vine tunnel to the waiting Elvish medical team at the entrance. They took control and carried off the wounded assistant, and her companion also left with the medical team. Maxx was deep in thought and feeling uneasy. He was wondering how the meeting was going between his father and Queen Haruntha. It was all playing on his mind more and more.

Allana Yana-Ash & General Hugo Brough

CHAPTER 7

The Delegation

(If you find the courage to stand and face the Laniakeean suns, your shadows will fall behind you.)

Lord Brough and the two UEL members, Ahmed and Villiers, were all feeling decidedly queasy when they finally landed at the leyline circle in front of the queen's palace. It took them a couple of minutes to pull themselves together and recover.

A couple of the queen's guards approached them, one of which spoke very good English, and offered the party a vial each of Voovo. "Please try this Earthans. It will immediately counteract the trauma of the ley line travel for you. Its effectiveness will last quite a long time, sufficient enough for the travel back to your portal later."

The guard was quite right, they began to feel so much better and quickly as well. It was then that they looked up and were taken aback by the sight of Venus. The guard explained what it was and all the details. The party were fascinated by it all. One of the UEL members was constantly sneezing from the sulphuric gaseous eruptions emanating from Venus.

They made their way to the palace, through the outer rooms, and then came to the large wooden doors of the great hall. The doors slowly opened, and in they trooped, accompanied this time by two more of the queen's personal guards. Lord Brough would insisted that he be at the head of the party, in his usual conceited way, waddling forward as he did.

The queen was standing just in front of her wood throne, waiting for Brough. Again, ten feet from the queen, two more guards stepped forward and crossed bows in front of the party. Brough squared up to the queen and with hands on hips stared at her face on, legs splayed in a wide stance. The bowmen accompanying the delegation were bowing low. Brough turned his head to the side and glanced at them, and just went "Hmm," in a disdainful way, and turned to continue looking at the queen.

Queen Haruntha, on the other hand, looked at him with a sideways look and smiled demurely. No matter how rude and crass Brough was, she noticed a flicker of a smile on one side of his mouth. In front of her was an unpleasant human, she had guessed that from the moment Brough had walked through the slice. She had been monitoring his thoughts since he had arrived in Laniakeea. He would have had no idea whatsoever of course that she could read thoughts at any distance, that he didn't need to be in her presence. This was a skill only the queen or Elfistra were able to utilize.

What a difference in character and manners there was between Brough and Hugo she thought even more difficult to understand, considering Brough in front of her was Hugo's father. So much more to learn about this species.

"Welcome to Laniakeea," the queen graciously said, "You are most welcome. I am greeting you in the spirit of friendship, and with the express hope and conviction, that our two species can learn and ultimately develop with each other. To exchange knowledge to the extent that it can help our understanding of each other, our culture, language and technology."

The two UEL members were smiling from ear to ear and nodding vigorously. Brough said nothing for a moment, before replying, "Well, I agree with most of what you have said queen. I realize we are a little behind the advances you have made, particularly in the areas of magic, which I think could be very helpful to us. I do realize that there were some initial fatalities on both sides, but as explained by my son Hugo, whom you have met, I accept that mistakes were made, and in the spirit of understanding and the forging of a new special friendship, those matters will be put on one side and we can move ahead."

"Thank you," said the queen, "I was hoping you would say that. Now I have made my introduction, I wish for you and your delegation to meet my sorceress, Elfistra, and her aide Mandaz. She deals with the security of this dimension and only wants to meet you and understand you, and will answer any of your questions."

With that the queen turned around and started to walk up the steps with the intention of sitting down on her wooden throne. As she was walking up the steps with her back to the delegation, Brough, in particular, couldn't help but notice glimpses of her attractive rear end that revealed itself, when her costume swished to one side then the other as she walked up the steps.

The Queen knew what she was doing of course, and putting him off guard would be to her objective. Manipulating him would be a challenge to her, and although you would never know it, she was smiling inside and enjoying the manipulative hold she was having over Brough.

Brough's eyes were as round as saucers, and he thought to himself, *'Hmmm, just give me five minutes with her, and I could show her...'* But Brough was interrupted mid-thought by the queen announcing that Elfistra and Mandaz were approaching. Brough moved his massive body around to look, and Elfistra was gliding along towards them with Mandaz slurping and hopping behind her.

When they were only fifteen feet away, Brough said out

loud, "What the hell is that stink?" The noxious putrefying odor from Mandaz had reached his nostrils.

Brough quickly turned his head around to look at Ahmed and Villiers, and whispered, "Have one of you farted? For God's sake control yourself." The two UEL members also slowly shook their heads. Brough was mystified, could it be that the stench was coming from these two in front of him?

As he turned to face Elfistra, she seemed furious. The queen had mentioned to her earlier to curb her feelings and anger, and that way they could gage the truth coming out of the delegation's mouths and now it seemed, particularly Brough's mouth. Elfistra, at this point, wanted more than anything to obliterate him. But she was following the queen's command and stood firm. Mandaz, however, was bombarding Elfistra's mind with ways they could make this uncouth human disappear forever.

She turned to Mandaz and said, *'Be quiet will you. Have patience.'* Next, still directed at Mandaz, came the queen, *'You will cease now Mandaz, or I will have you removed from the hall.'* Mandaz stopped immediately and slid back a couple of steps. He leaned on his staff, kept still and watched the proceedings.

Elfistra turned to look at Brough and said, "So human, do you have questions for me?"

"Yes, I do," said Brough, "As you appear to be much

more technologically advanced than we are, how soon do you think we could start working together to advance our knowledge of technology? We have ley lines as you do. I have now experienced how yours work. They are so efficient. The technology behind them would be particularly helpful to us, since we have had to revert to more primitive forms of travel."

"That all came about," continued Brough, "because now we have no nuclear capabilities. A worldwide disabling of all types of nuclear facility was carried out to prevent any more catastrophic nuclear wars that had already decimated our world's population. That on top of global warming meant that the polar caps started to melt, so nearly ninety percent of the surface of our planet is now underwater, and what land is still on the surface is drastically overpopulated."

"The urgency of finding a logistical solution to transport, food, medicines and essentials is paramount. Will you show us how to harness the power of the ley lines?"

Elfistra looked at Brough; she wanted to tell him that he was still too primitive to understand the concept in her mind only one step up, in evolutionary terms, from an ape. A degree of magic was involved. Earthans brains were too small and primitive to enable a ley line.

So instead Elfistra said "It is possible, we could certainly spiritually clear out all your natural ley line conduits, set the natural coordinates, teach you how to use and travel with ley lines, but a degree of magic would need to be used initially Over time, once the ley line has 'matured,' as we put it, a specific incantation, in our own dialect of Elvish, would have to be issued telepathically, but could be adjusted to accept a verbal incantation, possibly in your language, to initiate travel to whichever destination is required. But for the time being, a Laniakeean would need to be stationed at every conduit for it all to work. So, the brief answer to your question is: yes, in principle."

Elfistra went on to describe the workings of Laniakeea, how old the Elves were as a race, how they believed that Earthans shared the same ancestral lineage. After approximately twenty minutes, Elfistra finished by asking the delegation if there were any more questions.

"Yes," said Brough. "I find the subject of your wand fascinating, how it seems to be a central part of your beliefs, and that in fact you would describe it as a sentient being? Is that correct? "What in fact what can it do?"

"Why are you so particularly interested in our wand, or Elvina, as we know her?" asked Elfistra.

"Erm, no particular reason," Brough stuttered, "Mainly curiosity, that's all." Brough wasn't a particularly good liar. At this point Elfistra could see images in Brough's brain of him holding a wand, not the shape of Elvina, because he had never seen her, but just a wooden rod, and from the end of which was shooting sparks, and a maniacal look on Brough's face, then from his point of view looking out over millions of people who were all bowing down before him. Elfistra could feel Brough reveling in the attention and admiration he was receiving from the masses of people.

'Does this human really believe that one of the purposes of Elvina is to give whoever is holding her, unequivocal power and adulation from the people he would rule over?'

Elfistra was convinced that here was another typical Earthan power crazed leader. Earth dimension has had them since the beginning of their time. Elfistra's studies of Earthan history showed that there were these types of megalomaniacs cropping up time and time again.

Elfistra started to amble slowly towards Brough, who unusually for him, was feeling a little uncomfortable, and she whispered to him, very slowly, in that raspy intimidating voice of hers, "You wouldn't be thinking about attempting to steal our wand Elvina, would you human?"

Immediately, there was a look of confusion on Brough's face. Suddenly flooding Brough's head, under his own volition, were images of Earthan seaside beaches, sandcastles and seagulls. Again, and again and again these images repeated themselves.

This made Elfistra inwardly smile. This fat human had suddenly realized she was reading his thoughts.

Brough remembered what Hugo had told him at the debriefing, about how they were able to read thoughts. He mistakenly thought they haven't had chance to read any of his thoughts so far. Elfistra laughed inwardly at this imbecilic way of trying to put her off the scent.

Suddenly into Elfistra's head came Mandaz's telepathic thoughts. They were coming very fast, one after another, almost the equivalent of telepathic screaming, '*See! See! He wants the wand. He wants it for his own use. We have to stop him now. Why don't we kill him now and have done with it. It makes sense!*' The queen interjected at this stage, '*Mandaz, calm down, that doesn't make any sense at all. I agree, we have to make sure Brough is out of our dimension, and I agree he has an uncommon interest in Elvina, so that temptation will be taken away from him. We won't give him any more information. Luckily, they are not all alike in their thoughts. The human, Hugo Brough I like and I am beginning to trust.*'

Elfistra and Mandaz exchanged knowing glances, but left their minds blank, just in case the queen was observing them.

The queen got up and stepped down slowly to the dais where Brough was and said, "Well, I believe that was an informative first meeting and hope that more will come and be as fruitful as this one. We will be preparing to start introducing you to our ways of life, and we will begin with the clearing of your ley lines. For now, though, we need to escort all of you back to your portal. The other members of your delegation, Hugo, Maxx and Ding Ling, and the two Earthan soldiers, have been invited to stay for the night, and will stay at Allana's dwelling, and then they will travel back to you tomorrow."

No sooner had the queen said this than Brough said, "Fair enough." He turned on his heels and waddled down the hall to the main door. Ahmed and Villiers couldn't believe Brough's complete disregard for protocol, so very quickly they made their bows, said their thank you's and goodbyes, and trotted after Brough. And they were gone.

If there is an equivalent of an Elvish sigh, the queen did one then. She turned to Elfistra and Mandaz and told them, *'Something else you need to be aware of Elfistra, Allana was demonstrating the use of the bow and skaeloth in preparation for the upcoming Gruthanda competition, at the national stadium, to the other Earthans in Nymlarii, when the Morg'Umist attacked them. None were killed, but Sheedra, one of Allana's assistants was injured. I want you to find out why the Morg'Umist were here and why the party were attacked, and more importantly, who set up the contract.'*

'Yes, my queen', said Elfistra, *'I am already aware of this incident and have already sent out guards to find and follow clues.'* Elfistra by now was bowing low.

Mandaz did the same, and they turned and started to make their way out of the hall. As they were departing, Mandaz in particular, looked very excited and was rubbing his ungainly hands together, Elfistra had a face like thunder and her withering stare towards Mandaz made him wipe the lopsided smile off his face. Mandaz was convinced Elfistra had hired the assassins, which is why he was so upbeat.

Elfistra was thinking intensely. An attempt made on the lives of the Earthans? or Allana and her assistants? or both even? It was Elfistra's duty to find out who had done this. First things first. She would find the guilty Morg'Umist, interrogate them and discover who had hired them.

By now, the party at the Gruthanda competition grounds had made their way to the ley line circle. Allana had explained to them that she had asked permission for them to stay overnight at her dwelling, and Queen Haruntha had granted this request. She was also informed that the meeting between Brough's delegation and her queen had been satisfactory, but with security reservations with Lord Brough, and that the party were leaving to transport back to the Earthan dimension on her orders.

They reached the ley line circle. Both Maxx and Ding Ling and the two Earthan soldiers immediately went down on one knee and closed their eyes and tried to relax. Hugo stood there, feet apart, hands on hips. Allana looked at him and decided to persuade Hugo to adopt the same position as

Maxx and Ding Ling. But he stood his ground.

Maxx looked up and said, "Just do it Hugo, don't be an idiot."

Hugo turned his head to look at them. As he did so, Ding Ling glanced at him through a now opened eye and he smiled and said, "Master, confucius say, when called an idiot, better to kneel like us, than stand there and remove all doubt."

As Ding Ling said this, Maxx, Ding Ling and the soldiers started chuckling. It caught Hugo as well, who ended up smiling and went down on one knee. Allana simply nodded her head and just said "Finally."

They all arrived without incident at Allana's dwelling without incident, and walked towards the round open door. They noticed in the doorway that there were two Elves, a man and a woman. They were smiling. Allana had already alerted them that the humans were staying overnight.

The male Elf was very well built, with very blonde hair that cascaded down his back. He was a good foot taller than Hugo and Maxx. He was wearing a purple wrap of some sort that came to just above his knees. There were green straps that were connected to the front part of the wrap and which then wound around his shoulders and the back of his neck. It all seemed a very relaxed article of clothing. He did have a number of quite startling tattoos on various parts of his body, which were Elvish symbols.

On the other hand, the female Elf standing next to him was dressed quite unusually. Everything she was wearing was painful to look at, with clashing colors and completely mismatched textures. But her hair grabbed your attention. It was a shock of golds and blues, the hair itself looked almost 'punkish' in style and was no longer than chin length. This was very unusual in Laniakeea. She was a 'rebel,' and in Elvish parlance, she would be known as a Dakathor. (one who doesn't comply). Because the general population did all conform, she stood out from the crowd.

All the women Hugo had seen had a similar colored marking, albeit in different colors, which went as a band from one eye, across the bridge of the nose, and over to the opposite eye. Not so with this Elf. Her make-up again was entirely different. It was reminiscent of red Indian markings, with bold white and black lines traveling across her cheeks. A very bright yellow color had been applied to her lips. She wasn't unusually tall, and this became apparent, when she strode over to Allana. She wore black fabric boots inlaid with metal, but which seemed to be two sizes too big for her.

She stopped very close to Allana, reached up with her arms, cupped them around Allana's head and pulled her face towards her own, then she appeared to be sniffing the air around her face. Then a little too sensuously, she lightly kissed Allana on the lips. She backed off slowly, smiling at Allana.

This did not go unnoticed by Hugo and the others. They watched in silence. They couldn't quite make out what was happening. That was a greeting that was bordering on slightly intimate, and they weren't sure what to make of it.

Allana sensed their unease, and immediately introduced them. She gestured to the male Elf and said, "This is Hanale," They all nodded their heads and acknowledged this, then she gestured to the female Elf, and said, "This is Hounani, and we all live here together."

Hounani seemed pre-occupied and was looking suspiciously at Allana and Hugo, who were now exchanging glances and smiling. Hounani was also looking at Hugo and Allana's auras, and her eyes narrowed a little more.

Again, Hugo and the others held a hand up and said "Hello," but Hounani had already turned around and disappeared inside. Hanale turned to them all and welcomed them. As they entered, a creature, the size of a cat darted around their legs, then went straight up to Ding Ling, scrabbled up his trousers and tunic and sat curled up around his shoulders.

At first Ding Ling was dancing around as if possessed, but Allana said it was their pet and was very friendly. Ding Ling started to calm down and said to Allana, "What is it?"

Allana explained, "It is called a Jarjam, and her name is Shalish. The Jarjam is very common in Laniakeea. They come in a multitude of colors. They are very warm to the touch and are a little like a cat in your dimension, but a lot rounder, with no sharp claws!"

The face is similar to that of a teddy bear, and pleasing to look at. Their eyes are round and large, like a marsupial's eyes, which makes them very appealing to look at.

The state of their mouth is such, that they look like they are always smiling. So on the outside, a very pleasing pet that would also go down well on the Earthan side. However, it did have another feature that was a little different, and that was its tongue.

The Jarjam's tongue is three times the length of its body, silvery in color, and in many ways acts like a tail on a monkey. It's very dexterous, slightly sticky on the top and can change color almost instantly. Its diet consists of a type of insect, which is similar to an Earthan dragonfly, which is called a Riktapath. If a Jarjam creeps up to within striking distance of a Riktapath, the Jarjam's tongue quickly changes color to the color of the Riktapath.

The Riktapath's eyes lie on the side of its thorax, and its own body color infuses into its eyes. The Jarjam converts its tongue color to that of the Riktapath, so when the Jarjam flicks out its tongue, it is too late for the Riktapath to react, and it quickly gets wrapped up and eaten.

But they are very clever, they can also send thought messages to other species, and crave attention, in the form of wanting to be held close, with lots of petting and stroking, and so on.

By now, Ding Ling had Shalish in his arms and was stroking her behind her ears; this produced a very attractive soft howl. Shalish unraveled her tongue, which gently started wrapping itself around Ding Ling's head, and ended up covering one eye, making Ding Ling look like a pirate from the days of old.

Ding Ling was quite happy playing with Shalish, which had taken a great liking to him, so Hugo continued into another room where the atmosphere was decidedly frosty. Hanale approached him and offered Hugo a small bowl with a mixture of what looked like various forms of small fruit.

Hugo was convinced this was to draw his attention away from Allana and Hanale.

These fruits seemed quite unlike anything Hugo had seen before. They were strong basic colors, but it was the shapes of the fruit that were unusual. One was round, orange in color, and looked like it was covered in barbs.

When he touched the barbs, they immediately fell away to produce a yellow liquid, so then he was left with an oval ball, the size of a grape, which was now covered in sticky yellow liquid. Hugo tentatively picked it up and sniffed it. It reminded him of an old English sweet flavor called parma violets.

Hanale said, "That one is called a *'Kraldan'* in Laniakeean Elvish, but translated the closest I think would be something like 'Sensaas fruit.'"

He popped it into his mouth, and it effervesced slightly and melted away to leave a little seed, similar to a large pumpkin seed.

Hugo started to raise his fingers to his mouth to remove the seed, but Hanale quickly said, "No, eat. It's very nice. Enjoy the mental sensation." *Mental sensation?* thought Hugo, and he noticed Hanale, nodding vigorously up and down. *'I wonder if Hanale is nodding because he is reading my thoughts?'*

"Yes," said Hanale, "Oh, I just remembered that Allana said it would be rude to read your thoughts, so I am sorry. I won't read them anymore Hugo."

Hugo bit into and chewed the seed. Immediately Hugo had the sensation of flying through clouds, high up in the sky. He knew he wasn't really up there, but the sensation was very real. If he pointed his arm up, he appeared to go up sharply, and the same downward when he pointed down.

But it was the sensations he was experiencing that were most noticeable. It was leaving him with butterflies in his stomach, he was now enjoying the sensations, twisting, turning and when he closed his eyes, even though he couldn't see anything visually, the sensations were all there. This whole process lasted only thirty seconds or so, then pretty quickly, he started to feel normal.

When it did all stop, he looked at Hanale. Both of them with a serious face, but then after a second or two, they fell about laughing. "Did you enjoy that Hugo?" said Hanale.

"Oh God, yes," said Hugo. "It could be likened to mild drugs that we used to use at one time where I come from, but nothing as sophisticated and quick acting as this. Is this a real seed from a tree or has it in some way been engineered?"

"Oh, most definitely a real seed," said Hanale, "In fact, do you see those trees in our garden landscape, the ones whose big fleshy purple leaves reach up and then droop down to touch the ground?"

"Yes," said Hugo

"Well they are called Melroon trees, and they constantly produce these seeds. We have a close symbiotic relationship with the Melroon trees, in that, we tend to them, help them reproduce, and in return, their seeds, over a period of a couple of milley? Malanni?..."

Hugo guessed the word Hanale was searching for and said, "Do you mean a million?"

"Yes, yes," said Hanale, "Over a million years, these seeds have evolved genetically to be very attractive to all Elves in this dimension. And it seems Earthans as well now." And Hanale started laughing.

"This dimension?" queried Hugo.

"Has Allana not explained?" said Hanale, "The Elves in this dimension are only one of a multitude of different species of Elf. All the other Elvish dimensions can be accessed via the collection of portals in the North of Laniakeea, beyond the Windfell mountains."

"Even here in Laniakeea," continued Hanale, "we have quite a different species of Elf that has been here from about the same time as we have. They are the water Elves, and are called the Pharaas, and live in a very large and deep blue lake in the North of Laniakeea, called Salnalyn Lake."

"They are quite different in appearance to us, in that their bodies are covered in blue-green scales, similar to your fish scales. The fingers and toes of their hands and feet are webbed, and on each side of the neck, they have small gills. They can come onto land for almost up to a day, but then have to return to water. They have a semi-permeable covering that can instantly cover their eyes when in the water, but moves away when in the air. It has been suggested that our Elfistra, because she has scales, is a genetic combination which includes the Pharaas."

"They don't have a nose such as we have, more like a small bump and two slits. The females all have very long hair, bright fluorescent green in color, which when in water, converts into a swimming aid. The hair becomes as one and moves from side to side, a little as I would imagine your water snakes in the Earthan dimension move. Their speed under the water is remarkably fast."

"Their homes are in deep caves under the lake, and their eyes have developed to be able to see in very low light conditions, which is why, when they come to the surface, they have to wear some form of filter to cover and protect their eyes from the brightness of the light, and to stop them drying up."

"Apart from that, we also share a common ancestry with them in that we can communicate telepathically, although the words and images are a little difficult to understand at times. Similar to the accents in your dimension. They are our allies. Whenever we have been attacked or provoked by enemies that come through our portals, they have come to our aid, and they accept our queen as their queen."

"They are unable to use a bow and arrow, but can jump and move extremely fast, and can disable an enemy by using a form of wrestling technique."

As Hanale was coming to the end of his explanation of the Pharaas, there were raised voices outside the dwelling that sounded very angry. Both Hanale and Hugo looked each other, then made their way to the opening.

Outside was Allana, holding out her hands to Hounani, apparently trying to appease her. But Hounani was having none of it. She looked visibly upset, and was crying. Hugo noticed the tears were light blue. As soon as Hugo and Hanale appeared in the doorway, they both stopped and looked at them, then Hounani, seemed to start up again, but telepathically. Both Allana and Hanale started to move towards her in a placating way, but Hounani turned on her heels and ran off.

Allana looked very upset and Hanale went up to her, put his arms around her and they went inside. Hugo decided to let them go in on their own, then he followed himself.

When he went in, they were not there, but Ding Ling and Maxx were. The Jarjam had now wrapped its tongue around both Ding Ling and Maxx's heads, but they sat still and quiet when they heard the noise from outside.

Maxx stroked the Jarjam, and it slowly withdrew its tongue. "What was that all about?" said Maxx to Hugo.

"No idea," said Hugo, "But Allana looked very upset. I want to help, but think it's best not to interfere. Ah well, we will find out sooner or later."

No sooner had Hugo said this when Hanale came out of another room and told them all, "Allana is ok, It's just a little problem, which I am sure will be resolved. In the meantime, can I help in any way? Are there any questions about Laniakeea you would like to know?"

Right away Maxx butted in. "Well," he said, "There is this one question I have for you." Maxx walked to the far end of the room and picked up what looked like an ancient page paperback book, and brought it back to Hanale and said, "I hope it's ok, I saw this lying on the table and was glancing through it, and it seems to be a book showing the ley line circles?"

"Yes, you are right," said Hanale, "They are, if you like,

public ley line circle maps. Each drawing will indicate the position of a ley line circle in each of our districts.

"Each district, depending on its size, will have between one and six ley line circles. On the front cover is ours which you have been traveling to and from, but inside are all the other circles, of which there are currently fifty-four in use. Some are being refreshed, and new ones are being planned all the time."

Maxx seemed to be particularly interested in this book, so much so, it caught Hugo's attention.

"Well," said Maxx, "I think I understand the principle. Let's look at this one here, which looks like a large tree in the description at the top of the page?"

"Yes," said Hanale, "That's our Sola Tree, our spiritual home."

"Yep," said Maxx, "And isn't it also the home of your wand, Elvino?"

"Yes," said Hanale, "But our wand's correct name is Elvina."

"Yes Elvina," corrected Maxx. "Well, say I wanted to travel there, I would stand on the circle in the direction of that arrow there," he pointed to a page in the book, "the white one, the one with the image of a tree at its arrow head, I would have to speak some Elvish, and it would transport me there?"

"Exactly." said Hanale. "You are a very quick learner

Maxx," said Hanale, who was obviously impressed.

"And how difficult would it be for me to speak the Elvish incantation?" asked Maxx.

"Well," said Hanale, "see the bottom of the page? That is Elvish script. In fact, it is an Elvish script in our own specific Laniakeean accent, just as security, so that other Elvish enemies couldn't use the ley lines."

"What does it sound like?" said Hugo

"It goes like this," said Hanale, "Kreeth na hay na sans T'la."

"Kreeth na hoe no son T'lana?" said Maxx

"Almost," said Hanale, but he started laughing. "You actually said, 'Your body is wrinkly.'"

Another few tries, and Maxx was word perfect, and Hanale was slapping Maxx on his back, congratulating him. Hugo was frowning, as now Maxx was looking at the ley line circle that would take you back to the circle close to the Slice, from the Sola Tree circle, and he was making Hanale recite that incantation as well.

Maxx said to Hanale, "That is a lot of Elvish for me to cope with, I'm not sure I could do it. I can imagine standing there and saying something completely different and getting nowhere."

Hanale laughed hard at this and said, "Maxx, even we Elves can forget the direction incantations sometimes, some are very long, so there is a failsafe built in. And that is in the form of just one word, and that one word is **'Krandoo'!**

"When you stand on a ley line circle, all the direction arrows are fixed, except for just one, and this one can swivel all the way around. It is red in color. All you have to do is to move the arrow to point in the general direction of where you want to get to."

"Then," continued Hanale, "You would just need to say **'Krandoo,'** and you would travel in a straight line until you come across a ley line circle on that path. Remember, all ley line circles are connected in straight lines. This was invaluable to me in my youth when maybe I had eaten too many nuts from the Melroon trees and couldn't think very well!"

Hugo was now seriously wondering what Maxx was up to. This wasn't like Maxx at all. But Hugo noticed he was looking decidedly uneasy all the time now. And Hugo couldn't put it out of his mind that his father had something to do with it all.

Allana walked in. She looked composed as always with a nice smile. "So, what have you been doing?" she said.

"Maxx seems to have a great interest in finding out where the leylines can take you, and learning the magic words to transport you." He then turned to Maxx and said, "But he hasn't told us why he has such an interest in getting to the Sola Tree and Elvina? Have you Maxx?"

Maxx shuffled his feet, and came out with, "I was just interested that's all, I find it all fascinating." Hugo's look told

Maxx he wasn't satisfied with his answer.

Hanale then chipped in with, "And his Elvish accent is perfect. Would you all like to come outside? The night air is growing dark, and I can show you the smaller planets that are visible at night. In your dimension, you would need a telescope, but here you will feel you can almost touch them. I will also show you some of the nocturnal types of insects we have here. Some of them will be quite dangerous and frightening to you, but if you stay with me, you will be safe."

Ding Ling didn't like the sound of that at all. He imagined monster like proportions of beetles and spiders that he detested.

Hanale said, "Sorry Ding, I couldn't help listening to your thoughts. Yes, we have large Laniakeean spiders here as well. Maybe the size of a large dog from your dimension. The fur on its body is needle-like and shoots out under pressure if challenged. The tips contain a muscle relaxant, which would simply make you collapse on the ground helpless and paralyzed while the spider comes up to you, wraps you up in a little shroud of webbing and then drags you back to its lair, which is normally at the first branch level of a certain species of tree. But the good news for you is that they live deep underground in small caves."

"Ahh," said Ding Ling, "Very good news for me, I think. My name Ding Ling by the way."

"Yes," continued Hanale, "but they are commonly

known to come to the surface at night to capture victims. It is called the Furanell. It is the greatest cause of deaths of smaller children in Laniakeea, which is why all children under the age of six are always be in their dwelling as the light goes down."

Ding Ling said, "I'm going to hide behind you all the way, please Hanale."

They all laughed at this. Then Ding Ling continued with, "Confucius would say, 'Your life is what your thoughts make it.' My thoughts are giant spiders everywhere, so run like hell."

Again, everyone laughed.

Hanale then said, "Everyone follow me, and I will take special care of you Ding." Immediately, Ding Ling went running after Hanale shouting, "My name Ding Ling, like a bell, Ding Ling."

As they were all trooping outside, Allana held onto Hugo's arm and said, "Hugo, please can we talk? I have some explanations for you, and misunderstandings to clear up, and its better it is all done now than wait for another time."

Hugo said, "Sure, where shall we go?"

"Follow me. There is a little structure at the side of our dwelling, a little like a gazebo in your dimension. We usually use it to meditate or practice our magic techniques."

And so, they came to this little gazebo-like structure. It was laden with large yellow flowers draped all over and around it. The scent was so intoxicating and heady; it seemed to be entirely relaxing Hugo. They went inside and sat on a couple of large round pillow-like structures on the floor. Hugo wasn't sure what was in it, but when he sat down, it moved. And it moved into a chair-like shape that felt comfortable and relaxed. Allana sat very close and opposite to him.

She looked deep into his eyes and said, "In your dimension, do you sometimes have times when you want to say something, but are not too sure how to start?"

Hugo laughed, "All the time Allana."

"Oh good." said Allana, "Well, let me explain how a family unit works in Laniakeea."

And so Allana started to explain to Hugo that in Laniakeea, a family unit is composed of three Elves. A male and two females. Elvish females are not able to produce children. They don't have the necessary reproductive capabilities.

In fact, she was telling Hugo, it is the male Elves that produce children. The males are in fact hermaphroditic, in other words, they contain both male and female sexual reproductive organs.

It is not known for a male and a female Elf to have a sexual relationship and has been that way for millions of years; however, two females can still have a happy and all-encompassing relationship, which is sexual. When two females are comfortable in a relationship, which is called 'Kelmenanth,' they then seek out a male Elf, to form a 'family' unit when the time has come to produce a child.

Allana explained that it sounds very matter of fact, but feelings and attraction are very crucial here, and all three undergo a ceremony, known as Latadjin, whereby all three commit to form a strong family unit. The male Elf, leaves on a lone quest to the Sola Tree to receive the tree's spiritual blessing. It is a three-day affair, where the male Elf has to come to terms with his own failings, to face up to his demons, and be prepared to have a child and bring it up with love, care and attention.

The sex of the child, through evolution, would more likely than not, be a female, so that the balance of two-thirds of the Laniakeean population being female, and a third male, is not disrupted. This process is overlooked by the Sola Tree, who is responsible for determining whether a baby should be a male or female. There is never any argument over the choice made by the Sola Tree.

And now Allana started to explain, the problems of last night, and the arguments between herself and Hounani, who was Allana's partner within the Latadjin. Allana explained how most Elves are honest because to lie or be deceitful is difficult because of the physical attributes they have or that surround them, such as the color of the eyes, the strength and intensity of color of an Elf's aura, and even in the changes of the pheromones that surround an Elf.

And this, she explained to Hugo, was what happened last night between herself and Hounani. She explained that Hounani is a rebel, is very different to the mainstream female Elves, and it is this quality that she found very attractive. And they have had a close relationship for many years.

"And then you come along Hugo," said Allana, "And the status quo has been turned upside down. Hounani could see and experience how I felt about you, concerning my eye color, my aura and the subtle change in my pheromones, which is what she was able to experience when we came close to greet each other. Of course, she then felt threatened, and couldn't understand how I could even begin to find a male attractive, especially a male of a different species."

There was a moment's silence as they both gathered their thoughts. Hugo then said, "Remember when you went to the medicentre? whilst you were in there, and still recovering, the chief medic explained then that you couldn't produce children. He was very confused, trying to understand how you could ever populate Laniakeea if you couldn't have children. He was able to ascertain, that the internal workings of your body, were not as a result of an accident, surgical operation or other phenomena, that it seemed pretty conclusive to him, that it was the evolutionary norm, and he suspected all the females in Laniakeea would be similar."

"Yes," said Allana, "But there is another side to this Hugo, which involves you." Hugo looked up at Allana's face, trying to search for what was coming next.

"Just as you have vestigial organs or parts of your body, that once worked, and now don't, just like the coccyx at the base of your spine, which are the remnants of a prehensile tail, so it is with the Elves of Laniakeea. By that I mean, at the beginning of our existence, it would have been males and females that had sexual relationships and produced children, but over the millennia, our evolutionary changes took place. In effect, what I am trying to say is that a female Elf could have a relationship with a male Elf, we have everything for that to take place, but it is simply not done in our society now."

Allana was now trying to be very careful with what she was going to say next. "It is possible for me, as a female Elf, to have a form of sexual relations with a male, especially if that male was from the Earthan dimension as you are. You are geared up for this to happen with a woman in your dimension, are you not?"

Hugo just nodded slowly but didn't speak, allowing Allana to continue. "Remember what I said earlier and telepathically at the Gruthanda competition grounds, that I needed to tell you something? Well this is it. And I need to tell you again that my queen has strictly forbidden anything to happen between us, and the Elfistra knows of this as well now, as is her right."

"So, last night, after Hounani and I talked, and the fact she could see I had these feelings for you, a male, and you as another species, she became distraught and angry and stormed off. She can be very hot-headed at times and clearly lives up to her name as a 'Dakathor,' one who doesn't comply. She will come around. And I will explain that no matter how much I have feelings for you, and I know you have feelings for me, they cannot go anywhere."

Allana was beginning to look visibly upset. Hugo felt he wanted to get close and just put his arms around her to comfort her, but he wasn't sure what to do, so he just sat there looking at the floor, twiddling his thumbs.

A minute or so later, they both looked up at the same time to say something and interrupted each other. They stopped mid-sentence, and then they laughed, which somehow broke the tension. Hugo said, "You wanted to say something Allana?"

"Yes," said Allana, "I wanted to say, I am allowed however, to perform a special spiritual fusion of mind and body with anyone I choose. It could be male or a female. This never normally would challenge the family set up in the Latadjin. I have never had the interest to enter into this with anyone at all. But Hugo, I would like to perform the Sootalanash, as we call it, with you. In fact, I have had permission from the queen to do this. So, I hope you will agree to this?"

Hugo pondered this, only mainly because he had no idea at all what was involved. So, he turned to Allana, and asked her briefly what sort of experience he would expect.

Allana, burst out laughing, "Oh Hugo, from what I imagine it could be for you, possibly like having the feelings of a passionate sexual relationship with someone, but without actually physically touching them."

"Oh, I see," said Hugo, unable to hide his sudden interest, but also frustration, "Did you want to try it now?"

Again, Allana laughed. "No, not now. We would have to prepare, collect our thoughts, think about the other person, and there is a form of sensual 'connecting' massage that is involved as well. And we would have to go to a special private place to perform this. Dotted around our dimension are small round huts, which we call, Arkhrun.

"When it is time to enter, there is subdued light, magical candles that bathe the inside of the Arkhrun with warm glowing light and a mixture of scents similar to your ylang-ylang, patchouli and sandalwood infusing in the air. The floor is soft and sensual, with a material that is similar to your silk, that moves and caresses your skin. I think it will how do you say the phrase in your dimension? 'blow your mind.'"

"And Hugo," continued Allana, "you would have to promise me that you would not get physical with me in any way, that is not how it works. The effect, I promise you though, is just as enlightening as the physical aspects you would expect in your dimension."

You could see all this turning over in Hugo's mind, but with a big sigh he said, "Yes, alright then, I promise."

And with that they both got up and ambled back to Allana's dwelling, slowly chatting about what to plan for the next day. Within an hour they all settled down to sleep, except Maxx, who was disguising the fact, he was very wide awake. He was nervous and was trying to formulate a plan that was swimming around in his head.

Maxx looked at his watch. He also looked at the two soldiers who were also pretending to be asleep in his room. They were also in on the plan, whatever it was. They all synchronized their watches, set the time and waited until they were sure everyone was asleep.

Elfistra bonding with Elvina the Wand

CHAPTER 8

A Rude Awakening

(Once you begin to believe in yourself, you will find others will begin to believe in you.)

It was very early morning. Hugo, Hanale and Ding Ling were fast asleep. It was already light and the sunlight was streaming in through the open window. Ding Ling was also fast asleep.

Suddenly, quickly and very silently, two of the queen's bodyguards came into the room. One went straight over to Ding Ling, the other to Hugo and they started to shake them aggressively, and then drag them both out of their beds onto the floor. While this was going on, Hugo was trying to collect his thoughts and started protesting, asking what the hell was going on.

Telepathically, all Hugo and Ding Ling got were, '**Dress now, be quick, don't talk.**' This was repeated again and again. Hugo and Ding Ling did as they were told, and were exchanging glances at each other, wondering what was happening. They had just dressed and were being led out of the room when in came Allana running at full pelt.

You could see Allana was imploring the guards to explain, and she was now jabbering quickly in Elvish to the two soldiers. Although telepathy is widely used, verbal Elvish is used in emergencies to get a message across. They replied, but it didn't take a genius to realize that their answers were curt and to the point. Allana looked at Hugo and Ding Ling. She was distraught. As they were marched out, Allana shouted to them that they were being arrested, and that Elvina had been stolen, but that she was going immediately to see Queen Haruntha to try to find answers.

When Allana said Elvina had been stolen, Hugo stopped in his tracks, and he suddenly realized there was no sign of Maxx or the two Earthan soldiers. He asked Ding Ling if he had seen them, and Ding Ling shook his head. The guards were getting a little more aggressive now and kept saying *'Quiet now!'* into their heads.

They arrived at the queen's palace, but instead of going through the main palace door, they were paraded around to the left of it, where there were steps leading down to a large basement room. It was dark and stuffy, and had a musty smell, that both Hugo and Ding Ling found unpleasant. There was damp red dust on the floor, and various forms of chains and tables were strewn about.

They were both led to a very long table and were pressed into chairs at one end, then what looked like a thin silvery thread was wrapped around their wrists. Ding Ling thought they felt very loose and it would be no problem to squeeze out of that looped thread when they were alone. However, no sooner had he thought this than one of the guards, said something in Elvish and stroked his finger across the thread, and immediately the thread tightened up so much, it made both Hugo and Ding Ling wince and screw their faces up.

No amount of straining was going to break those threads. In fact, the more they struggled, the tighter it became, so for now, they just relaxed as much as they could and sat there.

The two bodyguards left. Hugo turned to Ding Ling and said, "You know Dingy, these last few days Maxx has been acting suspiciously, and it all started just after the second meeting, when Allana was with us at UEL central. I noticed Maxx looking sheepish after he had come out of Father's office, who I am convinced now, must be behind all this. It now seems all too obvious now I have put two and two together. Maxx would never do something like this on his own."

"When Allana mentioned that the wand had been stolen, it all fell into place for me, how Maxx was so curious about the ley lines, and using them to get to the Sola Tree where apparently the wand is kept and protected. He even got Hanale to teach him the Elvish incantations to travel on the ley line from Allana's dwelling to the Sola Tree, and from there back to the slice."

"Why have we been arrested?!" shouted out Hugo frustratingly.

Ding Ling was quiet, mulling things over, then he said, "Master, yesterday evening when you were outside with Allana, I remember Maxx telling me of powers that wand has but is protected by maze. Hanale tell him, it has a name, Uthaross, which translates as 'maze of many troubles.' Maxx was asking Hanale lots of questions about it, so much so, I noticed Hanale looking suspiciously at Maxx. So, Maxx stopped right away."

"Maxx also look worried," said Ding Ling, "when Hanale explain how wand can only work in special people's hand, and if not the right person, that person can die."

Ding Ling fell quiet, and they both were contemplating what to do next, when in came Allana with one of the guards.

"Hugo? Ding Ling? Are you both ok?" Allana was working her way nearer to both Hugo and Ding Ling, but the guard slapped his bow on the table in front of Allana preventing her from being able to have any contact with them both.

"The queen knows now that Maxx and the two soldiers

have stolen the wand. At the foot of the Sola Tree, one of your soldiers was found, who has been killed. I find that so difficult and upsetting to understand, the maze is very difficult to get through. Search parties have been sent out, but the feeling is that Maxx and the remaining soldier have managed to make their way back to the slice and have gone back to your dimension."

"To operate the ley lines, they would have needed a basic ley line circle map. Every dwelling has one, but more importantly, knowing the right Elvish words of the incantation that would initiate the travel. I mean, the incantations are especially in our Laniakeean dialect, just so other warring Elves cannot use the ley lines to their advantage."

As Hugo heard this, he then told Allana what Maxx had been up to, how he was acting suspiciously, how he was asking Hanale to teach him the Elvish incantation words and so on. "I am pretty certain now," said Hugo, "that Maxx has committed this crime, and I feel partly responsible. My overriding concern now is to do whatever I can to get the wand back."

"We have a problem Hugo," said Allana, "The queen at this moment, at the insistence of Elfistra, has to accept that you are all suspects. What worries me more than anything is that the penalty for stealing the wand is death. A most horrible death, which I feel I can't tell you about at the moment. I have to inform you that Elfistra is urging the queen to issue the death penalty against you both, saying she is convinced you must have been accomplices."

Allana began to pace up and down. The guard was giving them all of the immovable stare. Hugo and Ding Ling were deep in thought. But it was Ding Ling who suggested that they try to see the queen and plead for her to release Hugo and himself, and to go to find Maxx and bring back the wand.

"Let me ask the queen now if she will allow an audience with her. I will plead your case. Elfistra will not want this to happen, so I am going to let the Queen know, without Elfistra suspecting what I am trying to do. Because I am an 'Elfanda,' one who is granted special powers. This is a partly hereditary, partly a titled power passed down from generation to generation. One of those powers is that I may communicate with my queen purely on a one-to-one basis. For us, that means that Elfistra would not need know."

Allana turned away from them and went to one end of the room. Ding Ling said, "Master, if Maxx stolen wand and back home, there will be plenty trouble for us, especially if your father behind all this plan."

"You're damn right there Dingy," said Hugo, "But it will be sorted, mark my words. By hook or by crook, I will hold my father to account for press-ganging Maxx to steal Elvina. He won't get away with it. What mystifies me most is why? What did my father promise Maxx? What could he hope to accomplish by having Elvina in his possession. I know Maxx hates my father, and I do sympathize with him." Hugo was seething as it seemed the truth was making itself known.

"You are in luck Hugo, thankfully," said Allana who had now come close to them from the other side of the room. "The queen has said she will grant you an audience. It has to be now though. Are you ready to go?" As Allana said this, the guard lifted his bow, went to both Hugo and Ding Ling and with a few Elvish words, lifted the slivery thread binding their wrists."

You could see Hugo and Ding Ling wondering who had told the guard to release them. Allana noticed the looks on their faces and said, "Our queen has very potent telepathic abilities and can send not only one message to one person, but multiple messages to a multitude of Elves simultaneously, to the further reaches of our dimension, and all this can happen in a fraction of one of your Earth seconds."

Since they were already in the basement of the palace, they were escorted up and were in front of the queen within five minutes. Hugo noticed there was no sign of Elfistra and Mandaz and was thankful for this. Not having Elfistra and Mandaz breathing down his neck, would make Hugo's chance of putting forward a case to the queen, so much more convincing."

The atmosphere now was a lot tenser since the last time Hugo was introduced to the queen. Maybe it felt more intimidating due to the fact that six of the queen's bowmen closely surrounded Ding Ling and Hugo. Their arrows were already nocked on the bowstrings of their bows, although the bows were pointing downwards. All the bowmen were standing in a stance with their left feet slightly in front of their right feet, ready to go on the offensive at the first sign of any movement on the part of Hugo and Ding Ling.

"I am very disappointed Hugo Brough," said the queen, who was sat on her wooden throne at the top of the dais, "I felt sure that the word 'trust' is just as crucial to a human as it is to an Elf, but obviously not. The stealing of Elvina, our sentient wand, is a serious crime. The whole of Laniakeea will pursue the perpetrator of this crime. Allana pleaded your case to me to listen to what you have to say. I will tell you I will be closely monitoring your thoughts in detail. You have five of your Earth minutes to plead your case. Begin now."

With that, the queen sat very upright on her throne. There was absolute silence. Everyone's eyes were boring into Hugo. Hugo noticed the queen's eyes were almost scarlet and knew she was angry.

Hugo looked at Ding Ling and Allana, just to know there would be someone there to help and back him up. He faced the queen and began.

"Queen Haruntha, I haven't known about your Elves and Laniakeea for very long. But with the help of Allana, and the kindness afforded me from everyone I have met, I have nothing but the utmost respect for your dimension and its Elves. I still have a lot to learn, but I do know a little of the history of Laniakeea and in particular the wand Elvina. I do know where it resides within a maze under the Sola Tree. I have never been there of course. The whole of my being is against this terrible crime, and I feel partly responsible, in that it could have been some members of our party that stole Elvina, and particularly my half-brother."

"I have no words to describe how that one fact alone makes me feel. I do know this though: I would like your permission to recover the Elvina for you. Without a doubt, I am the best placed to do this, since I am from the Earth dimension and would know how to investigate, and discover Elvina's whereabouts."

"I promise you I will endeavor to recover the wand for you, and make the perpetrator of this crime pay for what they have done. Please allow me one Earth day, and if successful, I promise I will be back here handing the wand back to you with my apologies. I request that my aide Ding Ling accompanies me and if possible Allana, since the use of mild magic could be very helpful. Finally, I have to stress that the amount of honesty and respect varies from Earthan to Earthan, and is not as immutable or as respected as the Elves of Laniakeea."

And with that Hugo stepped back and waited. The queen looked like a statue. She was in deep contemplation.

Her eyes never left Hugo's eyes once. By now Hugo was aware of mental probing in his mind and thoughts. He was sure it was the Queen, so he kept himself very open. And indeed, she was inside his head.

Everyone was very still, even Ding Ling with his little tics, was not moving. Allana didn't move her head but strained her eyes to look at Hugo. She didn't think he could have pleaded his case any better.

The queen stood up, she took in a deep breath and said, "Hugo Brough, I will allow you to pursue the thief. I would urge you to do whatever it takes to bring Elvina back to us. Allana will accompany you, rather than any of my guards, I believe that way, it will not raise any suspicions or be in any way antagonistic. Allana has my permission to use magic, only, though, if absolutely necessary."

"It seems 'trust' and its meaning is similar in both our dimensions, although you say it occurs in varying degrees with Earthans, and that is what I am offering you now Hugo Brough. If you break that trust, you will be banished from Laniakeea, and the ramifications for all of us to work together lost forever. Do you understand exactly what I am saying?"

"Yes," said Hugo, "I understand completely. But I assure you, I will re-unite Elvina with you. I give you my word, and I have never broken my word. And thank you for trusting me at this time."

"So be it Hugo Brough," said the queen, "And I would expect you to look after and protect Allana to the best of your ability." At this point, the queen turned to look at Allana, and she could see Allana was not only looking at Hugo but a slight hint of a smile was on Allana's lips. The color of her eyes didn't escape the Queen's attention for one second either."

"You may go," said the queen, "Take great care." And with that, the queen came down the steps. As she reached the bottom step, Elfistra seemed to appear from nowhere and indicated she would like to have an audience with the queen, and to include Hugo, Allana. and Ding Ling, since it concerned them as well. 'My Queen, I have managed to find the Morg'Umist responsible for attacking the party at the Gruthanda competition grounds.'

'In fact, there were three of them. The assumption that they had been contracted to try to kill the Earthans, was unfounded. In fact, it was a Laniakeean family called Rilitonath, that has had a continuing grudge against Alana's family, the Yana-Ashes. It all stems from enviousness and jealously. The Rilitonath appear to have come just behind the Yana-Ashes in the Granthanda competitions for generations, and the head of the family hired the Morg'Umist to, in some way, only disable Allana and her assistants, so their family would have an advantage in the upcoming competition. The family maintains they only wanted to disable, not kill, but realize that what they have done was wrong and unforgivable and await your *sentencing.'*

The queen carefully turned over the information. It was a serious crime and needed to be dealt with. The one punishment that would fit this crime would be to conduct a Kralapal ceremony. It was the only way forward. If conducted correctly, the queen felt very sure it would not happen again.

'Thank you Elfistra, well investigated.'

The queen then commanded Elfistra to arrange the Kralapal ceremony as soon as possible for those members of the Rilitonath family members that had come up with the idea and employed the Morg'Umist. The Morg'Umist were to be released and banished back to their own dimension with a severe warning. Elfistra bowed low before the queen, and they both went their separate ways.

Meanwhile back at the dais at the bottom of the queen's throne and steps, Hugo, Allana and Ding Ling all looked at one another, then turned and left the hall, closely followed by all the Queen's guards. The three of them all stood on the ley line just outside the palace. Allana set the transportation in motion.

Twenty-five minutes later they were standing at the end ley line circle close to the slice. Hugo felt fine this time; he was obviously getting used to traveling this way. Poor Ding Ling, however, looked a little gray, and Hugo thought he was going to be sick at any moment, but after a few deep breaths and some Voovo, the color came back to his face and he was smiling again.

They all collected their thoughts, and as one, Hugo, Allana and Ding Ling strode into the slice. On the other side, as they were making their way to Brough Manor, Hugo turned to Allana and said, "What is this Kralapal ceremony the queen said the guilty members of the family that wanted to disable you would have to attend?"

Allana said, "Hugo, it is a ceremony older than time itself, and as far as we are aware, is only used on Laniakeea, to positive outcomes each time it has been used. You know by now, we Laniakeeans, are peace and harmony loving, and we believe that physical punishment for crimes is not the way to solve the issue, and can in fact lead to more problems."

"And so, the Kralapal ceremony was devised. Basically, if someone has done something wrong in this case the father and eldest son of the Rilitonath family they will be taken, where possible, back to where the crime was committed in this case, the base of the Gruthanda competition grounds. Then anyone and everyone that knows the two accused, are urged to attend. This includes all their relatives and friends."

"Usually," continued Allana, "there are many people attending. They will surround the two accused, and then speak of all the good they have done. Nothing negative is allowed. This will continue until everyone has finished, this can sometimes take up to two days."

"You see," said Allana, "we Laniakeeans believe that everyone is good, yet sometimes we make mistakes, which is really a cry for help. So Laniakeeans will unite in this ceremony to encourage the Elf or Elves to reconnect with their true spiritual nature. The belief is that unity and affirmation have more power to change behavior than shame and punishment. This is the essence of the ceremony known as Kralapal, 'Elvish kindness towards others.'"

Elvina the Wand
(The most powerful and magical wand to be found on Laniakeea)

CHAPTER 9

Elvina the Wand

(I came. I saw you. I conquered my fears. I fell in love.)

Earlier on that morning, it was still dark when Maxx and the two soldiers silently rolled out of their beds. They crept out of their room, down a corridor, turned left through the kitchen area and made their way to the front opening.

Gently they opened the door, which was a very thick fabric-like structure. They had to use their watches to light the way. Once outside, dawn was beginning to light up the horizon with pinks, golds and lilacs. They made their way quickly to the ley line. As they were doing so, Maxx was mumbling the Elvish incantations to himself, over and over again, to make sure he remembered them.

They reached the circle and stood in the middle. Maxx pointed out that they had to face the direction of the white arrow. You could see, from the looks on the soldier's faces, they were a little unsure of Maxx's ability to remember the correct pronunciation of the incantation. Once in position, Maxx uttered the Elvish words, **"Kreeth na hay na sans T'la."** He must have said it correctly because twenty-five seconds later they arrived at the ley line circle almost opposite a massive tree, the Sola Tree.

For Maxx and the soldier's, it was an impressive sight. The tree rose to two hundred and fifty feet into the air. The trunk wasn't solid as the trees on Earth in any way, but a combination of a multitude of fine white or gold wooden solid tubes that all interlocked and twisted and came together as one 'trunk-like' body.

What was strange, was that the main body of the 'trunk' was twisting sideways in all directions, then returning back to where it started from. It was also expanding and contracting all the time. At its widest point it must have been almost thirty-five feet in diameter. The roots formed a cave-like structure at its base, with the solid wooden rods expanding outwards to create a sort of igloo. At the bottom of this, facing the circle was an opening, with two Elvish guards leaning up against either side of the opening snoozing. From the entrance and descending down some natural stone steps, there looked like what appeared to be a cave entrance.

The Sola Tree must have had branches that started to shoot out from the sides from around twenty-five feet above the ground, but you couldn't see them. There were no leaves as such, apart from a smattering of very fleshy green round leaves. What there was were strands of very long fine gold colored filaments. There were masses of them. Very closely knit, and they must have been from four to five feet long.

They were stretching up and sprouting all over the tree, so the whole effect was similar to a very large mushroom shape. The slightest of breezes would waft this multitude of fine gold colored filaments, which caught the light and created a sparkling light effect. And there was a form of music in the air. As the wind caught the filaments, they vibrated in harmony forming a harmonic scale that rose and fell depending on the direction and intensity of the wind. It was so beautiful to see and hear, Maxx and the soldiers stood there and were mesmerized for a few seconds.

"Right," said Maxx, "you were not told of this mission until now for security reasons. Our objective is to steal this wand they call Elvina." The soldiers looked at one another in disbelief. "Yes, yes," said Maxx, "I realize the enormity of what we are about to attempt to do, but orders come directly from Lord Brough."

"This is not going to be some military maneuver like we would conduct back on Earth. On the contrary, there may be situations that are very alien to us, and we will have to think hard and fast on our feet. Ready?" The two soldiers nodded, but not very convincingly. They crouched down and quickly covered the ground to the entrance of the Sola Tree. The soldier's orders were to disable, not kill.

As Maxx and the soldiers reached the entrance, they split up to tackle the Elf guards who were still leaning half asleep against the Sola Tree roots. One Elf was rendered unconscious very quickly and was laid down and his feet and hands secured with zip ties the soldiers had brought with them. The other though woke up just as the other soldier pounced. The Elf quickly side-stepped and caught his elbow under the soldier's chin. The soldier staggered back dazed. The Elf went in again with a short dagger, wrestled the soldier to the ground and was about to plunge the dagger into the soldier's throat, when the first soldier came to his colleague's aid and wrestled the Elf's head and neck to the side and up. There was a loud crack, and the Elf's body went limp.

Maxx said angrily, "You've killed him. That wasn't supposed to happen." They dragged the bodies out of sight.

Maxx and the remaining soldier came to the entrance of the steps leading downwards into a cave-like structure. Down they went slowly, prepared for anything that would come their way.

They both grabbed some stick-like candles and continued down into the dim light. At the bottom of the steps, the floor leveled off. It was red laterite dust that felt slightly damp. They continued, now under the roots now of the Sola Tree. Above them at first were interlocking roots, but these gave way to a solid round tunnel shape.

Two minutes later, they noticed shafts of light coming

into the tunnel from the left and right, and as they came abreast of the light, two tunnels were extending into the distance on either side of the main tunnel they were standing in, maybe ten feet in diameter.

The soldier then looked at Maxx and said, "Can you hear that sir? That sound? Sounds like horses or something like that?"

How wrong the soldier was! They were not horses. They were a form of wolf. A wolf that is nearly seven-foot-tall at its shoulders. Its fur is pure white, very thick, and along its back there are a number of razor-sharp appendages, which can be used very effectively to cut its enemy into pieces, and if they don't do that, then their enormous teeth and fangs certainly will.

This is the Zo'Sah wolf from the Denetrine district. It has been known to be possible to domesticate them partly. In fact, Allana's family rescued two pups once when their Mother had been killed by a Kroleeth lizard, a huge dinosaur type of reptile which is on average, seventeen feet long. One pup died shortly after it had been rescued and Allana was given the responsibility of raising the remaining pup to adulthood. Again, as with most of the animals on Laniakeea, the Zo'Sah wolves were intelligent enough to telepathically send thought images as a way of communication.

As Hugo and the soldier, each looked down his respective tunnel, there was a Zo'Sah wolf in each tunnel bearing down at them, at great speed and they looked extremely aggressive. Maxx and the soldier were panicking now. They really didn't know where to run, and even if they did, there would have been no way to escape the ferocity and speed of these wolves.

Flashing into their heads were disjointed images of gruesome parts of bodies that had been ripped apart, and as the images pulled back, they showed the Zo'Sah wolves feasting on them both

They gritted their teeth and prepared themselves as best they could, as the wolves came quickly towards them. The wolves must have been running at close on forty miles an hour. Hugo and the soldier could hear the hissing of the wind rushing over and through their fur. The maniacal growling, grunting and gnashing of teeth were the most frightening sounds they had ever heard.

At the last minute, there was another sound mixed in with everything else. What was it? A tinkling? A rattling? When suddenly, the wolves were almost upon them, they had crouched down while running and now began to leap up.

In mid-air, both wolves came to a very abrupt stop, as the chains had reached the limit of how far they could stretch. The saliva of the wolf aiming for Hugo slopped itself in a diagonal line across Maxx's face. They both had sturdy collars on and attached to them were large linked metal chains. They were growling and chomping their jaws only a foot or two from Maxx and the soldier. They both were frozen at the spectacle before them, but it only took a couple of seconds for Maxx to grab the tunic of the soldier and carry on down the tunnel.

They turned a bend, and only then did they stop to take in great gulps of air, and bent over, hands on knees trying to catch their breath.

However, Maxx couldn't understand why they were wearing collars and chains, what was the purpose of that? To scare and frighten? Maybe, but if that is all it did, then no harm was done, and wouldn't delay them.

They continued down the tunnel. It curved gently to the left, and it was then they came across skeletons on the floor. These were not whole skeletons, they were broken up, with a pelvis on one side of the tunnel and the upper section of a skeleton on the other. There were skulls that looked like they had been punctured or containing large holes, as if the heads had something long and sharp, a spike of some sort, forced into it under high pressure? Worryingly, even the long canine tooth of a wolf maybe?

What they also came across in all this debris were partly dissolved links from chains, and there were even some parts of collars. Maxx knelt down to pick up the chains and collars and they disintegrated into dust in his hands. How strange?

Suddenly, it was all starting to make sense. The chains and collars those large wolves were wearing, once activated by movement, had started to dissolve and disintegrate slowly. Any others in the tunnel were then going to have the fright of their lives, realizing that the wolves were now free to roam, and indeed kill their prey.

Maxx stood up quickly and shouted at the soldier to run like hell down the tunnel. They only had a limited amount of time, and Maxx had no idea what that was going to be, so best go all out now to grab that wand, wherever it may be.

They were now sprinting down the tunnel which started to bend to the right, and without warning, they came to a cliff edge. They were both scrabbling to stop from tipping over the edge, Maxx only just managed it to stop, but the soldier slid over the edge. Luckily, in mid-air he managed to twist his body and grab onto the edge with his fingers. Maxx grabbed the neck of his tunic and hauled him back up onto the edge.

They gingerly stood up, then bent over to look over the edge. What they saw was a drop of around five feet, into a green fluorescent thick looking river. It must have been twenty feet wide.
They didn't like the look of this river. In fact, it was giving off an enormous amount of heat. The soldier saw a couple of small rocks on one side and threw them into this river. They quickly erupted into flames and sank beneath the surface, so any ideas they had of swimming across were not going to happen.

Something was swimming in this river. It had fins. It briefly came to the surface turned on its side and looked at them both with one eye, and then quickly slid down under the surface.

At first, they didn't notice a ley line circle to one side. It was partially covered in dust, which they quickly scraped off. There was nothing on it except for one red arrow, and it was pointing directly to the other bank. When they peered, they were sure there was another ley line cycle on the other side.

"Oh great!" mumbled Maxx "How are we going to use this circle to get across?" Then he remembered Hanale telling him, if anyone was stranded, not knowing which incantation to use; there was a failsafe word that could be used. Always use a red arrow he said, and say "Krandoo," which in Forlasath, the Laniakeean Elvish dialect, meant 'straight.'

Once transporting, it would take you in a straight line till it reached another circle in its path, whether that be a foot away or the other end of the dimension. And since the red arrow was pointing directly across to the other circle, they stood on it and took their chances. Maxx closed his eyes and said "Krandoo" and they were across.

"Phew," said Maxx. Momentarily they were both collected their thoughts, but set off once again, and within thirty seconds they came across a vast round cave. It was bathed in soft gold light, and there in the middle, on top of a very ancient stone-carved very ancient column sat the Spiriten, that hopefully would be containing Elvina.

They gingerly made their way forward, expecting other nasty surprises, but there were none. The soldier reached up for the Spiriten, and handed it back to Maxx.

Maxx could feel the Spiriten vibrating, it was warm to the touch. It was wooden, a light teak color, but you could tell right away, it was old seasoned wood. Inlaid into it were ancient Elvish carvings and what looked like rare metals embedded into the wood. He undid the small clasp on the side, and the lid slowly rose of its own accord, and there nestled on a bed of purple and red velvet was Elvina.

Elvina was composed of two distinct parts. One part was beautifully carved wooden stock which must have been seven inches long. The wood was intricately carved with shapes and swirls and other Elvish markings. At the top was a blueish/green orb, that appeared to be filled with gases that were swirling around. It was in here that the heart of the Sola Tree was kept. Maxx didn't even think about touching it, after everything he had learned about it from Hounani and Allana. He gently closed the lid, closed the clasp, and put it securely into his shoulder bag, then they turned around to make their way back.

Negotiating the river on the way back was simple, and they started to run back up the corridor, then they passed the skeletons and dissolved chains and collars, and were coming up to the two adjacent tunnels that the enormous wolves had run down.

They were almost tiptoeing along at this section. They had reached the two tunnels and were two or three feet past them, when all of a sudden, they heard the wolves again. His assumptions had been right, once activated the chains would begin to dissolve. The chains were not making the tinkling sound they made previously, but more a dampened dull sound. *'Elf magic, just what we need,'* thought Maxx.

They stopped for a second, looked at each other in horror, then set off at full speed back up the tunnel. Their running speed was no match for the wolves that were gaining on them very quickly now. Maxx didn't dare look around. He knew it would be touch and go if they made it out at all.

Around another bend, and ahead of them were the Sola tree roots and freedom. They scrambled to try to wedge themselves into the roots of the tree, which they managed to do in the nick of time. They were approximately ten feet into this protective cocoon of roots, but this didn't stop the Zo'Sah wolves thrusting in their huge paws, brandishing their nine-inch-long sharp claws, trying to dig their way in to drag Hugo and the soldier out.

Unluckily for the soldier, one of the thinner roots gave way under the continued pounding from the shoulder of one wolf, which meant the claws managed to bury themselves into his chest. As they hadn't penetrated deep enough, so it ripped the soldier's skin but was unable to drag him out.

Maxx and the soldier squeezed even further back. The wolves started to pace and look at the both of them out of the corner of their bright yellow eyes. Images of feasting, blood and gore continued to pop up in their heads, but after a few minutes, some howling and growling, scrabbling at the ground, they seemed to lose interest and make their way back down the tunnel.

Hugo and the soldier waited and listened, and as quietly as possible, made their way out and into the entrance proper. There were the dead Elf guard and his companion, who luckily was still unconscious. After Maxx had put a temporary dressing on the soldier's wounds, they made their way to the ley line circle.

They stepped into it. Maxx found the right arrow, and tried to remember the incantation to transport them to the slice. Again, and again, Maxx tried, but it must not have been quite right. By now, the unconscious Elf guard was coming around.

"Come on Maxx", Maxx shouted to himself, "Remember." He tried one more time, and suddenly they were off. The soldier wasn't prepared, but nonetheless, they arrived at the circle close to the slice. The soldier on his knees was now retching and bleeding profusely from the claw wounds on his chest.

The slice was approximately two minutes' walk away, and they had to negotiate some tall undergrowth to get there, so they took the opportunity to check if there were any Elves around. There were three, just to the left of the slice, in deep telepathic conversation.

Hugo whispered to the soldier, "We have to create a diversion." The soldier had an emergency flare in his kit belt, and he thought it might give them enough time to entice the Elves away from the slice to investigate. The soldier cocked the flare and threw it with all his might up in the air to the far left.

The pink hissing smoke of the flare did its job. The Elves looked around, and sped off towards it, and Maxx and the soldier took their chance and ran up to and into the slice. A few moments later they were on the other side, facing a contingent of Earthan soldiers who immediately lowered their guns.

Maxx shouted for the commander, directed the medics to attend to the soldier with him, and asked for a horse. As he said this, one was brought up for him, and he set off at full speed for Brough manor. *'At last,'* thought Maxx, *'I am going to get what I justly deserve.'*

A Trickle of Blood
(As Maxx pressed the point of the dagger slightly into the neck of Lord Brough, directly above his jugular, a small trickle of blood started to drip down his neck and onto his tunic)

CHAPTER 10

A Trickle of Blood

(Be gentle with the Earthan's. Be understanding. Be patient. They have a lot of catching up to do.)

In a cloud of dust, Maxx arrived at Brough manor, jumped off his horse and went to find his father. On the way, Maxx communicated with his father via his HC, and Brough told him brusquely to make his way the East Wing library.

There were two libraries within Brough manor. One was quite large and doubled as a casual living room, where family members and children and friends would collect. However, there was a private library, that only Brough usually had access to. Everyone knew of its existence, but only Brough could give permission for someone to enter, and it didn't matter who they were. It was situated in a cold, damp annex at the rear of the manor. To access it, you would have to go through two doors, both of which were lockable when Brough wasn't in residence.

Maxx came to the entrance of his father's private library, took in a deep breath, and then went through both doors into the library's inner sanctum. There, at the far end of the library, was a huge open fireplace with logs already roaring away.

Brough was standing with his back to the fire, having lifted up his tunic coat, and was warming the backs of his legs.

"Well?" said Brough, "Did you get your hands on it?"

"Yes," said Maxx, "But it wasn't easy, one Elf dead, one unconscious, and one of our soldiers dead and the other receiving medical attention while we speak."

However, Brough wasn't interested in the slightest in that sort of information. Even if more had been killed, this was of no importance to Brough. He just wanted the wand, and more importantly, it's unbelievable power he had been so eloquently informed about.

Maxx swung around his backpack, undid the straps, and carefully lifted out the Spiriten containing Elvina. He carefully placed it on the massive thick oak table in the middle of the room, and he stepped back. Both Brough and Maxx looked at the Spiriten for a few moments. They both could hear the buzzing and humming emanating from the box.

"Well?" commanded Brough, "Open the damn box up,

now!" With that, Maxx approached the box, undid the little clasp on the side, and slowly, of its own accord, the lid lifted up.

Brough took a step forward and peered into the box, and in all her resplendent beauty, there was Elvina. Brough stared at the wand in awe, licking his lips and rubbing his hands together. He asked Maxx if he had held her.

"What?!" exclaimed Maxx. "You have to be joking. Only certain Elves can hold her. If you are not a 'chosen' one, you will evaporate into thin air." Then a small smile spread across Maxx's lips and he said, "Why don't you grab her then?"

"Ah well," said Brough, who was looking decidedly pleased with himself, "After grabbing one of the Elf guards at the slice, and making him an offer he couldn't refuse, we managed to get out of him, an Elvish phrase, that will allow someone to hold her in their hands for around two minutes. Enough time, of course, to alter everything I want around me, the way I want it."

This was false information, of course. The Elf that had been pressured into saying something, but was never going to give out the true facts about Elvina, and was secretly hoping these stupid Earthan's would grab her. It would be the last thing they ever did.

As Brough leaned down to take the box, Maxx quickly got in before him, snapped down the lid, and moved the box to his side of the table. "Aren't we forgetting something?"

Brough immediately started to get angry, the anger building in him like a volcano, "What the hell do you mean?" he spat out.

Maxx let out a long-drawn sigh, and said in a very condescending way, "The papers? The ones you had drawn up showing that I had equal rights to this estate, its lands and title and full acknowledgement as your son. Or had you conveniently forgotten?"

"This is how it's going to work." said Maxx very calmly. "You give me those papers and I pass over Elvina into your grubby hands. You do that now, or I am taking the wand back to Laniakeea. No discussion."

"Ok, ok," shouted Brough through gritted teeth, holding his hands up. Brough stomped over to his window desk, unlocked and opened a drawer and pulled out some documents, then waddled back to Maxx and thrust them into his hands. Maxx gave the documents a cursory look, and then handed the Spiriten, containing the wand to Brough.

As Brough started to turn around and walk away, Maxx was still looking through the documents. "Hang on a minute," said Maxx, as he looked more closely, flipping through the documents again. "You haven't signed, dated or sealed any of them? They are worthless as they are. Sign them now!"

Brough slowly turned around to look at Maxx. There was a malicious look in his eyes, and as he slowly put the

Spiriten down on the desk next to him, he squared up to Maxx and said, "Well, you win some, you lose some. Circle of life and all that. I've detested you from the moment you were born to that whore of a mother of yours. It wasn't easy at the time, but I'm glad now I was able to make sure she wouldn't live to tell the tale."

"This is a world of the haves and the have nots, and guess which side you belong to? And to top it all, you prance around in your designer clothes and fancy hairdos and to cap it all, you're a bloody homo!" By this stage, Brough's face was contorted with rage.

"I'm arranging for you to have that permanent vacation in that desolate area of the Eastern landmass, where there will be plenty of your kind there to practice your filthy up's and down's with. So, clear off before I have you arrested."

While Brough was coming out with this tirade, Maxx's temper was snowballing rapidly. He was, by the time Brough had finished talking, trembling with rage. He bolted forward, running full into Brough and head-butting him at the same time. Even the massive bulk of Brough couldn't withstand this assault, and he staggered backwards.

Luckily the wall behind Brough prevented him from falling, and in fact what it did do, it gave Brough the leverage to push forward with his hands off the wall and punch Maxx square on the nose. This time Maxx staggered back, wiping the blood away from his nose that now started to bleed profusely. His eyes were watering so badly, he couldn't see properly for a moment or two, which gave Brough the opening to shoot forward and bring his knee high up into Maxx's solar plexus.

Maxx bent over thoroughly winded, but managed to move back to assess where to go next. They started to circle themselves, slowly, in complete silence. This was no play fighting. It was as serious as it gets. Brough had forgotten that Maxx was a champion wrestler, and to Maxx, all those competitions and hours of training started to kick in automatically. Maxx had spent considerable time in parts of the American landmass with a cult American wrestling club.

Again, Brough rushed forward towards Maxx to grab him in a bear hug. At the last second, Maxx bent down and put his head between Brough's fat thighs and clasped his arms and hands around the outside of each leg.

At the same time, using Brough's momentum, he started to stand up. Brough's upper body was now falling onto Maxx's back, so Maxx quickly changed his position, so that now Brough's body was pivoting straight up. Maxx was still holding Brough's legs, and let Brough's massive body continue curling back until he landed with great force on his back onto the floor. Maxx heard all the air being expelled out of Brough's lungs, plus the cracking sound of Brough's head on the hard-stone floor. This was the classic 'Alabama Slam.'

Whilst Brough was lying there, Maxx jumped into the air, and landed with the back of his arm straight across Brough's windpipe. This was called the 'Cactus elbow,' All these moves came to Maxx automatically; he didn't even have to think about them.

Maxx could have taken Brough there and then, but he let Brough recover a little, Maxx was enjoying being in control, physically, over his father. Brough started to haul himself up onto one knee and gradually he pulled himself upright, rubbing his throat but by then Maxx had moved quickly behind him and grabbed him in a classic firm headlock, and there was nothing Brough could do about it. A little more sustained pressure and Maxx could suffocate Brough, but to Maxx, that would have been too easy. He reached down deftly, and pulled out a seven-inch dagger from his boot sheath. He brought it up and exactly into position where Brough's jugular would be, just to the side of his windpipe.

They were both breathing heavily. Maxx then started to shout in Brough's ear, "You are going to sign those papers, or I am going to sever your jugular."

"Not a chance," spat Brough, "You haven't got the courage to do something like that. It takes a real man to do that, and we both know you are not one of those!"

Brough started to struggle, but the combination of the headlock and the tip of the dagger just above his jugular kept him quiet.

By now, the tip of Maxx's dagger had dug even deeper into Brough's throat, and a little trickle of blood started to meander down Brough's throat and drip onto his shirt and tunic.

Hugo, Allana and Ding Ling had arrived on the Earthan side of the slice. Their horses were already prepared, so Allana and Hugo doubled up and Ding Ling got on his own horse and they set off towards Brough Manor.

While galloping along, Hugo tried to reach both Maxx or his father on his HC, but couldn't raise either of them. He was discovering that it took a short while for HCs to re-boot once they are back on this side of The Slice.

They arrived at Brough Manor, just as Lady Brough came to the entrance. They all dismounted, and Hugo said to his mother, "Have you seen father or Maxx at all?".

"Yes Hugo," said Lady Brough, "I know your father was in the private library, and Maxx arrived in a rush around twenty minutes ago and also ran to the library. Hugo, what is going on?"

"I'm not sure at the moment mother, But I'm going to find out. Please, can you look after Allana and Dingy?"

"Of course, my dear," responded Lady Brough.

As Hugo was turning a corner to the first door of the private library, he could hear raised voices. He flew through the first door, then flung open the second, and what confronted him stopped him in his tracks.

Here, facing him was his father, and behind him, holding his Father in a powerful headlock, was Maxx, with a bloodied nose, who was holding a dagger to his father's throat. Hugo immediately noticed the blood running down Brough's throat from the point of the dagger.

"What the hell is going on?" shouted Hugo. "Maxx, for God's sake, put down the dagger!"

"You haven't a clue as to what's going on, have you Hugo?" said Maxx. In less than a minute, Maxx explained everything to Hugo: his mother's murder, his persecution by Brough all his life for him being gay, the fact he was never going to be an equal family member. Brough had promised all that, if he was to steal Elvina and bring it to him, and that he never had any intention of signing any document for him and finally was going to banish him to some godforsaken remote place on the other side of the world.

You could see Hugo was struggling to take all this in. But there were priorities here, and no matter how much Hugo despised his father, he couldn't have Maxx cutting his father's throat.

"Maxx, you know that Helena and Kayon and I always treated you as our brother, not a half-brother. We all know our father is one of a kind: aggressive, rude, thoughtless and cruel. The despicable ways he manipulates people, and we are included in that, and this now, is another example of him thinking only about himself. He is a megalomaniac. No two ways about it, but if you cut his throat with that dagger, you will only make it worse for yourself."

Maxx was listening intently to Hugo. He trusted Hugo and loved him as a brother. Hugo continued, "I've just spotted Elvina there on the table, I've come to take it back to the queen, and I know you know it's the right thing to do Maxx. As to our pig of a father banishing you somewhere, it's not going to happen, and I expect him to pay for murdering your mother."

Maxx was wavering now and suddenly pushed Brough away from him so hard, Brough fell onto his hands and knees. Brough slowly pulled himself up, and stood there shaking a little, breathing heavily and wiping his throat with a handkerchief he had pulled out of his pocket.

Hugo ran to Maxx and hugged him tightly, and whispered to him, "It's going to be ok. I'm going to get father arrested and to have him come to account for killing your mother. Maxx, a far as I am concerned, you will always be my brother, and a part of my family."

As Hugo was saying all this to Maxx, neither of them noticed that Brough was leaning down slightly to grab something from inside the top of his right boot. He had a small gun in his hands, and he was slowly was walking towards the two of them.

At the last minute, they turned sideways to face Brough, and both of them noticed the gun, which was pointed in their general direction. By now Brough had disheveled hair and a wild look in his eyes. He looked quite mad.

Brough said "Thick as thieves, aren't we? You just can't get it in your thick skulls" as he said this, through gritted teeth, he was jabbing his forefinger on the side of his head, again and again "I have a plan, and it involves that wand over there" he carelessly wafted the gun over to where Elvina was "and you lot are just some flotsam in the way. Well, I won't have it."

And with that Brough took a step forward, and as he did so, he started to point the gun at Maxx's heart. He pulled the trigger. The recoil made the gun jump up in Brough's hand, and the smell of cordite filled the air.

Hugo was transfixed. He couldn't believe what his Father had just done. He just stood there in absolute shock. No sooner had Maxx crumpled to the ground, than Brough took yet another step forward, pointed the barrel at Maxx's head, and shot him again at point blank range. A dark pool of blood started to spread out quickly around Maxx's head.

Brough turned the gun around and offered the barrel to Hugo, who took the gun. Brough told him, "And this is where you arrest me Hugo," and put his hands up in the air.

For a second, Hugo was in shock, and then just backed away a little, touched his HC and shouted for the sergeant at arms to come immediately. Literally ten seconds later, in came the sergeant and a private. They were both carrying intelliguns, and they looked first at Hugo, then Brough and finally at Maxx lying on the floor.

"What's going on sir?" said the sergeant to Hugo.

Hugo replied, "You need to arrest my father, Lord Brough for the murder of his son and my brother, Maxx Brough." The sergeant and the private stood in disbelief. "Now!" shouted Hugo.

"Wait a minute sargent," said Brough, "Just look at the evidence here. That is NOT my gun, it's my son Hugo's gun." Hugo glanced down at the gun very briefly, and realized it was his own. *Where had he got that from?* he thought.

"If you were to check the bullet in my son Maxx's chest, and the one Hugo fired point blank into his head, you will find forensics confirm they both came from the same gun. And since he is holding the gun, it's quite apparent that it has his fingerprints all over it. I suggest sergeant, that you arrest my son, Hugo for his brother's murder, and as soon as possible before he shoots you both as well!"

At that the sergeant and the private leapt onto Hugo, wrestled him to the ground, zipped his wrists behind him and started to frog march him out, protesting, but not before Brough went up close to Hugo, and whispered into his ear, "You see Hugo, I win, you and Maxx lose."

"Right," said Brough to the soldiers, "Take him away

now." Hugo was taken straight down into the basement beneath the manor, where there was a holding cell. He was thrown inside, the
door was locked and the private sat just outside on guard.

Luckily, in their rush to arrest him, the soldiers had not disabled Hugo's HC, so Hugo quietly called up Ding Ling and briefly explained briefly everything to him. "Can you meet me down here? But be careful, you will have to disable the guard. I need to get out as soon as possible, and retrieve that wand before my father hides it somewhere."

Hugo sat and played over the events of the last half hour. It seemed like a fairy tale. And he was becoming upset now, he loved his brother, and swore that his priority would be to make his father pay for his senseless murder of his brother. He buried his head in his hands and wept.

Six or seven minutes later, Hugo thought he had heard a noise outside the cell door when suddenly Ding Ling's head popped up. There was a turning of a key, and in came Ding Ling closely followed by Allana. They removed the zip ties from Hugo's wrists, and both were saying how sorry they were. Anger started to well up into Hugo now. He knew he had to control it. That way he could think more clearly.

"First things first," said Hugo, "We need to find Elvina."

'Master, look," said Ding Ling, who took off his backpack and inside, carefully wrapped up was the Spiriten containing

Elvina.

Hugo couldn't believe his eyes, "How…?"

"Master," said Ding Ling, "we sneaked into library. You know small washbasin closet? Just to left of snooker table? Your father was in there, looks like he was cleaning blood off face and hands, so we grab wandy thing, and we sneak out again and come down here pronto."

"Well done, both of you. Right. We need to move now before he realizes what's happened, and get the wand back to your queen Allana." As Hugo stepped cautiously out of the cell, he noticed the private, sat on the chair facing the wall smiling. "What's wrong with him?"

"Oh, I just used some mild magic on him Hugo. He thinks he is at the cinema watching a movie. It will wear off in ten minutes."

"The private suddenly shouted out, "Popcorn, I want popcorn now." They all left quickly and quietly, out through a hidden door that Hugo knew about, around the corner of the manor, grabbed their horses and they were off at full gallop back to the slice."

Just over half an hour later saw all three of them walking up the grand hall in the queen's palace. Ding Ling had already handed Hugo the Spiriten containing Elvina, and as they walked up to meet the queen, she came down to meet them.

"Oh Hugo Brough," said the queen, "I can't begin to thank you. I trusted you, and you have repaid all of us by rescuing Elvina."

"Well, it was certainly a team effort," said Hugo, "If it hadn't been for Ding Ling here and Allana, I probably wouldn't be standing here in front of you now."

"We must celebrate, Hugo Brough." said the queen.

"I would love to, but there have been some unfortunate circumstances that will need my immediate attention, and so need to return immediately to the Earthan dimension."

"I am sorry to hear that," said the queen, "Anything I can help you with?"

"I think it may take a little too long to explain now, so think I will just leave, if that is ok?"

As Hugo said this, Allana stepped forward and put her hand on his forearm, and he could see she was in conversation with the queen. The queen then came down and stood quite close to Hugo.

She said, "As you know we can read thoughts as you think them, but retrieving thoughts, and past memories, is a little more of a physical process. For you everything that has happened in the last two hours I can retrieve in a fraction of a second, if you give me permission, that is. It is a way of possibly helping you."

"Erm, ok then." said Hugo. The queen then lifted her hands, which she then spread out over particular strategic points down both side of Hugo's face. As soon as she closed her eyes, Hugo was in a different world. Everything that had happened in the last two hours was being replayed back to him, but insanely quickly, and not just from his perspective, but weirdly, from the perspective of everyone else that was in the scene. And no sooner was it was replayed, than it was all over.

The queen removed her fingers, opened her eyes, and with utter compassion simply said, "I am so sorry Hugo Brough. How upsetting for you. I now understand. Thank you for allowing me to see your memories. You had best go now, I think it may be better for Allana to stay here on this occasion while you go with Din Din to put everything right."

At this Ding Ling stepped forward, and while he was bowing down low, said to the queen, "I Chinese ma'am. My name Ding Ling, not Din Din, which is food you feed chicken to make them lay eggs. Thank you so very much for understanding." Not a lot was going to bring Hugo out of the mood he was in, but this did make him smile.

On the journey to the slice, he knew there would be soldiers ready to arrest him. Hugo was racking his brains for a way around this, to let the truth be known. Any feelings he had for his father had disappeared when he shot and killed Maxx.

Hugo and Ding Ling had reached the circle just before the slice, when suddenly Hugo grabbed Ding Ling's shoulders and said to him, "I've got it! I've got it!"

Ding Ling stepped back a pace and looked quizzically at

his master, "Got what Master? A headache? Crabs? No deodorant?"

"No Dingy," said Hugo, "Remember a month or so before all this happened, before we discovered the slice, we overhauled all the security at the manor house?"

"Ah so Master, remember well," said Ding Ling, "I fell off ladder, then electricity went through body when I touch broken wire. My hair stands on end, and I glow like lightbulb and everybody laugh, but not you Master, you check that Dingy is ok."

"Erm, yep," said Hugo. "Now we completely upgraded all the CCTV cameras, and even installed them in rooms where there had been none before, including the private library. In fact, I installed four cameras in there, so every aspect of that room will have been covered, and any movement and also importantly, voices, recorded. And as luck would have it, I never got around to telling my father that they had been installed."

By now Hugo was looking pleased with himself. "Right Dingy," said Hugo, "As soon as I am back on the other side, you sneak off to the security hut at the Manor, and grab the SD cards for that period of time that it all happened, from the moment Maxx arrived and met my father in the library, including the time I entered. It is crucial we have all the footage that shows my father shooting Maxx."

"I want you then to go straight to Joel Langley, who is

as you know, commander in chief of security within the UEL, and ask him to report to the main court, because that is immediately where I will be taken, and set up screens so that all will be able to see what in fact happened. Can you do that for me?"

"Oh Master," said Ding Ling, "you very clever person. And I know evil prevail when good men fail to act. And you acting like you step on rusty nail. You are good man. I so glad I am your family Master. It will be done."

As they walked through the slice, sure enough, there was a contingent of guards there who immediately arrested Hugo. The commander, who Hugo knew personally, said to Hugo as he was zipping Hugo's hands behind his back, "I'm sorry sir, I have my orders, but all the men know the accusations being flung about are unfounded. I am ordered to transport you to the UEL command center and to the court there to conduct a preliminary session to decide whether you will stand trial for the murder of your brother Maxx. Anything you say may be taken down and used in evidence against you."

Maxx was led away to a horse, and they all started to make their way to the UEL headquarters.

By now, Ding Ling had just reached the manor and made his way to the security hut. He searched for the relevant footage he needed, briefly watched the pertinent parts of the recording (which he found very upsetting), made a copy, then made his way to the UEL command center.

Hugo was escorted in. The main court was at the back of the ground floor. The thick wooden double doors were flung open and Hugo stepped into the packed hot stuffy courtroom.

The Barboski
(A magical horse related to the Earthan unicorn. They live in the Queen's garden. They are telepathic, and can levitate to thirty feet or more off the ground)

CHAPTER 11

Unfounded Accusations

(One body. One mind. Two hearts. This is Elf perfection.)

The courtroom was certainly heaving. The public gallery, which would normally hold forty people, had extra chairs brought in on each side, so now it was at full occupancy with sixty.

It all smacked of age-old traditions in this courtroom: the carved wood paneling on the wall, the wood benches and so on. Hugo remembered from somewhere that beeswax polish was still used to treat and polish all the wood, even though there were no more bees left on Earth, and substitute technology was now used to pollinate plants.

Hugo was led down some steps, and to the left, then up some more and into a category A shielded witness stand. This was a stand that was surrounded on four sides by bulletproof glass. The zip ties were removed from his aching wrists, and as he rubbed them, he looked around the courtroom.

He noticed immediately his father sitting in the witness gallery, and of course that is where he had to be, because he was related to Hugo. He had that same infuriating smile on his lips, and Hugo wanted to wipe it off. Hugo also noticed an oblong white plaster on the side of his father's neck where Maxx's dagger had penetrated his skin.

The court's judiciary were sat in an imposing looking line of desks. There were five desks. The desk in the middle was set a little higher than the others. Four of the judges were already sat either side of the raised desk, which, for the moment was empty. Hugo knew his father would normally be sitting there, in his role as the local judge.

Below Hugo and to his left, were what he presumed were the prosecuting team. To his right, on the other side of the courtroom were the defense counsel. All of them wearing black court gowns, short old-fashioned wigs and white collars. Behind both the prosecutor and defense, there were a couple of rows of short-wigged legal assistants.

Hugo caught the eye of the leader of the defense counsel, who immediately came over. Hugo knew him. He was called Jeremy Unsworth. "We have a slight upward battle here Hugo," whispered Jeremy to Hugo. "No witnesses, it was your gun, and your fingerprints are all over it, never mind the fact you escaped from custody."

"Possibly the only thing we can hold onto is the fact you came back on your own volition and gave yourself up. We are stumbling from the start. Is there anything we can use to help in your defense?"

"Yes," said Hugo, "There should be clear CCTV footage of all the events that led up to my brother's death, that will show conclusively, that my father shot Maxx, that I had nothing to do with it other than doing my best to prevent it all happening, and that my father orchestrated the whole thing. I also want some other evidence that should be apparent to be officially noted, that my father premeditatively arranged to have Maxx's mother murdered. Again, this will be substantiated by the CCTV video recordings."

Jeremy took a step back and raised his eyebrows, "Is your father or the prosecution aware of this video evidence?"

"Nope," said Maxx.

"And who will be submitting this evidence? The court will come into session in only five minutes time."

"My aide, Ding Ling, is on his way now with the recordings." As Hugo was saying this, he noticed technicians were setting up various LED screens around the court. Ding Ling had managed to get all that side sorted already.

Each judge had a mini screen in front of them, and these were all being coordinated from the sound and visual booth at the back of the court. This booth had only one entrance, and that was just outside the double doors that led to the court. But it would be guarded.

Hugo continued, "He should be here any minute. Please look out for him."

"You may be aware Hugo," said Jeremy, "that once the court is in session, we will not be able to open the doors to anyone?"

"Yes, I am aware of that," said Hugo, "which is why I have instructed Ding Ling to hand the video evidence straight into the sound and visual booth.

"Good. Good," said Jeremy, "I will make sure the sound and visual technicians have my permission to submit this as evidence and inform me as soon as they have the evidence to set up and ready to play."

By now, it seemed, everything was ready. Raised up on the sides of the court, were monitors showing the heads of all the UEL members. Large cameras were already running, capturing every moment of the proceedings.

A hush descended on the courtroom, as a door behind the row of judges opened, and in came Lord Justice Oldham, a seasoned murder trial judge. The clerk of the court shouted out, "All rise." Everyone in court stood. Oldham walked up three steps and along to his chair and sat down. Everyone else then sat. There was silence.

He sat upright, and for a couple of minutes was making copious notes on a pad in front of him. The tension in the room was rising and whispered conversations had started up in the witness gallery. Oldham grabbed the gavel in front of him, clapped it down on the wooden stock in front of him and shouted out, "Silence!"

Oldham then nodded to the barrister leading the prosecution, who stood up, and proceeded to lay out the circumstances behind, and then the eventual demise of Maxx, He explained that the evidence to hand was irrefutable and that it could be none other than Hugo who was the person that had murdered Maxx. As he said this he was emphatically pointing straight at Hugo. He held this pose for a few moments and then went and sat down.

Brough was slowly nodding his head in the witness gallery. He had that infuriating smile across his face that he always had when he thought he was right, and everything was playing out exactly the way he wanted.

Judge Oldham then looked over his half-glasses at the defense, and in particular at Jeremy, who stood up. "Well?" said Oldham, "Have you any evidence you wish to submit?"

"Yes m'lud, we have unequivocal evidence to show that Lord Brough was indeed the perpetrator of this heinous crime, and also have an admission, by his own tongue, that he was also responsible for the demise and consequent murder of Maxx Brough's mother, a" Jeremy looked down at his notes "member of the cleaning staff at Brough manor, one Shantell Williams. I have the all the information to hand which I would like to submit as evidence."

At this stage, unusually, the judge said, "I wish to consult with both the prosecution and defense in my chambers. There will be a recess for fifteen minutes."

At this, those in attendance rose and the judge walked out of the court and made his way to his chambers, closely followed by Jeremy and the prosecution barrister, Clifford Hinckley.

In the chambers, the judge looked carefully at both barristers. "You realize gentlemen, that this is a high-profile case. And even more awkward due to the fact that Lord Arlo Brough is also a circuit judge and head of the UEL. We cannot have a botched-up case here. All facts have to be proven beyond a reasonable doubt."

The judge continued, "Mr. Hinckley, you have already submitted all points of evidence, which the court proceedings ensure has to be admitted to the defense counsel and court in general. But you, Mr. Unsworth, are claiming you have clear evidence that Lord Brough is responsible for the murder of his son Maxx, of which there has been no mention of it at all previously, and certainly hasn't been submitted as yet? And now you claim there is evidence that he murdered his son's mother. Can you unequivocally confirm all of this?"

"Yes m'lud, the evidence has only now just come to light, and is already set up to play and admit as evidence, and I am informed, will conclusively prove that Lord Brough not only killed his son, that he tried to blame Hugo Brough, and was also responsible for the murder of Maxx Brough's mother, a case that is still open and unresolved."

The judge let out a big sigh, and said, "Right. Let us continue, and hope we can reach a satisfactory conclusion quickly as to where we are going with all this." With that, all three of them made their way back to court. The two barristers went in first, then the clerk announced the arrival of the judge, and everyone stood. Judge Oldham then came in and sat down, slowly followed by the rest of the court taking their seats.

The judge said, "The defense wishes to submit important evidence, in the form of recordings from CCTV cameras in the second and private library situated within Brough Manor where the alleged murder took place. Although this evidence should have been previously submitted, due to circumstances beyond anyone's control, I have now allowed its submission. I have also decided, that the defense councils' evidence be submitted before the prosecution's evidence. Mr Unsworth, you may proceed."

All the while, Hugo kept glancing at his father, and he could quite clearly see that Brough hadn't a clue as to what was going on, but when the judge mentioned the CCTV cameras in the library for the first time, he felt sure he could feel and see the panic in Brough's eyes. He wasn't smiling any more. In fact, he was looking decidedly queasy.

All the lights dimmed, and then on all the monitors, in

full color and sound, were the events that had transpired, in minute detail, from the moment Maxx walked into his father's library, to the moment that Hugo was arrested and frog marched away to the holding cell. The lights in court were switched back on. There was the sound of overpowering silence. Nobody moved or said a word. Everyone drew in his or her breath when Brough shot Maxx first in the chest and then through the head at point blank range. They shook their heads in disbelief when Brough offered the handle of the gun to Hugo.

Brough himself suddenly stood up, purple in the face, shouting that it was all lies and a fabrication, and didn't the court recognize who in fact he was, or who they were dealing with? "Don't you lot realize," shouted out Brough, "I am a high court circuit judge, for God's sake?!"

The public gallery was now booing him and calling him names, but he continued to sprout out all his titles and deeds.

Judge Oldham brought down his gavel on the stock and immediately ordered the arrest of Lord Brough.

Already, three guards had Brough in handcuffs and were leading him, shouting and swearing at the top of his voice, out of the gallery.

The Judge then ordered quiet in the court and summarily dismissed all accusations against Hugo, ordering that Hugo be released immediately. The judge also remarked that Lord Brough was now accused on two counts of murder made against him: the murder of his half-son, Maxx Brough, and that of Maxx's mother, Chantell Williams. A date for the commencement of the double murder trial would be decided upon at a later court session. In the meantime, Lord Arlo Brough would be kept in remand in a high security prison.

Hugo just sat there for a few moments to try to gather his thoughts. *'What a day,'* he thought. *'Life throws us these curve balls, and sometimes we wonder how we will ever survive.'*

He took in a deep breath, and stood up and smiled at Jeremy, as he was released. "Well that was short and sweet," said Jeremy, "I will, of course, keep you apprised of all proceedings against your father, not only for the murder of Maxx but also Maxx's mother. I wouldn't be surprised if these accusations open up a whole new can of worms as far as your father is concerned, with lots more accusations of other crimes now surfacing, since your father is in custody."

"Thank you, Jeremy." said Hugo, and he made his way out of the courtroom. Outside the command center, he took in a deep breath of fresh air and met up with Ding Ling, who he thanked for literally saving his life. They made their way back to Brough Manor, to tell Allana, and also of course, Hugo's mother Romilly, who would have no idea of what had happened at all.

"It was also time to tell his brother and sister, Kayon and Helena, everything that had been happening. Ding Ling had already organized this as well.

Hugo rubbed the top of Ding Ling's head, and with a smile said, "What would I do without you Dingy?"

"Not a lot master," said Ding Ling, "You make lots of worry for me, make me not poop for many days, now sorted, time for me to take care of backlog."

"What?" said Hugo, then realized what Ding Ling had said, saw his creased-up smiling face, and burst out laughing.

As Hugo approached Brough Manor, a weary Hugo, noticed Allana, standing at the entrance with his mother, Kayon and Helena.

"I thought you had decided to stay back in Laniakeea, Allana?" said Hugo, as he dismounted, "Has something happened?"

"No Hugo," said Allana, "I just felt it could be more important to be here to offer you some support. I hope you don't mind? You have had lots to deal with."

"Allana has been very comforting for me as well Hugo," said his mother.

"Of course, that's ok," said Hugo, "Thank you for being so thoughtful." He then addressed everyone and said, "Shall we retire to the study? I know you will have been following all the developments, and would like to explain in a lot more detail for you all."

Everyone made their way to the study. Allana, his mother, Kayon and Helena. He explained to them all, everything that had happened. For a few moments, nobody said a word. Helena started to cry softly, and Kayon went up to her and put his arms around her shoulders to comfort her. But it was the reaction of Hugo's mother, Romilly, that surprised everyone. She didn't seem the least bit upset?

Hugo said, "Mother? Are you ok?"

"None of you realize what a horrible brute of a man your father was behind closed doors. I have had to live with that for years. The times I have taken beatings on your behalf just so he wouldn't vent his anger on all of you. I loved Maxx as if he was my own son, and I know you all also loved him in your own ways. All that has happened was inevitable, the writing was on the wall as they say. It's important we bring some happiness into our lives and move forward." And with that Romilly stood, slowly went to all of them, hugged them tightly and left the room."

Little did Helena and Kayon know, but they would begin to become a much closer part of Hugo's life in many ways. Hugo noticed how affectionate Kayon and Helena were towards Allana, she had impressed them very much.

Hugo went outside into the walled garden with Allana. They sat on a swing seat overlooking a little pond, the surface of which was rippled by the koi carp feeding. Surrounding it were lilies of all species, so their heady scent filled the air. The grass lawns had just been mown, and so mixed in with all that was the smell of cut grass.

Jemima, the head cook, had brought out a wonderful

cream tea of freshly baked scones, clotted cream and homemade strawberry jam. She had set up a little table to one side, laid out a very old lace French tablecloth and also brought out a huge china teapot of Lapsang Souchong, that wonderfully smoky tea, that was Hugo's favorite. Hugo loved Jemima's homemade jams. She managed to include whole pieces of fruit in the jam, making it a meal in itself.

Allana and Hugo just sat and swung gently back and forth. Allana reached out tentatively and just held Hugo's hand, more than anything, as a comfort. Already Hugo was beginning to relax and took in a deep breath. Then he looked at Allana and said, "Shall I be Mummy?" Allana just looked at him with a look that said, 'What are you talking about?'

So, he smiled and got up, poured Allana some tea, put in a little milk and handed it to her. She took the cup and saucer tentatively and first smelled the tea, then tried a sip. Then she smiled, and continued to drink. Hugo went on to twist the scones, that were still quite oven hot, so the homemade butter melted almost immediately, spread on a spoonful of jam and carefully put a large dollop of clotted cream on the top and handed this to Allana.

Allana wasn't too sure what to do with it at first, but she watched Hugo tackle his. She twisted the hot scone in half, just as Hugo had done, and took a bite. You have to remember: this was an Elf, with completely different taste buds, and that would have no idea what the ingredients she was trying were or how they tasted. It was like watching a three-year-old eating something new for the very first time. A look of amazement flooded across Allana's face. She was searching for some reference of anything that she had eaten in Laniakeea, but of course nothing would come close.

Behind them, Hugo heard a noise, turned around to see Ding Ling hovering around five feet away. "Sorry Master," said Ding Ling, "didn't want disturb. Urgent message from UEL. They want speak urgent."

"I wondered when that call would come obviously to do with my father being arrested and so on. I had better go. Allana, may I leave you with Ding Ling? Get him to tell you of his work at the intelligun research facility. We will be going back to Laniakeea as soon as I get back. You must also be very tired, and need to catch up on sleep."

Hugo got up and started to walk towards the stables, which was off to the left of where they were sitting. He called Ding Ling over and explained to him to watch over Allana and make sure she was comfortable. With that, Hugo went towards the stables and disappeared.

Ding Ling turned around, put his hands on his hips, looked at Allana and gave her a beaming smile. He walked over to her, and sat down beside her. For a moment they both looked straight out at the variety of garden flowers.

Then Ding Ling said, "You call me Dingy, ok? My friends call me Dingy. You are friend of Hugo, so you my friend also, it ok?"

Allana smiled at this, "Yes, thank you Dingy. And you can call me Allana, ok?"

"But Allana your name?" said Ding Ling, "It no sound different to last time?"

"Yes, I know Dingy. We don't have nick-names like you do."

Ding Ling thought this very funny. His laughter had always been infectious, and he ended up sounding like a chipmunk. This then set Allana off. It was what they needed after all the tension of the day.

"So, Hugo tells me you work at a gun factory, in research and development?"

"Hmmm," said Ding Ling. "My research make you laugh. It makes everybody laugh. I end up with lots of little bruise all over body." Ding Ling could see Allana didn't know what he meant, so he said, "I put on protective body armor. On chest, on arms, on legs, on head, and even here" he pointed towards his crutch, "Where sun never shine. Then soldiers and scientists get new gun and fire at me to see how good it is."

"Oh, I see!" exclaimed Allana, looking very worried, "Does that not hurt you?"

"No silly," said Ding Ling laughing hard now. "Only joking. I am very good with all sort of guns and rifles. We test speed, accuracy etc by firing at targets or using computers. No one hurt of course. Company is called intelligun. Gun is ordinary, but bullet is super special. Very clever. Can sniff DNA which is programmed into it. Only programmed target will be hit. Bullet go anywhere up, down, around corners. It can hover and is able to remain undetected until it senses target. Everyone on Earth has DNA signature. All are individual. Bullet can be programmed for one person only."

"On Laniakeea", said Allana, "we only use bows and arrows and a form of magic to disable unwanted guests. However, we don't like war. Unfortunately, in the North of Laniakeea, in the district of Gareen, there are a number of portals. And ever since Laniakeea was formed, we have had warring species coming through to attack us, or attempt to steal Elvina and so on. So far, we have managed to resist, but always have to be, how do you call it? 'on our toes'? Always ready. We have soldiers patrolling the portals all the time. What do you think of war Dingy?"

"No like war, never have liked it. Me believe very strongly that war not determine who is right, it only determine who is left. But that doesn't stop me liking guns. Not because they can kill people, but the engineering that makes it."

"For pleasure I like to track an animal, only using cleverness, sometimes may take many hours. If lucky, I find I in position, with animal head in my sights, only then I pull trigger. Good news for animal is, I have no bullets in gun. Animal lives on, and I get excitement of tracking it and seeing it in my gunsight."

"Now, I have a favorite gun. Me very proud of it. It is very old gun and very popular on Earth many years ago."

"Why do you like it so much Dingy?" said Allana, "Can you describe it to me?"

Ding Ling's face lit up. Here was someone who actually wanted to know about his gun. He became very excited, and didn't know where to start. So, he took in a deep breath and said, "Well my favorite gun called Kalashnikov AK47. Very beautiful. I kiss and polish it every night before I go sleep. We call it retro gun now, from the past. So AK47 is a weapon all fighters used to love. It was once the world's most popular assault rifle. A simple nine-pound amalgamation of forged steel and plywood. It will shoot whether covered in mud, or filled with sand."

"Even a child can use it," continued Ding Ling, "And in the past they did. The Russians put that gun on a coin, the old African country of Mozambique, put it on their flag. Russians make best gun in world, but guess what? They couldn't build cars that last!" At that Ding Ling burst out laughing again, but Allana failed to notice the humor in that.

"And you Dingy?" said Allana, who thought it time to change the subject, "Have you a partner, as is the custom on

Earth?"

"Custom?" said Ding Ling, "Partner?" His face morphed into lots of laughter lines, "No Allana, I married to my work, and my duty to my master, Hugo, who as you know, is my family now. Anyway, I have simple life. To me marriage like poker. Poker is a game using small cards. You can start with a pair, but end up with full house. I can only cope with me, never mind lots of little me's. No, Allana, having partner, not my cup of china tea."

"And Hugo?" said Allana, "Is there anyone, a woman, who is special in his life?" She tried her best to keep it very low key, almost a throwaway question, but Ding Ling understood the real meaning behind that question. He had to be very careful, and wanted to mention someone, who was pivotal in ensuring Hugo became a man, and that someone was called Charlie Andover.

To Hugo, Charlie was for many years the epitome of sexuality in a woman. Who needed rude magazines under the bed, or porn on a laptop, when there was a living sexual machine on his doorstep? She had a shock of tumbling red hair, usually tied into a pony tail. Charlie was the stable manageress. Her boots and jodhpurs, and open blouse, revealing her ample bosom and sensual sexy perfume, made the then seventeen-year-old Hugo go weak at the knees every time he saw her.

Although she was twenty-three years older, here was a

woman that knew men found her sexually very attractive and used it for her own advantage. Even at seventeen, Hugo was a handsome strapping lad, full of testosterone shooting out of every orifice, and Charlie wanted a piece of the action before anyone else stepped in to claim the spoils.

And so it was, one balmy summer evening, in the hayloft attached to the stables of Brough Manor, on the pretense of wanting to show Hugo one of the horses, she lured him into a quiet spot, and slowly seduced him. She spent most of the time trying to hold him back, to slow down, and he looked like he was going to explode at any minute. But Charlie knew what she was doing and managed to orchestrate everything the way she wanted, and more importantly, the way he wanted. After the fumbling, heat, passion and stickiness of the moment, Hugo lay back on the bed of hay, breathing heavily and fell head over heels in love with Charlie. Hugo was a virgin no more.

'*Shall I mention Charlie?*' thought Ding Ling. He knew how a woman's mind can latch onto something so simple, let it fester, and bring it up at the most inopportune moment. '*But then again,* he thought, '*Allana is a completely different species. She is an Elf. From a dimension where women like women, and not men. Yep, he will be safe, I am sure of it.*'

"Well," said Ding Ling, "Hugo did have an interesting and special time with stable manageress, a woman called Charlie Andover, who still works here. It is fair to say he has feelings for her, but that is as far as they go now." Ding Ling felt as pleased as punch with the subtleties of that explanation, but it was Allana's reply, that poked him like a frosty finger.

"I see," said Allana. It was the way she said it: very slowly. Already Ding Ling was having misgivings. Should he explain to his Master that he had told Allana about Charlie, or just leave it alone, and hope she never mentioned it? Dark clouds were looming in Ding Ling's mind. *'Damn this Chinaman!'* he thought to himself.

Hugo, by now, had reached the UEL. The Adjutant in charge was ready to meet him, and ushered Hugo into the command center. As he stood there, and he looked carefully around, he noticed every member was present, even those on monitors from whichever part of the UEL they governed. At the same time, the main raised Dias facing him was empty. That is where his father would have sat.

The deputy head of the UEL, a Croatian called Miroslav Zivanovic welcomed Hugo from his position just to the left of the vacant seat that would have been occupied by his father.

"Welcome, Hugo. Unanimously, we all agree that the circumstances surrounding the murder and subsequent arrest of your father are quite shocking. We offer our sincere condolences on behalf of the whole of the UEL over the very sad demise of your brother Maxx. We have called an extraordinary emergency meeting to discuss these developments.

"After only a short time to deliberate, a motion was voted on, and passed, to promote you to the position of Head of UEL security, particularly, since you appear to have forged a tentative friendship with the queen of Laniakeea. I myself have been sworn in as Commander in chief of the UEL. Both our positions take effect immediately. Have you anything you wish to comment on Hugo?"

Hugo took a deep breath. "Dear members, first of all, thank you for your condolences. It has indeed been a tumultuous day for me. It will of course take a little time come to terms with everything that has happened, but at the same time, I appreciate the fact that there cannot be any delay in forging our friendship with Laniakeea. I understand already, that some of the Laniakeean scientists are already here and working on several ley line conduits, clearing them out, in preparation to use them to travel great distances in a very short time.

"This one action alone on the part of the Elves will prove to be the deciding factor in our world's ability to prosper and be more self-sufficient. I think it prudent, and would ask the member's permission, to spend more time in Laniakeea, building up the all-important trust, after the debacle of the stealing of the wand, which has now been returned to Queen Haruntha by myself."

There was a general discussion between all members. They were all then busy pressing buttons, and when they had all finished, all looked towards Miroslav. You could see quite clearly that Miroslav was taking on board all the messages that the members had sent to him. He looked up Hugo, smiled, and said, "Of course Hugo, we will be happy to allow you free rein to conduct your business in Laniakeea for as long as you require. However, we also realize, now is a time for you to rest and recuperate. Please take as long as you like to do this, before engaging with your duties."

"Thank you, sir," said Hugo, "I plan to return to Laniakeea shortly, and will endeavor to rest there until ready. Thank you again." And with that Hugo was then back outside, on Firemaker, galloping back to Brough Manor.

He caught up with Allana and Ding Ling. Allana knew he had been told to rest, so immediately told Hugo they needed to go back to Laniakeea. Hugo asked Ding Ling to accompany them. Before they left the manor, he had a quick meeting with his Mother, Kayon and Helena. They both agreed to help their mother with all to do with readjusting the finances and workings of Brough Manor.

Hugo, Allana and Ding Ling said their goodbyes and began to make their way back to the slice. As they headed that way, Allana was suddenly having strong feelings of unease. Nothing to do with Earth, or with Hugo. All Elves possess a degree of clairvoyance, and Allana, as one of the Elf chosen ones, Allana's abilities were more acute.

She turned to Hugo and Ding Ling and told them she had a very strong feeling that something terrible may be about to happen on Laniakeea., and that they needed to get back as soon as possible. With that, they galloped off towards the slice.

Rand Raneth
(The leader of the Mandaxon. A rogue species of Elf, that wears all black and carry black bows and arrows)

CHAPTER 12

The War of the Black Arrows

(Don't ignore the planets that come close enough to touch. They will always be a part of the grand spiritual cosmos. Embrace them with your hearts)

They reached the slice, jumped off the horses, and went straight through the portal. On the other side, they were met by one of the queen's guards, who was quickly communicating telepathically with Allana.

She turned to Hugo and Ding Ling and said, "We have to make our way to the palace as soon as possible. I will explain on the way."

They stepped onto the ley line circle and transported immediately. They arrived to bedlam. Bowmen and bow-women were running this way and that, with an urgency and determination that Hugo hadn't seen as yet. You could cut the tension in the air with a knife.

They made their way to the queen. As they were en

route, Allana explained to Hugo and Ding Ling, that they were under attack, from an old adversary, collectively known as the 'Black Arrows,' a term given to them because they wore all black and their bows and arrows were also black. She explained that as a species they were rogue Elves, that are called the Mandaxon. For many centuries, the Mandaxon had tried to take control of Laniakeea. Laniakeea, she explained to them, was an important dimension, not only from the fact that Elvina resided here but the base of the sentient being, the Sola Tree, was also established in this dimension.

It wasn't just the Mandaxon that wanted control of Laniakeea, but many other warring factions from a multitude of other Elf dimensions. The only downfall for Laniakeea, was the fact that in the district of Gareen, in the north of the dimension, were all the various portals, open doors if you like through which all nefarious types and species of Elf, and indeed unknown non-Elf species, could gain access.

There was nothing that the queen could do to block the portals. They were part of the natural fabric of their dimension and had been established since the beginning of the formation of Laniakeea. As with all great ideas, the portals had been in-built to give free access to all, hoping that knowledge and close relations could be developed if there were inter-species portals. Sadly, the opposite has generally been the case, and now it was too late to turn back time and close all the portals. Only Elvina could do this and would have to be sanctioned by the Sola Continuum, (a collection of the six oldest and wisest Sola trees), and this would never ever happen.

The Mandaxon were led by a very unpopular Elf called Rand Raneth, an evil looking Elf. Very powerfully built. He had small piercing yellow eyes, and no hair anywhere on his body, including his eyebrows. He had intimidating tattoos on his head. He also had a nasty scar running from the corner of the left side of his mouth, up to and half way to the lobe of his left ear. More than seven feet tall. He was, in fact a Laniakeean, who defected to the Mandaxon. All their soldiers wore tatty black cotton-like material, which was wrapped around themselves from head to toe, only leaving slits for the eyes and mouth. When in battle, they never spoke, could disguise their thoughts and had their own peculiar Elvish accent that no one would ever hope to understand.

They used bows and arrows, which of course were all black, but the tips of the arrowheads were dipped in a mixture of poison, taken from the back of a rodent from their dimension, called a Krass. This was simply a very powerful muscle relaxant, which immediately made the victim fall to the ground paralyzed. But mixed with this was a magical potion, that incubated very quickly to produce purple/black looking boils all over the body. When these boils burst, inside were black spores, that could be carried on the wind to infect other innocent Elves. Only a few Elves would need to be hit with an arrow, for the effects to be spread far and wide.

Once someone was infected, by actually being struck by an arrow, he or she would generally will survive for only one day, in rare cases two days. There was no known cure. Only on two occasions, the use of Elvina had reversed the process. If, and as happened in the majority of those cases, where Elves had breathed in the spores, this could be counteracted by careful monitoring and the administering of an anti-toxin, that the scientists on Laniakeea had been able to develop and produce. But each time the Mandaxon attacked, they have managed to develop an even more lethal complex of spores. Again, time was of the essence.

The anti-toxin had to be spread all over the body, within six hours of the symptoms becoming apparent. This was a very delicate process, ensuring that none of the boils were ruptured. In fact, a new anti-toxin spray had been developed, one which removed all possible chances of the boils being ruptured, and of course, was much quicker to apply. There were masks the Elves wore to filter and denature the spores when in battle, which fit very snugly over the nose and mouth.

Allana, Hugo and Ding Ling were now in the palace's great hall walking quickly towards the queen. As they got nearer, Hugo and Ding Ling noticed the queen had changed into a type of armor suit. It looked as if it was a type of leather fabric, fairly close fitting and dark brown in color. The queen had her own bow. This was strapped to her back and on her waist was a quiver containing six or seven blue arrows. She wore a protective helmet with a 'T' shaped opening from her forehead to her chin, and also across where her eyes would be.

But Hugo then also noticed to the left of the queen, were two species of Elf, he had not seen before. He assumed one was female and one male. One was smaller in stature with very long hair, and the other a good head taller and very powerfully built. Their suits or skin (he couldn't make out the difference at this stage) were silver scales, and depending on how the light reflected off the scales, could change color to that of an iridescent dark blue. They were standing in a pool of water. On closer inspection, Hugo noticed minute secretions of water coming from between each scale and running down the body. This was obviously to keep the body moist.

The female, the one with the long hair, turned to look at Hugo. Hugo noticed strangely, that her hair seemed to become as a single flexible block of hair, like a single muscle, and was constantly moving, sweeping across her buttocks then would curl up and rest on one of her shoulders, then flip back down again. Both of the Elves wore minute eye protectors, as if they were about to go swimming, when in fact they were protecting the eyes from drying up when on land. The webbed large feet and hands didn't go unnoticed to Hugo and Ding Ling, who just looked at each other in amazement.

But it was the five little oblique gill slits on each side of their necks that fascinated them the most, opening and closing constantly.

By now, they were quite close to the queen who broke off to address Hugo and Ding Ling.

"Ahh," said the queen, "Hello Allana, Hugo and Ding Ling. We are in the middle of a war with a faction of Elves called the Black Arrows. I know Allana has filled you in with some of the briefest of details and would welcome your help in defeating them. It is your choice entirely, and you will not be looked on unfavorably if you thought this is none of your business."

"We would like to help in any way we can," said Hugo. Ding Ling gave Hugo a piercing glare, sighed, then he also nodded his head.

"Good, good," said the queen, "Let me introduce to our allies, the Pharaas. The Pharaas are a species of water Elf that live deep in the Salnalyn Lake. The lake is in the furthest north of Laniakeea, in the district of Baern. At its deepest point, it is in the region of almost twelve miles deep. There is a whole submerged city down at those depths. The Pharaas came to our dimension three million years ago, having been persecuted by another species of Elf from the dimension that was once their home. We support them where we can, and they help us repel factions of warring Elves that try to infiltrate our dimension."

"Now," explained the queen, "they cannot speak your tongue but have a much more advanced state of telepathy, and with your permission, I wish to give their king, Dathbiyra and Queen Faelath here, the chance to communicate with you telepathically. Don't expect a conversation, just very vivid images, which are worth a thousand of your words. You will have no trouble understanding them."

"Their greatest asset is that they can implant very real thoughts into their enemies' heads, and not just one individual at a time, but many at the same time. They are able to determine their greatest fear, enhance it, and make them believe they are in the middle of their fear. Many a battle has been won with this one offensive tactic."

At that moment, the King, Dathbiyra, removed the eye protectors and looked towards Hugo and Ding Ling. For a second or so, Ding Ling was convinced an inner membrane swept across each eye, with a slight clicking sound.

Immediately, an image, in full color, of the king and queen, smiling at Hugo, appeared in Hugo's head. When Hugo turned his head, the effect was a full three hundred and sixty degrees. Hugo was convinced he was in the queen's garden. He could smell the scent of the flowers, feel the sun on his face.

They came up to him, one at a time in his head, held his shoulders, smiled and stood back. Hugo had great difficulty imagining this was telepathy, it was so real! After thirty seconds, the images stopped abruptly. Hugo was slightly unsteady on his feet for a second or two, but his composure came back very quickly.

Hugo tried to reply by telepathically sending them an image of his hand waving and the letters 'Hi' in bright yellow, underneath the image. Both the king and queen stopped what they were doing and stared at Hugo and acknowledged what he was trying to do with smiles.

They also started shrugging, which Hugo found out later, was the Pharaas way of laughing politely. Even Queen Haruntha was smiling, and she quickly sent a telepathic message to Hugo which said, *'That was amusing Hugo. We saw what looked like you chasing after your hand that had left your body and the 'Hi' letters were so bright, it was difficult to make them out. But rest assured, the king and queen very much appreciate your efforts in sending them the message, especially since telepathy is something very new to you. They have both taken to you.'* At the same time, Ding Ling also had the images in his head, and when the images stopped, he looked more than a little perturbed.

"This terrifying stuff Master," said Ding Ling to Hugo, "Wish I could draw curtains, so they not see inside my head. They very fishy Master, and the woman fishy, has tail growing out of head. Ahh, I remember a Confucius saying, 'Everything has beauty, but not everyone sees it.' All I can see is two pieces of strange looking cod."

"Stop it Dingy," said Hugo, "They may be reading your thoughts."

"Dingy not thought of that," said a worried-looking Ding Ling. And immediately he composed a scene in his head of feeding the koi carp his nasty uncle used to keep in a pond in his garden. Of course, Ding Ling was going over the top, forcing a big smile and orally saying at the same time as he was trying to generate the images, "Lovey fish, lovely fish," over and over in his mind, and throwing handfuls of food pellets into the pond to feed them.

Hugo noticed that Dathbiyra and Faelath were looking intently at Ding Ling and had huge smiles on their faces. *'I wonder what Ding Ling is thinking up in his head now?'* thought Hugo frowning.

In the background, Allana couldn't help but catch Ding Ling's thoughts and was stifling her laughter. Ding Ling caught her eye, and furrowed his eyebrows and stared at her as if to say, "Are you reading my thoughts?" But she turned away, more than a little embarrassed.

"We are now making our way to my generals," said the queen, "They are close to the insurgents. Just to the West of Salnalyn Lake, which is where the portals are. They have been pouring in from portal number five, which is a direct link to their dimension. We have heard already that Rand Raneth is leading them. He is a very clever tactician."

And with that they all started to make their way to the queen's circle to transport straight to the circle almost on the west shore of Salnalyn Lake. Once they arrived, they noticed over a thousand Pharaas waiting for their king and queen. They all saluted, by raising their crossed wrists into the air. In and around them must have been five thousand Laniakeean Elves. In the midst of the Pharaas, was a very ornate structure, a little like a wigwam, but on an enormous scale. It was constructed with what looked like a crushed red velour material. The queen pointed it out and told Hugo and Ding Ling it was the 'tactical' tent.

When they went in, both Hugo and Ding Ling looked up and around. It seemed like there was no roof or cover at all. Allana explained that it was more or less impenetrable from the outside to arrows and so on, but inside, the view reversed and the material became transparent. In the middle was a very long table with maps and measuring instruments. Two male Laniakeeans were standing there looking down intently at a sort of 3D map of the area.

Hugo couldn't help but notice that the two Laniakeeans were a little older, and had snow white hair. They both wore helmets of sorts and masks. To their side, three Pharaas were also bent over the table studying the map.

As the queen and the rest of the party approached,

those around the table stood up and bowed low to the queen. The queen introduced Hugo to the two Laniakeeans as generals Rhyfonaldas and Androthacan. And all three of the Pharaas were military leaders. They had gold stripes running down the outside of their arms, denoting the equivalent rank of general.

They all turned towards the map and looked down. This was amazing to Hugo, the map transformed into a complete 3D structure, so that height and width could easily be judged. Now for Hugo, there was no verbal speaking at all from this point. Everything came as images into his head. It didn't take long to understand what they were discussing, but he knew if he was to give any input at all, it had to be telepathically, especially images for the Pharaas.

General Androthacan was pointing to a large wide gully that ran along the border of the district Gareen, where the portals were, and the district of Baern, where the Salnalyn Lake was. One of the Pharaas generals was suddenly placing very vivid images in all their heads. Each one told a story in sequence.

It showed the Mandaxon led by Rand Raneth, emerging out of one of the portals, and already were making their way across the border, via a raised piece of ground towards Salnalyn Lake. From there, they were turning a hard right to make their way south towards Spiritwood, which they would skirt, because the natural magic was too powerful for the

Mandaxon to deal with.

They would then deviate to the right, work their way down the length of Spiritwood to the bottom, where there was a gap, then straight up towards the Sola Tree and Elvina, the prize that Rand Raneth was aiming for.

Hugo was a very astute general, and had won many campaigns using his wits and guile. As a tactician he was excellent. He knew they were trying to think of some way of stemming the flow of the Black Arrows. Hugo bent over closer. He was feeling his way along the 3D model of the border and noticed a gully that ran down the border, cutting deep into the ground. It must have been ninety-five feet wide at the bottom and relatively flat, but both the sides rose sharply, and at an acute angle, to the surface either side of the gully. Immediately a tactical plan came to him, and he would give it a ninety-nine percent chance of success.

He turned to the queen and said he had an idea that could solve the problem. But how would he get this across to the generals, especially the Pharaas generals?

"Hugo, I will explain to them all you wish to contribute your ideas. The way to achieve this is to make up the images in your head, just think them, that's all, just as you have observed the Pharaas doing for you. Don't worry; they will pick them up clearly. But keep it in a running timeframe, don't jump from one scene to another. Imagine you are a bird from your dimension, that is looking down at everything that is happening, and try to get those visual ideas across."

So, he looked at the generals, who were politely waiting for him. Hugo decided to close his eyes. He felt he could form the ideas and images more easily, and in fact, this proved to be the case.

From a bird's perspective, he showed the Mandaxon starting to come out of the portal and attempt to cross the border, but being prevented from doing so, by a large contingent of Laniakeeans on the edge of the border.

His images showed the Laniakeeans, guiding the Mandaxon into the deep gully that ran down the border. As the last of the Mandaxon came out and were ushered down the gully, they suddenly discovered there was no retreat for them, blocked by more Laniakeeans that were hiding in waiting.

This would spur the Mandaxon to progress further into the gully, simply because the sides of the gully at this point were too steep to negotiate, only then to be attacked by the thousands of Pharaas on both sides of the gully, who would be using their superior mind-altering telepathic abilities, and making it impossible for the Mandaxon to retaliate. Suddenly both Laniakeean generals came up to Hugo and saluted him, and following that, the Pharaas implanted strong images of the same from them in Hugo's head.

The queen approached Hugo, and quietly said. "Very well thought out Hugo. You have impressed them all. The only extras we will be adding to your plan is to introduce some Kroleeth lizards to block their retreat, at the front and rear of the gully. Thank you for your suggestions, Hugo."

Hugo noticed Allana smiling at him and slowly nodding her head. Ding Ling, who was just to the left of Allana, just looked completely bewildered, so Hugo went over to him to explain what he had suggested.

"Very clever plan Master," said Ding Ling, "I glad I am on your side."

The Kroleeth lizards reside in the district of Kroleeth, which also happens to be the district in which Elfistra and Mandaz reside. They are a little similar to a dinosaur species from Earth's past. In fact, its appearance is similar to an elongated version of the Tyrannosaurus Rex, at least in the front and middle. It is completely covered in diamond-shaped scales that are purple, and each one edged in a very bright yellow.

They have three pairs of eyes: two on the left side of its head, two on the right, and two, next to each other on its forehead. What is remarkable about the eyes are that they all work independently of each other. If you have seen the eyes of a chameleon, that is exactly how they work.

They have a pair of small claw-like appendages on their upper body, perfect for gripping and holding, but their legs are very powerful and muscular. All along its back running all the way from the top of its head to the base of a tail, there are many scales that don't lie flat, rather, they are vertical and each one can rotate three hundred and sixty degrees.

If we were to look at these vertical scales more closely, we would notice that the surface is covered in mirror-like minute circles so light can be reflected very easily and brightly. Continuing down to the base of the body we come to an unusual tail, which is approximately the length of the Kroleeth lizard's body, again covered in scales, but at the end of the tail is a club-like appendage composed of very hard, short keratinized vicious spikes.

This tail can be maneuvered very quickly and at its most efficient, is brought forward towards its enemies in a whip-like motion. If the Kroleeth thought its life was in danger, it can whip the tail so hard that the club-like end can detach and travel towards its enemy, embedding itself and therefore debilitating its enemy. Immediately, a new club-like end of the tail would then grow back.

But as a precursor to the action of the tail, the scales running down the lizards back rotate to catch any light which is directed straight into the eye of its enemy. While blinded, the lizard then brings its tail into play. So, in most battles, the Kroleeth lizard is a formidable part of the Laniakeean military force.

Finally, we have the jaws. A multitude of three rows of teeth, broken up, on the front sides of the jaws by some very long canine teeth. So gripping, then shaking the head, will ensure that huge lumps of flesh are ripped from the enemy's body. If a tooth breaks off, another pops up in its place instantaneously.

By now, Hugo's plans had been taken on board by the generals, and already were being implemented. Streams of Mandaxon were now being forced down and into the gully.

Behind the main body of Mandaxon, came the Laniakeen bowmen who were driving them farther into the gully. Approaching on both sides were the Pharaas, using their telepathic visualization skills, that implemented very realistic images of a huge tsunami body of water that was now rushing down the top end of the gully. The effect on the Mandaxon was spectacular; they felt they had to run as fast as possible further forward down into the gully to avoid being swamped and drowned.

Panic was written all over their faces, and they all began to run headlong into a dam of large rocks and earth that had been quickly built at the bottom end of the gully. Over these rocks were now streaming dozens of Kroleeth lizards towards the oncoming Mandaxon.

Rand Raneth and a contingent of his warriors had managed to run up a slightly less steep side of the gully to a long and large shelf, where they were now in formation, and loosing off a myriad of black arrows, whose arrowheads had already been dipped in the poisonous secretions of the Krass rodents, and would prove to be fatal to any Elf they hit.

From inside the tent, they all emerged to witness the

events as they were happening. Hugo and Ding Ling were also given masks to filter out any of the Mandaxon spores that would affect them.

As they were running alongside the top of the gully, they were being warned by the others not to get caught by any of the Mandaxon arrows which would be fatal.

As Hugo and Allana were running along, Hugo turned to his side and noticed that Ding Ling wasn't with them. He grabbed Allana's arm, and they started to look around. Then Hugo noticed a body, lying prone on the floor, thirty feet back.

Hugo shouted out "Dingy?" and the arm of the body lying on the floor raised itself into the air. They rushed back, and indeed it was Ding Ling. Into the back of his left calf, was a large thick black arrow was embedded. Hugo and Allana looked worriedly at each other, then started to examine Ding Ling. Already up and down his leg, small black boils were starting to form. Ding Ling was now semi-conscious, and looked suddenly very weak and pale-looking. The whites of his eyes were starting to hemorrhage, so were turning slightly bloody, his pupils turning from brown to black. To Allana, Ding Ling's aura was normally very energetic, but already it was looking very weak and only half its size.

"We now have to help Dingy as quickly as possible," said Allana, "We have less than six hours. We need to get permission from the queen to administer Elvina. It is the only thing that will save him. I have already messaged my Queen, and she will be here any moment. I'm so sorry Hugo."

Hugo couldn't believe how quickly Ding Ling was being affected, how the energy was draining from him, and how quickly the black boils were developing, already on his arms, his neck and across his chest.

Hugo felt so very frustrated, there was just nothing he could do, and it was churning him up inside.

Suddenly the queen arrived, knelt down and examined Ding Ling. She stood, looked at Hugo and Allana, and told Allana she had permission to administer Elvina. The queen had already sent word ahead to the keeper of Elvina, who was preparing an area just inside the roots of the Sola Tree. It would be very well protected.

Hugo scooped up Ding Ling, and ran with Allana to the nearest ley line circle and transported straight to the Sola Tree. When they arrived, there, to their surprise, was Elfistra.

"The queen has fully informed me of what has happened, and I am here to protect all of you while you perform Elvina's magic on Ding Ling. Remember, we are still at war with the Mandaxon, and Elvina will be in a more vulnerable state because she is more exposed than I would like to see."

With that, Hugo carried Ding Ling, into a quiet place deep within the roots of the Sola Tree. The roots were so thick, it was almost like being in a small igloo-shaped room.

There was a white table in the middle, and Hugo laid Ding Ling onto it. Allana then turned to Hugo and asked him to stand at the back of the room, and no matter what he heard and saw, he was to keep perfectly still.

As Hugo walked towards the wall, he could see Elfistra in the entrance; she was waving her arms in a very peculiar way, when suddenly there seemed to be a golden transparent globe surrounding the room. Elfistra stood there, legs shoulder width apart, looking up, her eyes closed, concentrating. Hugo turned and felt the back of the room. It felt hot. He was sure he could feel a pulse running through it. It is strange, but it felt vaguely comforting. He turned to see an assistant approach Allana with the Spiriten, the magical box containing Elvina.

It slowly opened up of its own accord, and immediately a bluish glow came from the box. Allana seemed to be issuing incantations, then she slowly reached in and held Elvina firmly in her right hand and brought it out of the box. The assistant closed the Spiriten and moved away.

Allana stood upright and started to raise her right hand into the air. At the same time small electric blue ripples of energy were beginning to envelop her hand and travel first down her arm, then across her chest and other arm, down her body, both legs and further down to her toes.

Finally, these electric blue tendrils worked their way up to Allana's head and covered it completely. Hugo could see it was Allana's body, but now couldn't make out any discernible features. There was a humming in the air. The hair on Hugo's arms, legs and head started to stand on end, as if there was suddenly lots of static electricity.

A large blue bolt of energy then started to stream from Allana's right hand, and in particular, from the magical globe that was on the top of Elvina. As a cloud, it hovered over Ding Ling's body, then shot into him and enveloped him. As it did so, Ding Ling arched his back and his body left the table surface and hovered approximately a foot above it.

All this time, Hugo had been leaning on the wall behind him, using the palms of his hands to soften the hardness of the walls. He started to notice the walls beginning to move, to pulsate, to almost feel like they were breathing. They seemed to be breathing in sync with the breathing of Allana.

Hugo was also beginning to feel very energized. Once, when he was injured back on Earth, he was given pure oxygen. And that is how he felt now. Wide awake. Any feelings of anxiety and tiredness were melting away.

Ding Ling's body continued to hover above the table, but Hugo noticed from all over his body were a stream of minute black dots, like a swarm of houseflies, buzzing and rising up towards the ceiling. When no more were left, a golden stream from Elvina encircled the little black dots, and suddenly, with a very loud 'swish,' the black dots were evaporated in a flash of blinding golden light.

Ding Ling's body slowly started to descend to the surface of the table. At the same time, the effect of Elvina taking over control of Allana started to reverse its transformation, ending up with Elvina being held in Allana's outstretched hand.

The assistant was already there and opened the Spiriten so that Allana was able to place Elvina back inside. With the box still open, but before the assistant left, a few moments of what Hugo assumed were thanks, were being issued to Elvina, before then the assistant closed the box and disappeared to take Elvina back to her secure place deep within the cave within the Sola Tree.

For a few moments, there was absolute silence. Elfistra glided in, and looked intently at Ding Ling, nodded, and then left. Hugo noticed that Allana now was slumped on the opposite wall, but smiling. She had little blue tears rolling down from her eyes, and very tenderly, she said to Hugo, "Dingy will be just fine now. He won't be able to respond for a short while, while his body readjusts, but he will bounce back better than before. Whenever Elvina enters the body, she will re-energize everything inside and out."

Hugo ambled slowly over to Ding Ling, who appeared to be in a deep relaxed sleep. He smiled. He then looked up and walked slowly over to Allana, brought her into his arms, held her close and whispered into her ear, "Thank you so much."

She looked up into his eyes and smiled. Little tears were still running down. If nothing else, on the rare occasion she had used Elvina in the past, it was for her always a very emotional, spiritual experience. Elvina connects with the very soul of someone who is holding her.

Hugo noticed a movement to his left, and there just inside the edge of the doorway stood Elfistra.

Hugo felt uneasy with Elfistra hovering away in the background. He wished he knew what it was about him she didn't like. She had made that apparent on a number of occasions now. For now, Hugo would let it go, but he would confront her at some stage in the future.

By now Ding Ling was beginning to stir, Allana and Hugo went to him. Allana used a small cloth to wipe his forehead. She was very gentle. Ding Ling looked at her. He started to cough pretty badly, and was bringing up an evil smelling black phlegm that Allana was wiping up from the corner of Ding Ling's mouth. Allana said the coughing will pass, it was just his body trying to get rid of all the toxins.

He continued to look at Allana, and said to her, in a croaky voice, "I will forget my injuries, but I never forget kindness." Allana continued to smile at him and said, "Dingy, you still have boils on your face and body, but they are drying up already. You will feel very weak for a while, but we will give you some of the blue Voovo, and it will help you recover very quickly." And with that, she disappeared to bring the Voovo to administer to Ding Ling.

When she had gone, Ding Ling turned to Hugo and said, "Master, do I look like the Chinese dragon monster with all these boils?" Hugo just shrugged, and confirmed what Allana had said about them already drying up. But Hugo could see he was worried about his appearance, and Ding Ling said, "Master, I want to see me in mirror."

Hugo said, "Dingy, that is not a good idea. Just let them settle down. You will be looking fine very shortly I am sure."

Ding Ling thought about this and then said, "Hmmm, everything has beauty master, but not everyone sees it, especially when you look at me like that."

"Have some patience Dingy, don't rush it."

"Master?" said Ding Ling, "I know, I know. It is impossible to trip and fall while walking slowly. I will wait." Ding Ling started coughing again, a lot more violently than before. He was coughing up more of the black evil smelling phlegm.

"I hate this cough Master, maybe best way is to take two laxative pills, that way I be too afraid to cough?"

Hugo burst out laughing, and so did Ding Ling, in between little bouts of coughing. And into the room came Allana with a large container of Voovo. She decanted it into a small vessel, and then held Ding Ling's head up while she helped him to drink it.

The change was miraculous. His color came back, the

dried-up boils were disappearing, and his coughing seemed to have gone. He sat upright. His leg, where the arrow had penetrated his skin was still swollen and black looking and very tender to touch, like a very bad 'bruise' according to Ding Ling. But all in all, it was beginning to all end well.

The relief on Allana's face that Ding Ling was on the way to a full recovery was very apparent.

"You are very thoughtful Allana," Hugo said, as he sidled up behind her. She turned around and stood very close to Hugo.

"Well, I have fallen for Dingy, and can understand why you both have such warm feelings for each other." Ding Ling's ears pricked up at this (Allana deliberately said this a little louder so he could hear). "So I just wanted to help," continued Allana, "Being a part of Elvina is very draining, but so worthwhile, and it will make you happy too." With this, she moved even closer, lent across and whispered into Hugo's ear, "Now is the time Hugo."

"Time for what?" Hugo said.

Allana continued to whisper in his ear, "Time to explore the Sootalanash. We will have to prepare. I have already booked a beautiful Arkhrun, we will go tomorrow. Are you ready?"

Hugo thought, *Oh God! Am I ready? Does a bear shit in the woods? Although I have no idea what it is I am supposed to expect?* Allana couldn't help but pick up his thoughts. And when she did, she burst out laughing.

Hugo realized she was reading them, and he laughed embarrassingly as well, and both of them moved even closer.

As this was happening, Ding Ling was carefully watching Elfistra in the background. Pacing back and forth. He was sure she was reading their thoughts, which she was able to do and didn't need permission to do, and could do so without any knowledge to those whose thoughts she was reading.

But he didn't like the look of her body language, not that he felt he could read the body language of such an alien looking thing. Once or twice she looked directly at Ding Ling, and her stare seemed to pass straight through him. He didn't like it. He made a mental note to warn Hugo to be aware of her.

Elfistra's face was showing the absolute contempt she had for the growing intimate feelings that Hugo and Allana had for each other. The contempt she had for Ding Ling, in fact for all the Earthans that were being welcomed with open arms by her queen.

She turned on her heels and swept out, vowing that she had to be the one to put a stop to this, once and for all! She would need to consult Mandaz as soon as possible.

The Sootalanash Ceremony
(The path that leads to the Arkhrun, where the ceremony is performed)

CHAPTER 13

The Sootalanash

(From this day. From this night, and forever more, love unconditionally)

It would be arrogant to think that for every species that exists, a demonstration of affection could only be physical. Procreation ensures the continuance of a species, and that act has to be associated with pleasure, for it is the pleasure that is part of the incentive.

Of course, so many other factors will come into play: how a species is built physically, the degree of intelligence, how different their reproductive and sexual orientations are, and so on. What would be an act of pleasure to one species, could be an unthinkable act to another.

In the case of Hugo Brough and Allana Yana-Ash, we do have two entirely different species. We already know that Earthans at this time will have sexual relationships to demonstrate affection and the need to procreate to produce offspring. It is, compared to other species, basic and primal. There is nothing wrong with this at all, it is in-built into our blueprint, and as far as the development of the Earthans goes, and where they are now, it would be deemed 'normal.'

However, we also know, in the case of the Laniakeeans, who although are linked ancestrally with the Earthans, they have differing needs of comfort, of closeness, of reproduction and procreation. The men are hermaphrodites, they conceive and produce the children. The sex of the children is decided by the Sola Tree so that a balance of one male to two females is always maintained, and it is the women who have the release of intimate, sensual relationships, and to a certain extent, these relationships demonstrate love, affection and romance. Over a million years of evolution for the Elves of Laniakeea has meant that they have moved along an entirely different path to that of the Earthans.

However, because of the similarities within the DNA helix signatures between the two species, elements such as the feelings of romance, and of sexual gratification are present, albeit in different forms. Laniakeean females do not now have the physical capabilities to produce children (i.e. no fallopian tubes, uterus, or indeed eggs), but do still have, as remnants of a time in the past when sexual reproduction was a common act between a male and a female Elf, those physical attributes that means that they can have a sexual union of sorts, still exist. They have a vagina, but for example, breasts are almost non-existent, since they would not be necessary in a species where the males raise the children, but are present. In present-day Laniakeea, it is only the females who may achieve any sexual gratification, and only between other females.

Males do have ways to release the tension that may build up, but they use various forms of meditation to combat this. The hormone testosterone, for example, doesn't exist in this species, so all the negative side effects of this hormone are not present i.e. the urge to procreate, aggression and so on. Laniakeean males have other unusual hormones that stimulate their body shape, strength, deepness of voice and others that encourage the need to prepare their bodies to have children when the time is right. Moreover, other specific hormones will prepare the males for aggression, protection and so on.

So Laniakeean women form relationships, between themselves, that are loving, sexually releasing and lasting. A typical family unit would be a male and two females. There is a ceremony, which two females can enter into that affirms their union and feelings for each other. The males enter into this union, but only to confirm that they are happy to produce children on behalf of the family unit and to look after and care for the child within this union. Generally, this works very well and very efficiently.

From the moment that Allana met Hugo, there was a spark. Something that meant they were drawn to each other. It started developing, and is now picking up speed, even though Allana couldn't quite understand why this attraction should be there. Maybe because of their ancestral links? A male human to her is not that physically different from a male Elf. She knows that pheromones play a large part in both species to help with the 'attraction' process. Also, there is personality. Hugo makes her laugh; he is warm, kind and thoughtful to her, all the attributes that a Laniakeean female would look for within her species.

This growing affection and a 'wanting' to take it further, physically and spiritually, became apparent to Allana, long before Hugo's more basic instincts started rising within him.

Allana has been warned many times not to pursue her feelings towards Hugo by her Queen and, even more vehemently by the sorceress, Elfistra. It has long been a rule passed down since time began, that any inter-species union would be frowned upon.

In the beginning, Allana was quite happy to uphold this fundamental ruling but has now begun to realize that affection, and to a certain extent, love, is one of the most powerful of emotions, for both species. So powerful in fact, that Allana, does not want to be held back by this ruling any more.

She has been trying to think of a way to demonstrate to

Hugo how she feels for him, without incurring the wrath of the queen and Elfistra. It would have to be non-physical, certainly for now. Luckily, for both of them, there is a way, and that is the ceremony known as the Sootalanash.

The Sootalanash is a special ceremony, generally reserved for two Laniakeean females, but also on rare occasions between female and male Laniakeeans. Allana had an audience to discuss this with Queen Haruntha, in the presence of Elfistra, and much to the annoyance of Elfistra, the queen gave permission for Allana to perform this ceremony with Hugo. The queen's thinking is that this may be the best way to put an end to any further escalation of feelings between the two.

The queen loves all her subjects, but a status quo has to exist. Nipping a possible problem in the bud has worked well for the queen so far.

The problem for Allana is that she knows how fulfilling it would be for her, but trying to persuade Hugo that it could be just as exciting and fulfilling as the physical activity he is used to, could be difficult.

Essentially the Sootalanash is a spiritual union between two people. This is a ceremony that is performed in special domed huts, covered in fur pelts from the Zo'Sah wolf, dotted around Laniakeea called Arkhruns. It involves meditation, and the burning of essential oils. Then the union of the necessary spiritual makeup of one person, with that of another.

When these spiritual manifestations come together the feeling is one of all senses being heightened. It will appear very physically, very sensually and to a certain extent sexually, but at no time, during any stage of the ceremony, do their bodies actually physically come together and touch.

The result, as any Laniakeean who has performed the Sootalanash will attest to, it is one of pure pleasure and fulfillment. Love and feelings of romance will stay with the couple for a very long time.

Allana knew she needed to guide Hugo very carefully, and to try to stem his basic Earthan instincts from coming to the fore, and to rely on her guidance. If he did that, she was convinced Hugo would get as much satisfaction from the ceremony as she would have.

One little element was worrying her, and that was she was feeling the need, more and more, to be physical with Hugo, such were her feeling towards him. She knew physically it would be possible, but she was feeling as if she was being pulled in two directions: on the one hand, her obedience to her queen and Elfistra, and her now physical feelings of attraction towards Hugo. Physical sensations that had remained dormant and buried in Laniakeean females for over a million years.

The Arkhrun is set in a beautiful, peaceful setting, surrounded by the most fragrant species of flowers and herbs that Laniakeea produces. Within this, the shrubs and trees are also sentient, so become a part of the whole creative spiritual process.

Mild magic is applied to create a sensation that from the moment you walk into the area, a feeling of relaxation washes over you. There are also the vines, as found in the queen's garden, whose tendrils gently brush your legs and hands when walking along the grassy path towards the Arkhrun. They deposit a very mild natural ecstasy-like drug into your system that slightly heightens your senses. Everything starts to become pleasant, you begin to feel excited, you begin to anticipate the journey of the ceremony.

On their way to the nearest Arkhrun, she explained in detail to Hugo the various stages of the Sootalanash. They had made their way from Allana's dwelling, and when she greeted him, she was wearing a very beautiful diaphanous green-colored fine lace all-in-one covering, similar in some respects to the beautiful saris that the women in India wear.

To Hugo, there didn't appear to be any sort of fixing, he couldn't understand how it was all holding together, and nothing was left to the imagination as far as he could see of Allana's body. She had also prepared her make-up that works well with the Sootalanash ceremony. It complemented her clothes, and accentuated her lips, ears and cheekbones, but it was her eyes that were the most striking.

They were alive and sparkling and pinky-red. Hugo felt he wanted to dive into them. She looked stunning. It almost took his breath away. That, together with the semi-transparency of the garment she was wearing, created an image that was sensual, sexy, and desirable.

Hugo too had been presented with clothes of sorts to wear for the ceremony. These were very light, almost silk-like and felt wonderful on his skin. They ensured he had complete freedom of movement.

It was this desirability, especially the physical aspects, that Hugo was now having for Allana that he was finding very difficult to control. He wanted to rush towards her, like a bull in a china shop, but he promised Allana he wouldn't. Also, he knew without his promise, there would be no trust, and if there was no trust there would be nothing. So, control was foremost in his mind.

They arrived eventually at the start of the green grassy path that leads to the Arkhrun. The path is just wide enough to accommodate both of them walking side by side, which they did. Occasionally Hugo's hand would brush Allana's, or Allana's arm would sweep gently across Hugo's arm. Each time, the anticipation of what was going to happen, heightened this fleeting touch so it felt like a mild electric shock.

The mild sedatives from the vines, the heady scents, prepared them well for when they then stepped into the

Arkhrun. Inside, and against one wall was an intricate carved long pot, standing on four legs, purple in color, with gold markings across its surface, which was slowly burning a mixture of dried herbs.

By the side of it, strange looking collections of small glass-like vessels were pouring different colored liquids from one vessel to another, and the warmth from the pot was gently warming the oils. In doing so, beautiful sensual scents were pervading the air, similar in many ways to the Earthen sandalwood, ylang-ylang and patchouli oils.

Against the wall and opposite each other were two strange looking recliners. They were moving, slowly pulsating, but in one spot. Allana indicated to Hugo that he was to sit in one, and she went and sat in the other.

As Hugo sat in his, it felt like he was melting into the recliner, almost like a piece of wax that was being warmed up. He relaxed totally. He felt his eyelids closing, but strangely, he could still see. Allana said this was all normal, so he let it all unfold before him.

He noticed then small golden butterflies came fluttering into the Arkhrun. One landed on his nose, which made him smile, then off it fluttered. Others were very gently alighting on his arms and legs and shoulders. Then, as if someone had waved their hands, they all took to the air and went across the Arkhrun to Alana.

He didn't know why but felt these were no ordinary butterflies. These too were intelligent and were making him feel more and more relaxed. Earlier, he remembered Allana mentioning that the Sola Tree would be there also, sharing in the ceremony, in a form that would be decided on. In this case, he now discovered, as little spiritual manifestations of the Sola Tree which presented in the form of beautiful delicate butterflies. Hugo smiled as he began to understand all that was happening.

He 'looked' over towards Allana, who had now started the ceremony. He could see her lips moving and could hear the Elvish incantations she was saying, but she was almost singing them. She was also holding her arms and particularly her hands in beautiful shapes, almost as if she was making shadow figures against a wall. Moving them slowly, purposefully and with lots of feminine grace.

As Hugo continued to accept and take in these beautiful feelings, he mistakenly thought this was what it was all about. How wrong he was. What began to happen next was simply mind-blowing for Hugo.

Allana started to glow. Gold at first, then slowly, different shades of rainbow colors would replace the one before, and so on. This changing of colors started to speed up, faster and faster, until the blur of colors produced a silvery glow, which by now had enveloped Allana from head to toe. Hugo could see her body, now lying motionless in the recliner, but it was as if her spiritual body was disassociating from her physical body.

The silvery form of Allana then stood up and away from her body. She looked intently at Hugo. Hugo could sense that her form was smiling. She began to hold her arms up towards Hugo. When this was done, gold sparkling thin rope-like ribbons started to circle Allana's spiritual body slowly. Faster and faster they circled, and now there was a sound in the air, a sort of humming. The intensity of the silvery form started to increase and grow brighter and brighter.

Even though Hugo was 'looking' through his closed eyelids, he was finding the intensity of the brightness of Allana's form difficult to look at.

Suddenly, without any warning, when Hugo thought he would have to turn away, this silvery form shot up into the roof of the Arkhrun, and then continued to bounce off all its sides, like a silver ball in a pinball machine. Faster and faster it bounced. Hugo was finding it hard to follow. The air was now feeling very charged. The hairs on Hugo's arms and his head were almost standing on end.

Finally, Allana's spiritual form shot to the furthest point of the Arkhrun, and hovered there for a couple of seconds, before then shooting straight into Hugo's body like an arrow. It went straight into his chest and into his heart.

Hugo's mouth opened. His arms and legs shot out, and he lay there like a starfish. He took in a long deep breath and held it. His eyelids opened, and to Hugo, it was the most pleasurable feeling he had ever had in his life. He felt as if every atom of his body had fused with Allana's. Pulses of energy were cruising through his body again and again, like a powerful repeating surf on a seashore.

He wanted it to last forever. He couldn't help it, but his eyes were stinging, and then he was weeping. He looked at his arms, his legs and body, and Allana was there, in his body with him. He knew it. He could feel the warmth of her. The emotion. The feelings of sexuality and love. Everything. There was nothing negative. Nothing was left out. It was as pure as it comes. Nothing could ever surpass this feeling for Hugo.

However, just a quickly as it had started, Allana then removed herself from Hugo and returned to and integrated with herself back into her own physical body.

For both of them, there had to be a period of acceptance, of letting go, knowing they had both been in a place so private, so intimate, that it had to take their breath away.

As they both started to readjust, they both felt as if they were sinking back into their bodies, slowly, and one at a time, their physical sensations were returning.

Hugo knew, even at this stage, that these feelings on all the emotional levels he had been on, would stay with him for the rest of his life. As they were both were readjusting, they were looking at each other. Allana was beginning to laugh, almost as a release, but it was the look on Hugo's face, which had the biggest of smiles, that made her laugh even more. And as she laughed, so did Hugo. They laughed for a long time; then they decided to slowly stand up.

"Wow!" exclaimed Hugo.

"Wow?" said Allana, "Is that it?"

"I am speechless Allana. I don't know what to say. It was the most amazing experience I have ever felt. I couldn't think of a warmer person to have experienced this with. I have to tell you Allana, my feelings for you are now so deep, I don't want them ever to end."

Allana smiled, and that smile said it all. She came up close to Hugo, held him close, and said to him telepathically, *'What I have done today Hugo is very special. Very trusting. Very loving. So we will remember this day for ever. No false feelings can exist in the Sootalanash ceremony, only pure honesty. And now you know the feelings you have for me, and the feelings I have for you, are genuine.'*

With that, they brushed themselves down, made their way to the entrance of the Arkhrun, along the path to the ley line circle and back to Allana's dwelling.

As they walked in, Ding Ling was standing there with crossed arms. "Master, you have been long time somewhere? Wait a minute Master," said Ding Ling, who now stepped forward and peered into Hugo's face with a quizzical look,

"What is wrong with face? Have look like love sick puppy? What you been doing?"

Allana couldn't help but laugh at this, Hugo caught her looking out of the corner of his eye, and he too started laughing.

Ding Ling looked at them intently, back and forth, waiting for an answer. When none came, he frowned, shook his head, sighed and went outside muttering to himself "It seem I only get proper response from Allana's pet, where she gone?"

Ding Ling's reaction made Hugo and Allana laugh even more.

A Laniakeeean Storm
(These are dramatic, mostly electrical. No rain but very high humidity. The Kroleeth lizards fly in them to soak up the charge from the lightning bolts. These storms also spiritually re-charge the Sola Tree.)

CHAPTER 14

Mandaz and the Cursing Spell

(Open your mind fully. You are an explorer, so go forth and explore.)

Throughout Laniakeea, all the Elves find Elfistra objectionable. They also find her very intimidating, and rightly so, as the sorceress, she has magical powers beyond the normal Laniakeeans wildest dreams.

They also respect her, because they love their Queen and the queen supports Elfistra with the security of their dimension.

Mandaz is different; he is repulsive, spiteful and short tempered. What the Laniakeean's can't quite fathom out, is why Elfistra makes it public that Mandaz is her aide? It is true though, that he normally never leaves her side.

The Laniakeeans know he is always around, but don't understand why he is there or where he came from.

When Mandaz he loses his temper, he is rude and aggressive, Elfistra is always there to calm the situation and always supports him.

Why? What could he possibly contribute to their partnership? From the outside this ugly, smelly slug of a being, so unlike any other Elf, including Elfistra, is present whenever Elfistra is called before the queen. Even the queen has a lot of respect for Mandaz, but he doesn't on the outside contribute to the workings of Laniakeea, or so it appears.

To understand why, we have to go back to the very formation and colonization of Laniakeea by the sentient treelike being, The Sola Tree. The Sola Tree had been searching for a suitable dimension for many millennia. It then came across this dimension. It was vast, it had air, water, flora and fauna, mountains and with slight variations, suitable ambient weather. The Sola Tree decided that this dimension should be called Laniakeea. In ancient Elvish, this translates as 'the immeasurable dimension.' The perfect name, when you consider that if you squashed the Earth flat, and placed it on a map of Laniakeea, the Earth would appear as a small dot.

Other Sola Trees were searching the cosmos also looking for suitable resting and colonization dimensions. There has always been one certain rule, a rule that cannot be broken, in that there has to exist good and evil, light and dark, yin and yang etc. One balances out the other, and generally creates harmony. They would typically exist together in one dimension, but there would be times when an imbalance of bad would attempt to suffocate the good and attempt to control it.

All the Sola Trees from all the other dimensions respected this rule. It just so happens that Laniakeea was a pleasant dimension to be born, and grow up in. It was a 'good' dimension. It was light and spiritual; however, it would be subject to darker forces that would want to try to colonize it, hence the reason, that every dimension would have a district that contained portals, enabling other Elves and species free access.

The Sola Continuum, as they were collectively known, ensured that every dimension they colonized had a district that had some portals. Unfortunately, 'bad' can be clever and cruel, and Laniakeea, over many millennia, has learned this to its detriment. Constant security is now placed in the district of Gareen where the Laniakeean portals exist, ready to repel those wishing to colonize or cause harm.

So, in those very early days of colonization, the Sola Tree decided Laniakeea needed a protector, not only that, a protector that would be very responsible and have the ability to learn from each insurgency, from evil forces that tried to attack. So, Elfistra the sorceress was created.

Half Elf, half a genetic construction decided upon by the Sola Tree. Elfistra (which means 'the magical one') also had the ability to regenerate. Every one hundred and sixty years or so, the present Elfistra would die, and a new baby sorceress would be born. A search would be set up to determine, which of the new babies born at the time of the passing of the old Elfistra, was the reincarnated Elfistra.

There is a simple series of tests that the babies would undergo, to find the true Elfistra. These were the babies that were just about able to send messages telepathically. They were presented with a series of objects, for example, five ear adornments, which are laid out before them. They were all very slightly different, but the reincarnated Elfistra would immediately pick out the one she had used since time began. In total there were collections of five types of adornments or objects, that were laid out in front of the baby the authorities suspected was the reborn Elfistra.

The correct item from all five tests had to be right, before that baby was raised and became the ruling Elfistra. Magic was used to accelerate the growth of the Elfistra from baby to young woman in the space of two weeks. The beauty of reincarnation was, that all the experiences, the highs and lows of battles, in effect the total memory would also be transferred into the new Elfistra.

Every dimension colonized by a Sola Tree, would have its own sorceress, whether that dimension be solely 'good' or 'evil,' and that dimension's sorceress would act accordingly, so some sorceresses were to be feared.

After a short while though, after observing the development of the Elfistra in Laniakeea, the Sola Tree decided Elfistra should have a companion, not to procreate, but to share in the decision making and for company. Moreover, in the true spirit of opposites, the Sola Tree decided a male sorcerer should be created. Laniakeea was unique in this respect. All other dimensions had only one sorceress, and that sorceress would be a female.

So, a male sorcerer was formed and was named Mandaz (which means the 'powerful one'). It didn't take very long for Elfistra and Mandaz to work together on all their duties, to the extent that they became inseparable.

This Mandaz, was quite unlike the present day Mandaz, in that he was powerfully built. Had full use of his arms and legs. He was to be admired, and although he looked fierce and intimidating, he had a very gentle, compassionate and gentle character, quite the opposite to Elfistra. He still had the same construction of scales all over his body, and had intricate magical tattoos on his lips. He wore a permanent crown of intricately worked silver filigree and was in possession of a magic staff. The staff called Tazareth, was a potent magical tool, especially when both Elfistra and Mandaz pooled their collective magical sources to use it to protect and serve.

There was an unusual sheen to Mandaz's scales, unlike Elfistra's that appeared to be solid, with a red flash of color between each scale, that showed itself when she was walking or was angry. Mandaz's scales could change into different iridescent colors, and so his colors were continually changing.

Such is the nature of the Sola Tree, that all of its constructs had to have the ability to love and to care for each other. This is indeed what happened between Elfistra and Mandaz. Imagine, falling deeply in love with someone, and it lasting not only for one normal lifetime but in the case of Elfistra and Mandaz, for countless lifetimes.

This was how it was between the two for approximately three millennia. They were inseparable. They both lived a long life, both died, both reincarnated and both met again, with their memories, not only of all their experiences but of their love for each other intact. This love, if such were at all possible, was a stronger bond after each reincarnation.

Once Mandaz said to Elfistra, "*I would be devastated if anything were to happen to you. I would lay down my life for you, to save you from harm.*" Little did Mandaz realize when he said that, how prophetic his words were to become.

Four hundred Elvish years to the day after Mandaz had said that to Elfistra, they were then attacked by a dark, and sinister spiritual species of Elf called the Lazanath. Their dimension called Rapaeva, was over a millennium older than Laniakeea. They were more advanced in many ways but were on a crusade of re-colonizing established dimensions, that had a Sola Tree, and in the case of Laniakeea, a wand in the form of Elvina. It was a dark and evil dimension and was led by a powerful magician, Lord Ransan.

Every dimension that had a Sola Tree, also had its own wand, and in the case of the Lazanath, their wand was called Elvak. It is worth noting that all the wands that were to be found anywhere were neutral on their own. It was the species of Elf that held it, operated and melded with it, that imbued that Elf's character and thoughts into the wand. So while Elvina in the hands of Elfistra, or Allana, would be used in a good and ethical way, Elvak, when melded with the Lazanath sorcerer would become dark, cruel and unpredictable.

The sorceress of Rapaeva at that time was a female and called Negran. She had very smooth dark skin, and was stunning to look at. The whites of her eyes were luminous, so it seemed like her eyes were glowing all the time. She also had a partner, but he stayed behind as protector on Rapaeva. Her hair was long and black, but had weaved throughout it many strands of silver thread.

Lord Ransan's scouts had discovered Laniakeea and reported back to him to say that Laniakeea it was ripe for the picking. They prepared and set off to re-colonize Laniakeea for themselves. They would use the tactic that had successfully served them well many times before when they assimilated another dimension, and that was stealth and speed of attack, get to the head of that dimension and neutralize their sorceress and gain control of that dimension's wand.

The Lazanath managed to disguise themselves when attacking. They all wore featureless gray clothes, reminiscent of monk's habits from Earth, but were able to render themselves transparent. They could be seen, but only just. They didn't use bow and arrows, but short daggers, that they were able to shoot towards their enemies using very advanced telekinesis.

The daggers would move so fast that it was difficult to follow them with the naked eye. Also, they were able to pinpoint with great accuracy where the end of the dagger would touch or plunge into an Elf, targeting pressure points that are similar in an Elf to that of a human. So, they could render their enemy's unconscious or paralyze them from the head down or kill them.

They entered Laniakeea via one of the portals, quietly and quickly, using their transparency and magical daggers very effectively. From previous scouting escapades, they already knew of the layout of Laniakeea, and the use of ley lines (for which they needed a knowledge of the Laniakeean dialect of Elvish,) which they were able to negotiate and use using their own system. The plan was to capture Elvina and then meet up at the queen's palace, where Lord Ransan would give Queen Haruntha the chance to surrender and be re-colonized. If she refused, the threat would be that many more Laniakeean's would die.

As with all best-laid plans, things can go wrong. They

reached the Sola Tree, neutralized the guards but discovered that the Spiriten containing Elvina wasn't there. They couldn't understand why it wasn't there? Immediately though, they decided to press on straight to the queen's palace to confront the queen, Mandaz and Elfistra, whom they were informed by their scouts, were already there, but oblivious to the fact that there was an attack. Or so they thought. This was their first major mistake

Luckily for the Laniakeeans, they had over many millennia, built up a very efficient early warning system around the portals that would warn Elfistra and Mandaz of insurgents. These would include sophisticated movement sensors that were virtually undetectable. It was these that first alerted Elfistra. She knew time was of the essence, so immediately ordered one of the guards at the Sola Tree, close to Elvina, to bring the Spiriten containing Elvina to the queen's palace and to place it in her hands.

Elfistra knew that Elvina was very much sought after, and was usually the focus of any insurgent attack. So, first things first: Elvina would be placed as soon as possible in her hands for protection, and if need be, to use.

Within a short space of time, the Spiriten containing Elvina was being cradled in Elfistra's arms. She was by now, in the hall with Queen Haruntha. No sooner were they all together than they heard a commotion at the great doors leading to the great hall, and in stormed Lord Ransan, closely followed by his sorceress, Negran who already had the wand Elvak beginning to integrate into her body.

Delicate black tendrils were wrapping themselves across her arms and hands, ready to be assimilated fully on command. Laniakeean guards were dropping like flies left, right and center, and still Lord Ransan strode forward, stopping a few paces in front of the Queen. Mandaz and Elfistra were just to her right.

Lord Ransan looked at both Elfistra and Mandaz, and wasn't aware that Laniakeea had two sorcerers. This was mistake number two.

Several Lazanath warriors were flanking Lord Ransan and Negra, each in a pose that meant they could deploy the daggers at the slightest movement towards Elfistra, Mandaz or the queen's bodyguards. They too were poised, bows were drawn, with arrows ready to let loose.

There was a standoff. No one moved an inch. It was Lord Ransan who slowly and gently moved. He reached up and drew his hood back over his cropped head and onto the back of his neck. He was a scrawny looking thin man, but his face was heavily lined and his eyes a dark green. Although his head moved slowly, his eyes flicked around taking in all that was before him. He then looked at the queen and smiled. It was not a genuine smile of course. It was a smile of contempt. A smile that is displayed towards a conquered soul from someone who believes he or she, is a conqueror.

Lord Ransan drew in a deep breath and said verbally, in a general Elvish dialect, "My queen, there is no need for this unpleasantness. Let me introduce myself. My name is Lord Ransan. I, like yourself, am an Elf. We are called the Lazanath, and we come from a dimension called Rapaeva. We are an ancient order of Dark Elves, but we are also explorers, and we have come to offer you terms for our colonization of your dimension."

Elfistra and Mandaz were bristling at this. It was taking all Elfistra's time to telepathically prevent Mandaz from using his powers with his staff, Tazareth, to attack Lord Ransan.

Elfistra telepathically said to Mandaz, *'Don't Mandaz, it's what he wants. Put down Tazareth, please, for all our sakes. Let us listen to see what he has to say.'*

At this, Lord Ransan slowly turned his head in the direction of Mandaz, as did all the other Lazanath warriors. Lord Ransan then said, "Hmm. A male sorcerer, how unusual. However, I think it would be very wise to listen to what your sorceress is advising sorcerer. We could destroy you before you had time to raise your staff, which I assure you would be ineffectual against our combined magical abilities."

Lord Ransan then slowly turned back towards the queen and said, "We are more advanced and older than you. We collect and colonize dimensions we feel could be of use to us. The kindness within me is offering a way for you to accept our take-over without the spilling of any more Elvish blood. How do you feel about my kind and generous offer?"

But Lord Ransan continued by saying, "Of course, the alternative is death and destruction of the Elves of Laniakeea, and the capture of your wand, that we know is called Elvina. You, Queen, would be reduced to the status of an ordinary Elf, and I would immediately take my seat on your throne to rule Laniakeea. Not such a pleasant alternative, would you agree?"

During this whole time, Queen Haruntha had been very quiet. Watching, observing, listening, assessing. She took in a deep breath and spoke very softly and calmly considering the circumstances. "Lord Ransan, you have come into my dimension. Unannounced and uninvited. You have already needlessly murdered a large number of my subjects and warriors.

"This is unforgivable," the queen continued, "I will never bow down to a tyrant who rules with fear and intimidation. Also, what is the point of it all, if not for pure greed and evil? We will fight to the death to protect that which is dear to us. My emphatic and definitive answer to you is no. I expect you to leave my dimension immediately and never come back. If you don't, neither myself nor my sorcerers will hold back using every source of power we will use to repel you.

Lord Ransan, rolled his eyes upwards, and let out a big sigh and said, "Why is it that many species of Elf are blind to the fact that they agree to their extermination. Ah well, you were given a chance."

At this Lord Ransan, pulled his hood back over his head and slowly started to step back behind his warriors and his sorceress, Negran.

By now, Negran had fully integrated with their wand Elvak, and as Lord Ransan came abreast of Negran, he merely ordered her to kill them all, except the queen.

Negran wasn't stupid though, she knew the key to winning this battle was to eliminate her counterpart, Elfistra, whom she could see was seething with anger. It is worth noting at this stage that it is virtually impossible for one sorceress and wand to kill another sorceress and her wand. Reincarnation may be thanked for that, but it was also a failsafe in-built by the Sola continuum. The most she could do was send a form of incapacitating spell, of which there are numerous to call upon, so very quickly she decided to use the cursing spell.

What happened next, happened so quickly, it was difficult to follow. Elfistra was so engrossed in the conversations; she had only just now taken Elvina out of the Spiriten and started to integrate with the wand. Negran was smiling because she knew she was already integrated with Elvak and was ready to issue the spell at Elfistra. Elfistra simply wasn't ready

She brought her arms together and pointed them at Elfistra, Negran's arms were now writhing black tendrils of energy and she could be seen mouthing the magical incantation for the cursing spell.

Mandaz could see what was happening and already was issuing an expansion spell. This is a spell that enlarges the body the spell is directed at, so the body swells to twice its size. It is excruciatingly painful, and in some cases the body itself will blacken and explode. The spell was directed towards Negran and the Lazanath warriors with his magical staff. At the same time, he could see that Negran's curse spell was leaving her arms and wand towards Elfistra.

He leaped towards Elfistra, shouting "Noooooo," and managed to jump in front of Elfistra and intercept the curse spell. It hit him full on into his chest. Mandaz's expansion spell, at almost the same time, hit Negran, and the Lazanath warriors.

Within seconds their bodies had turned black and expanded quickly and popped with large explosions, leaving a black goo on the floor. What Negran had not accounted for was that it was Elfistra holding the wand not Mandaz, so Mandaz was able to destroy her.

Immediately, Lord Ransan, who now was sprinting towards the hall doors was surrounded by more of the queen's warriors and arrested.

Suddenly there was screaming coming from Elfistra,

who by now was cradling Mandaz's head in her hands. The curse spell is the cruelest of spells. It completely changes and deforms the body that it is directed at. His arms and legs started to wither away, leaving behind the large hands and feet. The structure of his face changed, and so did his skin texture. The screams of torment and pain were not coming from Elfistra, but from Mandaz as these horrendous changes were taking place. Everyone knew this was a selfless act of sacrifice by Mandaz to save his love Elfistra. Red tears were silently running down Elfistra's cheeks. There was nothing she could do. This was all beyond the power of Elvina, who couldn't help either. All Elfistra could do was comfort him and try to soothe him as the torturing waves of pain washed throughout his body. When it had all finished, he had passed out, and looked exactly as he looks now.

Elfistra reached down and gently opened one of his hands and placed his staff into his palm and whispered into Mandaz's ear, "My love, I promise I will make the Lazanath pay for what they did to you. I will always love you and look after you." At this, Mandaz, who appeared to be unconscious, raised a shaking index finger of his right hand, and with great effort tenderly stroked the side of Elfistra's cheek.

Suddenly there was a loud bang in front of them. They all looked around to see the guards that had arrested Lord Ransan, lying on their backs.

"Where has Lord Ransan gone?" shouted the queen.

The warriors looked dazed and shook their heads. Then from above their heads, Lord Ransan's voice boomed out, "Some advanced magic, and I have gone. We will meet again queen, and when we do, you will not be so lucky. We will always be one step ahead of you, remember that."

Elfistra implored the queen to keep what happened to Mandaz a secret. For all spells that are directed towards another sorcerer or sorceress, especially those that are reincarnations, means that they will keep that curse every time they reincarnate. That curse will last forever. Mandaz would always be deformed until the end of time. Three millennia later, and now in the present, it becomes perfectly understandable why Mandaz is the way he is and also why, even now they are inseparable. Queen Haruntha has asked permission from Elfistra, to make it public. However, even when she has explained to Elfistra that the Elves of Laniakeea would accept the circumstances, and Elfistra and Mandaz would be widely accepted and respected, she still refuses.

The queen accepts that Elfistra's reasons are her own and are to be respected, and has decided she will not mention the subject again until such a time as Elfistra is ready.

Elfistra the Sorceress
(She is very powerful magically, and has the ability to re
incarnate. She is over six million Earth years old)

CHAPTER 15

Return of the Lazanath

(Remember, we are all on a journey. Enjoy that journey. This is the way to become a better Elf.)

It is 4 pm on a pleasant summer afternoon in the walled garden at Brough Manor. Lady Romilly Brough, Kayon, Helena, Hugo, Allana and Ding Ling are present. They are all sat at a round table, covered with the most delicate French lace and embroidered gold colored shot silk. They have all just eaten a light savory tea.

They were all feeling a little jaded. They had spent the afternoon at the sentencing of their husband and father, Lord Arlo Brough.

His time spent in prison awaiting trial was very foreign to him. Not getting his way, having to do what he was told to do. The taunts and mild to severe acts of violence from other prisoners towards him were frightening. Many of them he had sent down in his capacity as a judge. It was a rude wake-up call for Brough.

As with many prisoners who find themselves in this position, with time to think, he was beginning to have regrets for everything he had said and done. He had requested on many occasions, that a family member be given leave to visit him.

Indeed, messages from the prison to various family members had been sent out and received. It was in fact Lady Brough, who took it upon herself to pay him a visit, early on in his incarceration pending sentencing. She endured his ranting and raving and table thumping at her from behind his thick Perspex viewing wall. Not once did she react or reply.

And when he was spent, she just got up, turned and walked away without uttering a single word. Whilst it was upsetting to a certain degree, she was pleased with herself for being able to stand up to his controlling actions. For the first time in her life, she reacted the way she wanted, by not reacting at all!

The double trial and the gathering of evidence, took quite a while. When they appealed to prosecution witnesses to come forward with evidence that could be of relevance to the case, the prosecution counsel was inundated and awash with people coming from far and wide that had been touched by his cruelty.

Brough didn't have a defense to speak of. All the damning evidence against him was irrefutable, and the jury retired at the end of the case for only half an hour. They came back with a verdict of guilty on all counts, both for the murder of Maxx and the murder many years before, of Maxx's mother.

The family had collected earlier today to attend the crown court to hear the judge issue a sentence of twenty-two years for the murder of Maxx and nineteen years for the murder of Maxx's Mother. Both sentences were to run concurrently.

So here they all were, sat around a table in the walled garden. Conversation, which would usually be flippant and light and full of humor, was now unusually somber. One thing they all agreed on, was that he was beginning to look like a broken man, and when the judge read out the sentences, he gripped the rail of the witness box so hard his knuckles turned white, he appeared to take in big sobs.

He was shaking, and at one point, his legs looked like they may give way. Two guards came to him and supported him under his arms, which he accepted with grace. Hugo remembers thinking tht his father allowing something like that a little kindness and support would have been unthinkable a few months earlier. Brough would have kicked off in his usual insulting and crass way.

Hugo couldn't understand why he was having the slightest pangs of regret for the state his father was in now. He deserved everything that was coming to him, he knew that, even so, he couldn't get that little seed of regret out of his head.

But now, he needed to lighten the mood, and he kicked it off by standing and saying, "Oh, I forgot to mention, it is only two months before the grand finals of the Gruthanda competition takes place in the district of Nymlarri on Laniakeea, and guess whose team is favorite to win?" Hugo turned to his side and pointed towards Allana.

If it were possible for an Elf to blush, then Allana was blushing now. Her aura, for those that could read it, was like a firework display of emotions. Everyone was clapping as Kayon shouted out, "Come on Allana, tell us a little more about what will happen. I understand Hugo failed to draw back the bowstring last time he tried. Maybe it's time for a real man to step forward and have a go."

They all laughed at this, and then Allana stood to speak. "Thank you everyone, and yes Kayon, you will get your opportunity, but I warn you, you won't fare much better than Hugo, who did rather well for an Earthan weakling." To this they laughed and thumped the table.

"But," Allana continued, "You are of course all invited, including you Lady Brough, and since it will your very first visit to Laniakeea, it has been agreed that you will be sitting in a very enviable seat, next to my queen, Queen Haruntha."

At this there were false shouts and groans of "Why not me?" and "Oh I see, I'm I not special enough then?" and so on.

At this point, Lady Brough tapped a teaspoon on the side of her bone china cup and saucer, and said, "Well I have a little announcement as well. Firstly though, thank you Allana for the invitation. I look forward very much to meeting your queen and watching the spectacle of the Gruthanda competition. I will be cheering you on of course."

Allana bowed her head and gave a beaming smile.

Lady Brough continued, "So much has happened, highs and lows, but now I'm feeling very pleased with the way everything is starting to settle down. I'm feeling very positive about the future, and wish to plan something I had always wanted to plan but was never able to do, and that is to put on a grand ball.

There were murmurs of appreciation and clapping from around the table.

"I have already set the plans in motion, and will be inviting my friends, and all of yours and of course members of both our communities, to show we are all moving on to bigger and better things. Planning a ball will be the most exciting event that I have ever been involved in. It is also a gesture on my part; a thank you for all the help and support that has been afforded to me since all our troubles began, and what more exciting way could there be than to have a ball."

"Also, I would extend my invitation to your queen as well Allana," continued Lady Brough, "I believe I am right in thinking she has not visited our dimension as yet? This would be a wonderful introduction to the ways and manners of our Earthan dimension and its people. I have an official invitation here for you to hand to her when convenient."

"I am sure Queen Haruntha would be delighted to receive your kind invitation," said Allana, "and more than excited to accept. We may be different species, but essentially we are women, and all of us like to dress up for an occasion."

By now, two of the kitchen staff had arrived with fresh tea and Allana's favorite: homemade scones, jam and clotted cream. Allana held her hands together and beamed.

Hugo saw this and jibed, "Hmm, might be a good idea to shop for some looser fitting clothes, don't you think Allana?" Allana turned to him and shook her finger at him. She was becoming very au fait with all the little mannerisms and body language of the Earthans by now.

They all sat and started to eat. Allana couldn't wait to eat a scone; they were still hot from the oven, and she quickly and deftly twisted the scone in half, spread on the jam and clotted cream and was just about to lift it to her mouth, when she saw two Elves running towards them. She put the scone down, excused herself and went to meet them. They were communicating telepathically. She then bowed her head down and just stood there.

Hugo went to her and grabbed her hand and said, "Allana, what is it?" She looked towards Hugo and simply whispered to him, "A dark order of Elves, the Lazanath are attempting to return to Laniakeea, which will now be in great danger. I have to leave immediately. Please, will you and Dingy come with me Hugo? I believe we will need all the help we can get."

"Of course, Allana," said Hugo, and he then turned to Kayon and Helena, and said, "Would you like Kayon and Helena to help as well? They have both indicated they would like to be more helpful if needed."

Kayon and Helena vigorously nodded their heads at this. "Of course," said Allana, "Your help would be very gratefully received. I will explain what the threat is on the way to the queen's palace."

Both Kayon and Helena were militarily trained. Kayon was a powerfully built individual. He had prepared his mind and body. His physique was superb. A specialist in various forms of hand-to-hand combat, street fighting and martial arts, meant he could hold his own in any situation. He was, as was customary within military circles, pretty much covered in tattoos. He also had half his left ear missing. That happened during a training session when he was on a street fighting course. With short cropped red hair and stubble and square jaw, he was quite fighting military man.

Helena, on the other hand, was very feminine and pretty. She was an expert in logistical intelligence gathering and was very bright intellectually. She had always had a soft spot for Ding Ling though. In fact, the family wondered if they would pair up.

We all know Ding Ling played the fool, but underneath that comical facade, Ding Ling was sensitive, thoughtful, a good listener and of course had a wonderful sense of humor. He ticked off all the boxes that Helena would look for in a man. And although Helena was not at all tall, she was still an inch taller than Ding Ling, and that she appreciated as well.

From Ding Ling's perspective, she was very desirable, and he knew she knew the real Ding Ling. She was very tactile with him, and he with her. They reveled in each other's company. The humorous repartee between them was always quick and entertaining.

The best news Ding Ling had from Hugo many years ago was that he called him over once and whispered in his ear that Helena had a soft spot for him, and why didn't he take her out on a date? Well, to Ding Ling, this was the seal of approval from his master, and he treasured those words enormously.

In the past, all the suitors seemed to be six foot tall or more. From the outside, Helena was delicate, the picture of an English rose. Very white flawless skin, jet black shoulder-length hair. Her beauty preceded her, and because of it, had always been the envy of other women in their social circles.

On their way to collect their things, Ding Ling said to Hugo, "Master, I have been working on brand new state of the art intellibullet, that can hone in on a specific person's DNA signature. It can stun, paralyze, create hallucinations and of course kill. I will bring. Might be helpful. Will explain more later."

"Fine," said Hugo, and off they rushed. Ten minutes later they had all collected at the front of Brough manor. Ding Ling noticed Helena had already changed from that lovely feminine-looking woman with long hair, into her military fatigues, with her hair scraped back into a bun, all make-up removed (even though her femininity still shone through).

Ding Ling just stood there, hands on hips looking at her, slowly shaking his head and smiling.

"What now Ding Ling?" said Helena. They had always had a good rapport with each other.

Ding Ling said, "You looking like man now Helena, such a shame. I like you better as sexy woman."

"Well," said Helena, "I am ready to fight. I need to look the part. And it's not just the outside that is now the part, I am even wearing undergarments that will keep things protective and tight."

"Hah!" said Ding Ling, "Reminds me of Confucius who says, 'Woman who wear jockstrap, have make-believe ballroom.'"

She play-smacked him on his arm, and in mock shock said, "I wasn't talking about jockstraps."

They had mounted their horses, still laughing at this little exchange between Helena and Ding Ling, but the mood quickly became a little more serious as they wondered what the emergency on Laniakeea was all about.

Allana rode side-saddle with Hugo in charge of the reins, and they galloped off towards the slice. Ding Ling was doing his best to keep up. He closely followed behind them all, but he was on his donkey, which made him judder all over the place and threatened to throw him off.

When they arrived at the slice, Ding Ling looked positively punch-drunk after being shaken around so much. Hugo turned to him, trying not to laugh and said "Dingy, why don't you get a decent horse rather than that flea-bitten donkey?"

"Master you know my short legs no work on any decent horse. Donkey might be crazy. We all know he can't gallop like others, but at least he small, so good for me."

Helena chipped in with, "Dingy, why don't you put your donkey out to pasture, and stick to walking or running?"

"Ah," said Ding Ling, who realized he was becoming the butt of all jokes to do with him, and his donkey said, with a serious face. "You know me Helena, I live by Confucius, he clever Chinaman, and he said, 'Man who keep feet firmly on ground have trouble putting on pants'! This means nobody wants to see Dingy running around with nothing on lower body with dangly bits flapping in wind."

His face creased up, and his infectious chipmunk-like laugh filled the air. They all soon calmed down, and saw that Allana wanted to say something.

Allana thought this an excellent time to brief them all on the history of the Lazanath. Of course, Allana had not been born when the Lazanath last visited, but as a 'special' one to the queen, she had become privy to all the details and had to promise that regarding Mandaz, it would have to be kept a secret.

The queen deliberately left out what happened to Mandaz last time the Lazanath were in Laniakeea, out of respect for Elfistra. She also explained that since the last time the Lazanath visited, the Laniakeeans had a magical spell to neutralize the workings of the Lazanath daggers, but of course, since all that time had passed, the Lazanath no doubt had other more efficient ways of attacking and killing, so they had to be on their guard.

Allana knew that Elfistra and Mandaz would need to be restrained. The moment they found out that an invasion of the Lazanath was imminent, it would bring back all those horrible memories for them of the last time they met.

Elfistra would be ready to do what it took to destroy the Lazanath, every single one, after what they did to Mandaz. Mandaz too, although grotesque and deformed, knew his staff, Tazareth, that was a magical gift from the Sola Continuum, was as strong and as potent as it ever has been. With all magical objects, like Elvina and the Tazareth, there is a period of continuous learning, to discover just what it is capable of doing, and so it was with Mandaz's Tazareth.

He has had time to understand its powers, he has practiced using it, and in secret unleashed its powers on various objects, to great success. There was now very little that could come between Mandaz and his Tazareth. Elfistra was aware of its powers, but everyone else on Laniakeea, and even the queen, thought its only use now was to help Mandaz move, with the occasional prodding into the ground that erupted in a display of bright flashes and sparks.

How mistaken everyone was. This observation is exactly what Mandaz wanted the subjects of Laniakeea to think, because this is what his enemies would think, until he unleashed its incredible powers. The element of surprise would be instrumental indeed in attacking an enemy.

The Tazareth was as powerful as Elvina, but in different ways. It could change night to day and vice versa, it could create thunderstorms and lightning and even recreate a landscape that looked, smelled and felt real, but wasn't. And against an enemy, it could create powerful force fields to protect the bearer. It would only ever become active for Mandaz. The Sola Continuum made sure of that.

For anyone else, hoping they could access its tremendous powers, it would just feel like an inert stick in their hands. It would catch them off guard. Even though he was deformed, he still had a bright mind, and at some stage in the future, everyone would suddenly realize he was their savior.

From unpleasant gross looking object to becoming a hero overnight - this scenario has played over and over in Mandaz's mind for many millennia, and until now, he has been keeping it all a secret. Now, with the possible return of the Lazanath, this was the one moment he had always been waiting for to make them pay for what they had done to him. Underlying this though was his strong responsibility that was instilled into him by the Sola Continuum, as protector of Laniakeea, with his Elfistra, by his side.

So, these two powerful motives would mean he would be a powerful force to reckon with. Elfistra knew this, and because of it, she admired and loved Mandaz even more.

The party then stepped onto the ley line circle, prepared themselves and arrived at the queen's palace. By now, all of them had to adapt to traveling in this manner, and Hugo, more often than not, arrived standing up. It was still the butt of many jokes, not only with the Earthan's, but with the Elves as well, when they recounted his stubbornness, and ended up arriving by sliding along on the floor, with his mouth open and collecting the dry laterite dust.

Even he could see the funny side of it now, and if the story was recounted, he would glance at Allana, and she would smile, and her eyes would glow pinky-red. It was those days that they started to become very attracted to each other.

They arrived in front of the steps leading up to Queen Haruntha's throne. The party all bowed with respect before her.

"Ahhhh," said the queen, as she slowly 'glided' down the stairs. Ding Ling thought to himself again, *'How does Queenie do that?'*

"Very simple Ding Ling," said the queen, as Ding Ling cursed himself for thinking that out loud again, "A mixture of feminine charm and a little seductive magic."

"Thank you all for coming along to help," said the Queen, "I know Allana has filled you in to a certain extent with the bare facts about the Lazanath. And so kind of you Kayon and you Helena for also offering your services."

"Elfistra and Mandaz will be present, and Elfistra will be prepared with Elvina. In that horrible escape so long ago, the Lazanath used magical daggers to effectively kill anyone they sent them to. We are now prepared, and with work that Elfistra and our own scientists have carried out, we have devised a spell that will protect you from this particular form of attack. If the daggers are used, once they reach a matter of inches from your neck, they will be rendered ineffective and fall to the ground."

"If you could each individually make your way to Elfistra, she will administer the relevant spell. It will only take a matter of seconds, but can only be administered individually."

No sooner had the queen said this than all in the party

started to notice the unpleasant smell reaching their nostrils. They turned around, and behind them came Elfistra. Mandaz was just behind her, with his Tazareth, helping him to move forward. It was spectacular to see Mandaz hammer the Tazareth on the floor, and from the bottom of it come a shower of rainbow-colored sparks, and his whole body seemed to shift forward three to four feet.

Ding Ling noticed the wet yellowy green three-foot slime mark Mandaz left on the floor behind him, but he was careful not to think his observations as thoughts because he knew Elfistra would pick them up.

Also, anything he could do to keep out of her mind and way suited him. Normally a fearless man, Elfistra did intimidate him, and it showed in his body language. He would sweat a little, hop from one foot to the other, wring his hands, start to breathe more quickly and do his best not to make eye contact at all.

"And here are Elfistra and Mandaz," said the queen, "Good. Ding Ling, you might as well go first."

"Hmm," said Ding Ling. As he walked hesitantly towards Elfistra, he was thinking of a quote he remembered that said, *"I wish I could say that the one who hates me most, is one who doesn't scare me." The problem is, this woman scares me to hell and beyond, and she hates me as well.'*

Elfistra didn't want to admit that she did not understand any of Ding Ling's last thoughts, so she just gave him the 'come here and be devoured' stare.

"Stand here little yellow man, close your eyes and try to relax." And with that, she waved her arms in a particular way then pointed them at Ding Ling and called out, "**Nas taneth zarros neh heharandath kelmenanth.**"

All Ding Ling felt was a slight tingling, that started at his feet, traveled up his body and ended at the top of his head.

"You can go," said Elfistra, still giving him the stare that was making him squirm. He couldn't wait to move away. One by one the others had the same spell applied.

Once Elfistra had inoculated everyone, Queen Haruntha began to explain in as much detail as possible, the history, features and peculiarities of the Lazanath. Ding Ling and the others noticed that Mandaz seemed to be more agitated than they had ever seen him. Even Allana looked perturbed.

The queen concluded by saying that it was it was a completely different approach by the Lazanath to offer the queen proposals, whatever they would be.

The previous day, when suddenly and without any warning, a holographic image of Lord Ransan suddenly appeared in front of her. Not his whole body, just a grotesque swirling image of his magnified head. She could just see his eyes hidden in the folds of his habit hood that was pulled over his head.

"Queen Haruntha," began Lord Ransan, "We met under unpleasant circumstances last time. I wish to apologize for the way it was executed. Ah! I see Elfistra your Sorceress and Mandaz are in the background. I can see the effects the cursing spell had on you, Mandaz. Not very pleasant was it?"

When Lord Ransan said this, Mandaz started hopping around incensed with anger, and it took all of Elfistra's time to calm him down.

"Still, we all suffered during that time," continued Lord Ransan, "As you know I lost my sorceress, Negran, and we both lost warriors dear to us. However, I implore you now to consider a truce. A chance to parlay, to understand the benefits that a working amalgamation between the Laniakeeans and our dimension of Elves, Rapaeva, could bring to us both."

"A considerable time has passed since our last meeting," said Lord Ransan, "And we have technological advantages we would wish to share with you. Since our sorceress Negran was destroyed, we applied to the Sola Continuum to grant us another. This time, however, we were presented with a male sorcerer called Rass. He is quite unusual and very powerful."

"May I suggest," continued Lord Ransan, "that we meet with you at the next change of your moons?"

And with that, the holographic image disappeared.

The queen was addressing the party before her. She was explaining that she did not trust Lord Ransan: and that the improvements to the early warning systems built into the dimension portals in Gareen had alerted them to the imminent approach of the Lazanath.

On that basis she had sent out a telepathic message to Lord Ransan, asking him to explain his movements towards Laniakeea, when he approached her with his holographic message. She was convinced that her message to him must have come as a surprise, and that possibly he was planning, as last time, to enter Laniakeea under cover and covertly. But now the element of surprise on his part was now lost, so he had changed tactics to make it all appear as though a convivial meeting could take place.

"We will all have to be prepared and be ready for the worse," said Queen Haruntha, "We cannot afford not to be. Having consulted with my Barboski, he sees nothing but upset and a battle on the horizon, which could be devastating for Laniakeea, unless we can meet his challenge forcefully right at the beginning."

"Elfistra," continued the queen, "you will integrate with Elvina, and be fully prepared for both Lord Ransan and his sorcerer, Rass. You all now are protected in the event Lord Ransan uses the magical daggers. Allana has explained the workings of your new intellibullets to me Ding Ling, and how it works, but explain in more detail please, to all of us, what we need to do to initiate its effectiveness. However, before you begin, I implore all of you, that this is a last resort retaliation."

"We are a peaceful Elf species," said the Queen, "And don't want to be dragged down to the baser warring instincts that are found in other species, including the Lazanath. At the same time that doesn't mean we can't protect ourselves against the evils that prevail in other dimensions. Ok Ding Ling, please proceed."

Ding Ling stepped forward and said, "These new intellibullets, Z1, are indeed very special. They read the DNA of each enemy. When fired they are controllable by in-built intelligence, in the intellibullet itself, and guidance from myself."

"These intellibullets can hover, create hallucinations and follow its enemy wherever it goes. They are impossible to catch. They will follow the enemy for months if necessary. Big advantage is Lazanath know nothing of its technology, so should be defenseless against them."

"However," said Ding Ling, "one drawback. We have to assess and record each of the enemy's DNA signatures. Only way to do that is we have to get enemy to have contact with tiny DNA sensors called Danobots. They are invisible to naked eye. Best way is to spread them on floor, then when enemy walk across them, sensors read DNA. I can prepare that before this meeting looks like it going arse over titties."

"Dingy," said Hugo, "you can't say it like that! Anyway, they wouldn't understand that terminology. said Hugo,

Please put it another way." Helena was trying her best not to smirk in the background.

"Ah, so sorry master," said Ding Ling, "Before it looking like meeting going to all-out war, I will capture DNA signatures before it all kicks off. We make a big circle, scatter on Danobots, and then they will step across them and assess specific DNA signatures. Ok?"

"Thank you, Ding Ling," said Queen Haruntha, "You might as well do that now, we are not sure when they will turn up. Let us be prepared."

Ding Ling brought out a little pouch from his tunic. He connected his HC to the DNA sensor interface. Once he did this, he would be able to communicate with the sensors and give instructions He took a handful of what appeared to be fine dust from the pouch and spread it onto the floor.

The dust appeared to move under its own volition to spread out to form a circle around the group from between ten to twenty feet from them. Each Danobot, is robotic, with small mechanical legs, which transports them quickly and purposefully to form the circle surrounding the group. Ding Ling then turned to the rest of the group and said "It is done. When each enemy step on a sensor, DNA result come to my interface and embeds itself in an intellibullet, it is then ready to fire. Then I verbally or manually key in instructions to tell each intellibullet what I want it to do."

Queen Haruntha, looked around, at the group facing

her, Elfistra and Mandaz, and several of her warriors and said, "Well, we are ready, so now we just…"

The queen was interrupted by the air around them being sucked in, then out, and suddenly in front of them, thirty feet away, out of thin air appeared Lord Ransan, his sorcerer, Rass, holding Elvak the wand, and eight Lazanath warriors.

This took everybody by surprise. How could this happen, with no warning at all? What advanced technology were the Lazanath's using now?

Lord Ransan slowly lifted the hood of his habit off his head to reveal a wicked smile. "So, you like our new mode of transport Haruntha? Our advanced technology scientists on Lazanath have finally developed what we are calling 'transporter capabilities.' Quite impressive, isn't it, and in the right hands, very valuable, wouldn't you say?"

Lord Ransan started to stroll towards Queen Haruntha, with his entourage a pace behind and moving with him. As Lord Ransan was coming forward, he began, to explain the reason behind his visit.

"I see you have some Earthans with you as your advisors. Is that wise, considering the fact that their dimension is relatively new?"

"To me Lord Ransan," said Queen Haruntha, "being genuine and honest count more than how long a dimension has been established." As the queen said this, Lord Ransan stopped just short of where the ring of DNA sensor Danobots were lying. Ding Ling was beside himself with frustration and was willing Lord Ransan and his group to take just one more step as a whole.

"I see," said Lord Ransan, "Ah well, it's of no consequence to me. I am here to put forward some convincing reasons why it would benefit you, and me of course, to amalgamate our dimensions into one."

It was now that Elfistra and Mandaz managed to get a closer look at Rass, the Lazanath sorcerer. Rass was very powerfully built and was in a humanoid form, but that is where the similarity ended. The whole of his body was perfectly smooth and silver in color. It was also very shiny.

You could see the arms, legs, torso, neck and head, but they were featureless, except for one eye in the middle of the forehead, a nose, ears and a mouth.

Elfistra was doing her best to calm Mandaz down, who wanted to move in immediately to confront Ransan and Rass. In fact, his Tazareth was glowing and sparking, and picking up Mandaz's mood, thoughts and feelings.

This didn't go unnoticed by Rass, who slowly turned his head towards Mandaz and just stared at him.

"Well," continued Ransan, "Let me tell you what we can offer. We can offer ourselves as allies in the event your dimension is attacked. We can share with you many advance technologies, some of which you have no idea exist, including our new transportation method. In fact, let's offer you a little demonstration of what this can do."

Suddenly, one by one, each of the Lazanath warriors would disappear in a swirling mist, then reappear either in front or behind or on the other side of the group. Then another warrior would do the same, and then all the warriors were moving all the time disappearing and reappearing somewhere else. Whilst this was happening Lord Ransan and Rass kept very still and in one place.

It was very unnerving to Queen Haruntha and the others. They didn't know where to look next, and the process was speeding up. As suddenly as it had started, it stopped, and all the Lazanaths were back in their original positions - unfortunately for Ding Ling, still a few inches outside the ring of Danobots.

After this demonstration, Ransan, started to move forward slowly again while saying, "And so besides all of this we can offer, we both know that your Elvina is a white wand, and our Elvak is a black wand. Exact opposites. Each has their own unique powers, but we now know, that if the two were to be brought together, their combined powers would be magnified a thousand times. Our dimensions would be the most powerful throughout the whole of the dimension system. Certainly, the most powerful of dimensions that contain a Sola Tree."

By now, Ransan, Rass and the Lazanath warriors had stepped into the band of DNA robotic sensors, and already Ding Ling's HC was buzzing with the information and results of the DNA sampling. Ding Ling had already pre-programmed the results to be installed into all the intellibullets.

At the press of a button, all the bullets could be released from Ding Ling's intelligun, and would speed towards their targets. He had already programmed them to aim for the neck of each recipient, and hover approximately one foot away.

Wherever that recipient would move, the intellibullet would follow, until such a time that Ding Ling would issue further instructions.

"To what end though," said the queen, in reply to Lord Ransan, "To have absolute dominance over all dimensions? To enslave all the Elf species in those dimensions? This sounds suspiciously like the thoughts of a conqueror, and at the end of it all, you Lord Ransan, would self-promote yourself to - what? - King Ransan, ruler of all dimensions?"

"No." continued Haruntha, "I will have no part of this. This is against all our teachings and ethos. Our very existence is based on peace, not war. You will never control Elvina, or our dimension. I would ask you to leave and never come back!"

As Haruntha was saying this, Ransan started to visibly shake with anger. This must have been a new experience to him, to have a dimension and its figurehead stand up to him.

Everyone was beginning to feel the tension. The Lazanath warriors had already brought out their magical daggers. Mandaz had primed his Tazareth staff, and Elfistra had integrated with Elvina. Rass, was slowly turning from a smooth silver shape to black and shiny as Elvac was incorporating into him.

Kayon, Helena, Allana and Hugo could only stand still and watch and feel the tension grow. It seemed that Queen Haruntha was the only one who looked calm and in control.

Ransan blurted out, "You leave me no alternative Queen. You have been offered a more than generous way to amalgamate with our powers, and yet you still refuse? We will do what we came here for then, and we will overcome you this time." By now Ransan's face was a deep purple, and blood vessels running across his temples were pulsating as if they were going to pop.

He turned to Rass, to set everything in motion. Rass ordered the deployment of the Lazanath warriors' magical daggers, which in an instant sped towards the group facing them. The daggers reached only a few inches from the throats of their intended victims, then stopped and fell powerless and inert onto the floor.

For a moment, there was silence. The incredulous look on Lord Ransan's face was a picture. He could not understand what had happened. Just as he was beginning to turn to Rass to unleash the power of Elvac, Ding Ling quietly stepped forward and raised his hand and said: "Hold it right there Ransack!"

Ransan shouted out, "And what does this fool think he can achieve when faced with all my innumerable power? He can't even pronounce my name correctly."

"Ahh," said Ding Ling, "Always expect the unexpected Lord Ransack, You so old and experienced, you do not know this piece of wisdom? You need read Confucius."

Ransan's face was a picture, as were those of the rest of his troop. They couldn't, try as they may, get a handle on what Ding Ling was talking about. But it didn't matter, it was what Ding Ling wanted: the element of surprise.

At that moment, Ding Ling pressed the 'initiation' button on his tunic, and from his gun, silently and extremely quickly came ten intellibullets which all moved to the necks of each of the Lazanaths, including Rass and Ransan, and stopped abruptly one foot away.

A few of the Lazanath warriors took a couple of steps back, and they all noticed that the intellibullets followed them, still precisely a foot from their necks.

"Rass," said Ransan, "Get rid of these Earthan trinkets or whatever they may be immediately."

But try as he might, nothing Rass threw at the intellibullets worked. And why should it? This was something entirely new to the Lazanaths.

Ransan was becoming angrier now, when calmly, Ding Ling continued, "You see Ransack, you cannot know everything. These are special. At signal, each bullet will release five small darts, that implode into your necks. At same time, force-field is generated around each body and at precisely two-tenths of one-second, darts explode, equivalent to a very powerful thermonuclear device, known as MK-41, and equivalent to twenty-five megatons.

You look confused? Quite right. Your body would evaporate, last thing you would say is 'What the …?!', then that is end. Good news for us is that explosion self-contained within force-field. Sure, we would hear explosion, and feel heat, but we are safe."

Ding Ling was on a roll, and he knew it. By now he had their attention, so he continued by saying, "But Ding Ling have more good news for you. These bullets can hover and follow you wherever you go, for long, long time. Don't have to blow head off either, can paralyze you, stop you breathing, so lots of lovely ways of saying Sayonara."

Finally, Ding Ling said, "Would you like me demonstrate on one of your warriors?" Ding Ling sauntered over to one of Ransan's warriors, pointed at him and said, "This one?" The warrior nervously stepped back, and of course the intellibullet moved with him. "Or this one? or this one? or even you Ransack?

At the top of his voice, and now visibly shaking with

anger, Ransan shouted, "My name is Ransan?! Lord Ransan!"

"So now, time to make quick decision Ransack. You go now, don't come back, and I will call intelibullets back to me, or you stay and say goodbye to your ass!"

Ransan simply knew he was beaten. He turned on his heels, and one at a time, in swirling puffs of smoke, his contingent transported back to their dimension.

For a minute there was silence, then everyone cheered. Helena came and hugged Ding Ling, as did Hugo, and even the queen and Allana, bowed low before Ding Ling.

He had never felt so important in his life. The feeling was wonderful.

The queen went to him, and said, "My Barboski hinted that this may happen, and from the most unusual quarters, and it has come to be true. Ding Ling, Laniakeea is indebted to you, you will always be very welcome here."

"Thank you, my queen." The way he said this with a gracious bow, made everyone smile. "Trouble with Ransack, for someone so old and thinks he knows it all, he doesn't know that real knowledge is to know extent of one's ignorance."

"Very wise saying, and true, Ding Ling," said Queen Haruntha.

As they all caught their breath, Ding Ling collected the intellibullets from his gun and identity marked them for if they were ever needed in the future. He placed a small electronic box on the floor that collected all the remaining millions of DNA Danobot sensors and packed them all away.

The queen indicated they were all invited to a form of spa in an area of the queen's garden that had hot springs. From here they could sink into the deliciously inviting warm scented waters, having already walked along the path with the sentient vines that stroked their legs and hands and left them slightly heady and intoxicated.

As they relaxed and chatted, Saturn came slowly into view, and it filled the entire pale mauve sky, came Saturn, looking as resplendent as ever. For Kayon and Helena, this was the first time they had experienced this, and were awestruck by the whole planetary experience.

Charlie Andover
(Manageress of the horse stables at Brough Manor and love interest to a young Hugo Brough)

CHAPTER 16

Hello Charlie Andover

(Experience the feeling of contentment when all is good, and all is right.)

Almost two weeks had passed since the Lazanaths had tried unsuccessfully to take control of Laniakeea, and life in both dimensions had slowly reverted to its normal state of affairs.

Lady Romilly Brough had been working very hard organizing the preparations for the grand ball that was to be held in an enormous marquee in the spacious grounds of Brough Manor.

The landscaping, the extensive gardens and the weeping willows along the banks of the river that meandered across the bottom edge of the lawn, could have been a Turner oil painting.

It was beautiful, and the setting perfect. The marquee itself did not stand alone but was attached to the leading edge of Brough Manor itself. An entrance on one side led back and forth to the extensive kitchens. The kitchens themselves were a hive of activity. Everyone, from the potato peeler to the maître'd and head chef, were prepared and knew exactly what they were doing. The smell of roasting boar and elderberries and honeyed parsnips and poached pears in a Murdei red wine filled the air.

Since half the guests were Elves from Laniakeea, there was even a comprehensive selection of Elvish delicacies. Allana had been invaluable in offering her suggestions on what would please all the Elvish guests. Most Elves are vegetarian of sorts, and the choices of salads, honeyed nuts, cheeses, edible flowers and so on were innumerable. All of these were spiced with Elvish spices, that created unusual tastes that humans had never tried.

There were also some so-called delicacies that were alive, like a form of warm-blooded worm, some insect-type creatures, and unusual nuts and fruits, like the Kraldan or Sensaas fruit that Hugo had tried previously, imported in from Laniakeea, that if eaten, would instill a feeling of being slightly tipsy.

On the other side of the marquee, there was a larger entrance, that led straight into the grand hall within Brough Manor, through which guests would arrive, be greeted and ushered into the marquee.

The marquee layout was extraordinary. Besides the

beautiful cotton and lace tablecloths, the chairs had also been decorated, and adorned with carefully tied red silk bows. All the tables were round, therefore enabling all the guests at each table to interact with each other, a particular requirement of both Queen Haruntha and Lady Brough.

The tables themselves were adorned with free-standing candles and bouquets of sweet-smelling peonies and pure white lilies. As a special requirement of Lady Brough, the lilies were all to be of the 'Casablanca' species, which had the most delicate scent of all the lilies she could have ordered, and the long slender pure white heads had a gracefulness to them that caught the eye.

However, there was something that set the whole ambiance of the marquee above all else that had been seen. With the gracious permission of Queen Haruntha, magic had been applied to a number of spectacular candelabras that seemingly were just floating in the air.

As the guests (mainly the Earthan guests), stepped into the marquee, the sight of the floating candelabras took their breath away, and for a few moments they could only stand and stare open-mouthed at the spectacle before them.

When Queen Haruntha arrived, she looked simply stunning. Even though this was a formal affair, her choice of dress was still enticing and attractive. She was wearing a large headdress of gold and silver thread woven in and around small delicate white roses, that had been cleverly fashioned into a magnificent crown. Her make-up, her choice of material and its color, ensured that everyone had to stop and look. She certainly made an impact. Moreover, she finished it off with the gliding motion of her steps. Beautiful.

Allana, in electric blue, also looked equally as stunning. She was wearing a backless off-the-shoulder dress. The material seemed to float around her and accentuated her every move.

Hugo was wearing his army temperate 'dress blues' uniform with a red belt. His service ribbons stood out on the left-hand side of his chest. He was handsome, no doubt about that, and he turned many females' heads when he entered the marquee. This didn't go unnoticed by Allana.

Ding Ling accompanied Helena. Certainly, Helena was an 'English rose' and wore a classic retro ball gown that was cream shot silk, underneath which were layers upon layers of netting to create a full and voluminous gown from the waist down. Around her waist, a broad red patent leather belt, that accentuated just how slim her waist was. The top was again classic off-the-shoulder, and she was wearing very long white gloves. Her hair was plaited up and fashioned into a French pleat.

Ding Ling, it was quite apparent to see, was feeling uncomfortable with what he was wearing. He had never in his life worn a hand-tied bow tie with an old-style starched collar, which was just fractionally too tight, which is why he kept straining and pulling faces as he tried to wedge his finger between the inside of the collar and the skin on his neck. The rest of his tuxedo suit looked fine, although there was a slight whiff of mothballs every so often, but his black shoes were army issue, and with their bulled up black shiny round toe-caps, looked out of place.

When Helena was helping him to dress earlier on, she started giggling and said he looked as if half of him was coming to the ball, but his feet were going to the army parade ground. Usually meticulous in his planning for everything else, procuring the right shoes had utterly escaped him. The other problem was, that the shoes were a tad too tight and had not been broken in, so they were pinching his toes, instep and ankles. He had to keep his feet moving all the time to gain some relief from all the pinching.

Unfortunately, it didn't have quite the desired effect. One guest whispered behind her fan to one of the organizers, that she thought the tap dancer was rubbish and needed sacking immediately.

Hugo and Allana had promised Lady Brough that they would go straight to the kitchens to check that the food preparations were on schedule. Hugo for the Earthan food and Allana for the Elvish food. Ding Ling suggested to Helena that she continue to mingle with the guests which she loved to do, and he would accompany Allana and Hugo, if nothing else than to get out of the public eye to rest his now sore feet, that he was sure were developing blisters.

As the three of them were approaching the entrance to the kitchens, Hugo noticed that Ding Ling was developing an unusual gait, and with each step he was pulling faces and grimacing.

"Whatever is the matter with you Dingy?" asked Hugo

"Ah, so sorry Master," replied Ding Ling, "Shoes causing me plenty of trouble, blisters bigger than boiled eggs, nothing that comfy plasters won't cure. I go very soon and sort them out."

No sooner had Ding Ling replied to Hugo, than from across the noisy din of the kitchens came a voice that Hugo and Ding Ling recognized immediately and which stopped both of them in their tracks.

"You're not trying to ignore me now are you lover boy?"

Hugo and Ding Ling snapped around. They both looked at each other and simultaneously said "Charlie Andover." They both knew that from this moment on, where this night would go, would be anybody's guess.

Charlie Andover. Thirty-two years of age. Stable manageress of the extensive horse stables at Brough Manor. One of the most vivacious women to have walked the Earthan dimension. There was just something about her that had men going weak at their knees. Hugo and Ding Ling both slowly turned to see Charlie waving at them from across the busy kitchen. It was Charlie that had released Hugo from his seventeen-year-old virgin status, to that of a man, in one fell swoop one steamy evening in the hayloft behind the stables.

Hugo always had a 'thing' for Charlie, and why not? Her natural red hair, ample bosom and pert rear were the stuff of Hugo's wet dreams. He fantasized about her constantly; she was always awash with the most alluring perfume imaginable, garish red lipstick and her blouse always unbuttoned a little too far down, so Hugo's eyes would invariably follow the line down to feast on her bosom.

Ding Ling had a mini panic attack. He said to himself that Confucius would say that 'if buttocks start to clench, then very bad news was on the horizon.' First and foremost in Ding Ling's thoughts was him remembering telling Allana some time ago that it was Charlie Andover who had orchestrated Hugo's first passionate sexual fling, at the end of which he fell head over heels in love with her. Luckily, she saw it for what it was, a handsome young teenager, and yes, she took advantage of the fact he had the hots for her, knowing it would help him move on as well. That evening ended well for both of them, and Hugo, an evening never to forget.

It was the 'forgetting' part of all this that Ding Ling was praying for as far as Allana went. He hadn't told Hugo at the time that he had mentioned Charlie was Hugo's first proper sexual encounter to Allana, which he was now regretting with a passion.

It was too late. Up to this point, Allana was quizzically looking at Charlie, until that is, Charlie sauntered seductively up to Hugo, put her hand behind his head, pulled it down and kissed him on his right cheek. The thick red lipstick left its mark on his cheek, which she slowly started to wipe away as she said, "I wondered when I would bump into you, darling."

She stepped back a little, and now we notice her red hair coiffed up into a French pleat, with a strand or two tumbling down seductively across the right-hand side of her cheek, with a beautiful diamond comb buried into the fold of the pleat. She wore an off-the-shoulder emerald green taffeta dress, which followed her womanly contours to her small waist, then the bottom half of the dress ballooning out. She had dainty feet, and we could catch the occasional hint of green diamond encrusted Fred Wang custom-made shoes.

Hugo was spluttering; it had completely taken him off guard. This amused Charlie who threw her head back and laughed out loud. As she did this, Hugo had a waft of the glorious scent that Charlie always wore, the vintage *Diorella* by Christian Dior, and in throwing her head back, revealing the smooth white skin of her neck. How he didn't throw himself onto her at that point and kiss that neck he would never know, but he did control himself, managed to take a shaky step back and said: "Well fancy seeing you Charlie."

For a moment or two, Charlie stared at Hugo with raised

eyebrows, then she said, "Is that it, Hugo? Seriously?" Charlie laughed again, "Surely you have something more intimate you would like to say to me?"

By now, in quick succession, Allana was cottoning on fast to who this woman was. She could see the effect she was having on Hugo. She looked, with an open mouth at Hugo, then turned slowly to look at Charlie. Her eyes by now had narrowed and had changed from their pinky color whenever she was usually around Hugo, to an angry bubbling red.

Charlie caught the stare and stared back at Allana almost defiantly, as if she knew she was being antagonizing, and then said to Hugo, "Darling, this must be your little Elf friend, I have heard so much about, and you haven't introduced me."

Ding Ling could see what was happening. To him it was like setting a match to the wick of some Chinese firecrackers. What was going to happen was inevitable, loud and have people running for cover.

"Oh yes, of course, sorry," said Hugo. And in a very nervous animated way Hugo said, "Allana, this is Charlie Andover, manageress of the stables here at Brough Manor. Charlie, this is Allana Yana-Ash from Laniakeea."

Poor Ding Ling, he had heard that an ostrich, when under threat, tries to bury its head in the sand to hide, and this is just what he wanted to do now. In his mind, Ding Ling was imploring Hugo to get his thoughts together and see that Charlie was teasing him, and started to think of diversions before the 'thunder' came.

Charlie though, then turned to Allana and said, "I hear that riding our horses is a challenge for you? Why don't you come to the stables one day? I could put you in the kindergarten class with the other four to six-year-olds. They start off on donkeys, might be just the thing to help get you riding like an adult?"

Ding Ling was frantically trying to move them away from each other. "Erm? Oh, look Master, time flying very fast, you need to meet guests. NOW!"

"Oh, be quiet you little man," said Charlie with the hint of a frown on her forehead. She was enjoying this so much now; she didn't want it to end. "In fact, you should come along with Allana, Ding Ling, I hear you haven't progressed to a horse as yet, and are still on that boneshaker of a donkey?"

"We could take one of the smaller ponies and pack up the saddle underneath with two pillows. That should give you a little more stature?"

Ding Ling was sweating profusely now, stretching his collar that he felt was trying to strangle him, and his shoes were agonizing, so he rapidly started shifting his weight from foot to foot.

Charlie noticed his prancing up and down and around with his feet and said, "Whatever is the matter, little man? Do you need to go to the toilet? If you do go, will you? You don't need my permission."

If those present could see Allana's aura, it would have been all over the place. She began to dislike this Earthan woman. Who did she think she was? Everything that she had been told about Charlie Andover by Ding Ling came back to her in precise detail. She really didn't like this woman one iota now.

"Oh master," said Ding Ling, tugging frantically on Hugo's sleeve, "remember you told me that you wanted to show Allana your, your? yes! your army 'medal collection? so we need to go NOW, please?"

This snapped Hugo out of the reverie he was in, and he blurted out, "Yes of course, sorry Charlie, have to go. I did promise Allana I would show her my collection."

This couldn't get any more comical. Allana standing there mouthing the words 'medal collection?' not having a clue what Hugo was talking about, with Ding Ling tugging furiously on Hugo's sleeve and looking as white as a sheet. Hugo himself looking partly concussed. In fact, it was Charlie who slowly put her hands on her waist, and said to them all, "Ok Hugo, you and Ding Ling toddle off and show Allana your medals.

"I don't need to come of course, I have already seen your 'medals' first hand, haven't I Hugo darling?" And with a flourish, she turned on her heels and was looking for another unsuspecting victim to annoy and tease.

Allana was discovering and understanding the subtle human use of sexual innuendos very quickly, and knew exactly what Charlie was getting at. For a moment, Hugo just stood there and rolled his eyes up to the ceiling. Ding Ling took out a handkerchief from his pocket, was mopping his brow and was looking like he had single-handily managed to prevent World War Four.

What was very unnerving, and to which Hugo and Ding Ling were completely oblivious, was the way Allana was looking intently at Hugo, knowing that when the time was right, she was going to cross- examine him on every sordid detail of his liaison with Charlie Andover, and he had better get all his facts right. Everything that had been passed onto her by Ding Ling, every minute detail was buried in her memory, ready for such a time as she would need it, which would be sooner, rather than later.

Allana didn't like Charlie Andover. The way she was able to manipulate Hugo, the way she aggressively took control of the conversation and especially her rudeness. What she just couldn't understand was, what did he see in her? Surely her perfume alone was enough to make anyone, human or Elf, gag?

So, a little later than expected, Hugo had dusted himself down, and he and Allana sauntered into the marquee proper as if nothing had happened. As they went in, Hugo caught Kayon's eyes (he was acting as master of ceremonies and was introducing all the guests). He spotted Hugo and started tapping his watch, meaning to enquire where the hell he had he been.

Allana and Hugo made their way over to Kayon. Hugo simply whispered the name 'Charlie Andover' into Kayon's ear. Kayon just rolled his eyes upwards and nodded. He understood completely.

Ding Ling, on the other hand, couldn't stand the awkward pinching of his black military boots anymore and managed to get one of the kitchen chefs to swap shoes with him. Trouble was, this particular chef's shoes were multicolored trainers, but to Ding Ling they felt like the most comfortable slippers he had ever worn

Ding Ling also managed to undo the brass button on the collar of his dress shirt, so at least he could breathe again. Luckily, he met up with Helena who wanted to know what had happened and where had he been. "I explain later Helena," said Ding Ling.

As for Queen Haruntha, she was enjoying the whole spectacle and was so pleased to see how well the Earthans and the Laniakeeans were integrating and making friendships. For the first time since the slice had been discovered and the Earthan dimension was revealed, she felt pleased that both species were getting on so well together.

As the queen was thinking this, she was casting her eye across the dance floor in awe at how complicated the

Earthan custom of dancing appeared to be. She spotted Allana and Hugo, just as the music changed to a slow dance, and Hugo was showing Allana how it was to be performed, by bringing their bodies close together.

It reminded the queen to re-visit how Allana and Hugo were coping with not letting their emotions run away with them. She was aware of course she had given permission for Allana to perform the Sootalanash with Hugo, hoping that would satisfy any desires they had for each other. With what she was observing now on the darkened dance floor, with Hugo and Allana inseparable and gazing into each other's eyes, she began to think the Sootalanash may have had the opposite effect.

Since time immemorial, throughout Laniakeea, there had always been the unspoken rule stating that for the betterment of general progress, that inter-species relationships should be deterred wherever possible.

She made a mental note to have a word about it all with Allana when they were both back in Laniakeea.

Kroleeth Lizards

Terrifying lizard-type creatures. Are able to communicate using a basic form of telepathy. Their tail is also a weapon that can detach and embed itself into its enemies. A new tail grows back almost instantly)

CHAPTER 17

A Difficult Decision

(A humble Elf will compete in Granthanda thoughtfully and with care, so as not to injure others.)

A week had passed by since the grand ball at Brough Manor. It had been an enormous success. More than anything an element of trust was developing between the Earthans and the Laniakeeans.

Already the instigation of the ley line network system was well under way. The Laniakeean engineers and scientists had been working hard seeking out the network of ley lines that were buried beneath the earth across the United European Landmass (UEL), in particular, the main spiritual and Earth electrical conduits, from which the circles would be formed.

The whole of the United England States (UES) had finally been signed off by the Elf in charge of the project. Twenty-one circles had been formed, and after a period of teething problems - mainly by the Earthan's who were trying to use them - it all seemed to be working according to plan. There was a circle at Brough Manor, the headquarters of the UEL and of course, close to the slice.

Earthan's in their droves were queuing up to try them, and for this purpose, the Laniakeeans had built a practice ley line section, which was comprised of two circles, one mile apart. Travel was almost instantaneous since the distance traveled was so short, but was very helpful in demonstrating to the Earthan's how to stand, or kneel initially, to take deep breaths, not to move and the consequences if they did, which wouldn't be very pleasant, and so on. There were regular sessions set up to instruct the Earthan's how to use them.

As on Laniakeea, the greater the distance traveled, the longer it took, and a side effect of that, for Earthans only, was a feeling of nauseousness. So back in the Earthan dimension, for those feeling confidant of using circles to travel greater distances, there were hints on how to prevent the nauseousness, either using medication, applied via the HC units just behind the ear or by using deep breathing techniques. Small phials of the blue Voovo liquid were starting to be distributed to all those wanting to use the ley lines, and of course, Voovo had many other health benefits in addition to helping feelings of nauseousness.

There were arrows, of various colors, fixed into the circles, to show the destination choices, and how long the journey would take. Besides the Laniakeean engineers constructing the circles, clearing out old energy lines and replacing them with new vibrant lines, there had to be a series of commands that needed to be spoken once a person was on the circle, to transport them to their destination.

This had been a little more difficult. The magical incantations were all in Laniakeea's Elvish dialect, and had to be translated into English, and this caused some problems. For example, either nothing would happen or a completely different destination would be reached, or even worse, as happened in one case, someone ended up in the black gaseous ether between dimensions. So, it was decided that new magical incantations would be created, that could be spoken in English.

Maps were sent to all HC's of every Earthan detailing all numbered circles so far constructed, the destinations that each circle would transport to and the English incantation for each destination. These could be easily be accessed at any time, and with a simple command, a holographic 3D version of the map would appear just in front of someone, at eye line level. They were vaguely similar in looks in some ways to the old London Underground maps in combination with an old style sat nav.

The correct pronunciation of a specific destination incantation was of course very important, so to help with this, a recorded voice pronouncing the incantation could be accessed, again via the HC. Sometimes the incantation simply could not be directly translated from the Elvish to English, so there were a few cases where the incantation would be a mix of English and Elvish. For example, the destination of Stonehenge (the most powerful ley line conduit on Earth) was 'Panath ston raylo henge sonam'.

Finally, at every ley line circle there would be a guide to help if anyone was still unsure how to use them. These guides, it was decided, would be available for three months from the commissioning of a circle.

Allana had been summoned to the palace to meet with the queen. She wasn't told what the meeting was about though, so her mind was racing ahead when she stepped into the grand hall of the palace and was making her way to the queen on her throne.

She noticed that Elfistra and Mandaz were to one side. As Allana approached, she bowed down low, out of respect for her queen.

Since no Earthan's were present, all communication would automatically be conducted telepathically, and Allana knew Elfistra and Mandaz would be listening in, as was their right.

'Hello Allana', said the queen, 'Thank you for coming. Allana, I just wanted to find out how your relationship with Hugo was coming along since we last discussed this. I did permit you to conduct the Sootalanash, to exchange your feelings, but essentially was hoping it would put to rest any further thoughts of entering into a deeper relationship.'

'My Queen', replied Allana, 'thank you for permission to conduct the Sootalanash. It was everything I had wanted it to be, and more, and I believe it was a wonderful experience for Hugo as well. As to whether that satisfied our desires for each other, and could have helped us go our separate ways, I am afraid that has not been the case.'

'Love', my queen,' continued Allana, 'I have discovered is a very potent powerful emotion, much stronger than I ever thought would be possible. I realize it is common to ourselves and the Earthan's, and even though I know Hugo and I are completely different species, we have fallen in love with each other. Unequivocally.'

The queen, for a moment just stared at Allana, then Elfistra came in with 'You realize we have our rule Allana, that forbids relationships between different species. That rule is there for a number of reasons, and I am quite sure you know what they are but I wish to reiterate them.'

'At the formation time of Laniakeea by the Sola Tree,' Elfistra continued, 'It was strongly felt, by the Sola Continuum, that any fraternization between species would dilute the Laniakeean ethos that stood for progress, truth and honesty.' Elfistra continued by saying, 'The elimination of any other inferior element that could disrupt this ethos would be paramount, and that included the fraternization with other species, whether they were more or less evolved than ourselves.'

All the while that Elfistra was saying this, Mandaz was nodding and agreeing with Elfistra. The queen was studying Allana's aura and body language, for any signs of an adverse reaction to what was being said.

The queen could see that Allana was feeling uncomfortable with what she was being told. It seems as if she and Hugo have entered into a deeper relationship, even though Allana was warned not to do so. The queen realized she needed to be very careful. She didn't want to alienate Allana. Allana was very special to the queen. Besides being an Elfanda (special one), a term given to a handful of Laniakeeans that had more expansive magical powers naturally, and which tied in with ancestral links to the Queen, Allana had been instrumental in forging essential links between the Earth and Laniakeean dimensions.

The knowledge she gained when she was a scientist and given the responsibility of studying the Earthan's and their language, has proved to be invaluable, in ensuring a basis of trust between the two dimensions.

'Well', said the Queen, 'We can put all this on one side for now Allana, because I am aware you are practicing hard for the Granthanda national championships which are only three days away. But please, make no mistake, however difficult it may be for you, and for Hugo, your relationship cannot develop any further. I don't want to be in a position of demanding that Hugo return permanently back to his Earthan dimension, and you not being permitted to cross over to see him.'

By now Allana's eyes were watering up - or should I say, 'bluing' up, since an Elve's tears are blue. She couldn't believe the queen was saying this, after all that Hugo has done so far to help Laniakeea. Even in the queen's heart, Hugo was already established as a trusted aide.

The queen herself was finding it very difficult to ask this of Allana. She knew only too well herself of the disruption and heartache of an affair she had with a handsome king who came from a dimension called Paniso, many millennia ago. Even though the Panisoans themselves were half Elvish, King Brentan and Queen Haruntha were dissuaded from continuing their relationship by the Sola Continuum.

Usually the Sola Continuum would not interfere, but in this case, an example had to be made of the king and queen, being the heads of their respective dimensions. It broke both their hearts. Allana did not know of this, since all this happened between the queen and King Brent before Allana was born. Even so, the queen was struggling with the decision and felt the turmoil Allana must be going through.

Even Mandaz, who full well knows the power of love, had to side with the law of the dimension and with the queen and Elfistra. Mandaz indicated he wanted to say something to Allana. This took all of them by surprise.

This was a very uncharacteristic Mandaz that said, with a complete feeling of tenderness in his voice, 'Allana, even I am capable of love' – he glanced at Elfistra who acknowledged his look – 'even though I know I am repulsive in many ways, but the rules are set for a reason for all our sakes, and especially for yours. Please, you must call off this relationship you have with Hugo Brough. We are servants to the Sola Continuum, and we have to abide by their rules.'

Allana stood very still for a few moments. She was in deep anguish. How could they demand this of her? She knew she would never abandon Hugo. The emotions in her were building up. Now she just wanted to run away and hide; to get away as far as possible from the queen, Elfistra and Mandaz.

Allana blurted out, as blue tears were now starting to stream down her cheeks, 'I'm sorry my queen, I love Hugo. I can't help it. He is part of my life, and always will be. Why am I being punished? It is not fair.' Her two hearts were pounding in her chest, so much so, she thought they could all hear them. She was furtively wiping the tears away, trying to cover up how upset she felt at this moment

Allana had never felt this way for anyone. At first, she tried to resist, but that was futile. The strength of the emotion took her by surprise. She would do anything for Hugo and just wanted to spend every single second with him, and she was convinced he would want the same.

After the Sootalanash, she knew the ceremony, no matter how beautiful, was not enough. She wanted more, much more. Hugo had unlocked a million years of primal feelings in her that had been made to lie dormant. She had already had an inkling of this in the way she felt when he held her close.

Even thinking about him, made her hearts quicken, and at the beginning she knew she had to resist for all the reasons that have already been explained, but this was so much more powerful, and now was beyond her control.

Allana said quietly, trying to control the sobs that were now running through her body, 'My queen. Please, may I have your permission to leave?'

Queen Haruntha let out a big sigh. 'Yes of course Allana. But before you go, I want you to know, I too have been in a similar situation to you, many millennia ago. I do know what you are going through, to have to say no to someone that should be a part of your life.'

'Your father, Kalama,' continued the queen, 'has been a tower of strength to me for over eighty years, and your mother's Kakalina and Kalea have the kindest hearts of any Elves I have known. And when you became a "special one," I promised all of them that I would always be here to protect you and nurture your best interests. Sometimes laws are passed by authorities much higher up than mine, and they are decreed for a purpose that can seem very unfair to those that have to adhere to them.'

'My heart goes out to you Allana,' said the queen as she slowly walked to within a foot of Allana. She put her arms around her and hugged her as she whispered into her ear, *'I have asked for an audience with the Sola Continuum, to discuss your case. I can't promise anything. They may dismiss my audience right away once they know what the subject is, but I promise I will try my very best.'*

The queen kissed her index finger, then gently stroked it down Allana's right cheek, as is the Elvish custom, between an older Elf of high order and a younger one, when one formally wishes to show a sign of affection. She released Allana, who thanked her, then stepped back two paces, bowing. Allana then turned and ran out of the great hall.

Allana made her way back to her dwelling, and as she stepped off the circle, and was walking back, she broke down. Tears were flowing down her cheeks. She looked a sorry sight. The make-up across her eyes had run. As she was approaching her dwelling, in the doorway was Hounani, her legal female partner. She had her hand on her hips and a scowl on her face.

Allana hadn't seen her since she stormed off that evening a while ago when she was upset with Allana's affections for Hugo. Allana had tried to contact her a number of times, but the answer always came back that she didn't want to be disturbed, so Allana respected that

Allana tried to disguise the fact she was so upset as she

approached Hounani, who then noticed Allana, and the state she was in. Hounani's face suddenly changed from what it was to one of concern and she softened immediately and came running up to meet Allana. They stood to face each other, less than two feet away, and just looked at each other.

Hounani made the first move as she came up to Allana, held her head in her hands and sniffed the air around her face. Then they hugged. As they were hugging, Hounani said, *'I'm so sorry Allana. I have had time to think and reflect, and I was wrong to storm off like that. I love you of course, but selfishly wanted you all to myself. You know me, I'm hot-headed, and sometimes put actions before words, so I'm sorry.'*

They pulled away slightly, then Hounani was looking intently into Allana's face and said, *'Well that is me, but whatever is the matter? why are you so upset?'*

As they went inside, they also met up with Hanale, who was equally perturbed that Allana was upset. Allana started to tell them both everything that had happened at the meeting with the queen, Elfistra and Mandaz, and what they were demanding.

As all this was happening with Allana, Hugo was back at Brough Manor and had been in meetings all day at the UEL central offices, sorting out security issues, and bringing the council up to speed on how the integration was coming along between the Earthans and Laniakeeans. The council were very pleased with the improvements already that they had received from Laniakeea, especially with the intallation of working ley lines. They thanked Hugo for his continuing work with the Laniakeeans.

Hugo, Ding Ling, Kayon, Helena and Lady Brough were enjoying a hearty, rich roast dinner. It was all talk about the upcoming Granthanda grand championships. How Lady Brough was excited about traveling over to Laniakeea for the first time, and the fact she would be the guest of honor and be sitting next to the queen. She was in deep conversation with Helena as to what she should wear, and would her diamond tiara would be over the top, would the matching shoes, dress and handbag she had just bought, be formal enough and so on.

Kayon was discussing with Hugo and Ding Ling what technique he could use to draw back the bowstring of a competition bow successfully. How then Helena butted into their conversation urging Ding Ling to have a go with the bow, knowing full well the bow was taller than him, knowing it would end in failure and having Helena sniggering in the background, and so on.

One thing they were all oblivious to, especially Hugo, was wondering how Allana was feeling at this precise time, and the decision she had to think about that could alter both their lives drastically.

A month ago, Allana had given Hugo a magical amulet. It was only small and heart-shaped, fashioned out of precious metals and leather. It once belonged to one of Allana's grandmothers. The metals that were used to fashion the amulet were unique, and in this case, it meant that Hugo could speak to Allana, and vice versa, telepathically. Hugo's HC was never in a million years going to be able to secure a line of communication between the Earthan and Laniakeean dimensions, but Allana's amulet could. Not that he was necessarily worried, but he had been trying to reach her all day, and there was no response.

The last he heard was that she had been summoned to see the queen, but Allana at that time had no idea why, so out of curiosity he was trying to find out what it was all about. And since that last communication, while she was on her way to see the queen, there had been no response since.

Nope, he wasn't worried – or at least he was trying to convince himself of this - it was just curiosity. He would try one last time though, if for nothing else than to understand the details of the itinerary that had been put together for their arrival in Laniakeea tomorrow morning, ready for the grand championships the following day. They were to be put up, Hugo understood, as guests of the queen, in a palatial dwelling to one side of the queen's magic walled garden.

Hugo excused himself from the dinner table and decided to try to call Allana just one more time before retiring. He held the amulet in his right hand, closed his eyes and repeated the incantation to open up the telepathic communication between himself and Allana. '**Raltoo leyno pandan eso.**' His mind was blank, so he tried again, and this time it was answered. But it wasn't Allana. Someone else's thoughts that came flooding into Hugo's head. '**Hello Hugo. It is Hounani here, Allana's partner. I picked up your telepathic messages to Allana's amulet. I wouldn't normally do this, but she has been very upset and at the moment is sleeping. I don't think I can tell you why Allana has been so distraught, but I am sure she would prefer to tell you herself. Please don't worry too much, she is feeling a little better, and I am sure she will contact you first thing in the morning.**'

This all took Hugo by surprise. For a few moments, he didn't know how to respond. He had only met Hounani briefly, and she was very upset at the time and ran off. It was only later that Allana had explained to Hugo what had happened.

'**Oh right,**' thought Hugo, '**Erm, I understand, I think. More than anything I was just wondering about the itinerary for tomorrow, timings and so on, since myself and my family have been invited to the Granthanda Championships.**'

'**Yes Hugo,**' said Hounani, '**If you can all arrange to meet myself and Hanale at the circle on the other side of the slice at nine o'clock your time, that would be good, and no doubt Allana will be with us as well, and I am sure she will explain everything to you. May I take this opportunity to apologize for how I acted *when we met briefly a few months ago?'*

'Of course, Hounani, continued Hugo, *'We will see you tomorrow at nine in the morning, thank you.'*

Hugo let go of the amulet, and tried to make sense of what Hounani had told him. Not the meeting arrangements, they were simple enough, but what was going on with Allana? Why had she not contacted him about it? What on Earth could it be about? Questions were firing in his head one after another. At least she wasn't injured or anything like that. Well, he would bide his time. He was sure all would be revealed tomorrow.

Hugo then joined everyone and informed them that the arrangements were to meet tomorrow on the other side of the slice at nine in the morning. He didn't mention anything to do with Allana, that was private to him.

By now everyone had finished and all made their way to organize and pack, after which they all retired early.

The next day, it was a cold misty morning at Brough Manor. All had a mini breakfast and met at the front of Brough manor for half past eight. Hugo had managed to second some motorized transport in his capacity as security chief for the UEL and the whole group were transported to the slice.

Once in position, they all walked through the slice and arrived in Laniakeea. Sure enough, there were the two obligatory Laniakeean guards, but also Hounani, Hanale, and to Hugo's relief, Allana. They were all smiling and came up to introduce themselves to anyone that hadn't met them already.

Hugo at once went straight to Allana, who smiled at him and whispered to him not to worry; she would explain everything later. With that, they all transported to the queen's ley line circle, and from there to the queen's walled garden dwelling. While everyone was unpacking, Hounani and Hanale were answering questions about everything to do about Laniakeea and the Gruthanda competition.

Allana took this opportunity to grab Hugo and disappear to a little dwelling that was situated on the edge of the queen's forest on the other side of the walled garden.

Allana sat Hugo down, held his hands and told him of all that had happened with her meeting with the queen, Elfistra and Mandaz. She also talked about the surprise she had at seeing Hounani again after so long, how she had tried to contact her, but now she was back and fully understood Allana's feelings for Hugo, and wanted to help in any way she could.

Hugo took all this onboard. Then said, "So I guess we now wait for the outcome of the meeting between your Queen and the Sola Continuum?"

Allana was quiet for a moment. Searching for how she could say what she felt she had to say next. "Hugo, this is all causing so many problems and unease not just for me, but for you as well. Do you really love me enough to stay with me? And weather this through to the end?"

Hugo turned to Allana, gripped her hands tightly and said, "Allana, I love you with a passion I never knew existed. I honestly couldn't imagine life without you. Nothing will drag me away from you, nothing."

"Then we have to wait Hugo. It may be that the Sola Continuum may want to see us as well. I know though that my Queen will be doing her very best to come up with something that means we can be together. The Queen normally gets what she wants, not every time, but she can be very persuasive. We have just to wait. But Hugo, if she says the decision is made so we can't see each other again, for me, it would be devastating. I don't know what I would do. I feel I would disobey them. What could they do?"

"I know," said Hugo, "I am always one to wait and see what a result is before making a decision, but like you, I would refuse to take on board a decision that was designed to keep us apart."

"I'm glad you feel the same way Hugo, so now we will put it to the back of our minds. I need to clear my head and prepare myself for the Gruthanda competition. Once we have had some refreshments, I will explain the rules to everyone, so hopefully, it will make their spectator experience so much more enjoyable."

"I have even organized," said Allana, "for you all to meet my two assistants, Zenthan and Vashtal. I have very carefully selected them. Their magic, when it comes to maneuvering the arrows, works so well together, so much so, I do believe we have a good chance of winning again this year as well. Competition is always very high though."

"Well," said Hugo, "I am sure you will win again Allana. And know I will support you all the way, as will the rest of my family."

Allana suddenly felt so much better now, knowing Hugo was behind her all the way, and the excitement of the competition was making her feel excited. Tomorrow would be a day to hone her skills, make sure her ancestral bow has been properly prepared and that she has her pep talk with Zenthan and Vashtal. She had a good feeling about the competition. She came closer still to Hugo. They hugged closely then made their way back to the queen's dwelling.

The Lighting of the Flame Flowers
(A little magic is applied to the small insects that live in the Shantay-Nay-Sal flowers, causing them to glow gently, providing light outside in the evenings)

CHAPTER 18

And The Winner Is…

(An unconditional gift, be it love or materialistic, is the most precious of gifts.)

The next morning was clear and bright. Allana had already been up two hours before everyone had stirred. She was practicing her skills and each part of the drawing of the bowstring. As a whole, it was also very much a meditative spiritual process. It wasn't just her arms that drew that string back; it was her whole body and mind.

Tomorrow at one pm Earth time, the competition would begin. Usually it would commence three hours earlier, but the constellations and time of the Elvish year meant that at ten am tomorrow morning, the planet Uranus would pass by quite closely. That wasn't a problem in itself, but the proximity of the planet could cause a few minor disruptions. Being one of the coldest planets, the temperature for the three hours over Laniakeea, would plummet, and make it quite uncomfortably chilly.

There is also the atmosphere of Uranus, which is composed of hydrogen, helium and methane, which again, because of its proximity, would make the air on Laniakeea a little too flammable. And finally, there is the question of its brightest ring, Epsilon, and the planet itself, a huge distraction, not just to the competitors involved in the competition, but also the one hundred and ninety-five thousand spectators that would cram into the 'bowl' of the competition grounds.

Hence the reason, for safety and many others, it was easier to re-schedule the start time. For now, though, it was time to practice. Already everyone staying in the queen's dwelling had had a light breakfast and made their way out to the gardens in front of the dwelling to watch Allana, Zenthan and Vashtal. The group sat on wood benches, covered in thick scented purple moss and watched in awe as Allana went through the process of attaching the arrow, drawing the bowstring back, and the meditative process of the whole movement, which continued after the arrow left the bowstring.

Anyone would think the group was watching a fireworks display, the 'Ah's' and 'Oh's' as they watched with fascination just how far up in the air the Skaeloth flew, and then it's magical manipulation by Zenthan and Vashtal, who appeared to be doing a balletic dance.

The practice continued for ten minutes, and then they decided to rest. Allana took the time to explain the rules, and what the referee and his assistants would be wearing. She explained that they had permission to levitate to twenty meters above the ceiling height that the Skaeloths would need to reach.

There was a lower limit and a higher limit where the competitors had to place their Skaeloths. If it were too low or too high, they would be allowed two more attempts, and if they were not able to achieve this, they would be harshly disqualified.

Allana showed everyone the Lelurar abrasive string they would be using. Allana could not unwind it, because it had already been scrutinized and seals placed around it that could not to be broken until the time of the competition. In any case, very thick protective gloves would need to be used, the abrasive qualities of the Lelurar were very keen, and could quite easily sever a finger.

Allana pointed out the green powdered crystals that lined the Lelurar that would puff out in an explosion of green smoke if it was running against another competitor's Lelurar.

She also explained the basic game play for the benefit of Lady Brough, Kayon and Helena. "One end of the Lelurar here is attached carefully to the end of the Skaeloth. When I then loose the arrow into the air it pulls up the Lelurar."

"The other end is fixed to this machine here," continued Allana, "That is spring loaded and allows a movement of the arrow to move up or down or side to side during the competition. Once at the desired height, two small pieces on the sides of the Skaeloth fall away, as then two oblong banners, similar in many ways to the kites you use on Earth, but rounder, start to unfold and meet together. This in our case, is highly decorated and green, our team colours, so that the spectators and referees know who the Skaeloth belongs to."

"Essentially then, when all Skaeloths are in position, the referee blows a horn, and the competition begins. The two assistants of each team, using skill, timing, guile and using permitted mild magic, try to maneuver the Skaeloths across the sky, in an effort to sever an opposing team's Lelurar with their own."

"When this happens, the attacking team's Lelurar would rub against the opposing team's Lelurar and sever it. And- when this happens, because there are minute color capsules embedded in the Lelurar, a large puff of colored smoke is observed, and the team whose Lelurar has been severed has to retire.

"But it doesn't stop there," said Allana, "We are into the final phase of the competition. When three teams are left, there is a 'fire-off,' or Graldoth as we call it, and this is a series of tasks, that fall to the bowman or woman in the three remaining teams."

Allana continued, "Twelve semi-permeable balloon type spheres are formed and hover in the sky above the competitors' heads. There is a special referee who is responsible for this phase of the competition, and using mild magic he keeps them aloft and moving in the sky. He is called a Franzoth. Each of the spheres is filled with a colored gas, representative of the colors for the three remaining items left in the competition, four spheres for each of the three teams

"The designated archer has to loose an arrow, not a Skaeloth this time, into the air and try to pop their own spheres. If they pop someone else's, they are disqualified. But where it becomes more exciting, is that these spheres are constantly moving around, seemingly haphazardly, in between each other, so the skill and guile of the archer becomes very important. It doesn't even stop there, because each time a sphere is popped (in an explosion of colored dust representative of the family colors of the competitors) the remaining spheres start to speed up, so it all becomes more and more difficult. If, by accident a team pops another team's sphere, that team is disqualified, and the illegally popped sphere replaced.

"Eventually, the overall is the one that has popped their respective four spheres, before anyone else."

Allana also showed them the competition tunics they would be wearing, mainly green, with gold Elvish markings weaved into the chest plates. Their hair would also contain colored green and gold cloth. These were the Yana-Ash family colors. Finally, where they would compete from, they would erect a large green and gold banner, so that everyone would recognize the team.

At this point, she invited Kayon up to try to shoot a skaeloth in the air. As Kayon made his way to Allana, Hugo was nudging Ding Ling, and they both had smiles on their faces.

Allana showed Kayon what to do, how to draw the string back and so on, and passed on the six-foot tall practice bow and skaeloth to him. Before he took his position, he turned to Hugo and Ding Ling, and said to them, "Right, let me show you how a real man does this."

No matter how he strained, he couldn't seem to pull back the bowstring more than a foot and a half, which although more than Hugo, it still wasn't sufficient to fire the skaeloth high enough into the air. Instead, what happened was, as he was straining, he had the skaeloth pointing towards a large tree, thirty feet in front of him.

The string twanged as he inadvertently let his grip on the bow stock handle slip, the bowstring twanged out of the fingers of his right hand, resulting in the skaeloth shooting out of the stock of the bow, hitting the tree at great speed, and then ricocheting back and hitting him just to the side of his left eye.

Luckily, because it was a skaeloth, which doesn't have

an arrowhead but a tightly wrapped material end, he wasn't seriously injured. However, as the arrow itself is almost an inch in diameter and two and a half feet long and has quite a bit of weight to it, his eye was already beginning to swell and looking like a classic black eye.

Well, Ding Ling, Hugo, and Helena were apoplectic with laughter. It was only Allana and Lady Brough that seemed to be concerned about him and went to him immediately. Allana took some of the herbal ointment from her pocket and gently worked it in around his eye. She also gave him a small phial of Voovo, which worked wonders, and he was already feeling much better.

"Ok, ok you lot," said Kayon to Hugo, Ding Ling and Helena, "Fun's over. If I hadn't seen Allana pulling that bowstring back all the way, I would have said it was impossible to do. She must be damned strong."

Ding Ling chipped in with, "Ah but Kayon, remember famous saying which goes, 'A good archer is known not by his arrows but by his aim.'"

Kayon said, "And your point is, Dingy?

Ding Ling came straight back with, "Well, you aim for tree, and you hit it. Shame your eye got in way though. You must be very good archer Kayon."

Again, they all fell about laughing, except again for Allana who was smiling, out of respect for Kayon, and Lady Brough who was still fussing around Kayon, checking he hadn't hurt himself.

"It's ok," Kayon said to Lady Brough and Allana "Thank you. It's just my pride that's dented that's all."

However, Hugo wasn't going to let that be the end of it, with a big smile he turned to Allana, and said out loud so that Kayon could hear, "Allana, now Kayon's eye will be turning blue, purple and black, it won't clash with any of the other team colors will it?"

Again, laughter reverberated around the garden. Allana suggested this was a good time to all retire back to the dwelling for refreshments and a light lunch. On their way back, Allana said that after lunch, that she was arranging for them to meet a Barboski, since they already had been told that the chief referee would be riding one, as is customary, during the Granthanda competition, she thought it would be good for them all to experience these magical creatures face to face.

Sometime later in the afternoon, they all made their way to the edge of the queen's garden, and in front of them was the queen's forest, where the Barboski live. Allana explained to them all everything about the Barboski, that they were magical, could levitate generally to thirty feet above the ground, but considerably higher if needed; that they were related the Earthan unicorn, but of course didn't have wings or the horn on the forehead.

The Barboski also had dormant flaps on their shoulders that once many millennia ago would have contained wings, but as they have evolved, they don't need those physical attributes any more since they can now levitate at will. Finally, it was explained that they communicate using images that they will place in your head. To reply, think of a suitable image and the Barboski will pick it up.

Allana said to them all, "The queen has a Barboski called Halhaze, and certain members of our communities, through work they have done or because they are an Elfanda, ('special one') such as myself, are given permission to have our own Barboski."

A Barboski, when paired up with an Elf, is a bond for life, and the Barboski will always come to the aid of its bonded Elf. One other feature of the Barboski is that they are very clairvoyant, and also can transfer images into the heads of enemies that may attack Laniakeea.

They can completely disorientate the enemy, and over the millennia, have worked with or come to the aid of the Laniakeeans, which is why they hold a special place in the hearts of all Elves in this dimension.

"In fact," said Allana, "you are going to meet my Barboski now. We bonded around one hundred years ago. He is very special to me and he is called Julow. I have already sent out a telepathic 'Hello' to him, and he is making his way here now."

No sooner had Allana said this than at the edge of the forest, a movement caught everyone's eyes, and standing there, snorting, and pawing at the ground, was the most magnificent white Barboski. He slowly walked towards the group, and immediately everyone could feel they were in the presence of a magical animal with a higher intellect, far removed from the horses found in the Earthan dimension.

Everyone, except for Allana, had an image flash into their heads which merely said, '*Hello, I am Julow.*' Hugo was a little more aware of the Barboski because he had already met the queen's Barboski called Halhaze. The others though looked on in wonder and began to make their way towards him, to pat and stroke him.

Suddenly an image was flashed into Hugo's head. It was crystal clear. It was of a little girl. She had beautiful thick curly dark hair and Elvish make-up, and she had small Elvish ears. Her eyes were mesmerizing, large, round and blue, two different shades of blue, and she seemed to take two steps forward in Hugo's head and lifted her arms and smiled as if she wanted to be held.

Around her neck was an amulet that was almost an exact copy of the one that Allana had given to Hugo. Suddenly the image started to fade away. What did this mean? Who was the little girl? One thing he was sure about, was that he felt she was very much a part of his life, and the love and affection that was emanating from her to Hugo, was very real and powerful. At the very end of this replay, in came walking into the scene Allana, who was smiling. What did it all mean?

Then the images stopped for Hugo. The others in the group were still being communicated with, and Allana was telling them how to respond, with clear, pleasant thoughts. This interchange of images went on for five minutes then stopped. Julow walked up to Allana and nuzzled her neck. It was quite plain to see how much affection Julow and Allana had for each other.

Then Julow turned around walked, then trotted back to the forest, but was leaving the ground to approximately twenty feet in the air by the time he reached it, and with a snort and a flick of his long blonde flowing tail, was gone. Everybody was thanking Allana for introducing them all to Julow. So now they relaxed and talked about the itinerary for the competition tomorrow.

They all retired early, but not before Hounani, Allana and Hugo had a chance to clear the air. As the beautiful sunset shot the sky with mauves, pinks and orange colors, they sat under the canopy of a pergola bursting with large white flowers which the Elves call, **'Shantay-nay-sal,'** roughly translated as 'Lady-of-the-Night.' It had the most delicate of scents, which only started to release at night.

Even more mesmerizing was the fact that the stems, stamens and leaves had growing on their surfaces, minute types of insects that at night fluoresced, emitting a soft white gold light. There was no need for any other artificial lighting, they were bathed in this wonderful light, and with the added headiness of the scent, they all started to relax completely.

Hounani started it all off by apologizing to Hugo for her behavior the first time they met when she has stormed off. By now Hugo was realizing that honesty is the most important feature of the Laniakeeans. As Alana had told him a while ago now, what with reading auras, and sniffing the pheromones around an Elf, it would be next to impossible to lie convincingly.

However, more than that, they had found as they evolved that honesty can be very powerful. "Remember," Allana said to Hugo once, "we are not obsessed with money, such as you have in your dimension. We don't have or need money, we have advanced to the stage that everything we need we can provide, either naturally or magically, so the idea of being rich or poor doesn't come into our ethos, or way of thinking. We do have a social structure," said Allana, "In the sense our queen is at the top if you like, just as an ordinary Elf is at the bottom. But even then it doesn't work to the detriment of another, so that any Elf, no matter what their social standing in Elf society, can always seek an audience with the queen, and they can make joint decisions on many subjects that can affect life on Laniakeea."

"With a grand competition such as the Granthanda competition, then of course, the queen is respected and will be sitting in a private enclosure, but all the other one hundred and ninety-five thousand spectators, no matter what their status will all sit together. In other words, there are not some seats that are better than others.

"I understand the fundamentals of communism, as it used to be in your dimension, the idea of which is good, but money, politics and greediness put communism on an altogether different path. So, on Laniakeea, we have a form of communism, or better to call it community, which as you can see works well, when you remove the politics, power struggles and of course, most importantly of all, money. This all ties in with the Kralapal ceremony, for anyone that has committed a crime, and life on Laniakeea is as peaceful as it could possibly be."

Therefore, with this establishment of honesty, Hounani was very honest with Hugo, telling him what had upset her so much, and that she was hot-headed. She explained to Hugo that she was 'married' to Allana and Hanale, and she loved Allana very much and still did, but has come to realize, that Allana has her choices as well, and still loves her, but Allana's passionate deep love is for Hugo, and she now fully accepts this.

As she said this, Allana moved to her and hugged her closely, and Hugo was able to pick up her telepathic 'Thank you.'

Hounani was still looking different and dramatic compared to all the other Elf females Hugo had met. Still, the shock of bright red hair, the clothes that were unusual in the fact that they were not silk-like and flowing but a much heavier material, and the choice of materials almost deliberately chosen not to complement each other, did still attract his notice. It was somehow reminiscent of the 'punk' era fashion on the Earthan dimension.

Hounani smiled at Hugo, moved over to him and told him she hoped they would be close friends, and even joked with Allana, by saying if she ever got tired of being with Hugo, she wanted to have the first refusal. By now the atmosphere was convivial, and they laughed genuinely and happily.

So, it came them all to retire and be up early for the Grand Granthanda competition tomorrow - well, not too early. They would be able to experience the passing of Uranus, which should be a spectacle in itself for all those from the Earthan dimension.

In spite of not having to be up too early, they all were. They had their breakfasts and were already outside just before the skies had started to darken slightly heralding the passing of Uranus.

It took your breath away, the immense size of the planet, and trying to come to terms with the fact it was so very close. They had been warned not to light anything because the flammable gases of Uranus were starting to filter into the atmosphere of Laniakeea. It did become a little darker, and the air a lot chillier, so being advised to put on some extra clothing was advice to be heeded.

Uranus was a blue-green color, and none of the spectators could see a solid surface, but as Allana explained, the planet's atmosphere was very gaseous, which is why nothing substantial could be seen.

At half past twelve Earth time, they all made their way to the Nymlarii district, the home of the Granthanda competition grounds. They were all ushered into reserved seats that were set aside for them; they had already said their goodbyes to Allana and her team earlier on. Lady Brough was escorted to a separate enclosed seating that was set a little higher than those around. She was ushered into a rather grand chair made from wood and covered with the queen's livery of green, gold and red, but just to her side was a much more elaborate chair, and this is where the queen would sit.

One of the queen's guards informed Lady Brough that the queen would be along very shortly, and she was offered some refreshments.

Once the group took their seats, they then were able to take in the spectacle before them. It was awesome. The sheer scale took your breath away. It was hard to make out the other side of the vast cut away concave circle in front of them. From halfway up the bowl, thousands of seats had been carved, and by now it was close to full capacity of one hundred and ninety-five thousand spectators.

A rough estimate from the edge of the bowl to the bottom would be three hundred feet. The sides were not vertical but a shallow curve which descended then leveled out at the base, that was flat with the diameter being approximately half a mile. There were steps running up the sides at regular intervals, and all the seats were covered in a very lush purple moss, so the whole effect was quite colorful.

There were Elves, dressed in yellow garments that were handing out a choice of Voovo, or a vine sap drink, called Lalan, milked from the acres of vines that surrounded the bowl. It was a sweetish yellow looking liquid that tasted almost tropical, and also a hint of prunes, that Ding Ling had mentioned last time he visited here.

Ding Ling turned to Hanale and said, "Where are bathrooms?" Hanale replied, "Oh, there are none Dingy. We Elves have a slightly different system to your bodily functions, which means we can internally re-cycle our waste products, but not indefinitely of course. We could last up to three weeks before visiting a Raldan unit, as we call them, to expunge ourselves of the waste products of our metabolism.

"We have thought about your needs though," said Hanale, "and we have constructed a small shelter further back in the vines if you need to use it."

"Ah very kind Hanale," said Ding Ling, who then turned to Hugo, who was listening to this conversation and said, "Well master, as confucius says, 'Man who has constipation problems, will have to deal with backlog.'" They all laughed, except Hanale who didn't have a clue what constipation was, and Ding Ling believed it would take too long to try to explain to him.

Suddenly there was a fanfare of horns. The queen had arrived and had already sat in her seat next to Lady Brough. They both seemed to be enjoying each other's company, smiling and laughing together.

The queen stood up and announced the start of the competition. She welcomed her Earthan guests and wished all the competitors the very best of Elvish luck. Ding Ling couldn't understand how the queen's voice was so clear and loud enough, and how it was able to reach all the spectators. When he asked Hanale, all Hanale said was, "Magic Dingy, just a little magic."

The whole group also noticed that when the queen had finished her announcement, just as Earthans would show their appreciation by clapping and cheering, the Laniakeeans simply hummed, just one note, (probably a middle c), not too high and not too low, and indeed, if there were enough Elves, others would introduce harmonic notes, so that the air around them seemed to vibrate all the way through to your core. The Laniakeeans also brought the index finger of their right hand to their foreheads and moved the hand away, as a mark of respect for the queen.

Into view, levitating up from the bottom of the bowl, was the head referee who was sat on a beautiful Barboski. Suddenly, every one of the spectators, including the Earthans, had a bright image which said hello and welcome that came into their heads. All the spectators responded again by humming. The Barboski flicked its tail and turned three hundred and sixty degrees in a circle, bowing its head.

The referee looked resplendent in his yellow and orange strip tunic, with ribbons of the same color flowing out from his hair. He was joined by five side-helper referees, or Palraths, as they are known, and they stood out in their all yellow tunics. Again, they had long filaments of yellow cloth streaming from their hair. These didn't have a Barboski, but did have the queen's permission to use more advanced magic so they could move and levitate to any height.

Horns were being blown again, heralding this time, down on the bottom of the bowl, the competitors that were marching onto their designated competition spots.

Hanale could see the Earthans were peering a little, struggling to see and make out precisely who the teams were, so he turned to them all, and said, while reaching into a small bag, "I am so sorry, we Elves have very good eyesight. I realize it may be difficult for you to see as far as we can, so I have something here to help you see great distances with absolute clarity.

"All you do is place this in the middle of your forehead,"

continued Hanale. "Then when you blink your eyelids very quickly twice, you will see much more clearly and with greater magnification. We call them Mirrols."

And with that he passed along what looked like small mirrored circles the size of a thumb nail. He instructed each of them to place them onto the middle of their foreheads, and they seemed to adhere very well. As they blinked twice quickly, immediately, the clarity of their sight was improved by seventy to eighty percent, and the magnification was amazing. It seemed as if when they wanted to focus on something, it suddenly was magnified automatically. As soon as they quickly blinked twice again, their normal vision returned.

Hugo twisted around to spot his mother who was with the queen further up and to one side, and it was as if she was standing right in front of him. These are unbelievable, he thought. He turned to Hanale to ask him how they worked, but before Hanale said anything, Hugo just said. "Don't tell me, magic?" In response, Hanale just smiled and nodded.

They were all now looking down at the bottom, and all spotted Allana and her team. Their colors had been erected and Zentan and Vashtal were bringing with them the sealed box of scrutinized Lelurar and six skaeloth arrows.

All the competitors were ready, the bowmen or women of each team were in position, ready to loose their skaeloth's into the air. Each team's Lelurar had already been attached to the end of the skaeloths. Allana, they could quite clearly see, had her ancestral bow in her hands.

The competitors notched their respective skaeloths, which all now had their Lelurar's attached, onto the strings of their bows, awaiting the start of the competition, which was given by the Queen, who using some magic, created a dazzling display of what looked like fireworks high in the air above their heads.

Slowly, all the competitors seemed to move at once, very slowly, following the traditional meditative spiritual sequence of movements, and then, also as one, let loose the skaeloths vertically up into the air. Cumulatively, the sound of the Skaeloths zipping through the air cumulatively, sounded like jet engines. The spectators took in deep breaths as the skaeloths sped higher and higher, then started to slow down as they reached the official window at which they had to be aimed for, which happened to be just below eye level for Hugo and the rest of the Earthans.

The window was set at approximately four hundred feet from the base of the bowl where the competitors had loosed their Skaeloths. There was a leeway of three hundred and eighty to four hundred and twenty feet from the base.

The chief referee, or the Chansath as he is known, moving quickly around on his Barboski, blew on a horn to announce that all the Skaeloths had reached their desired target heights, and the team colours had deployed around each of the Skaeloths, and indeed they did look like brightly colored kites from Earth.

The competition was now set to begin. Allana's assistants began maneuvering their Skaeloth back and forth across the sky. And it seemed they had decided to attack the family team called Raldath, whose team colors were bright red and silver

Back and forth the Skaeloths flew, dragging the Lelurar behind them. Two or three times it seemed Allana's team's Lelurar would almost touch the Raldath's, but they had managed to maneuver away in the nick of time. But the fourth pass, manipulated by Zentan and Vashtal proved to be successful. There was a ripping sound, and a bright flash of green powder as their Lelurar severed the other team's Lelurar, and their Skaeloth fell to the ground.

It was the end of the competition for the Raldaths. By now, Allana's team had already focused on another team closing in on them from their right, the Vancalth, who teams colors comprised of cream and dark pink. These were one of the favorites to win.

This was a frustrating time for Allana. Her part of the competition is in two parts. There is the loosing up into the sky of the Skaeloth, and then, if her team ends up in the top three, there is the 'shoot off' to decide the overall winner. So this stage of the competition was out of her hands, but she had absolute faith in the expertise and skill of Zentan and

Vashtel who were among the best Gruthanda maneuverers on Laniakeea.

The competition was now progressing well, with clever dodging and maneuvering in ways too subtle for Hugo and the other Earthans to see. The excitement was growing as, one by one, various other competitors were loosing their arrows or another team's Lelurar was severing their own. Eventually three teams were left in the competition, one of which was the 'Yana-Ash' team. This signaled the end of the first phase of the competition.

The Earthan camp must have looked a little strange and sounded strange to the thousands of other spectators, with their standing, stamping, cheering and manic clapping of hands. Allana caught the movement and noise way down in the bottom of the bowl, looked up, smiled and waved her arms at all of them. There would be a break now for approximately twenty minutes, before the final phase of the competition began. Whatever happened now, Allana's team were sure to get a medal, but it was the first prize she and her team had their eyes on.

Thousands of little bowls containing Lalan, the vine sap liquid was being handed out to all the spectators, as a form of refreshment and re-hydration. The two suns were shining (one is considerably larger than the other, and a deep golden color, the other much lighter and greyer) and it was becoming quite warm and humid.

The final, and arguably the most challenging phase of the competition was to begin. The bowman or woman, from each of the three teams, will stand in the middle of the bowl. This time they are issued with real arrows. High up in the sky, overlooked by the chief referee, still on his Barboski, was a special referee called a Franzoth, whose particular skill it was to magically form the colored spheres and move them randomly across the sky. Using magic, he would form twelve colored spheres. The spheres were similar to balloons, and approximately two feet in diameter.

There were four spheres for the Yana-Ash team, which were green in color, and four spheres for each of the other two teams, the Vancalth's and the Greanan's, whose spheres were dark pink and gold, respectively.

Once the competition started, all the spheres would hover high up in the air at one level. The object was for each bowman or woman to loose their arrows to try to hit their own colored spheres. If they did, that sphere would explode in a cloud of colored powder, and the first to hit all of their spheres would be the overall winner.

It is not that simple of course, because the spheres were not static. They were magically made to move around each other, quite close, and at great speed. Suddenly, trying to hit the spheres seemed next to impossible. And to make matters even more challenging, the first bowman who happened to pop another competitor's sphere by mistake, was immediately disqualified and placed in last place.

The Franzoth, using his magic, started the spheres randomly moving around. The Chansath, then blew his horn, and the 'loose-off' began. Arrows were 'screaming' into the air - screaming because minute attachments to the sides of the arrows emitted a single musical note. Each team had their own musical note, and when all arrows were in the air, the musical notes harmonized and produced a very pleasant sound. This was all done for the spectators, who would hum to show their appreciation and touch their foreheads with the two fingers of the right hand.

By now the spheres would start moving around more quickly, in and around each other sphere, faster and faster. Allana was now moving very quickly, loosing off arrows left, right and center. It is very much skill-based, but the competitors are also allowed to use mild magic to anticipate where a particular sphere would be for when the arrow hit.

This was always going to be so very difficult to do, it was, if you like, 'multi-tasking' at the highest level. Imagine it, you may have loosed off ten arrows, and are maneuvering each one to be in a position to hit only your sphere.

There were plenty of near misses, naturally, because the last thing the competitors wanted to do was hit someone else's sphere. Suddenly, the referee's horn was blown, and the Greenans were in third place. Their last arrow had hit one of Allana's spheres. But another popped up almost immediately so the competition could continue. Of course, if a team managed to hit their own sphere, then that sphere would not be replaced.

It was now hotting up. The bowman from the Vancalth team, who was called Grandon, was an old adversary of Allana's, not only a good friend but an excellent bowman. Any balloons remaining belonging to the Greenans were dismissed, which left just Grandon and Allana's balloons remaining. Arrows were passing through the air and now popping the spheres until it appeared there were only two balloons left. The collective tension from the spectators was palpable. They were on the edge of their seats, willing their favorite team to win.

By now, the two remaining spheres were moving back and forth and around each other very quickly indeed. As a sphere was dismissed, the remaining spheres would speed up a little more. It was even difficult for the eye to follow the movement of the last two spheres, never mind trying to hit them, when suddenly, Grandon's arrow hit his last remaining sphere and it exploded in a cloud of dark pink dust.

So Grandon and his team, the Vancalths, were the overall winners, Allana's team came second, and the Greenans came third place. All the teams were hugging and congratulating each other, and shortly, there would be the presentation of prizes by Queen Haruntha.

Twenty minutes later, it was time for the presentation of prizes for the three winners. Each of the teams had arrived just in front of the queen's enclosure. The queen stood, and again, the loudness and clarity of her voice was incredible, Hugo glanced over to Hanale, who looked back and telepathically told him, *'It's a little of the queen's magic that allows this Hugo, as I explained to Dingy earlier on.'*

As we now know in Laniakeea, money doesn't exist. Material items don't count for a lot. But social structure does, which is always done with kindness and thoughtfulness. There are no 'poor' or 'rich' people. So, the third prize offered to the Greenan team was a holiday to the dimension of Linzadoth, which is the home of the Elf species called the Sraan. Linzadoth is to the Elves, a place of beauty, where visitors are pampered and looked after, and visitors are given the chance to generate a place of their choosing. A relaxing spa break if you like, in surroundings that you would never want to leave. Then we come to Allana's team, they also are offered a break to Lindazoth, but also a prized and ancient bow, fashioned by one of Laniakeea's most famous bowmakers, and is many millennia old and full of magical properties, was handed to Allana, who graciously accepted it from the queen.

Finally, we came to Grandon and the Vancalth team. Again, a visit to Lindazoth, a bow for Grandon, and also, permission to seek and bond with his own Barboski. To an

Elf this is an unbelievable prize. There are far fewer Barboski's on Laniakeea than there are Elves, so it is the queen, who has the power to offer a Barboski to an Elf. Also, Grandon was offered a little piece of land to call his own, and on which he could build a dwelling.

The atmosphere was amazing. Everyone was starting to make their way back to their dwellings. There was a little delay at the Grunthanda ground ley line circle, having to cope with so many thousands of spectators, so the queen, Lady Brough, Allana and the rest of the Earthan group held back for a while.

Hugo broke off to congratulate Allana, and they hugged, before then countless other Elves wanted to congratulate her as well, so Hugo left her to it and walked to the edge of the bowl to take in its vastness before they left.

As he was standing there, he felt a tugging at his left sleeve. He turned around, looked down and saw a small boy standing to the side of him. He was wearing unusually dirty disheveled clothes, and looked like he needed a good wash, with little scuffs of mud on his face, hands and feet. His eyes were unusually large and a bright turquoise blue, and he was looking intently up at Hugo.

Hugo could see this little boy wanted to communicate with him, but nothing was being said? The little boy reached across to hold Hugo's hand, and when he did, the following message appeared in his head, like the page of a book, 'Hello Earthan, I am called Kal. I am a Salatan, and are *what you would call an empath, in your dimension. I wanted to tell you that something special will happen to you in the future, but not too far in the future. It will change your life, and the life of Allana Yana-Ash as well. You must remember to love and support and nurture, and I don't just mean Allana. It will all become clear when the time is right.'*

And with that, the little boy turned and ran off. "Wait," shouted Hugo. "Don't go, tell me more?" However, the little boy had already disappeared into the vine forest which was very close to them. Hugo ran into the forest to see if he could spot him, but it was so thick, it was next to impossible.

Hugo turned back, and stood there with a quizzical look on his face, arms folded across his chest, deep in thought, and asked himself, *'What the hell was that all about?'*

The Sola Tree

(The spiritual and magical power on Laniakeea. Elvina the Wand is protected within its depths. The Sola Tree is part of the Sola Continuum that is responsible for the formation of dimensions)

CHAPTER 19

Kal The Empath

(Can kindness and love exist together? Yes. It's called 'Metta' or loving kindness)

It seems whether you are an Earthan or Elvish, having a celebration is part and parcel of life. And so, it was later in the evening following the Gruthanda competition, that there were lively celebrations.

Unlike the Earthans, it did not revolve around alcohol, or causing a nuisance, or necessarily damaging property of others. Nevertheless, they were generally very exciting affairs, with small magic games, a form of adult hide and seek, and of course variations on trying to hit objects with Skaeloth arrows.

They did drink copious amounts of Voovo, which if taken in excess rendered the drinker either over-excited or wanting to fall fast asleep, usually immediately wherever they were. So, by the end of an evening of celebrations, the odd body of an Elf would be lying prone on a floor, slumped over a tree seat or outside on the ground.

Others would either cover them to keep them warm or bring them into a shelter, whether they know them or not. One aspect of it all that Hugo and the others had not imagined is that the sense of humor of an Elf is almost the same as an Earthan. In all fairness, an Elf wouldn't find something amusing if they didn't understand the context, but if it were explained, they would laugh as much as any Earthan.

Small gifts were handed out and were much appreciated. Hugo and family were advised about this, so they came to the celebrations with their arms full of little gifts. "Not monetary gifts," advised Allana, "But gifts that are unusual, simple and honest."

"You have to help me here Allana," said Hugo, "I'm none the wiser as to knowing what you mean." So Allana spent the next hour, picking little gifts she thought would go down well, and most of them brought surprised looks on their faces of those from Earth."

Allana helped Hugo start to make a list, and then, very quickly Hugo cottoned on and added to the list himself. So, on that list you would find things like little lace pouches of fresh sweet-smelling lavender, photographs of Earthan Archers, even books about Robin Hood (these books could very easily be translated into Elvish), small train sets, puzzles of all sorts (Allana said any more of the old-fashioned Rubiks cubes Hugo had would go down a storm).

The problem with that, though, is that since the Elves have a much more advanced evolved brain, solving the Rubik's cube wouldn't be a problem. The fact that no other Elf would have anything similar, made it a wonderful gift anyway.

Lady Brough, accompanied by Queen Haruntha, was handing out small lace pouches of fresh English and French lavender she had been accumulating for a year. There were four drawers in a tall boy in her dressing room that were jam-packed with hundreds of lavender pouches and was pleased that at last, she had someone to hand them out to.

Hugo's gift to Allana, was an antique coloring book, full of illustrations, just called 'Cowboys and Indians.' It depicted the Indians in particular, who of course utilized bows and arrows. He was worried at first that since it was a children's coloring book, she may feel a little insulted. But this was not the case: she loved it.

She was particularly interested in the games the Indians played to hone their skills with the bow and arrow, and was particularly impressed with the Indians riding bareback at breakneck speed, then able to shoot an arrow at a moving target with an accuracy that she thought was unbelievable.

While she was quickly browsing through the book, Hugo slipped her another gift, which was a children's basic bow and arrow, and Great Chief's feather headdress. She was overwhelmed.

The Earthans in return received unusual sweets and nuts, some with mild psychedelic properties, as well as offers to ride on an Elf's Barboski. In all, it was a wonderful end-of-competition celebration.

As they were all making their way back to the queen's dwelling on the side of her walled garden, Hugo lagged behind a little to talk to Allana.

"Were you disappointed coming second?" said Hugo

"Not at all," said Allana, "Taking part and qualifying at the finals is always an achievement, and in any case, I was champion last year, and it was good to see my friend win this year."

"That's very magnanimous of you," said Hugo.

"Well," continued Allana, "we passed on many millennia ago from feelings of egotism, jealousy and so on. We do believe that taking part is more important than winning. That doesn't mean we are not competitive. We can be very competitive when we want to be, but don't get as upset as Earthans when we lose though. As a species, we don't have a problem with an ego."

They continued strolling slowly, just enjoying each other's company, when Hugo decided to tell Allana about the little boy, the empath Kal, and what he had said to Hugo.

Allana suddenly stopped and asked Hugo to repeat what

he had said. She then said, "We need to report this to the queen, Elfistra and Mandaz."

"Why?" asked Hugo.

"Hugo, do you know what an empath is?" said Allana.

"Well, yes: someone who takes on the feelings and emotions of another?"

Allana, turned to Hugo and smiled; "That is very basic Hugo. You have to remember that if it is an Elvish empath, or Salatan as we would call them, its powers would be unbelievable to you. The queen says that empaths are usually very vulnerable as well, and need to be protected. Evil Elves from other dimensions can abduct them, and use their powers against us. She is looking after five other empaths at the moment. Some are males and some females, and most of them are fairly young."

Allana went on to tell Hugo just what an Elvish empath can do. Mostly they will take on board anyone's emotions, but in addition, they will also act out those emotions as well. They are very knowledgeable, and use this knowledge to help people, unless misguided

It has always been known that they are non-violent, and can empathize with nature and animals as well.

"They can read thoughts and also memories. If there was something that happened to you that was upsetting, and it could have happened many years ago, the empath can relive the experience themselves, no matter how horrible. That is why they tend to be shy creatures. They can't take on everybody's emotions at the same time, which is why I found it surprising you said he spoke to you at the Gruthanda games."

"Well," said Hugo, "he did come up to me when it was all over I suppose, so there would have been far fewer people around."

"If you asked an empath what they like best," continued Allana, "they would tell you they want to be peacemakers. They hate violence and do what they can to stop it. They are also very clairvoyant, and can read memories of Elves, put them together, and correctly predict what will happen to them. In some dimensions, empaths are sought after for help and advice more than the resident sorcerer."

"As with all things in life," continued Allana, "there are some empaths that are stronger, more magical, more powerful even. And for a long time, there have been discussions among empaths that a special empath will come, that will not only be their savior, but Laniakeea's savior as well."

"Indeed, that is the opinion of the five empaths that my queen protects. They love my queen because she understands them well and provides for them and for an empath they have a relatively happy life."

"And these empaths the queen looks after," asked Hugo, "are they children as well?"

"Not all of them," said Allana, "Some are teenagers, which in our terms would be around seventy years old in

Earthan age. Sadly, most do not live to what we would call 'old age.'"

Allana also told Hugo that they are very creative and great story-tellers and used by trusted Elves to tell their children stories before bed. Even adult Elves are captivated by these stories which are normally amazing adventures. Empaths can't help being drawn to those of us that are suffering or have significant mental or physical problems. That is what being an empath is all about, and as a consequence they generally tend to be tired emotionally.

"So, they need lots of quiet time. Give an empath a pet, like my Jarjam, for example, and they will be so happy. Finally, thought has to be given to a gift you give an empath, because if that gift belonged to someone that had been involved in an emotional past, then the empath couldn't help but take those emotions on board."

Everyone met later in the queen's walled garden. The queen herself was there. Lady Brough had a wonderful time with the queen, and they both had hit it off together. Their thoughts and opinions on life in general were pretty much the same.

Hugo noticed Allana and the queen were in a deep telepathic conversation, and at one point, Allana looked intently at Hugo, then smiled at him.

'I wonder what that was all about?', thought Hugo, *'Maybe they were discussing the little boy empath?'*

He then noticed Allana walking towards him smiling, "So you can read minds, now can you?" laughed Allana.

"What do you mean?" said Hugo

"Yes," said Allana, "I was discussing Kal, to which end the queen wants to thank you for bringing it to her attention and has already instructed Elfistra to find him and bring him to her. She asks that you be present, as well as myself, since he mentioned me, and approached you. We have his name, and that he is a small boy. Elfistra won't have a problem finding him. Her magical powers are quite remarkable."

"I hope nothing happens to him," said Hugo, looking concerned.

"Of course not," said Allana, "It is simply to protect and nurture and look after him. Many times, empaths usually run away from their homes, because their own parents don't understand them or offer the special treatment they need and deserve."

It had been a very long day, for everyone, and most retired early. Next morning preparations were made for the Earthans to leave for their own dimension.

As Hugo drifted off to sleep, he was thinking of how far they had come, from that first evening when they stumbled on the slice, how Earth and Laniakeea met, to where they are now, becoming friends, sharing technologies and being able to adjust and live together in harmony. *'It was almost too good to be true,'* he thought as he drifted off to sleep.

He was woken early, by Allana gently shaking him.

"What time is it?" Hugo said groggily.

"Hugo please wake up," said Allana, "It is early I know, I'm sorry, but Kal has been found, and it seems just in time. The Morg'Umist were about to recruit him, but Elfistra made her presence known, which scared the Morg'Umist away, and he now has sanctuary with the queen, but he keeps asking for you. So, we must go. Hanale will explain to the others that you are just having a meeting with the queen, nothing serious, just a little chat, so that will leave us free to see what we can do to help and maybe have some answers to questions. I have prepared a little breakfast for you Hugo to eat on the way," said Allana.

Hugo smiled and said, "Ahh, you would make a good wife Allana."

Allana stopped in her tracks, looked at Hugo face on and asked him what he meant.

Hugo blushed a little and simply said, trying to laugh it off, by saying, "Oh it's just a common saying we have on Earth when a woman does something nice for a man, that's all, don't read anything into it at all."

Allana just looked at Hugo for a few moments, trying to read his expression. She knew what he said was making him embarrassed, but she didn't know why. Then almost as an afterthought, she thought to herself, *Does he want me to be his wife? Would being his wife be embarrassing for him?*

It was all getting to be a little complicated for Allana now, so she dropped it and off they went to the queen's palace, and in the background, Hugo just breathed a sigh of relief.

They both arrived at the queen's palace and started to make their way to the grand hall. They walked down to where they could just make out the queen. As they got nearer, they could see there was a small figure standing close to the queen. Hugo recognized him right away as being the little Elvish empath boy who approached at the end of the Gruthanda competition. They came to the queen and stopped. Allana showed her respects by bowing and so did Hugo.

They both looked at the boy, and he smiled back at Hugo and Allana. "This is Kal. He is going to be staying with us. We are going to look after him," said the queen. At this Kal turned his head, and looked up at the queen and smiled while he reached out for her hand to hold.

He looked considerably cleaner than when Hugo had seen him. He wore clean clothes and Elvish felt shoes, but nothing detracted from his huge round turquoise colored eyes. He appeared to tilt his head down a little and look up at you with those eyes. It was all very appealing.

He came over slowly to Hugo and said, *'Thank you for helping to rescue me. I am sorry I am unable to speak because of an accident; my vocal chords don't work properly. However, I can communicate telepathically. I hope you can understand me?'*

Hugo was coming to grips with communicating telepathically. Understanding was not a problem now, but sending a message back was still a little hit and miss, especially if it was required to send images as well to make everything more understandable.

The secret is that you have to clear your mind of any extraneous thoughts. This is very difficult for a human, although he did attend a Buddhist course once to be taught meditation, so through practicing a technique called 'the mindfulness of breathing' he has at least managed to slow down a constant stream of thoughts coming into his head. In fact, when he totally relaxed and meditated, he more or less was able to control one thought at a time coming into his head.

"You have a 'monkey mind,'" his Buddhist teachers told him, "always chattering away." But most do before using the discipline of meditation to control them, with thoughts 'chattering' all the time. So, when he was practicing with Allana, attempting to have a telepathic image conversation with her, a typical line of thought would read like this, '*I went out* (flash image of walking down a road) *this morning, and Jarjam* (images of cats and dogs) *came with me. I hugged a tree* (images of Earthan Canadian redwood trees) *and could hear what it wanted to say.*'

So now we come to Hugo's reply to Kal's question.

'*Yes,*' said Hugo, '*I can understand you very well. And your English* (images of schools) *is very good.*

But I am not so good yet at sending (images of a paper plane being thrown) **messages. So please bear** (images of brown bears) **with me.'**

The queen, Allana and now Kal were laughing at Hugo's attempt to send a clear telepathic image message. Hugo laughed as well, but knew he was being understood.

As always, Hugo's nose wrinkled when he could smell that Mandaz was somewhere close. And sure enough, from the shadows to the left of the queen came Elfistra and Mandaz with his Tazareth. At first, Kal, when he saw them, particularly when he spotted Mandaz, half hid behind the queen, then when they came closer and stopped he was looking at them intently.

He started to move away from the queen, and to everyone's surprise, started walking towards Mandaz. Kal didn't take his eyes off Mandaz as he was approaching him. He went up to him and put his hand on the top of Mandaz's deformed left hand.

As he did this, large tears were rolling down Kal's cheeks, and along his arm very small boils started to appear. Kal then looked up into Mandaz's eyes and said, **'I can feel your physical torment. It has been with you for a very long time. I'm so sorry. I can feel you love her so much'** – he pointed to Elfistra **'You won't believe me, but one day I can see your torment going, and you will be as you used to be, and he'** – he turned sideways and pointed at Hugo – **'will be the one who will help you.'**

Kal was displaying all the classic Elvish empath characteristics, but everyone was amazed with what Kal had come out with. It didn't make a lot of sense to Hugo and Allana, and you could see Elfistra and especially Mandaz were struggling to come to terms with it.

The moment Kal let go of Mandaz's hand, the boils that were starting to appear on Kal's arms also started to disappear. He made his way back to the side of the queen. They were all speechless.

The queen said, "This decision to help and protect him has to be a decision on both sides. In other words, it's what Kal wants as well. I have arranged for the other empaths to be brought here and have just heard they will arrive any minute. It will be good for Kal to meet the others. They are, in one sense, orphans, so not only will he begin to feel at home with the other empaths, but collectively their powers grow exponentially. The more empaths, the more they can do to help us and themselves.

"It has already been mentioned that there is an important feature with most of the empaths here in Laniakeea, and that is, they have the power to be excellent clairvoyants. There is always a 'leader,' in the sense that one empath will have the most significant powers, and it would be him or her that will organize the rest to create powerful clairvoyant readings."

"In my mind," continued the queen, "Kal is by far and

away, the most gifted empath I have ever come across, even when compared to empaths from other dimensions. Anyway, we will be able to tell right away when the others arrive."

Which they did, just as the queen finished speaking. In they came, a little characteristically a little cautious at first, which then turned to curiosity. They were already familiar with Elfistra and Mandaz, but not with Hugo and Allana. They were looking at them intently, then as one, they suddenly noticed Kal. He walked out to them, and stood there.

Without a word from anybody, each of the other empaths came forward and gently hugged Kal, then formed a circle. When it was formed they all simultaneously held out their hands and formed a hand-held circle, as if they knew they needed to.

Then again as one, they started to smile. Big smiles. Smiles that said they were comfortable with where they were, who they were and who they were with. The joy and happiness was emotionally powerful and palpable; it even carried across to Elfistra, Mandaz, the queen, Hugo and Allana, who found themselves smiling as well.

After a few minutes, they parted hands and started communicating telepathically. The queen had indicated that empaths normally like to speak verbally (It keeps their head thought free), but because Kal was unable to do so, they automatically spoke telepathically instead.

"Can you see what is happening?" whispered the queen

to Hugo and Allana, "See how all the others are collectively following Kal around? He is quite clearly the 'major' empath as we would call it. He will guide the group. However, don't be mistaken by assuming it's a kind of mind control. Far from it. Kal will be putting their interests before his own, their welfare before his, and even if one was not happy about something, Kal would do his best to help resolve the issue."

"In a very short space of time," continued the queen, "they will rely on Kal for everything, and he, because he is the 'major' empath, will look forward very much to the responsibility of doing just that."

"The reason for that," continued the queen, "is that they all know they understand their needs for each other. For example, times when they suddenly need to be alone, times when they want to connect with nature etc, and not having to explain themselves."

"One thing I did want to know," said Hugo. "I know Kal is a boy. He seems quite young. How old is he? He looks nine or ten to me."

The queen looked at Hugo and said, "Nine or ten, Hugo? Kal, although an empath is also Elvish, and as you know by now our lifespans are more than double an Earthan's lifespan. No, Kal is almost twenty-three, so not so much a boy as you would believe."

By now, while the empaths were playing, Elfistra and Mandaz, had been busy in telepathic communication. It seemed as if Mandaz had made an important decision about something and Elfistra was urging him to re-think. Quite clearly, though, Mandaz had made his mind up. They came over to join the queen, Hugo and Allana.

For the first time since Hugo and Mandaz had met, Mandaz said to Hugo (he had to communicate telepathically because his deformity meant it would be a struggle to speak verbally), *'You will be wondering, human, why the empath mentioned what he did, about myself and Elfistra. Secondly, where he mentions I will be as "normal" and you will be a part of it, I find impossible to put any rational explanation to. Now is the time to explain why I look like I do and my relationship to Elfistra.'*

'It would take far too long for me to explain why I have had to suffer what has been done to me for all these millennia, so I need your permission for Elfistra to place the events into your brain.'

'I believe our queen performed a similar procedure when she collected your past thoughts some time ago, over the incident with your father. Allana, it is just as important to you as well to know why, so I would like you to hold hands and the messages and thoughts will pass to both of you. So do you agree?'

"Yes, ok," said Hugo. Allana came up and held hands with Hugo. Elfistra came up as well, this time behind Hugo. She reached up and grasped his neck with her left hand and carefully placed the fingers of her right hand on the right-hand side of his face.

Immediately, Allana and Hugo were transported back to almost the beginning when the Sola Continuum informed Elfistra that they were introducing a male sorcerer as a companion, called Mandaz.

Very soon they fell in love and were inseparable. Allana and Hugo both took in a sharp intake of breath when they saw what Mandaz initially looked like. He was magnificent: powerfully built, and holding his Tazanath, which he still has now. No devastating deformity at all. He had arms and legs, whilst muscular and toned, were to extents normal, and the whole of his body was covered in scales in a manner similar to Elfistra, but the colors of his scales were constantly changing. He had red Elvish tattoos across his lips and a beautiful filigree silver round crown on his head that represented the leaves of a tree. The images that Elfistra was transferring into Hugo and Allana's head were so real, you could feel quite clearly that Mandaz was kind and compassionate.

Then into Hugo and Allana's heads came the terrible encounter with the Lazanath, and the cursing spell, which was directed towards Elfistra and would have killed her (because she was holding Elvina, which wasn't fully integrated into her body at that time). If it hadn't been for the fact that Mandaz threw himself in front of the spell, for which he received the full extent of its force, Elfistra would have been killed.

It didn't of course kill him, because he wasn't holding the wand, but created the deformed body Mandaz now possesses. However, what came across to Hugo and Allana was the depth of the passion and love that Mandaz had for Elfistra, and vice versa. This explained a lot to Hugo and Allana, as if the whole picture had been revealed, and suddenly they could understand.

As soon as the thoughts and images had started, they stopped as Elfistra took her hands off Hugo's neck and face and left Hugo and Allana almost dumbstruck and breathless. As Elfistra stepped back slowly, they could see she was distraught.

What they all then noticed is that all the empaths had come forward and surrounded them and started to place their hands on their backs. Immediately, feelings of calmness filtered through to them all. Some of the empath's eyes were filled with tears as they took on board the upset and suffering that Elfistra and particularly Mandaz had gone through.

After a few moments, everything seemed back to normal. Elfistra and Mandaz said their goodbyes and left quietly. Hugo and Allana turned to look at the queen, who also seemed visibly upset. She composed herself. She had been able to 'listen in' to the images and message that Elfistra had been transferring to Hugo and Allana, because she was able to, and had also been invited to by Elfistra.

The queen did know what had happened because she

had been there of course, but it still upset her whenever she was reminded of the events at the time. In particular, she would be upset by Elfistra's feelings for Mandaz, and the fact that he will be deformed till the end of time - or, that is, until Kal had mentioned that he may be changed? She too would like to know more about that.

Hugo said, "Well that explains lots of things to me, and I guess to you as well Allana?" Allana nodded. "Suddenly my attitude to them both has changed. What I can't understand is, why explain it now? In a way, they were forced to say something because of Kal."

"I agree with you Hugo," said the queen, "That has been my question to Mandaz ever since the incident, and he has always wanted to keep it a secret, until now. We will never know the reason why."

The empaths were back playing in their circle. Hugo and Allana went over to Kal, to see if they could get any more information on what he had told Hugo previously.

Kal happily broke off from the others when he noticed Allana and Hugo coming towards him. As they got closer to Kal, he held up his hand, smiled at them and said, *'You want more information, don't you? It is nice to see you both together. I don't want you to worry about things that are happening with you both now, you will be together for a long, long time.'*

Hugo and Allana looked at each other and raised their eyebrows. Almost unnoticed by everyone, Allana reached for

Hugo's hand and squeezed it gently.

'**Well thank you for that Kal, but I really wanted to ask you** (an image of lots of people talking at the same time in a room) **about what you said about something special** (image of a birthday cake with lit candles) **that would happen to me?**' By now the other empaths had formed a circle around Hugo, and could see him struggling to talk telepathically. Every time an unusual image came in the telepathic flow, all the empaths burst out laughing, and the more Hugo concentrated, the more they laughed, because his images became more and more bizarre!

'**And you also mentioned Allana** (an image of Allana with very few clothes on) **as being part of it all. But most of all about that "something" that I would have to nurture** (image of Hugo as a little boy, with little wellingtons and a plastic watering can, watering a little shoot in the ground that was growing through the soil) **and would change my life forever**' (an image of Hugo now looking like a bodybuilder, with huge muscles, and wearing some minuscule speedo swimming trunks).

By now, even Allana was doubled over laughing. So, Hugo just threw his hands in the air and asked Allana to take over from him. All the empaths came over to Hugo, and still laughing, all wanted to hold his hand.

So Allana asked the same questions of Kal, but much more clearly, and into their heads came Kal's message.

'**I can't say too much, because you may want to**

change your life because of it, but that will not happen. All I will say is, it will enrich your life, both of your lives, but it is something you will do together. It is a sort of destiny for you both, and you cannot change it, nor would you want to, when you discover what it is.'

'After a while, you will forget what I have told you, but will remember when it happens. Now please, can I not have any more questions? I'm tired and need to rest. Mandaz took a lot of energy from me. I like him a lot and predict his dreams will come true for him and Elfistra.'

Hugo and Allana thanked Kal, and then the queen, and started to make their way out, passing Elfistra and Mandaz. Hugo felt his manner towards them soften a little, and turned to Mandaz in particular instead and said, "I do hope what Kal is predicting will happen to you Mandaz." With that he smiled at Mandaz. Even though Mandaz is deformed, Hugo was sure he was pleased Hugo had said that and returned the smile, even though it made his face look a little more grotesque, and in his head, he heard, **'Thank you human for those words.'**

Approaching the queen's ley line circle, Hugo asked Allana if she was any nearer to understanding exactly what Kal meant? Allana simply shook her head. Hugo let out a big sigh and told her that he didn't either. "They tell me patience is a virtue," said Hugo, "so I guess we wait. Best to try to put it behind us."

The Melroon Trees
(These purple trees bear the popular Sensaas fruit. Within which are nuts that cause pleasant psychedelic effects)

CHAPTER 20

Lindazoth

(Stand up to the Kroleeth Lizard's. If you do, they will respect your courage.)

A week had passed since the Granthanda competitions. Hugo had been back in the Earthan dimension attending to security meetings as dictated by his role as head of security for the UEL. Many new parameters had to be set up, including security details referring to the Slice and Elf visitors from Laniakeea.

At the moment it was all very much trial and error, to implement security without being overbearing. The challenge was not to make it difficult for Laniakeeans from entering and leaving the Earthan dimension or vice versa, while still achieving a cumulative security system that would highlight any breaches by enemies coming into both the dimensions.

After a lot of hard work and cooperation on both sides,

the first basic rules had started to be implemented, and so far, it all appeared to be working well.

Part of Allana's prize as runner-up in the Granthanda competition, was a visit to the dimension of Lindazoth, home of the Sraan. Also, because both Hugo and Ding Ling had been very helpful and accommodating over the last few months in helping defeat the Mandaxon and the Lazanath, they too were given permits to visit the spa dimension of Lindazoth.

The numbers of beings given the chance to visit Lindazoth had to be very carefully monitored. Most dimensions are inhabited by sentient beings, not all Elves, of which there were trillions, and they had all heard of this beautiful paradise-like sanctuary and spa. Permits to visit were very few and far between, but Queen Haruntha was on excellent terms with the Sraan and their leader, a female called Queen Sanambal, and was allowed a certain number of permits to hand to those she particularly felt deserved a visit there.

So Allana, Hugo and Ding Ling, were preparing to visit Lindazoth for four days. They were leaving in the morning.

Lindazoth was a relatively small dimension, but the moment you stepped into it, you felt you had been sent to the most beautiful place imaginable. It was the only dimension known that used a particular form of magic that, without you realizing it, recreated whatever in your mind you would think of as the most welcome place ever. It wasn't holographic; it was more real than reality itself.

For example, as an Earthan, you could be stepping into a collection of Caribbean islands, with warm turquoise seawater, and small islands, covered in coconut trees. The sand would be fine and white and the consistency of castor sugar, the weather very pleasant.

Your mind and memories would be read so that there would be native islanders who would smile, cut down a coconut or two, chop off the top and present it to you with a straw, and you could relax and sip the coconut milk, sat with your back against a coconut tree and feel the warmth of the tree trunk that had been warmed by the sun, and a gentle sea breeze would gently flick your hair this way and that.

What was even more magical, is that whatever you wanted to do, or to be, it was instantly recreated for you. Usually an individual experience, it was also possible for two or more people to experience the same paradise. This did need a little prior planning in consultation with the Sraan, but mainly, it was entirely up to you what you experienced. The Sraan, it has been known for a long time, are a species of Elf that have the most advanced magical powers of any Elf species.

The moment you stepped into Lindazoth, you were in your world until it came the time that you needed to leave. The real Lindazoth, where the Sraan lived was quite different. Real Lindazoth was a dimension wholly covered in light blue warm oceans. There is land, but these are in the form of different sized islands that are suspended in the air, and slowly float around.

They usually are connected by a type of strong vine and exist in groups of between five to seven islands. There is a main island, where the Sraan will live. The islands are fairly tropical, have lush greenery, streams, and various species of animals. So good are the conditions that growing fresh eatable vegetation is easy.

The Sraan don't eat red meat, and in any case what animals there are that live there, are small and insignificant. But they are great fish eaters, and in the continuous oceans, there is an abundance of various types of fish, of unbelievable diversity.

In particular though, there is a species of fish, very similar in many ways to the Earthan killer whale, called a Scalox, which results in the deaths of eighteen percent of the teenage Sraan population every Earthan year, both males and females, in a type of 'coming of age' ceremony called the 'Fandrall'.

Hanging down from the myriad of islands are robust vines, that as already mentioned, connect groups of floating islands, but some of the vines hang down, and are long enough to touch the ocean surface, or at least just slightly above it.

The islands are in perpetual movement, but not only

that, they are dipping and rising at the same time as they move along. The primary object of the Fandrall is to climb down these vines until the young Sraan's feet touch the water. They are then are pulled along by the movement of the island and they surf the water using their heels. They can also run on the surface of the water, but sometimes, as the island dips, they can go in up to their necks, before the island moves upwards, and they are then hauled out to a few feet above the surface.

This ceremony has been happening for many millennia, and on its own, wouldn't be a problem. But the 'excitement,' if you like, of the ceremony, is that shoals of Scalox patrol those areas of the ocean, underneath those islands that are designated to allow the Fandrall ceremony.

This peaceful pastime now has the potential to become a bloodbath, and indeed, unfortunately, does. At any one time, off just one of the islands there may be as many as fifteen young Sraan taking part in the Frandrall, and the Scalox know this, and are swimming just under the surface of the ocean, patiently waiting.

Just as the Scalox know that the Sraan will be coming down the vines, the Sraan know that the Scalox will be down there, so now it becomes a bloody cat and mouse game. A Sraan will quickly ease himself down the rope and start to surf the water with his heels, but always on the lookout. A Scalox will suddenly catapult upwards to try to catch and eat him or her. At the same time the Sraan deftly pulls themselves up the vine and taps their feet enticingly on the nose and lips of the Scalox, which after a few moments has to sink back down into the ocean.

It is a form of highly sought-after bravery, to tap a Scalox on its nose and not get ripped apart or swallowed whole, which unfortunately does happen too often.

Queen Sanambal has tried many times to change the ceremony, so no-one gets hurt. Opinion is very strong amongst the Sraan, though, that this ceremony, as barbaric as it seems, is a definitive part of their culture and shouldn't be changed.

The 'real' Lindazoth, for all the right reasons, are kept secret to the trillions of visitors that come for some rest and relaxation. No visitors would never come into contact with the islands or the Scalox for that matter.

So, it was that Hugo, Allana and Ding Ling were happily chatting in Allana's garden. Hugo and Allana were on the swing seat, and Ding Ling sat on a log close by. They had just finished talking about the plans for the trip. For Ding Ling, he was going to a gun making factory, not any old gun making factory, but into factories that make well known guns known to man, including his favorite of all time, the Kalashnikov AK47 machine gun.

Hugo and Allana, were arranging to experience a deserted desert island together - as simple as that. It had to have a hammock between two coconut trees for Hugo, and Allana wanted a selection of ancient bows and arrows to play with.

They then were discussing Brough Manor, and some of the alterations that were being carried out to make it more accessible to visitors, and the plans to make it an equestran center. Allana had asked Hugo who he was getting to oversee the project, and Ding Ling chirped in with, "I suppose Charlie Andover will be involved, since she is the manageress."

As soon as he said that, he wished he hadn't. He saw Allana's ears prick up when he mentioned Charlie Andover and she slowly turned her head towards him. Hugo spotted this as well and quickly tried to change the subject.

"Yes, but just as much time, energy and money will be put into the refreshment area and the tours of the estate office." It was too late. Allana didn't respond at first. She was thinking. Hugo wondered what she was going to say next. It was not good

"So how is your Charlie Andover?" said Allana.

Hugo let out a nervous laugh then said, "She's not *my* Charlie Andover Allana."

"Oh really?" said Allana, "That was not the impression I got when I met her at the ball, and she was very rude to me."

Hugo felt like throttling Ding Ling for bringing her name up. He felt like he had walked into a plate glass window. Wham. He now needed to think very carefully about everything that was going to come out of his mouth. Ding

Ling could sense the impending doom and thought he might excuse himself and make a quick getaway, but no sooner had he stood up, and before he even managed to open his mouth, when Allana said to him, in the sort of authoritative voice that a dog trainer would use to a dog, "Sit! You are very much a part of this discussion Ding Ling."

Ding Ling knew it must be serious - she used his full name. She hadn't done that for a long time.

Allana turned to Hugo, and very sweetly said, "Why don't you tell me what Charlie Andover did that night in the stables? She seemed very proud of it. I think it will all tie in with what Ding Ling kindly told me about you when you…" Allana turned to Ding Ling and said "How did you describe it to me Ding Ling? Oh yes, 'became a man.' That was it, wasn't it?" Ding Ling didn't respond or move a muscle. She now turned to Hugo and said. "Yes, I'm pretty sure that was it."

Unconvincingly Hugo said, "Oh, it's so long ago Allana, I can't remember. Oh yes, I remember now. She was showing me how to clean saddles with saddle soap, how to oil the bridles and so on."

Allana burst out laughing. Hugo and Ding Ling exchanged worried glances, then they too started nervously laughing.

Suddenly, like a bolt out of the blue, Allana said menacingly, "Bullshit."

'*Jeez,*' thought Hugo, '*where the hell did that come from?* He had never heard Allana swear. Elves don't swear. Ever.

"I like that word," said Allana, "It's an Earthan word that says exactly what it means, Bullshit, Bullshit, Bullshit. Yes, I like that word a lot."

Ding Ling looked like he was going to faint. There were beads of sweat on his forehead. If this place Landazoth they were going to is was about creating a perfect place for them to be, it would be a dungeon with torture racks, if Allana had any say in it. He waited with bated breath to hear what Hugo would reply with.

Hugo was racking his brains to think what to say so that would allow him to come out of this unscathed, or even alive. He knew the Elves' whole culture was based on trust and honesty, and Allana, he was sure, knew the entire story by now about his involvement with Charlie. So, he decided to tell her what really happened, and leave nothing out, except maybe the fact that he found Charlie to be very attractive, but not in a 'let's have an affair' sort of way.' And if truth be told, he enjoyed his teasing by her, and the double entendres and so on. '*Here goes,*' he thought.

"Allana. said Hugo, "all human males go through something called puberty. It starts happening from one's young teens. The voice deepens, the body changes, becomes more defined, chest broadens and so on. The hormone testosterone begins to course through our bodies and we start getting the desire to procreate. Our first sexual encounters can stay with us for a lifetime, and yes for me, it was with Charlie Andover, I didn't realize it at the time, but I was infatuated with her."

"I too was quite a catch for women at the time. I came from a well-to-do background, was financially stable and was told I was handsome for my age. To some women, like Charlie, I was the object of their desires, but for different reasons. I was a catch, I was younger, very sexually active, and she wanted a part of it. Not just that, but to orchestrate the losing of my virginity is what she desired the most."

"I'm sorry she was horrible and rude to you at the ball, and I know it's no excuse, but it is her character, plus of course there was a touch on enviousness in there as well. You will no doubt be bumping into her again at some stage. So, there it is, for a human, a man even, to be honest, is not easy at times. I also didn't want to upset you, and was coming to terms with your reaction. For what it is worth Allana, given a choice between you and her, it would always be you. It's true, because I love you. I don't love Charlie, no matter how she may manipulate events to the contrary."

During this monologue, Ding Ling started breathing again. His master had a way with words, and if that didn't placate Allana, nothing would.

Allana was quiet for a few moments, then she looked at

Hugo and moved closer to him, held his hand and said. "Thank you for your honesty Hugo. Although I have studied humans and their way of life, I didn't research the nuances of puberty in human males. What a trial you had to go through."

"Our males don't go through anything like this at all. Although having said that, if we go back to the very early days of Laniakeea, when females were able to procreate, males would have had similar sorts of urges and a form of puberty to go through and so on.

They all sat there for a moment, then Allana looked at Ding Ling and said, "I'm sorry I raised my voice Dingy. When you told me about this at the beginning, I realize you were being honest and trusting with me. Thank you. And oh yes, we won't be going to a dungeon when we go to Lindazoth." Allana started to laugh, and Ding Ling tentatively joined in.

They all started to relax, and Allana proceeded to tell Ding Ling and Hugo about the real Lindazoth, and of the coming of age ceremony they perform.

The next day, they made their way to the dimension portals. They each had little backpacks. Portal number four was the one that would transport them to Landoz. They arrived into a reception dwelling, and already the atmosphere appeared relaxed and inviting.

There were a couple of Sraan's who welcomed them and

Hugo, Allana and Ding Ling handed over their permits. Once the permits were scanned in, they were then ushered to the rear of the reception dwelling, and at the back were some doors. Each one was brightly colored with large gold colored numbers on them. Hugo remarked that all the numbers were English numbers, to which Allana smiled and said, "The magic around here means that whichever species you are, you would see a number on the doors in whatever language you speak or telepathize in."

Hugo and Allana said goodbye to Ding Ling, who entered door number three. Allana and Hugo went up to and through door number seven.

No sooner had Ding Ling walked through his door, than he heard gunfire and fell to the ground and lay flat. All around him bullets were zipping past and over his head. Suddenly the noise, which was deafening, stopped. There was bluish smoke everywhere. The smell of cordite hung in the air. When he dared look up, he noticed a group of men crowded around a sizable barreled gun that was supported on a trellis and could be moved around on two large spoked wheels either side of it.

Ding Ling picked himself up and made his way over to the group of men; he wanted to see what this gun was. He realized that he was in a green field. It was slightly overcast. Ding Ling turned and looked behind him to see many targets with bullseye rings painted on them.

The group of men standing around the gun parted to see Ding Ling walking towards them; it was then that Ding Ling noticed the Gatling gun, which was essentially the very first machine gun, and said out loud, "Wow, Gatling gun, amazing. So new as well." Ding Ling said to one of the men, "This look very new, when was it built?"

The man indicated a large man opposite him with white hair and a medium white beard, "He is the man to talk to, he is the inventor."

"What? I can't believe it." To the large man in from of him now he said, "It's true? You invent this gun? If so, you must be Richard Gordon Gatling."

The man replied, "Indeed I am sir." Ding Ling nearly tripped over himself to shake the man's hand. "I love your gun. First automatic gun. Historically very important." The man turned to his companions, scratching his head, then back to Ding Ling and said, "History? My good man, this is my prototype and was just finished yesterday."

Ding Ling walked over to inspect the gun. He examined it from every possible angle, down the barrels, and was even given permission to let off a few rounds of ammunition. He stood back, with a huge smile on his lips, and as the blue smoke in the air around him started to clear, the scenery gently changed to that of a vast warehouse.

It was a lot darker and also a lot colder. Ahead of Ding Ling, again there was a group of men. This time they were wearing typical green Russian military uniforms, except for one man who was wearing a light gray suit. They were speaking Russian. Ding Ling quickly adjusted his HC to translate it, and such were the advances in technology with anything to do with communication, it also enabled him to even speak basic Russian, albeit with a slight Chinese accent.

The man with the light gray suit turned around. Immediately Ding Ling recognized his favorite gun and shouted out, "That's the Kalashnikov AK47 isn't it? and I don't suppose you are Mikhail Kalashnikov, are you?"

They all turned around to look at Ding Ling. The man with the light gray suit was wearing two gold stars with red ribbons, which were Hero of the Russian Federation medals.

"Yes," said the man with the grey suit, "That is indeed my gun, and I am Mikhail Kalashnikov. How did you know about it?"

In the brief notes that all visitors to Lindazoth were given, it mentions that the realistic scenery and peoples or species in them, would be interactive and would not question your presence. There were also lots of parameters that could be altered to make the whole experience as realistic as possible.

For example, if you wanted to experience a civil war, you had the choice of being an invisible observer, or dressed up in period armor, but not be touched, or the whole hog, and be involved in the battle and sustain minor injuries.

There are in-built failsafe's of course. Serious injury or indeed death would be prevented.

And so, as Ding Ling approached them, he was wearing the uniform of a heavily decorated general first class in the Chinese army, with enough gold braid on his shoulders to sink a battleship.

"I am General Ding Ling, and I have heard of your automatic gun, its efficiency and reliability and wanted to see it in action myself."

Kalashnikov gave Ding Ling a big smile, and said, "You are most welcome to try it out, General Ding Ling. One of my officers will instruct you on how to use it. Over there you will see a number of targets that you can use for practice."

"Thank you, General Kalashnikov, but I think I have the knowledge already. Please let me try."

Kalashnikov raised his eyebrows in surprise. However, he gave Ding Ling his Kalashnikov. It was almost new and Ding Ling looked at it and stroked it adoringly. He partly dismantled it, and quickly put it all back together again, showing everyone there that he knew his way intimately around every inch of this machine gun.

This made Kalashnikov and the other generals laugh out loud. Ding Ling walked over to the firing line and faced the targets, which were wood cut-outs of soldiers dotted around. He put on some ear protectors, then he pressed the trigger and expertly and efficiently decimated the heads of all the cut-outs. When he had finished, Ding Ling simply said, "Beautiful gun, very beautiful."

Kalashnikov and the other officers looked on with amazement at the skill of this Chinese general. They went up to Ding Ling and slapped him on his back praising him.

Ding Ling was beginning to enjoy himself, and to think that General Mikhail Kalashnikov, inventor of this machine gun was here in person praising him. He didn't want it to end. Already the scenery was dissolving away to another period and another favorite make of gun that Ding Ling admired.

Meanwhile, for Allana and Hugo, the experience they were having was completely different in every way. In fact, they decided to have their permit split into two parts. The first, to show Allana, just what Hugo would imagine as being the perfect break away. (from a human perspective): then Allana wanted to take Hugo to meet a species that he might find very, as Allana put it, "interesting and thought provoking."

As Hugo and Allana walked through door number seven, they stepped out onto warm fine white sand. The clear turquoise sea was lapping on the shore of the small island they had arrived on. On this little island, there were a number of coconut trees. There was the occasional seagull. The sun was shining and there was a warm gentle breeze.

As they walked through the door, Hugo found he was

wearing swimming trunks and some snorkeling equipment. Allana, a bikini and also a snorkeling mask and flippers. They were greeted by some local islanders, who put a ring of hibiscus flowers around their necks, and in the distance, a steel band was playing. A waitress handed them two rum punches and ushered them to a double hammock strung up between two coconut trees.

Hugo fell about laughing, watching Allana trying to get in the hammock. Twice now it had spun around and she had ended up on the sand. Hugo held it for her, and this time she managed to get in and he gently sidled in next to her. They were close.

They closed their eyes and relaxed and took in the whole ambiance of it all. "This just is beautiful Hugo," said Allana, "I know now why you chose this." Sometime later, they hopped out of the hammock and noticed a table in front of them laden with fish and lobster and lots of fresh tropical fruits, so they had lunch.

Afterwards, they noticed a dugout canoe for two people. One of the waiters said it was for their use, so they stepped in, grabbed a paddle each and started paddling towards a much smaller uninhabited island.

'This is simply perfect,' thought Hugo. He felt the worries and tensions of the past few months melting away. They were due to spend the night in a little ramshackle of a hut on the water's edge. Before that though, they sat and watched

the glorious colors of the Caribbean sunset on the horizon. Later, they lay back on the warm sand, breathing in the warm salty air and counted the meteors flashing across the sky.

They spent two days in Hugo's paradise, thoroughly chilled out and relaxed. Time as we know it doesn't work in Landazoth. They could spend what they believed to be four hours in a location, then walk out to find only an hour had passed. They went snorkeling, a completely new experience for Allana. Surprisingly, she wasn't very confident swimming in water, Laniakeean's have no need to swim, as they don't have any seas to swim in.

"Of course, there is the great Salanyn Lake in the Baern district, but that was the domain of the water Elves." One of the island staff even handed Allana a small bow and some arrows, and proceeded to throw either guava and lemons into the air for Allana to see if she could hit them, which she did, of course, every single time.

Next, it was Allana's turn to surprise Hugo. They made their way to the exit spot, and their door suddenly appeared in front of them. They walked through and back into the reception. One of the Sraan was there to guide them to another door, door number eight. This was Allana's surprise for Hugo.

"Can't you tell me anything about where we are going to?" Hugo asked Allana.

"It will all be explained when we walk through the

door," she replied. Allana had a very satisfied look on her face. Hugo could see Allana was very excited, not just for herself, but for Hugo as well.

As they walked through they stepped immediately onto a green grassy savannah, and just in front of them was the edge of a deep drop to a valley. When they looked up, there was the most beautiful mountain range. The air was warm and bright, and it looked like it was an early morning sunrise, with purples, pinks, golds and oranges developing in the sky on the horizon.

However, it wasn't this that took their breath away, no matter how stunning it looked. Their focus of attention was centered on a small unusual-looking planet, that looked a like the Earth's moon, but just as on Laniakeea, it appeared very close and you felt you could almost touch it. It filled the sky. It was somewhere over the mountain range ahead of them and almost looked like it was resting on the mountaintops.

As if that wasn't enough, quite quickly it appeared to be changing color from the whites and grays that Earthans are used to seeing on their own moon, to a deep gold color, then quite spectacularly, it looked as if there were rivers of thick dripping or flowing gold liquid from the planet, which ran down the mountainsides and disappeared into the valley way down below.

As they both stood and took all this onboard, from behind them came a friendly, slightly robotic voice which said,

"Good morning Hugo and Allana, welcome to Traeloth."

They turned around and in front of them stood a tall spindly being, that was very humanoid looking. It seemed to have very smooth lines to its body. It had no hair on its body at all. There was an excuse for a nose and ears, and no mouth as such, but two huge expressive eyes, that were welcoming and friendly. The skin color was a very light grey color, almost silvery, and almost translucent, but warm to the touch and real. It wasn't wearing any clothes; it didn't need to, it was entirely featureless.

When it walked, it was very humanoid looking, but its most interesting feature was that of its face. It was oval, and when it talked, images appeared in this oval, as if watching a film or images.

Hugo felt strongly that there was something familiar about this humanoid, and he couldn't put his finger on it, when into Hugo and Allana's head came a very clear telepathic conversation. There was no accent whatsoever, as if someone from Earth was talking to him. The tone was very friendly, not at all patronizing, and you just wanted to listen to it. It reminded him of his lovely Grandfather who passed away a few years ago now, a great storyteller. The inflection in the voice and the pauses were almost identical.

Speaking to both Allana and Hugo, it started off by saying that his species now only normally communicate telepathically, but for the sake of Hugo in particular, he was able to verbalize his speech.

It told them he was a species of humanoid called the Huumas. And what would interest Hugo the most, is that the Huumas were seeded with the same evolutionary DNA blueprint as that of humans that reside in the Earthan dimension now.

He explained that none of the Humaas had names. It wasn't necessary. One Humaas would only need to think of the personality of another Humaas, and be able to contact them. The complexities of personality are even more detailed than the fingerprint of a human.

But to make it a little easier for Allana and Hugo, he explained he would be using a made-up name, and they could refer to him as Rowel. As he spoke, images were playing out in the oval interface screen where his face would have been. When he stopped sending telepathic messages, his face would revert to normal, and the 'screen' would disappear.

'We are from the same mold Hugo, you and I. Long before you humans were seeded in your dimension, four and a half million Earth years to be exact, the Sola Continuum had already seeded our dimension of Traeloth. The Sola Continuum decided to seed Earth with the same DNA blueprint and then compare your evolutionary development to ours.

'Sure enough, we too started off as a type of ape, had a form of the bronze and iron ages, and were also intent on self-destruction and overpopulation, culminating in food shortages and wars that not only nearly destroyed ourselves, but our flora and fauna as well, but eventually as evolution progressed we went down the technological path.

'It wasn't all the same of course. We didn't have the ice age or dinosaurs as you did, we experienced other phenomena that would appear very strange to you.

'So, at the stage you are at, our evolutionary history so far has mirrored each other's. Because we were almost four and a half million years ahead of you, we are at the stage now where there are no wars, no children. Our lifespan is almost a million years; such are the advances in our technology.

We don't need food or water for sustenance, and we don't have any of the basic animal ape instincts that you still have. We are now twenty-five percent biological material, the rest robotic synaptic biometal. We have much larger sized brains than you Hugo, but, as Alana and other species of Elves have done, have understood the need to research the brain and utilize its capacity. So, we constantly utilize one hundred percent of our brain, all the time. We have a brain circulatory system composed of biological blood and tissue, but surrounding it is a thin layer of advanced electrical circuits, artificial neurones and so on, hence the almost doubling in size.

We have electrical implants that can detect any malfunction in our bodies before they happen. If I want our conversation to go to all the inhabitants of Traeloth, it is just a question of thinking that thought. We have harnessed travel in the form of what you would call spaceships, however, they are eighty percent biologically sentient beings. They move by harnessing this dimension's strong magnetic fields and can cover distances you would fail to comprehend at this stage of your development.

If we extrapolate your evolutionary development, we would say you would be identical, more or less, to where we Huumas are now in another three million years.

To say Hugo found this fascinating would be an understatement. "So, you are saying," said Hugo, "that you and I are humans, only you have been around a lot longer?"

"Exactly," said Rowell, "I too am fascinated with this real-life concept. We are if you like, 'related.' What a lovely thought that is. So, I would like to be your guide around Traeloth, and please, you must ask questions. I love questions." Although Rowell wasn't physically laughing, Hugo could feel it very strongly in the intonations of his verbal messages. Nobody would be able to resist the warmth and friendliness.

The first thing Hugo mentioned was the dripping gold planet. "Ah yes Hugo," said Rowel, "You may know from Laniakeea, that the planetary systems work in a different way to yours, and so it is with the planets we observe in the skies of Traeloth."

"In particular, the planet is very similar to your own

moon, and once in an Earthan month, the planet comes down very close to that mountain range in the distance. That dripping gold liquid is pure energy, and it boosts the energy systems on Traeloth. But even more than that as it is not necessary for us to eat food or drink water as you would do, the energy is pooled and all we need to do is tap into the energy source for instant sustenance. We call the planet Succor, without it we would perish."

"Similarly, with sleeping, it is not necessary for us any more, since we are continually regenerating our energy source and constantly repairing, we never feel tired. Sleep in your dimension Hugo is also a critical time to repair and rest. For ourselves, such is the technology, if anything inside us, or in our environment, shows the first sign of aging or breaking down, it is immediately repaired or replaced before it does."

"If it is ok with you both," said Rowel, "I would like to transport you to an area of the void which exists in-between dimensions. This area we call the 'blackness'. What is unusual about the blackness, is that only your spiritual body can only access it."

By now, Hugo was beginning to lose the thread of what Rowel was trying to explain. Rowel could sense this, so he decided to clarify a little more simply.

"You may have heard of 'out-of-body' experiences, or astral travel Hugo? In essence, it is important to understand that we are physical shells, and you are no different to us in that respect. Allana is aware of how you can leave your physical body."

"Hugo," Rowell continued, "Your physical body ages and then will physically die, but your spiritual being, your essence, your personality lives on eternally and it will transfer to another body. So when we are in the vicinity of the 'blackness' I will initiate and coax your spiritual body out of your physical body and show you some of the experiences that are there for you to experience. Please don't worry at all, there is no need, I will be with you guiding you. It is perfectly safe."

Hugo looked at Allana, with a slightly apprehensive look in his eyes. This made Allana chuckle. "You will be just fine Hugo," said Allana, "As an Elf on Laniakeea, we regularly use deep meditation to initiate the release of our spiritual body. I did it for you during the Sootalanash. I didn't mention it then because it would have been too much for you to take on board."

Rowel then approached them and asked them both to follow him. In a small clearing was a gleaming silver sleek looking space ship. It was almost like a futuristic car, but it didn't have wheels. Instead, it was suspended two feet from the ground. It was streamlined and looked a little like a silver dart. From the back, there were small steps that seemed to integrate into the body, up and into which they stepped. Once inside Hugo just stood in disbelief and looked around.

From the outside, this dart-shaped object was the size of a small car one would have found on Earth hundreds of years ago, but on the inside, the dimensions were huge. It must have had fourteen floors, all open. It was vast. Rowel was explaining it was taking them and others to the 'blackness,' but he also explained that every Humaas had the opportunity to have a much smaller version for their own personal use.

"We are travelers, explorers, just as you are Hugo, it is part of the human 'conditioning' and will always be so, no matter how many trillions of years we evolve into the future, so the 'blackness' is just one of the thousands of destinations that we have visited, but we are discovering new dimensions and species all the time. It's a very exciting time for all Humaas, and I hope it will be the same for you when you reach our evolutionary level."

Hugo in particular, attracted a lot of interest, and when one Humaas was asking him a question, all the other would physically connect, by placing a hand on each other's shoulder. This meant when Hugo answered, everyone would hear his response. Time was moving on, and a gentle humming in a harmony of three musical notes indicated they had to lie down on individual very comfortable looking beds. As Hugo lay down, with Allana on the bed next to him, he could swear the walls of the transport were breathing, a little like the walls of Allana's residence back on Laniakeea.

"Yes," said Rowel, "Although the first impression is that it is an inert metal ship, in fact, she is a biological sentient being, and we have a very much symbiotic relationship. We look after each other."

As they lay down, the lighting dimmed, and there was a intense sensation of movement, not at all jerky, very smooth and a very low hum emanating from the walls. No sooner had it started than it started to fade away. Hugo and Allana started to sit up, but Rowel was there to say, that they must continue to lie down. Hugo turned to Rowel and said, "Have we traveled far?"

"Almost a million light years Hugo."

Hugo just looked at Allana in disbelief.

"But there will be nothing to observe while still in our physical bodies, which is why I would ask you both to lie back and relax while I initiate your spiritual bodies to join us."

At this point, Hugo and Allana were feeling very relaxed but wide awake. The lighting dimmed. There was a combination of sweet-smelling air and harmonizing musical tones that seemed to relax them into a deeper and deeper trance-like-state, but all the while, their minds were very much awake.

For Allana, she knew exactly what was happening, but for Hugo it was a different kettle of fish. Very soon, he noticed that he seemed to be moving around in his body, like a ping pong ball in a balloon. It was a very strange sensation, and there was a strong pulsating strong vibration that was moving up and down his body in waves.

Suddenly in front of him was Rowel, who was now communicating telepathically, since being able to speak verbally wouldn't be possible. *'Just feel you want to be upright with me Hugo. Try to keep your mind clear. Now you are out of your body, your thoughts rule your movement. If you feel you are not in control, I am able to use my spiritual influence to control them, and explain what to do.'*

Hugo thought about standing upright and immediately he was upright. He noticed he didn't feel cold or hot - nothing in fact, but he could see very well, and he wasn't breathing as such. Rowel was coaxing him along and told him to think about moving to a small room up to his right which was about a hundred yards away, and suddenly he was there. Rowel was there with him as well, and was explaining he could move faster than the speed of light if he wanted to. There were no limitations when in the spiritual form.

He could move through walls, he could see three hundred and sixty degrees, simultaneously, he could split himself up so part of him was with Rowel and the other with Allana. But all the time, when he thought he was still, he seemed to be sinking downwards slowly. Rowel, with a lot of humor in his message, said, *'Don't worry Hugo, that is just remnants of your experiences of living your life in a dimension that has gravity. Your consciousness is so used to its effects, it's recreating the feeling of gravity for you. All you have to do is say to yourself, "There is no gravity."'*

Hugo did this, and immediately it all stopped. He was now enjoying this 'freedom,' being in a place where 'thought' rules. The applications to Hugo were enormous; there was really nothing he couldn't do. He could 'see' Rowel and Allana, but they were more ghostly images of themselves rather than flesh and blood.

'Please now let us hold hands Allana and Hugo, because I am ready to take you to the heart of the 'blackness,' although you will question why it is called the "blackness" when we get there.'

With that, they were off. To Hugo, it was a blur, but he had the impression of traveling at tremendous speed, leaving him with butterflies in his stomach, then they all came to an abrupt stop. They were floating in blackness. Not one speck of light was anywhere, Hugo didn't know which direction he was facing or whether he was upside down or the right way up.

Hugo felt unseen hands were manipulating him gently into a sitting position, and then they were gone. Next, he was immediately surrounded by vivid colors. They were block colors. Nothing moving, then, slowly at first, minute strands of colors were beginning to revolve around him, they were picking up speed, faster and faster, until they became white then translucent, and they were moving towards a planet.

Hugo recognized it immediately as Earth, and they all moved down towards its surface, until they were approximately two hundred feet up. They and were moving in a straight direction, parallel with the surface, moving up and down where the natural geography of the contours of the land dictated.

But Hugo couldn't understand, it was an angry looking surface before him - volcanoes, lava with no life at all. They then started to speed up for ten seconds, then slowed down, and now there were dinosaurs, lush greenery, lakes and seas. Again, they sped up for ten seconds, then slowed to see apes foraging in the undergrowth, saber toothed tigers, early descendants of birds and so on. They moved on and this time they saw early man of the bronze age, living in the tunnels of their encampments, and then to the colonization of the Americas and then to the building and development of Times Square in New York.

This continued onwards until the present day for Hugo. 'I'm afraid we have now to return Hugo, I hope you enjoyed a history lesson of the sort you have never have thought possible. Your Earthan dimension and its evolutionary path is fascinating to all the Humaas, but also very similar in many ways to our own. Just as fascinating is Allana's, and I hope one day you will visit again and allow me to take you on a journey of our evolutionary journey here on Traeloth. You will then understand the similarities.'

After a brief journey where they all re-integrated into their physical bodies, they returned in the ship back to where they started from. Hugo genuinely thanked Rowel for the experience of a lifetime. They walked to the transition point, where their door back to Lindazoth was waiting for them.

They walked through and Ding Ling was waiting for them, with some unusual rifles and machine guns strapped to his back. He asked Hugo and Allana if they brought anything back with them. Hugo told him that he didn't have anything. Then one of the Sraan approached them, and handed each one of them a small cylindrical flattened tube, that could fit in the palm of your hand. Hugo looked at it and scratched his head. He turned to Allana and asked if she knew what it was or what it did.

"It's a holographic memory pen Hugo," said Allana. "Just point it in front of you and press the little red button on its side."

Hugo did just that, and in front of him was a holographic recording of everything that had happened to him, from meeting with Rowel, transporting in the ship, coming out of his body and the history lesson of the evolutionary development of the Earth.

"That's amazing," said Hugo, "Something to treasure." The Sraan always leave a memento for all visitors that have visited Landazoth.

Ding Ling looked at his holographic pen, "Hah," said Ding Ling, "This will show me meeting my hero General Mikhail Kalashnikov, I am a happy Chinese man. Me can't wait to show my bosses where I work. Me now have plenty of street cred,"

Their visit to Landazoth came to an end, they said their goodbyes to the Sraan and made their way back to Laniakeea. Hugo and Allana eventually ended up at Allana's dwelling, but Ding Ling said he was going back to the Earthan dimension. He wanted to show his friends at the gun research factory in which he worked the selection of rifles and machine guns he had brought back, one of which was the Kalashnikov AK47, personally signed by the master himself, General Mikhail Kalashnikov.

The 'Dripping Moon' of Lindazoth
(Liquid spiritual energy drip feeds the dimension of Lindazoth. This is the energy source for the Humaas, the advanced human species, that is millions of years more advanced than ourselves)

CHAPTER 21

The Decision

(If you want to love others, you need to learn to love yourself first.)

Hugo and Allana spent the next day watching and re-watching the holographic recordings of their visit to Lindazoth. Allana told Hugo she had enjoyed every minute in the South Sea Islands, the warmth, the crystal-clear water and food. Now, she told Hugo, when she heard Earthans talk of 'paradise,' she knew what they meant.

For Hugo though, his visit to the Humaas, now knowing they were humans who had traveled so much further along the evolutionary scale, had a massive impact on him. Especially the fact that he had grown up with the near certainty that Earth would destroy itself, now understood that there was an excellent chance that they would weather it all and come out in a similar state of advancement as that of the Humaas. This gave him a great feeling of hope.

Although the visit to Lindazoth was a break, a sort of

holiday, they both agreed that it had been well worth going. They were nevertheless exhausted, so they all retired early to sleep that night.

Also, tonight was the first proper chance since they had had to sleep together since they entered into the Sootalanash. Not even to have sex of course, but because they just wanted to be close - to go to sleep together and to wake up together.

But they were aware they were still under the queen's edict, particularly Allana, that they were not to take their relationship any further. Oh, how difficult that was becoming, and each day they were questioning the decision more and more. They felt it was so unfair. They had lots of conversations about how an Earthan couple who were in love would live together. They also discussed how an Earthan couple would make love. Hugo explained it was a romantic union, a special one, between two people.

In his mind, it was the ultimate expression of love between two people, it was fun and satisfying and the natural progression on Earth was to produce an offspring, although not necessarily that alone.

More and more, Allana was letting repressed feelings of sexuality come out, after millions of years of suppressing them and moving on, particularly if we are looking at a union between an Earthan man and an Elvish woman. She had feelings. To make love to an Earthan, would be an unaccustomed experience to her. So much more physical, not spiritual like the Sootalanash. She had, even as an Elvish female, everything needed to embark on this journey with Hugo, and as time went on, she wanted it more and more.

Of course, she also knew she would be unable to conceive, and have a baby, certainly not Hugo's baby, not the way it would work biologically between a man and woman in the Earthan dimension, but the longing for that was also growing deep inside her. She also knew there were ways around those huge stumbling blocks, with the advances in biological science.

In any case, she and Hugo had promised the queen, to take it no further, and they wanted very much to respect that, but the conflict was growing in both of them. What kept it at bay was the faint possibility that the Sola Continuum was going to decide on it all - and hopefully with a positive decision. To be together was all they wanted. Was it too much to ask?

They were trying their very best to put it to the backs of their mind. They just had to wait for the decision, and they hoped it would come sooner rather than later.

It was almost laughable to see how they tried to be tactile and intimate with each other without crossing any lines. It was if they were young teenagers. It was exciting and frustrating at the same time.

So, they retired that night, exhausted from the trip to

Lindazoth, and both fell into a deep, dreamless sleep.

The next morning the two suns had already risen high in the sky. Both Hugo and Allana were woken by Hanale, saying there was an important message for them both from Queen Haruntha, and that when they had dressed and had breakfast, they were to make their way to the palace.

"It must be the decision," said Hugo to Allana, "What else could it be? We need to get a move on Allana."

"Hugo," laughed Allana, "if you eat your breakfast any quicker you will have heartburn, please slow down."

"Oh, ok," said Hugo, "I guess you are right."

They slowed the pace down a fraction, prepared themselves and made their way to the palace. Within half an hour they were standing in front of the queen. Also waiting for them was Elfistra and Mandaz.

The queen came straight out with it. "I know you both have been waiting for a decision from the Sola Continuum, and so have I. I did put a persuasive argument to the Continuum a short while ago, and early this morning they have requested that all of us here are to travel to the seat of the Sola Continuum itself to hear their decision. We are to make our way there now."

There are six members of the Sola Continuum, which includes the spirit from the Sola Tree that is present in Laniakeea. The Sola Continuum meet in deep space, in-between dimensions. There is a physical place that has been constructed so that any species from any dimension that has a Sola Tree, feels less apprehensive. To arrive floating in very dark black deep space wouldn't be very helpful.

So, in the case of Allana and Hugo, the construct was of a grand palace, since that is something that is present on Laniakeea now, and for hundreds of years was a symbol present on Earth, particularly from that part of Earth that Hugo grew up in (There are no palaces now in the Earthan dimension - the last one disappeared over two hundred and sixty years ago.)

In this palace, the six current members of the Sola Continuum form a circle. The wand Elvina, is also present, she acts as the conduit for any of the Continuum that wishes to speak. Any visitors are asked to stand in the middle. The physical structure of a Sola Tree is left in each of their dimensions; it is the pure spirituality and energy of each of the Sola trees that comprise the Continuum. Within this palace, once the group walk in, they are met with very subdued light, that very slowly revolves around all the colors of the spectrum.

At six points around the inside of the circular very tall walls, are six very bright white columns. These appear to be gaseous and seem to be continually moving. Not outside the perimeter of the columns, but within each were sparkling minute gold stars that were tumbling around. When one of the Sola spirituals wanted to communicate, then the column would be buzzing with little gold stars. It was spectacular to look at. Also, Elvina would be a mass of bright electrical blue tendrils that would wrap themselves around that particular Sola member communicating so that there was a clear communication.

There was also music of sorts being played, harmonic notes that would calm and lift the moods of anyone that would be in attendance. This was generated to put them at ease.

It was into this that the party from Laniakeea arrived. Getting there was also quite different. Each were transported on the back of a Barboski. Allana, the queen, Elfistra and Mandaz all had their own, but Hugo was able to ride on the leader of the Barboski, a magnificent looking animal that had two gold stripes running across his forehead to denote his rank.

This Barboski was called Trancer, and immediately put Hugo at ease. Once Hugo was on his back, the posse floated up and away, led by Hugo's Barboski. The journey time was a lot less than Hugo expected. They arrived and were dropped off outside the massive doors leading into the circular palace, where they collected in the middle.

The queen, Elfistra and Mandaz, had only twice been here amongst the Sola Continuum. Even so, they all stood there, mouths wide open, slowly turning their hands around and back again to look at the spectacular columns of light in front of them. The music in the background was having a relaxing effect on them all when suddenly a deep and heavy combination of telepathic voices came into their heads.

The voices were as one, but everyone was aware it was a combination of the thoughts and communication from all six of the Continuum.

Allana moved closer to Hugo and held his hand. Hugo responded by gripping back, but all the while he didn't take his eyes off the Continuum.

'Welcome,' boomed the Continuum's voice in everyone's head, 'We are simplifying our telepathic conversation with you all for the sake of Hugo from the Earthan dimension, so he will be able to process what we are collectively saying. Hugo, so much is new to you, but one of the Sola continuum colonized your Earthan dimension many millions of years ago, rooting in a land mass known to you as 'India,' before seeding with the Human DNA that would lead to Human Beings. The same DNA signatures that were seeded to produce the Humaas nearly four million years before your dimension was seeded.'

'We have discussed yours and Allana's plea to want to become partners, even though the rules for inter-species relationships are not permitted. The reasons for this you already know.'

'However, in this case, we are going to make an exception for the reasons we are now going to explain. We have observed over many millennia, the effects of greed, power and the need for self-destruction that has been observed in the Earthan dimension, but we have also observed how relationships between different cultures, races and people on Earth have proved to be welcoming and fulfilling.'

'The fact that it is possible to see a suitable happy conclusion between such different races is very welcoming and pleasing to the Continuum.'

'In a sense, therefore, we will permit you both to form a relationship, however you wish it to manifest. It will be to the Continuum, not so much an experiment, but you will be closely observed to see if interspecies relations can work, and if so, we would then remove this rule for all dimensions that we have seeded.'

'In essence, our only wish is for peace and harmony, but realize that there is a balance. So good and evil have to exist together, such is the rule of the grand cosmos. So this may well be the next step to see a more positive harmony existing between all species.'

'You may not have thought about it now, but if you pursue your relationship and then begin to think of children, which we would expect would be a natural progression, the only proviso we would make here is that you would still need to abide, certainly on Laniakeea, by the ratio of two females to one male. This is one rule that would still need to be observed. That decision would be ours as to what sex the child would be, and the condition is, you would have to accept our decision.'

With that, the columns started to settle down, becoming filled less with gold stars. In all their heads was a calling from the Barboski just outside to say that they were waiting to transport them all back to Laniakeea, which they did.

Before long they were all, once again, in the queen's palace. No one spoke for a while. They were all still in awe with where they were and what was said, but it was the queen who turned to Hugo and Allana to congratulate them. She was so happy it had turned out like this for them both. She found it hard to contain herself and found that as a handful of individuals, they were able to appeal to these makers of universes with their unlimited powers, and in turn, they were made to feel important and opinions listened to and acted upon.

Elfistra and even Mandaz, shuffling along as he did, seemed pleased for Hugo and Allana.

When finally, Hugo and Allana had reached their dwelling, they found themselves alone. Hanale and Hounani were out. They stood facing each other, they reached forward and came close together. Hugo reached up and brought Allana's face to his. Allana could feel Hugo's breath on her face, the warmth of his body, which was being pressed closer and closer into hers, and then they kissed. At first just the briefest of kisses, they looked deep into their eyes and then they kissed again with a passion that had been growing and building for months and months. They both couldn't believe that life, as they knew it, at this moment in time, for both of them, could be any more perfect.

The next few months for Hugo and Allana was a whirlwind of activity. Where would they live? Laniakeea or the Earthan dimension? And what about the notion of having children? Even in their wildest dreams they didn't expect the Sola Continuum to mention what they did.

They both knew they wanted a child. It was unspoken until this point, but they both brought up the subject at the same time, with the excitement of that growing inside them.

Would they need to marry? What would happen to Allana's Elvish marriage to Hounani and Hanale? What about her relationship with Hounani? So many questions. So many decisions. But Allana had a wiser head on her shoulders than Hugo did in these matters.

Time, she told herself, would move everything along in a naturally progressive way. They would tackle one little problem at a time. That way the whole picture would begin to look less complicated and much more achievable. They were certainly going to have their work cut out, and now would be as good a time as any to begin, so they began to lay out a plan of action.

Four months later, Allana was proved right. After much soul searching with Hanale and Hounani, they just extended their original dwelling. They would all live together, and if Allana and Hugo were to have a child, then Hanale and Hounani would be a part of the family.

Allana had special permission from the queen to dissolve the 'marriage' that held together Allana, Hounani, and Hanale. They all were in full agreement with that. It is as if they were starting afresh, but with completely different sets of values. There was nothing in the Elvish constitution that would fit now, so they decided they didn't need anything official and had accepted that the family unit was now all four of them, and if everything worked out well and they had a baby, they were all going to be responsible for his or her upbringing.

Hugo and Allana had a number of visits from an Elvish practitioner, together with his skills, and with two magical interventions from Elvina (sanctioned by the Sola continuum), it all meant that what was missing from Allana to make her as complete as any human Earthan woman, was now intact and fully working.

Just as Hugo experienced the Sootalanash and its feelings, it was now the turn of Allana, to be guided through the ways of sexual and spiritual fulfillment by Hugo. The experience for both of them was beyond words. They knew, in their heart of hearts, that they were destined to be together.

Two things started to crop up more and more whenever they had chance to talk: a baby and exciting new adventure. The Sola Continuum had seen both of them again, and they could see that what was happening was right, and asked them to be ambassadors when traveling to far and distant new dimensions.

They had word from the Continuum that if they did have a baby, this mixture of Earthan and Elvish, it would have to be a girl. Both Hugo and Allana accepted the decision. They really didn't care, they just wanted a little bit of each of them in one small package whom they could protect and love and nurture.

The integration of the Elves or Laniakeea and the Earthans was swiftly moving on in a helpful and useful way. Technological knowledge continued to be shared, and there was talk of other relationships starting between the two species. The whole basis on whether that would continue would be down to Hugo and Allana, so it seemed everyone, in both dimensions, and indeed many other dimensions, were observing them carefully.

A Baraladath Dwelling

(One of twenty-five throughout Laniakeea. They are special birthing dwellings. Prospective parents may choose. Hugo and Allana chose this one on the edge of Salnalyn Lake, home of the water Elves, the Phaaras)

EPILOGUE

(The beauty of a new life, excels all other things)

Fourteen months later, Hugo was doing his best not to be sick. He was constantly heaving. Beads of sweat were dripping off his forehead. His hands were full. His left hand was holding the smallest but cutest pair of baby's heels you could ever imagine. His right was holding some antiseptic wipes and he was attempting to wipe the stinkiest little bottom imaginable.

This baby was a wriggler. She had already eased one heel out of Hugo's hands and kicked the heavily soiled nappy into Hugo's crotch, and simultaneously flipped the dirty wet wipe, with the same foot, into his face, so it hung there draped over his left eye.

'That's it!' he was thinking. "Allana?" he shouted, at the top of his voice. "Where are you?" He needn't have shouted at all. Allana and Hounani, were giggling insanely. The round door to the baby's room was open a fraction, so that they could see in, but Hugo wasn't able to see them.

Every time Hugo gagged and retched, the baby girl giggled, and suddenly, Allana and Hounani laughed out loud, opened the door and walked in.

"Wow," said Allana, "that is a stinky smell Hugo"

"Yeah, well," heaved Hugo, "that's pure Elf shit, that's what that is. I have to get out of here before I pass out." There was more heaving, giggling and wiping, but then Hounani took charge, and quickly and deftly, tidied up the little girl, smeared some lavender cream and powder over her, promptly dressed her and sat her on a little padded wooden horse resembling a Barboski, which was now gently rocking after Hounani applied some mild magic to it. She was happily playing with a new Jarjam pet Allana had bought for her, and it was affectionately wrapping its tongue around her hand, making her smile.

Hugo came back into the room, having settled his stomach with some Voovo, and sat next to Allana on a comfy little log opposite the infant in front of them.

They looked adoringly at their baby. It had taken ages to come up with a name they both liked and wanted. They had agreed on Kia. She was perfect in every way, but her eyes were captivating. They were very round large and blue. The main part of her irises was a bright turquoise blue, then surrounding the irises, a thin band of deep blue. A deep blue that that could hold you, transfix you even. They were full of expression, and even at such a young age, Kia knew how to use them to best effect.

Kia was exactly four months old, but such is the norm

on Laniakeea, even though she was half human, she was maturing very quickly, compared to a human child. Not only her mind, which was large and more advanced, but her body as well.

This would continue until she was eight years of age, which is the coming of age for Elvish children. This would be the equivalent of approximately seventeen Earth years of age. They don't experience puberty in the same way as a human, but from eight, she would be able to think as easily and quickly as an adult Elf.

However, Kia was special. Very special. When she was born, there were queues outside their dwelling of Elves that wanted to see her, to touch her. But these Elves were not your normal Elves, oh no, these were highly spiritualized Elves, exceptionally advanced magical Elves. None of them would say why Kia was so special; they would only say "It's for you both to discover. The answer is there. You have to search and look for it. We cannot tell you."

Whenever they held Kia's small hands in theirs, they seemed to melt. Kia's eyes would look deep into theirs, as if telling a story. The Elves would leave looking happier and more fulfilled. All this was a mystery to Allana and even more so to Hugo.

It was only when they presented Kia to Queen Haruntha, Elfistra and Mandaz that they began to think that there was something special about her.

The change with Elfistra was remarkable, and both Hugo and Allana were doing their best not to laugh, with her cooing and clucking in front of Kia. Kia loved it, her infectious baby laughs reverberating along the walls of the queen's grand hall.

Even Mandaz, had sidled up, and for the first time ever, his whole demeanor changed. He reached forward and tickled Kia's left foot, and she squealed out with laughter. This in turn made Mandaz laugh. It was a sort of rumble from deep within, but a laugh nonetheless.

And then it was the queen's turn. "Well," she said impatiently, "When can I hold her?" Hugo smiled, lifted Kia out of the Elvish cot and handed her to the queen. She fussed Kia as well as the others, and then laid her back down in the Elvish cot very gently.

But what convinced Hugo and Allana, above all else that their daughter was extra special, was the reaction of Kal, the empath. He and the other empaths had come in with the queen at the beginning, and had been waiting patiently on the edge of the group, until they were summoned forward.

Allana noticed Kal, just behind and to the left of the queen, and motioned him to come forward to say hello to Kia. He tentatively crept forward, his eyes fixed on Kia, until he was only a foot away. Kia turned her head towards Kal, their eyes met, and immediately both were very still, this moment seemed to last an eternity and the biggest of smiles were on both their lips. Kia started to wriggle her little hands in front of him frantically, so he gently reached forward with his and held them.

It was as if a history of lifetimes were passing between them. The smiles never left their faces, then quite suddenly all the other empaths came crowding forward and each one put their hands onto the empath in front of them. It was as if Kal was acting as a conduit between Kia and the other empaths, so they were all simultaneously sharing the story. They too all started smiling.

Hugo, Allana, Mandaz and Elfistra slowly moved back to give them room. They were all amazed at the spectacle before them.

Elfistra telepathically said to Allana and Hugo, *'You do both realize that your Kia is an empath? And not just an ordinary empath, an extraordinary one. I can sense the greatness in her. We all have to nurture her because she will be not only be our savior, but the savior for millions of other species throughout the dimensional states. She will also be our protector, our guardian.'*

'The Sola Continuum were hoping this would be the case, but now she is born, they are convinced of this. But her life, I can also see, is heavily connected to that of Elvina the wand. At the same time though, I can see periods of great sadness. You won't be able to prevent it, you will have to deal with it, but deal with it you will and move on.'

When Elfistra had finished, she stepped back and joined

Mandaz, said her goodbyes to the queen, Hugo and Allana, turned and quietly, they both left. As soon as she left, Kal let go of Kia's hand and all the other empaths turned and made their way back to where they had been, just to the side of the queen. Most were still smiling at Kia and waving at her, and she was responding by giggling and waving her hands around.

Kal, instead of following the other empaths, made his way to Hugo and gently held his hand. He looked into Hugo's eyes and said, 'Remember the time we met at the end of the Granthanda competition? I said then that something special would be happening to you and Allana, that you would need to nurture? And that you would forget what I said at the time, but you would remember when the time was right? Well, now is that time. So, Kia is that something special that you both need to nurture.'

'When Kia has matured a little more, you will be seeing a lot more of us at certain times. Kia is an Empath, but far more powerful and stronger than I will ever be. However, our joint empathic qualities will come in to be so useful for Laniakeea, your dimension, in fact countless millions of other dimensions in the future. I look forward to being a part of that very much.'

With that, Kal and the other empaths left. Hugo and Allana went back to their home with Kia.

The years passed by. Those years were challenging times for Allana and Hugo. Besides minor battles with insurgents from other dimensions, Kia continued to grow and develop. She had magical powers that surprised not only Hugo but Allana as well. She was spending a fair amount of time with Elvina, and she was the only one, that Allana knew, that could properly communicate with her.

At eight Elvish years of age and five foot eight inches tall, she was stunning to look at. Her eyes would always be the focus for anyone meeting Kia. You were drawn towards them. She didn't have blonde or red hair like the majority of Elves, but inherited her father's very dark slightly curly hair. It was long and thick and was her crowning glory. Her expertise in magical skills was unbelievable, far better than Allana's ever would be. She was supernatural.

Kia learned fighting skills from her father, learned to laugh at her Uncle Ding Ling's crummy jokes and sayings, became a very accomplished young person in every way possible and now was pleading with her parents to be allowed to be with them when they next had to battle, or go on an exploration mission. Allana and Hugo were finding it increasingly difficult to say no, but the time was fast approaching when they would have to relent and say yes.

In fact, that time was going to be soon, a lot sooner than anyone could have imagined. And the terrible consequences of what was going to happen would be very difficult to contemplate. Hopefully the cosmos will be with them, helping them weather what was inevitably going to be coming.

Author's Note:

The first book of the series, The Prequel, gives a little insight into the adventures to come in all the books.

There is also the opportunity to join me at

www.thewand.me

I sincerely hope you have enjoyed this second book of the Wand Chronicles.
Be sure to read the continuing adventures in -
Book three: **Kia the Empath** and Book four: **Eternity**
Thank you,
Michael Ross
thewandchronicles@gmail.com

GLOSSARY
(Alphabetical)

ANDOVER:	Charlie. Manageress of the Brough stables, and lover for Hugo Brough.
ANDROTHACAN:	An older experienced Laniakeean General
AHMED:	A board member on the UEL (United European Landmass)
ARKHRUN:	A special Elvish hut only used to perform the Sootalanash.
BAERN:	A district of Laniakeea that holds Salnalyn Lake, home of the Pharaas.
BARALADATH:	The name given to special birthing Centers.
BROUGH:	Hugo. General. Son of Lord Brough
BROUGH:	Maxx. Illegitimate son of Lord Brough.
BROUGH:	Lord Arlo Brough. Head of the Brough estate
BROUGH:	Kayon. Brother to Hugo & Maxx Brough
BROUGH:	Helena. Sister to Hugo & Maxx Brough.

GLOSSARY
(Alphabetical)

BROUGH:	Lady Romilly. Wife of Lord Arlo Brough.
CEPNAEROTH:	The Laniakeean district that contains the Slice
CHANSATH:	Head referee at all Gruthanda competitions.
CIB:	Central Information Bureau.
DABITHYRA:	King of the Pharaas. The Water Elves
DAKATHOR:	An Elf that doesn't comply with normal Elf fashion and behavior.
DANOBOTS:	Microscopic intelligent robots that are able to retrieve DNA samples.
DTC:	The Diagnose, Treat and Cure machine.
DING LING:	Hugo's aide. From China. Warrior, humorist and weapons expert.

GLOSSARY
(Alphabetical)

ELFANDA:	'A Special One' An Elf that has above average magical powers and related to the Queen.
ELVAK:	A dark wand which belongs to the Lazanath
ELVINA:	The magical & spiritual Laniakeean wand.
EMPATH:	Elves and Human's that have special powers.
FIREMAKER:	Hugo Brough's stallion.
FAELATH:	Queen of the Pharaas that live in Salnalyn Lake in the district of Baern.
FANDRALL:	A 'coming of age' ceremony performed in Lindazoth by the Sraan species.
FASHNAL:	A family team entered into the Granthanda competition.
FRANZOTH:	Special referee in the final phase of Granthanda competition.
FORLASATH:	The Laniakeean Elvish dialect.

GLOSSARY
(Alphabetical)

FURANELL: Very large spiders that live underground. And will surface to capture young Elves.

GAREEN: The district in the North of Laniakeea that contains the portals to other dimensions.

GRALDOTH: The final phase of the national Gruthanda competition.

GRANDAN: Head of the Valcanth family team competing in the Gruthanda competition.

GREENAN: A competing finalist family team in the Gruthanda competition.

HALHAZE: The Queen's bonded Barboski.

HANALE: The male Elf in Allana's married family unit

HINKLEY: Clifford. Prosecution Barrister in the murder trial of Hugo Brough.

HOUNANI: The female Elf in Allana's married family unit

HUMAAS: An evolved species of Human.

GLOSSARY
(Alphabetical)

JAMJAM: A species of family pet found in Laniakeea.

JEMIMA: The Brough Family estate head cook.

JULOW: Allana's bonded Barboski.

KALAMA: Allana Yana-Ash's Father.

KAKLINA: Allana Yana-Ash's Mother. (No. 1) Every family unit in Laniakeea has two Mother's

KALEA: Allana Yana-Ash's Mother. (No. 2)

KELMENANTH: The official ceremony of 'joining together' two female Elves who are in a relationship.

KRALAPAL: A ceremony conducted for any Elf on Laniakeea that has committed a crime.

KRALDAN: Elvish name for the Sensaas fruit. When eaten instills a euphoric feeling.

GLOSSARY
(Alphabetical)

KRANDOO:	A failsafe emergency Elvish word to be used on a ley line circle to enable travel.
KRASS:	A toad-like rodent from the Mandazan dimension. Poisonous.
KROLEETH:	A species of Lizard that resides in the district of Kroleeth in Laniakeea.
LALAN:	Vine plant sap. Yellow. Tastes like prunes
LANGLEY:	Joel. Head of security for the UEL.
LATADJIN:	Official ceremony to confirm a family unit of one male and three female Elves.
LAZANATH:	A dark and spiritual series of Elf
LEY LINE:	Spiritual energy lines used by Elves and humans to travel great distances.
LINDAZOTH:	An Elf dimension where all species may go for some rest and recuperation.

GLOSSARY
(Alphabetical)

LULERAR:	The abrasive string used during the Granthanda competition.
MANDAXON:	A rogue species of Elf, dressed in all black. Commonly known as the Black Arrows.
MELROON:	A species of Elvish Tree that has large purple leaves that droop to the floor.
	It produces popular fruit that causes a pleasant euphoria.
MIRROLS:	Small mirror-like circles that are placed on the forehead. Enables Humans to see further and with greater magnification.
MOLASTROK:	The Laniakeean district that contains the queen's palace.
MORG U'MIST:	An Elf assassin species. Clothes and arrows are characteristically striped black and yellow.

GLOSSARY
(Alphabetical)

NEGRAN:	The sorceress of the Rapaeva dimension.
NYMLAARI:	The Laniakeean district that holds the national Gruthanda championships.
OLDHAM:	Lord Justice. A High court murder trial judge.
PALDARATH:	The name given to the touching of walls to access images from the past.
PALRATH:	Secondary referees that officiate at the National Gruthanda championships.
PANISO:	An ancient Elvish dimension ruled by King Brentan who had fallen in love with Queen Haruntha of Laniakeea.
PHARRAS:	A species of water Elf that reside in Salnalyn lake in the district of Baern in Laniakeea.
RALDAN:	A dwelling specifically for Elves to clear their internal waste products.

GLOSSARY
(Alphabetical)

RALDATH: A family team competing in the nationwide Gruthanda competition.

RANETH: Rand. Born on Laniakeea but defected to the Mandaxon, a warring species of Elf known as the Black Arrows.

RANSAN: Lord. Leader of the more advanced Lazaneth species of dark Elf.

RAPAEVA: The home dimension of the Lazanath.

RASS: The new male sorcerer of Rapaeva. He has smooth silver skin.

RHYFONALDAS: An elder Laniakeean General with white hair.

RILITONATH: An Elvish family that had hired the Morg U'Mist to disable the Yana-Ash family.

RIKTAPATH: An Elvish insect similar to an Earthan dragonfly.

GLOSSARY
(Alphabetical)

ROWEL: The name given to the Humaas that was a guide for Hugo & Allana on Lindazoth.

SALATAN: Lanakeean Elvish for Empath

SALNALYN: Lake. Where the water Elves reside. They are called the Pharaas.

SANAMBAL: Queen of the dimension known as Lindazoth.

SCALOX: A large predator fish similar to the Earthan killer whale.

SENSAAS: The fruit/nut from the Melroon tree

SHALISH: Allana Yana-Ash's Jarjam pet.

SHEEDRA: The name of one of the assistants to Allana in the Gruthanda Championships.

SHANTAY NAY-SAL: 'Lady of the Night' wall and tree climbing white flowers with a delicate scent. Also known as 'Flame Flowers' that illuminate the evenings with insects within, that glow.

GLOSSARY
(Alphabetical)

SKAELOTH:	An arrow with no arrowhead. Instead, tightly wound material forms a round ball on the end of the arrow. Used to practice, or for the first section of the Gruthanda championships.
SOLA	Continuum. Formed by six of the Sola trees.
SOLA	Tree. There are many trees in many dimensions, including Earth and Laniakeea.
SOOTALANASH:	A special ceremony between two Elves, usually females. A spiritual loving union.
SPIRITEN:	An ornate wooden carved box, inlaid with special magical metal incantations. This box is the holder of the wand, Elvina.

GLOSSARY
(Alphabetical)

SPIRITWOOD: A special forest surrounding most of the Sola tree. Very magical and acts as a protection for the Sola tree and Elvina.

SRAAN: The name given to the species of Elf that inhabit the dimension Lindazoth

SUCCOR: The small planet that drips golden energy onto Traeloth where the Humaas reside

TAZARETH: Mandaz's special and magical staff, given to him by the Sola Continuum.

TRAELOTH: The dimension in which live very early ancestors of the Earthan's called the Humaas.

TRANCER: The name given to the head of the Barboski.

UES: The United England States.

GLOSSARY
(Alphabetical)

ULTHAROSS:	The Maze that helps to protect Elvina the wand and translates as 'The Maze of Many Troubles'.
VANCALTH:	A family team competing in this years Gruthanda championships.
VASHTAL:	Allana Yana-Ash's second assistant in the Gruthanda championships.
WILLIAMS:	Chantelle. Maxx Brough's Mother who was murdered under suspicious circumstances.
WOODBEAD:	Romilly. Lady Brough's maiden name
ZENTHAN:	Allana Yana-Ash's first assistant in the Gruthanda championships.
ZO'SAH:	Wolf. A very large fierce wolf that lives in the Denetrine district of Laniakeea.
ZIVANOVIC:	Miroslav. First deputy, then head of the United European Landmass

Michael Ross

IMAGE TITLES

THE AUTHOR, MICHAEL ROSS 5
MAP OF LANIAKEEA 7
WINBERRY WOOD 8
THE SLICE 14
THE PLANET SATURN 38
QUEEN HARUNTHA 56
ELFISTRA & MANDAZ 78
DING LING 94
THE GRANTHANDA COMPETITION 120
ALLANA YANA-ASH & HUGO BROUGH 144
ELFISTRA BONDING WITH THE WAND 178
ELVINA THE WAND 194
A TRICKLE OF BLOOD 208
THE BARBOSKI 228
THE MANDAZON 252
THE SOOTALANASH CEREMONY 278
A LANIAKEEAN STORM 294
ELFISTRA THE SORCERESS 312
CHARLIE ANDOVER 342
KROLEETH LIZARDS 358
THE LIGHTING OF THE FLAME FLOWERS 378

PTO

IMAGE TITLES

(CONTINUED)

THE SOLA TREE 408

THE MELROON TREES 430

THE 'DRIPPING MOON OF LINDAZOTH' 464

A BARALADATH DWELLING 478

SELECTED PHONETIC PRONUNCIATION FOR SOME NAMES AND OBJECTS.

BROUGH : .... BRUFF
ARKHRUN : .... ARK-RUN
BAERN: .... BEAR-N
CEPNAROTH : .... SEP-NAH-ROTH
DABITHRYA : .... DAH-BITH-RAH
FAELATH : .... FAY-LATH
FRURANELL : .... FUR-AHH-NEL
HANALE : .... HAH-NAH-LAY
HOUNANI : .... HOW-NAH-NEE
HUMAAS : .... WHO-MASS
KRALDAN : .... KRAL-DAN
KROLEETH : .... CROW-LEETH
LANIAKEEA : .... LA-NEE-AH-KEE-AH
LATADJIN : .... LA-TAH-GIN
LULERAR : .... LOO-LER-RAH
NYMLAARI : .... NIM-LAA-REE
PHARRAS : .... FAH-RASS
RAPAEVA : .... RAH-PAY-VA
RHYFONALDAS : .... RI-FON-AL-DAS
RIKTAPATH : .... RICK-TAA-PATH
SALNALYN : .... SAL-NAH-LIN
SHALISH : .... SHA-LEESH
SKAELOTH : .... SKAY-LOTH
SUCCOR : .... SOO-COR
TRAELOTH : .... TRAY-LOTH

Printed in Poland
by Amazon Fulfillment
Poland Sp. z o.o., Wrocław